THE MONE

It starts with ... is partner, Pete ... ... Dr. Pantell who has just shot a man he found breaking into his office. Before he dies, the thief confesses that he was there to rob the safe, which though now empty, had earlier held at least a million dollars. So right away, Baron and Delanos know that something here is screwy. And then there's the thief's girlfriend who claims that Pantell set him up for the killing. Convinced that Dr. Pantell is not what he seems and that the cash in the safe is drug money, he and Delanos set about a robbery of their own. If only things had stayed that simple....

LOVE TRAP

What would you do if you were an aspiring architect, more or less happily married, and working for two guys who had made their fortune on your designs? You resent the hell out of them, but don't want to quit. And one day you overhear a plot to rob the business on payroll day. Would you warn your two bosses? Call the cops? Tell your wife? Harold Wilkenson doesn't do any of these things. He doesn't feel he owes the business a thing. But on the day of the robbery he's dragged along by his boss to deliver the payroll cash. There is a crash, a stickup, guns fired. Harold wakes up in the hospital. Now what can he do? If he confesses that he knew about the heist, he'll be arrested. If he rats on the thieves, they'll kill him. Quite a trap...

LIONEL WHITE BIBLIOGRAPHY (1905-1985)

Fiction

Seven Hungry Men (1952; revised as *Run, Killer, Run!*, 1959)

The Snatchers (1953)

To Find a Killer (1954; reprinted as *Before I Die*, 1964)

Clean Break (1955; reprinted as *The Killing*, 1956)

Flight Into Terror (1955)

Love Trap (1955; reprinted in UK as *Right for Murder*, 1957)

The Big Caper (1955)

Operation—Murder (1956)

The House Next Door (1956; first published in *Cosmopolitan*, Aug 1956)

Hostage for a Hood (1957)

Death Takes the Bus (1957)

Invitation to Violence (1958)

Too Young to Die (1958)

Coffin for a Hood (1958)

Rafferty (1959)

Run, Killer, Run! (1959; re-write of *Seven Hungry Men*, 1952)

The Merriweather File (1959)

Lament for a Virgin (1960)

Marilyn K. (1960)

Steal Big (1960)

The Time of Terror (1960)

A Death at Sea (1961)

A Grave Undertaking (1961)

Obsession (1962) [screenplay published as *Pierrot le Fou: A Film*, 1969]

The Money Trap (1963)

The Ransomed Madonna (1964)

The House on K Street (1965)

A Party to Murder (1966)

The Mind Poisoners (1966; as Nick Carter, written with Valerie Moolman)

The Crimshaw Memorandum (1967)

The Night of the Rape (1967; reprinted as *Death of a City*, 1970)

Hijack (1969)

A Rich and Dangerous Game (1974)

Mexico Run (1974)

Jailbreak (1976; reprinted as *The Walled Yard*, 1978)

As L. W. Blanco

Spykill (1966)

Short Stories

Purely Personal (*Bluebook*, May 1953)

Night Riders of the Florida Swamps (*Bluebook*, Jan 1954)

"Sorry—Your Party Doesn't Answer" (*Bluebook*, July 1954)

The Picture Window Murder (*Cosmopolitan*, Aug 1956; condensed version of *The House Next Door*)

To Kill a Wife (*Murder*, Sept 1956)

Invitation to Violence (*Alfred Hitchcock's Mystery Magazine*, May 1957; condensed version of novel)

Death of a City (*Argosy*, Jan 1971; condensed version of novel)

Non-Fiction

Sports Aren't for Sissies! (*Bluebook*, May 1953; article)

Stocks: America's Fastest Growing Sport (*Bluebook*, Nov 1952; article)

Protect Yourself, Your Family, and Your Property in an Unsafe World (1974)

THE MONEY TRAP
- - - - - -
LOVE TRAP
- - - - - -
Lionel White

Introduction by
Timothy J. Lockhart

Stark House Press • Eureka California

THE MONEY TRAP / LOVE TRAP

Published by Stark House Press
1315 H Street
Eureka, CA 95501, USA
griffinskye3@sbcglobal.net
www.starkhousepress.com

THE MONEY TRAP
Originally published by E. P. Dutton & Company, Inc., New York, and
copyright © 1963 by Lionel White. Reprinted in paperback by Monarch
Books, 1964. Copyright renewed April 18, 1991, by Hedy White.

LOVE TRAP
Originally published by Signet Books, New York, and copyright © 1955
by Lionel White. Copyright renewed December 31, 1983, by Lionel White.

"Lionel White: The Caper King—And More" copyright © 2022 by
Timothy J. Lockhart

ISBN: 978-1-951473-58-7

Book design by Mark Shepard, shepgraphics.com
Proofreading by Bill Kelly
Cover art by James Heimer, jamesheimer.com.

First Stark House Press Edition: February 2022

LIONEL WHITE: THE CAPER KING— AND MORE

Timothy J. Lockhart

One measure of a writer's ability and achievement is his or her influence on other artists. Lionel White, who published more than 35 crime novels from 1952 to 1978, had great ability and achieved a great thing—a large body of work that is consistently entertaining, invites repeated reading, and is at times unforgettable. Thus, one sees White's influence on other crime writers such as Donald Westlake, who, as "Richard Stark," wrote the Parker series of superb hardboiled caper novels (1962-2008), and on movie makers such as Stanley Kubrick, who made White's novel *Clean Break* (1955) into the classic noir film *The Killing* (1956), and Quentin Tarantino, who, in the credits for his fine neo-noir film *Reservoir Dogs* (1992), acknowledged White as an inspiration.

White wrote a number of heist, or "caper," novels in which a gang of criminals plans and executes a big score, usually with dire, even fatal, consequences for most or all of the gang. He even titled one such novel *The Big Caper* (1955, reprinted by Stark House Press in 2021). *The New York Times* called White "the master of the big caper," and well-known crime novelist Bill Crider said that White, "if he did not invent the caper story, is certainly one of the ablest practitioners in the field."

White certainly was the "caper king," as Ben Boulden characterized him in his well-researched introduction to the 2109 Stark House two-fer of White's novels *Coffin for a Hood* and *Operation—Murder* (originally published in 1958 and 1956, respectively). But White was more than that. He wrote many excellent novels that, although not centered on heists, are page-turning studies of people, many quite ordinary, drawn to commit crimes, sometimes for money, sometimes for love, often for both.

White had a genius for mixing hardcore career criminals with normal characters teetering on a razor's edge between straight and criminal lives, knowing that staying straight or going straight is the smarter choice, yet feeling a strong and often irresistible pull toward the dark side. Because so many people have wondered what it would be like to give in to temptation and break society's rules, readers identify strongly with White's more sympathetic characters as they struggle mightily with that decision. That is one reason Anthony Boucher, the highly respected novelist and critic, writing in 1958, praised White's dozen or so novels to date, which include this volume's *Love Trap* (1955), as "tense, cogent, convincing."

Moreover, perhaps because his novels are so well plotted—novelist and literary critic Rick Ollerman claims that "no one has ever been better at plotting a crime story than Lionel White"—filmmakers have seized on his books as source material for movies. White novels were the basis for, in addition to Kubrick's *The Killing* (with dialogue by Jim Thompson, author of *The Getaway* [1958] and other classic crime novels), *The Merriweather File* (1961), *Pierrot le Fou* (1965), *The Night of the Following Day* (1969), and more. One of the best "White movies" is *The Money Trap* (1965), made from the novel in this volume (with a few minor changes) and starring Glenn Ford, Elke Sommer, and Rita Hayworth. At the time of this writing the movie was available on DVD, although it is somewhat hard to find.

Despite his impressive literary output, biographical details about White are sketchy—and he may have wanted it that way. The 2001 *Contemporary Authors Online* entry for White quotes him as follows: "I am afraid that anything I may say may very well be fiction and certainly shouldn't be believed in any case." For example, we do not know precisely how many times White was married or to whom, and we do not know why, after enlisting in the Army during World War II (when he was almost 38), he served only five months before being discharged.

What we do know is that Lionel Earle White was born in Buffalo, New York, on July 9, 1905, (some sources give New York City as his place of birth) and died in Asheville, North Carolina, on December 26, 1985. He dropped out of high school after two years (not uncommon at the time) and soon became a newspaper crime reporter and then a copy editor before rising to edit various literary and true-confession magazines. White became a full-time writer in 1951 and published his first novel (in digest form) *Seven Hungry Men!* the next year.

He continued writing novels, along with some short stories and nonfiction, for 27 years, publishing them under his own name except for *Spykill* (1966). That one, a foray into the spy fiction so popular in the 1960s, came out under the pseudonym L.W. Blanco (a play on "white"). His novels sold well and received generally favorable critical attention.

In addition to Boulden's biographical essay about White, Nicholas Litchfield provides interesting information about the author in his insightful introduction to the 2021 Stark House edition of *The Big Caper* and *Steal Big* (originally published in 1960). And Ollerman's chapter "Crime à la White" in his excellent critical study *Hardboiled, Noir and Gold Medals: Essays on Crime Fiction Writers from the '50s Through the '90s* (Stark House, 2017) is essential reading for those who want a better understanding of White, his novels, and the movies made from them.

Neither *Love Trap* nor *The Money Trap* (1963) is a caper novel although each features an armed robbery as a key plot point. Whereas in *Love Trap* the protagonist accidentally becomes involved with a holdup, *The Money Trap* is a more straightforward and, probably for most readers, stronger story of a police homicide detective tempted to steal the money that he hopes will save his marriage to a wife with a taste for the finer things.

That detective, Joe Baron, the first-person narrator, likes his job and is good at it. He loves his wife, Carol, but the family trust fund that gives her about as much money as he makes has strained their marriage. Although he wants the couple to live on his salary, he finds that they can never quite do it, even having to charge, for instance, six bottles of scotch for a neighborhood party to Carol's account. Baron's junior partner and lifelong friend Pete Delanos told him before the wedding that "marrying a rich wife" wouldn't last. "It won't work—it never does."

Delanos, who likes to gamble, has his own money problems but comes across what he thinks is a solution to his and Baron's dilemmas. After a wealthy physician shoots a career criminal and drug addict who is robbing his safe and Delanos and Baron are called to the scene, Delanos takes the man to the hospital. The dying man—Phil Kenny—talks.

Delanos tells Baron that although no money was in the room when the police arrived, Kenny said there had been a million dollars in the safe. Kenny also said that even though he had been unarmed, Dr.

Horace Pantell had shot to kill, emptying his semiautomatic and putting "three of those lead slugs" in his back.

Delanos suggests there must be something crooked about Dr. Pantell, that the million dollars must be "hot money" the doc got from dealing drugs or heading a "high-class abortion ring." In that case, Delanos says, why shouldn't Baron and he take the money for themselves? Baron dismisses the idea, saying they can deal with the situation "by tipping off the Federals and letting them take over."

But the unusual circumstances make him wonder what really happened, and he begins to investigate, working his usual long hours while trying to deal with the troublesome situation at home, including the people in their upscale neighborhood who Baron thinks look down on him for being a cop. One is Dr. Jack Archer, a handsome and successful psychiatrist who gives Baron the impression that any time Archer wants Carol, "all he has to do is wiggle his little finger."

In the course of his investigation Baron comes across Rosalie Carver, an attractive, hard-drinking 22-year-old, who describes herself as "[t]he late Phil Kenny's girl—or common law wife, if you want to put it that way." Although initially reluctant to answer Baron's questions, Rosalie eventually gives him information about Kenny's relationship with Dr. Pantell and how Dr. Pantell made that million dollars, information that makes Baron reconsider Delanos's plan.

As one might expect, things go badly from there—very badly for some. The action begins to move with express-train speed and reaches an unexpected but satisfying chiaroscuro conclusion with its mix of light and dark shades.

In contrast, *Love Trap* is a tense psychological study of an ordinary man whose chance overhearing of the planning for a payroll holdup gets him involved in that crime as well as murder. Harold Granville Wilkenson, age 36, is a semi-failed New York City architect who has made his employers, the owners of the McKenny-Fleckner Construction Company, rich from building the "first four low-price houses" he designed when he joined the company "nine long, deadly dull years" earlier.

Now relegated to being the office manager, he is a bitter man, so resentful of his bosses' success—which he sees as due largely to his own efforts—that he refuses the generous offer of Sam Fleckner, one of those bosses, to set him up in his own architecture firm. His refusal is strengthened by the fact that his wife, Marian—who seems suspiciously close to Fleckner, a bachelor with a flashy sports car— keeps urging him to take the offer.

Wilkenson's humdrum world changes completely when in a neighborhood bar one Sunday afternoon he overhears two men talking about robbing his other boss, Tom McKenny. Leaving the bar he sees a woman in a silver convertible talking to the larger and more dangerous-looking of the two hoods. White foreshadows that she will be the woman to catch the hapless Wilkenson in a "love trap": "A slender, golden girl with flaming hair worn long and curled under at her shoulders. A girl with large azure eyes smudged on her perfect face. A girl with a glittering smile showing all of her perfect white teeth."

Once home, Wilkenson starts to telephone McKenny to warn him but stops when he sees Marian getting out of Fleckner's car in front of the couple's apartment building. Thus begins Wilkenson's ever-speeding spiral down into a noir nightmare in which everything he does to escape only drags him further down.

Having failed to prevent the robbery, Wilkenson is accidentally drawn into it when, at the last minute, McKenny asks him to come along as he distributes the weekly payroll to the firm's construction workers at their job sites. The robbery is successful, leaving Wilkenson slightly injured and a valuable witness for the police. Detective Lieutenant Shawn O'Malley's warm, sympathetic eyes and "soft Irish voice" conceal a steel-trap intelligence that, although Wilkenson badly underestimates his abilities, picks apart his evasions and lies one by one.

Wilkenson's struggles are further impeded by his fevered feelings for Sari Mizner, the beautiful young woman with azure eyes who is the lover of Roy Anders, the leader of the robbery gang. Wilkenson pays the owner of the neighborhood bar to tell him where Sari works—as a checkroom attendant in a hotel that has "a peculiarly fugitive air of licentiousness." The bartender, wiser in the ways of the world than Wilkenson, warns him that "Roy Anders eats guys like you for breakfast."

Told in the first person, *Love Trap* presents Wilkenson as an intelligent man (although not as intelligent as he thinks) who is self-centered and rather immature. He is also often impotent, which explains his relatively sexless marriage and his lust—although he imagines it is love—for Sari, who apparently feels sorry for him.

Wilkenson is not an especially likeable character, but he is enough of an everyman to engage and hold the reader's attention as he falls deeper and deeper into the pit he digs for himself with O'Malley constantly circling the edge. Wilkenson shifts from thinking of himself as an "innocent man" to someone who has a "natural criminal mind," and he drifts more and more into outright criminality as O'Malley and even Marian and Fleckner begin to see through his lies. *Love Trap* has the hypnotic effect of a terrible auto accident—you don't want to look, but you can't look away.

White's prose is always serviceable but seldom soars, reading almost like a factual account in a newspaper, perhaps because of his many years in journalism. But his ability to create compelling, well-rounded characters and to fashion intricate but still believable plots has seldom been matched and probably never exceeded in crime fiction. White is an author who well deserves rediscovery by new generations of readers, and the two novels in this volume are a fine way to start.

—November 2021

Timothy J. Lockhart is a lawyer and former U.S. Navy officer who worked with the CIA, DIA, and Office of Naval Intelligence. The author of the novels *Smith* (2017), *Pirates* (2019), *A Certain Man's Daughter* (2021), and *Unlucky Money* (scheduled for 2022), all from Stark House Press, he lives in Norfolk, Virginia, with his wife and daughter.

THE MONEY TRAP
- - - - - - -
Lionel White

Chapter 1

I was very tired; I had a lot of things on my mind.

He sensed my inattention. His hand moved, and he sort of half plucked at the sleeve of my jacket. He repeated the sentence.

He spoke in a low, almost inaudible voice, and if it hadn't been for the intense way he was watching me, I doubt if I would have understood, even then.

I looked across the naked top of the coffee-stained table, focusing my eyes, and shook my head in an effort to clear my mind. Pete had tipped the hat back from his eyes and leaned forward in his chair. He held the cup of tea in his right hand and his left elbow rested on the table.

"That's right, Joe," Pete said. "The report was wrong. Kenny didn't die without regaining consciousness."

He wasn't making sense.

I looked around the almost deserted cafeteria and noticed that the two cab drivers who had been sitting up front had left. A tired colored boy was banging dirty dishes onto a tray at one side of the room, and the faded blonde in the wrinkled tailored suit still sat alone, staring blindly at a tabloid, a dead cigarette in her hand. She was too far away to hear us and so were the two or three people behind the serving counters.

"Too tired for jokes, Pete," I said. "It's been a long night." It had, eighteen hours long.

"No joke, Joe," Pete said.

This time I didn't have to shake my head to come to. I was suddenly wide awake. I moved, leaning forward in my chair.

"What are you trying to tell me, Pete?" I asked. "I made out that report less than an hour ago. Are you saying you purposely let me make out a false report?"

"That's what I'm telling you, Joe."

I stared at him for a second or so, and then I took my time and lit a cigarette. I reached for the coffee which was already getting cold.

"So Kenny came to when you took him to Bellevue and ..."

"He talked."

"And then he died?"

"That's right, Joe. And then he died."

I nodded, very slowly.

"Thanks, Pete," I said. "Thanks for letting me get that straight, at least. It would be a little embarrassing for me to walk in Monday morning and have the chief explain that Phil Kenny was still alive. I wouldn't quite know what to say."

I took the cigarette out of my mouth and nodded and then pushed back in my chair and leaned forward to stand up.

"Sorry, Pete," I said. "I'd like to sit here and spend the rest of the night making small talk. But I do have to be moving on. You know—back to the squad room, Pete. And maybe you'd better come along with me. This time we'll try and get it straight. We have a little matter of a report to dig out and ..."

"Sit down, Joe," Pete said. "Sit down. We're not going back to the squad room. We're not going anywhere for a little while. I have a couple of things to say. I think maybe you'd better listen to me."

I tossed the cigarette into the coffee cup. For a moment or so I merely looked at him, staring into his dark, brown-flecked eyes. He didn't look as though he'd flipped. He looked just about as sober and sane as I had ever seen him.

I sighed and leaned back in my chair.

"Who am I not to listen to a police officer if he wants to talk?" I said. "Especially a detective. A detective second grade, no less. Of course," I added, making no attempt to keep the sarcasm out of my voice, "of course I do happen to be old Joe Baron, detective first grade and the senior member of this particular team. But after all, why shouldn't I listen? Especially when what you apparently have to say so vitally concerns me."

"There's no need to get snotty," Pete said. "Just listen and I'll ..."

"No need at all, Pete," I said. "And I wasn't being snotty. I was just explaining that my time is at your disposal. After all, we've worked together for several years; we've been buddies since we learned to walk and talk. The mere fact that you purposely let me make out a false report is hardly worth a second thought. So just go ahead and explain it away. You were saying something about Phil Kenny coming to before he died. Suppose you take it from there. Or better yet, perhaps you could tell me why you felt you had to hold back that enticing little gem of knowledge until after I had filled in ..."

"He came to, Joe, and he talked. He talked for quite a few minutes."

"So—he talked."

"He talked. I was the only one in the room. The only one who knew that he recovered long enough to talk before he died. The only one who heard what he had to say."

"It must have been pretty important, Pete," I said. "What did Kenny do, make you give some sort of deathbed promise that you would never reveal what he said? Did he think you were some sort of priest or something? And did you play along and promise this two-bit, second-rate hophead, this cheap ex-safecracker and burglar, that you would live up to the part and observe a vow of silence—even if you had to double-cross your partner, fail in your duty as an officer of the law, disgrace the badge ...'"

"Oh for God's sake, Joe," Pete said, "come off it. This heavy-handed sarcasm is getting a little tiresome. Why don't you just sit tight for a minute or so and listen to me? Do you want to hear what Kenny had to say or don't you?"

I shrugged my shoulders and slouched down in my chair and again I sighed. It was the last time that night I was to sigh. My eyes went to my watch and I saw that it was a quarter to five in the morning. I suddenly realized that already it was too late. The report would have gone on downstairs and would be on file by now.

"All right, Pete," I said. "All right, let's have it. Tell me what Kenny said."

Somewhere in the back, behind the counters, someone dropped a tray full of crockery and Pete jumped. It didn't bother me; someone was always dropping trays full of dishes in all-night cafeterias.

This time Pete leaned well forward and he spoke in an even lower voice, but I had no difficulty hearing him.

"Kenny told me that Dr. Pantell killed him deliberately. That he didn't shoot in self-defense but deliberately emptied his gun into him after Kenny had dropped the money and already had his hands up in the air."

I twisted my head on my neck and looked up at Pete. "The money, Pete? What money? There was no money in that room. Have you lost your mind?"

Pete shook his head.

"No, I haven't lost my mind. Maybe Kenny lost his, before he died, but I don't think so. I think he knew exactly what he was saying and that he was telling the truth. I don't think there is a doubt in the world he knew he was dying."

"All right. He was telling the truth. Again I say, what money? There was no dough in the room when we got there. There was no money anywhere around when those two uniformed men in the patrol car arrived."

"Just let me give it to you the way Kenny gave it to me," Pete said. "You remember the safe? The walk-in safe next to the bed on the north wall?"

I nodded. I remembered the safe. It was behind a screen, and the screen had been moved a little to the side so as to expose it. The door had been closed. I remembered it very well because at one point I had suggested that Dr. Pantell open it and check to make sure it hadn't been tampered with, nothing removed. Dr. Pantell had smiled and explained that the safe had never been used as long as he'd had the place and that it had been installed by a previous owner. He said that it had been open and empty when he'd taken the house and that, although he'd once had the combination, he'd lost it. That he'd never bothered about it after it had accidentally been closed and locked. He kept no valuables in that part of his establishment.

"My wife's jewels were given to relatives after she died," the doctor had explained. "I keep a few dollars in change around, but it is down in a drawer of my desk in the office. Of course there are drugs, but I keep them locked up. Also downstairs."

"What has the safe to do with it?" I asked.

"Kenny told me the safe has everything to do with it," Pete said. "Kenny's story is that when Dr. Pantell opened the bedroom door, he, Kenny, was standing in front of the safe and that he had already opened it. He was in the process of taking the money out of the safe when the doctor leveled the gun at him and told him to put up his hands."

"Again, what money?"

"The money Kenny knew to be in that safe. He wasn't quite sure how much money and he'd had no time to make a count before the doctor came in and found him. But he figures it was somewhere around a million dollars. In twenties and fifties and hundreds. All neatly stacked and bundled and labeled."

Pete pushed back his chair and stood up.

"Going to get some more tea," he said. "You want another cup of coffee?"

I didn't say anything.

"I'll bring you coffee," Pete said. "Think about it for a minute or two, will you? I'll be right back."

I thought about it for a minute or two. I thought of it all of the time that Pete was over at the counter getting the coffee and the tea.

It was just too damned crazy to believe. A million dollars. Dr. Pantell, a top Park Avenue diagnostician, deliberately murdering a man.

Phil Kenny had received a total of nine lead slugs in his body. It was amazing he had lived long enough to make Bellevue, without a DOA tag tied around his big toe.

Dr. Pantell had freely admitted emptying the automatic. His story had been that when he had entered the room, after hearing someone moving around, Kenny had been in front of the safe, standing next to the twin beds. The doctor had snapped on the light switch at the door and at once ordered the intruder to stand still and raise his hands.

Kenny, according to the doctor, had started to swing around and there had been a gun in his hand. It is quite true that an unfired, fully loaded .32-caliber revolver had been found under the body. No fingerprints were on it, but then Kenny was wearing rubber gloves.

But three of those lead slugs had entered Kenny's back. It doesn't take nine slugs to drop a man.

Then, too, Kenny was a known drug user and it had been logical to assume he had entered the doctor's residence in a search for drugs. Why then was he found on the fourth floor, in the doctor's living quarters, instead of somewhere downstairs in his office?

There was another thing. Kenny had a criminal record as long as your arm, but he never had been known to carry a gun of any kind, although he had been convicted in the past of safe robbery and burglary.

Yes, indeed, there were several little things that bothered me.

Pete was back with the tea and the coffee and a couple of pieces of Danish pastry. I waited until he slid the tray on the table and sat down.

"All right, Pete," I said. "Let's say that Kenny told you everything you have just told me. Let's say, for the record, that he might even have been telling the truth. That Dr. Pantell did actually murder him. And that Kenny had opened the safe and had found something like a million dollars and was in the process of removing that million dollars. Let's admit all that. Now just how does this explain why you felt it was necessary for you to keep quiet about it and let me put in a false report? Just what reason?"

Pete's brown eyes opened wide and he cocked his head, staring at me.

"What reason, Joe?" he asked. "What reason? Why the million dollars, Joe. The million dollars. Isn't that reason enough?"

Chapter 2

It had started just like any other day, except for the argument about the liquor.

I had been awake for perhaps ten or fifteen minutes, trying to get up the courage to get out of bed and close the window so the room would heat up. Wishing that it was Saturday morning instead of Friday. If it were Saturday, I wouldn't have to get up and close the window; I could just reach over and turn off the clock radio, pull the covers up to my chin, and go back to sleep.

A dull, gray, pre-dawn light filtered through the opened window into the room, but the room itself was still dark and so I closed my eyes, not wanting to think about getting up, not wanting to think about anything at all. But then the steam began churning through the pipes and the cold radiator, making the usual early morning racket.

Carol had fallen asleep, as she usually did, with one arm across my chest. I shifted, moved her arm, and she sighed gently in unconscious complaint. I got out of bed and crossed the room and closed the window and damned all old houses, no matter how charming, whose heating systems announced their lack of efficiency with a series of initial clangings and gurgles.

Stumbling over a pair of shoes, I returned to the table next to the double bed and flicked on the ten-watt night bulb under the shaded lamp. My terry cloth bathrobe was in a heap on the floor, and I picked it up and put my arms in the sleeves. I didn't bother to look for slippers, but left the room and went out in the hallway and down the stairs, which were lighted by another small-watt nightlight.

The coffeepot was on the electric stove in the kitchen and I turned it on. Carol had prepared it the previous evening.

There was frozen orange juice in the refrigerator, and I made up two glasses, using the blender to make them foamy. While I waited for the coffee, I used the downstairs bathroom, where I kept a spare toothbrush.

I returned to the kitchen and found a tray for the coffee and juice. I was playing it smart, saving a few precious early morning minutes by beating that clock to the punch.

By the time I had returned to our bedroom, the music was already filtering into the room, but Carol was still sleeping soundly.

I emptied one of the glasses of juice after putting the tray on the table at Carol's side of the bed. Then I crawled back under the covers on my own side.

I had been pretty crafty; I would have an extra twenty minutes.

She stirred and moaned slightly as my arms went around her. She didn't open her eyes but her own arms slid around my neck, and her small warm body drew close and her head lifted and moved until our mouths met.

She sighed then, the kiss awakened her. Her blue eyes opened wide and she stared into my face and then smiled and whispered something, pulling me toward and over her.

It is a little strange that I chose that moment to think of something I had read somewhere in a book recently. The author maintained that the sixth year of marriage was always the dangerous year. It was then that the bloom was supposed to have worn off, that a man and a woman must find something to replace their initial sex attraction.

The author didn't know what the hell he was talking about. Carol and I had been married for five and a half years.

It was better, greater, than ever.

The disc jockey finally finished spinning his platters and the early morning newscast came on. Carol was now sitting up, with both of our pillows supporting her head as she sipped her coffee. I was across the room, already dressed except for my necktie and jacket. I was strapping on the shoulder holster.

Carol said, "And, Joe, you won't forget the liquor for tomorrow night? Six bottles of Scotch. We have bourbon and gin."

That's what started it.

"Six bottles? For God's sake, honey," I said, "why six? Can't these bums stick to Martinis or something simple? You know damned well we can't afford ..."

Carol sighed. "Just charge them to my account, Joe," she said. "If we have to go through a budget inventory every time I want ..."

She had said the wrong thing.

I swung around and glared at her. "Your account! Listen, for the last time I am going to say it."

I didn't say it, I yelled it.

"I'm your husband. I have a perfectly good job. I make a decent living. Nine thousand two hundred dollars a year to be exact. Enough to support a wife in a fairly reasonable style. In fact, it's more than perhaps seventy-five percent of husbands in this country make and that includes husbands who support not only wives, but children as well."

"Why, we don't have any children, Joe," Carol said, smiling at me in that maddening fashion she has when she wants to prove that I'm acting like an ignoramus and a bore.

I took a long breath. I wasn't going to get anywhere yelling.

"All right, baby," I said. "All right. We won't discuss it now. I have to get to work. But, Carol, I'm not through with this. When we got married, you told me you'd be willing to live on my salary. You promised me ..."

"You promised me," Carol interrupted, "that you wouldn't let my income interfere or come between us. Well, this is a party I want. I have the money to pay for it; the people who are coming are my friends. There's no earthly reason you suddenly have to start standing on your pride ..."

"When I find I'm living on my wife's money, when I find that each year I personally go a little bit farther in debt ..." I was beginning to yell again.

Carol looked at me and pouted. "Then quit the force and go into business as I've wanted you to," she said. "You know perfectly well, with your education and brains, and with my capital ..."

I told her what she could do with her capital. I started to tell her a couple of other things, but again she just put her finger to her lips, shaking her head.

"Temper, temper," she said. "Now you just go along and be a good little detective and don't forget the Scotch. If it makes you feel any better, you can pay for it yourself. But be sure and get it, Joe."

So I kissed her good-by, and I went downstairs and out to the garage and got into the three-year-old Chevie sedan, which sat next to her MG, knowing that I'd lost another argument.

Because I was still sore, I forgot and pushed down on the gas pedal and, as usual, flooded the engine. It would have to sit for a few minutes before I could try again and that was when I realized I had forgotten to call Pete and be sure he was awake. Pete could sleep through a dozen alarm clocks, but for some unknown reason, the sound of the telephone would send him leaping out of the soundest sleep.

I started to get out of the car to return to the house and then shrugged and said to hell with it, under my breath. It had occurred to me that I was getting awfully tired of calling Pete. I'd been carrying Pete for a long time now, and I was getting fed up playing nursemaid.

Chapter 3

It had probably started when we were kids, living next door to each other out in Queens. We were the same age, but I had always been bigger and stronger than Pete Delanos. I'd been fighting his battles, going to bat for him, most of my life. We had grown up together, gone to high school and NYU together, and joined the department within a couple of weeks of each other. And we had come up through the ranks together, Pete usually one jump behind me.

Pete had a quick, agile mind and things came easy for him. It was just as well that they did because he also had a way of ducking the rules and getting into jams. As long as I can remember, I've been getting him out of these jams. Yes, I was getting tired of ...

I felt my face grow red. Getting Pete out of jams? It hadn't been completely one-sided. I was suddenly remembering that day, some three years ago, right after we had made the brains department and been assigned as partners. It had happened late in the afternoon when we'd gone to that apartment on the upper West Side on a tip that a kid named Katz, who was wanted for questioning in a homicide, was renting a room in the place.

I'd knocked at the door and when a woman's voice said to come in, had opened the door.

As I say, Pete always had brains.

No one had ever suspected that Katz, who was only fifteen years old, was really involved in the homicide. He was merely suspected of being an eyewitness. And so I had opened the door with my gun still snugly in its holster. Pete already had his in his fist as I stepped into the room. He had spotted Katz over by the window before he moved across the threshold.

Young Katz started blasting away without a hint of warning. The first two rifle shots would have taken me through the stomach if Pete hadn't leaped forward and pushed me to the floor. The bullets missed me and got Pete, one going through his left arm and the second catching him in the shoulder.

By the time I had my gun out, Katz was already sitting on the floor and crying, but of course by then it was a little late. Pete spent the next three weeks in the hospital, and if the shot which had gone through his shoulder had been two inches lower, he wouldn't have been in the hospital at all. He'd have been in the morgue.

I got out of the car and went back to the house and dialed Pete's number. He was still sleeping, but the phone only had to ring once before he was on the line.

He'd have plenty of time to shower and dress and have breakfast before he had to show up down at the precinct at eight o'clock. Pete had a bachelor apartment on the upper West Side of Manhattan; I had to drive all the way in from Westchester.

When a New York City cop finally gets to take off his uniform and moves into the "brains" category, or the detective division as it is more commonly known, he gets several breaks. To begin with, he gets more money. I've known a good many cops in the ten years I've been on the force, but I have yet to see one who couldn't use more money. I suppose cops are like everyone else in that respect. But money isn't the whole of it.

Once an officer gets into plainclothes, he starts to use a lot less shoe leather, and he finds himself sitting down more often than standing up. No more patrol duty, no more pounding the pavements or freezing to death on a windswept corner while dodging insane drivers as he tries to keep traffic crawling.

No more pulling water-logged cadavers out of icy waters. No more breaking your heart while you tell some tired, sick-eyed scrubwoman that her teen-aged son is downtown in the morgue with a dozen knife wounds in his body.

There's a lot of paper work, and it helps if you can type with more than one finger and a thumb. You do a good deal of traveling, but even if you have to use your own car and pay for your own gas in case the unmarked sedan which is supposedly assigned to you is in use, at least you don't take your life in your hands trying to get to the scene in nothing flat. You know that the uniformed boys will have arrived, so that there is no great rush. The dirty work will be over and you just move in to clean things up—if you can.

There are, as I say, a good many advantages as you move up in the ranks. You take better care of your health; your chances of living to an old age are a good deal improved. You can take a drink on the job; you can walk around looking just like everybody else, the more so the better. When you want to send out for coffee, you can do so.

A lot of the time your hours are your own—the same way that a great many of the decisions you make are your own. Of course, in theory, you only work an eight-hour day, five days a week, and you don't get paid for overtime, of which there is plenty. But there are compensations, some of which I have already mentioned.

Most uniformed men consider that the men in the detective divisions have it pretty soft. The boys in "brains" themselves figure that the eight-to-four stretch, daytime, is the best. Usually they are right. But this particular Friday proved an exception.

Chapter 4

Pete and I are assigned to homicide and we work out of headquarters down on Centre Street. On this particular Friday morning, we had an appointment over at the West Thirtieth Street precinct.

A girl had turned up dead in a man's room in a cheap tenement house late Thursday afternoon and the man was missing. By the time Pete and I had quit work, it hadn't even been determined for sure just how the girl had died.

In any case, we were due at the precinct house, which would act as a sort of clearinghouse, and if it was murder, or suspected murder, we would take over. If it wasn't, then we'd call in downtown and if nothing was stirring, drive on down and wait for something to happen.

When we met at the precinct, we learned that the girl had been found to have died from a heart attack—she was only twenty-three—and the man who rented the room had shown up and already had been cleared. So we called in and there was a stop we had to make on Canal Street: someone had reported seeing a man throw the body of a newborn baby into an ashcan. The newborn baby turned out to be a dead cat; so that didn't take very long, and by nine-thirty we were upstairs in the office having some coffee out of cardboard containers.

Pete always drank coffee up until twelve o'clock and then he switched to tea or coke.

It looked like it was going to be a nice quiet day and it was, up until five minutes to four when we were due to go off duty.

Pete was reading a scratch sheet, trying to figure a sure thing for the next day, when the phone rang. I let him answer it; I was busy with a pad and a pencil, adding and subtracting, but mostly subtracting. I was trying to figure out how a guy who made ninety-two hundred a year could owe something like sixty-eight hundred dollars, all long overdue.

Pete put the receiver back, looked at his watch, and said, "Damn!"

I guessed what he meant. "Apartment house. Greenwich Village," Pete said. "Somebody went out of a window. Wouldn't you know it!"

It was probably a suicide; they usually are. Especially in the Village. On the other hand, people have been known to be helped out of windows.

So we went downstairs and climbed into the department's unmarked Dodge sedan and headed north.

His name was Gerald Pickering; he was twenty-eight years old, married, and the father of three children. He lived out on Long Island and was in the insurance business. He made around twenty thousand a year, had a damned good-looking wife—we found her picture in his blood-soaked wallet—and on the surface he didn't have a reason in the world for wanting to go flying out of that twelfth-floor window.

But he had gone out of that window and no one had helped him.

It took a lot longer than you would have thought to get it all straightened out. To begin with, the girl who was in the apartment was half drunk and completely hysterical. There were several witnesses to round up, especially the woman across the street who had seen him teetering in the open frame of the window.

She was hysterical, too.

We had to wait around for a positive identification, which was ultimately made down in Bellevue by the pretty wife from Long Island, who was also hysterical and had the best of all reasons for being so.

There were a good many little odds and ends of details until Pete and I were ready to go back to headquarters and write out the report which would establish that it wasn't a homicide after all, so that, actually, we hadn't been needed in the first place.

Pete had tea as usual and I had coffee and I did the typing because I'm faster than Pete. And it was eight-forty-five by the time I was ready to sign the report. I had managed, somewhere along the line, to telephone Carol and tell her not to expect me until late. Pete, not being married, was saved this little difficulty.

I was reaching for my hat (contrary to television, detectives do not sit around in their offices with their hats on) when the phone buzzed again and both Pete and I looked around to see who was going to pick it up.

Nobody was going to. No one else was in the room.

"Shooting, off Park Avenue, at Sixty-eighth Street. The entrance is just around the corner," the voice on the phone said. "A four-story private house. The home and office of a Dr. Pantell. Dr. Horace Pantell."

"Listen," I said, "get someone else. We were supposed to be off at four—and it's almost nine now."

"I don't have the number; you'll see the squad car," the voice said. "Better get a move on. That's an important address."

"Goddamn it," I said, "didn't you hear me? We've been on duty since eight this morning...."

I jerked the receiver from my ear as the sergeant down on the switchboard hung up.

Chapter 5

It was while we were heading north on Park Avenue that I remembered about the liquor and realized I wouldn't have a chance to pick it up. By the time I passed through Armonk, the store where we traded would be closed. Well, I could always run in sometime Saturday afternoon. The party wasn't scheduled until eight in the evening.

Thinking about the liquor made me think about Carol.

I had a problem.

I'd had this problem for a long time, almost from the day we had been married. I knew that thinking about it wasn't going to do any good at all. The only thing which would solve that problem was going to be money and not the kind of money I could look forward to from the City of New York.

I remembered what Pete himself had said to me when I'd told him that Carol and I were going to be married. He had been absolutely right, too.

"I suppose I should congratulate you, Joe, marrying a rich wife. But, kid, you're out of your mind. It won't work—it never does."

"Rich hell," I'd said. "She may have come from a rich family, but she's no spoiled brat. Anyway, she isn't rich any longer. There's a trust fund and it brings her under ten thousand a year. That's it. She can't touch the principal."

"Ten grand!" Pete said, and whistled. "So that's almost twice what you're making now. What do you mean, not rich?"

"Look," I'd said. "Be sensible. Suppose she was working? Say some sort of career girl job or something. She could be making that in salary. It wouldn't stop me from marrying her. Anyway, Carol knows the score. We've talked it over."

"If she were working, Joe," Pete had said, "she'd probably quit her job when you get married. You can hardly ask her to quit a free ten thousand a year."

I hadn't wanted to argue. Pete was my oldest and best friend. He'd only met Carol a couple of times, but I wanted him to like her. I tried to explain.

"She understands all about me, Pete," I'd said. "She knows how I feel about my work, and she wants me to stick with what I have been trained to do and like to do. We've gone over it a hundred times. It isn't going to make any difference at all. Not the slightest difference. We'll live on what I make and ...

"And—well, that's it. If we have kids, and we certainly hope to, at least there will be dough for their education. In the meantime, I'm not going to hate the idea that she has some money of her own. So we can live in a little bigger house, she can have her own car, a couple of luxuries. It isn't going to make the slightest difference. Boy, you have to understand one thing. When two people love each other, really love each other, money isn't a factor."

It had sounded great. I'd even believed it. But it wasn't great. It was wrong from the word go.

It is true that when we started out, things were the way we'd hoped and planned. I guess I made the first mistake about the house. I'd wanted to take an apartment until we could save up a little, and it was while we were looking around for something that Carol found the old place near Armonk, up in Westchester. It came with some six acres, and at one time had been quite an estate. But years of neglect and just plain old age had left their mark. The roof leaked; the plaster had fallen off the walls; the furnace needed replacing; the ...

I don't have to go into details. The price was eighteen thousand dollars. You can figure the shape it was in.

I thought she must be crazy, but somehow or other she made it all sound reasonable and practical and I went for it. After all, eighteen grand would normally just about buy the small ranch house that I could really afford. And of course it was a tremendous bargain and we could work on it ourselves as we went along and, anyway, I was about due for a promotion and so on.

The long and short of it was that we bought the place and of course there were a lot of things that just couldn't wait doing if we were to live in it at all. So Carol started using her money, and we started fixing up the place. My promotion came along, accompanied by a raise in salary. It didn't help too much.

By this time I'd discovered that living in the country is a pretty expensive proposition. I'd also discovered that when you live in a neighborhood where your neighbors make about three times your own salary, your wife feels a certain sensitivity and you can't let her down, even if you have to let her spend her money and go a little into hock yourself.

In her own way, of course, Carol was great about it. No squawks because I didn't make more; no little subtle hints that I wasn't carrying my share of the load. No suggestions, at least at that time, that I might be smart to quit the force and find something more remunerative.

It was around the second year of our marriage that the doctor told Carol she never would have any babies. I think that was the turning point. It was about then she really started spending money as though the stuff was going out of style.

At first I didn't complain. I realized how upset she was, and I wanted her to do anything she could to get over her disappointment. It was at this time that something happened with the trust fund, something good I suppose you could say. Instead of a little under ten thousand a year, it started bringing in a little more than fifteen.

If you think that was good news, you are very wrong. Until then, it used to amuse me to refer to Carol as "my rich wife." When strangers would ask me what I did—and it has always amazed me the personal questions which strangers can ask—I used to laugh and say, "Why I married money—what else?"

The joke suddenly became a little stale. I could tell from the way some of them would look at me—the ones who were making thirty and forty thousand a year and who knew I was a cop, who knew how much money cops made.

Carol wasn't insensitive. She understood my pride and how I felt. She knows me better than I know myself. But she just figured I was being foolish to let it get under my skin.

"Cops are tough," she'd say. "Tough, hard, and callous. So just be tough and forget about it."

She was right about one thing. A man can't be a cop for any length of time and not be tough. You do get hard and callous. But that's just a matter of self-protection. You simply have to be able to put your feelings to one side. While you are on the job.

But not while you are off of it.

Some of the most completely sentimental, soft, easy-going men I have known are cops. Not on the job, but at home and with their families.

I wasn't tough with Carol. Maybe I have always been too much in love with her; maybe it's a basic weakness in my own character. And maybe it wouldn't have made any difference in any case.

I honestly don't think Carol could have changed any more than I myself could. She just went on being Carol. She'd been brought up with money and luxuries, and so long as she could afford it she wasn't going to pass them up. She liked nice things and expensive things and she was going to have them.

When things reached a point where I finally was ready to put my foot down, make a definite issue out of it, she had the answer.

She had the answer, but I didn't.

It had happened a couple of months back, when I told her that it had to end. That we were through running into debt, through using her money. That she would have to make a decision. Live on my income or else.

"All right, Joe," Carol had said, in that sweetly reasonable, infuriating tone of voice which showed perfect emotional control. "All right. I'll go along with you. We'll live on what you are able to earn. Now I'll make that concession, and you can make one in return. Go downtown today and quit. Resign from the force. You're a smart guy—the smartest guy I know, darling. You've been through college, and you've taken a night course in law. So quit the force and take up law. Or, if you don't like law, we'll find some business and put some money into it and you can go into ..."

I tried to tell her that police work was my life. I used about every argument in the book, including the very reasonable and logical one that if I were to quit the force and go into something else, it would probably take years before I made even as much as nine thousand two hundred a year.

I could have been talking to myself.

"I know you, honey," was all she'd say. "If you just quit the force, I know—I *know* you'll make it. So please don't be stubborn. You can have it either way, but not both ways. Stick to your job and I'll be completely happy to go along the way we've been going. Otherwise ..."

Otherwise ...

"Pick up the Scotch, dear, and just charge it to my account."

Chapter 6

"Goddamn it," I said.

"You can't win them all," Pete said.

"Hell, sometimes you can't win any of them," I said.

He figured I was talking about this second, after-hours assignment.

Five minutes later he swung the wheel and turned east into Sixty-eighth Street. There was a patrol car, its red dome light winking off and on, in front of a four-story brownstone house within a couple of doors from the Avenue. Behind it was a taxicab with its flag down and behind that a sleek black limousine, with a uniformed policeman at the wheel. It had a regular license tag and no official emblem, but we both knew what it meant.

"Must be important," Pete said, swinging in to the curb in front of the patrol car. "Must be at least a deputy inspector, if not the Inspector himself."

He was right. When the patrolman at the door checked our badges and let us into the ground-floor lobby, the first man we saw was Inspector Daniel Flood, and he was talking with a small, heavy-set, white-haired man who was wearing evening clothes.

The Inspector didn't have to check our badges. He may not have known our names, but he knew who we were.

He excused himself, a little deferentially I thought, and crossed over to us.

"Where you boys from?" he asked.

"Joe Baron," I said. "Homicide. This is my partner, Pete Delanos."

The Inspector nodded.

"Homicide eh?" he said. "Well, we don't need homicide. This is a breaking-and-entry job. Why didn't they send someone from the robbery detail as long as they had to have people here from downtown?"

"I wouldn't know, sir," I said. "They just told us that there'd been a shooting and I guess ..."

"There's been a shooting, all right," the Inspector said. "Only it doesn't come under homicide, although I don't think that the victim is going to be alive by the time the ambulance gets here. You see, Dr. Pantell—" he nodded over toward the short man with the white hair— "Dr. Pantell came home from the theater before he was expected. Had a headache. The doctor let himself in with his key—the servants are out for the evening—and he went up to the fourth floor where he lives. Heard someone in the bedroom and he opened the door and turned on the light and found a man standing in front of the wall safe. He ordered the intruder to put up his hands. The doctor had a gun which he has a license to carry. When the prowler reached for his own gun, the doctor let him have it. Simple case of self-defense."

Pete sighed audibly.

"Fine," I said. "That lets us out. We've had a hard day and as long as it doesn't concern ..."

"Just a second, boys," the Inspector said. "You are here, so you might as well handle it. Just routine. The fact is, we didn't have anyone free at the local precinct, and that's why I came over myself. Can't tell just when I can get a man over here. So you boys might as well take care of things. It won't be complicated. All cut and dried."

I started to say something, started to protest, but just then there was the sound of the ambulance siren wailing somewhere up the street.

"Glad they got here. You can never tell about Bellevue on a Friday night. We haven't got a make yet, but you—" the Inspector pointed his index finger at Pete—"you go on down with him in the ambulance, just in case he should regain consciousness. You—Baron, you said, didn't you?—you hang around and handle the detail stuff. Shouldn't take any time at all and the boys at the precinct will appreciate it. Just be sure, when you make up the report, you send a duplicate over to the House."

Again I started to say something, but before I could speak, the Inspector walked back across to the man he'd been talking to.

I could have squawked. Inspector or not, he had no right fobbing off his own men's work on us. On the other hand, he was an inspector, and if he didn't recognize me, at least I recognized him. Inspector Daniel Flood had a reputation of being one of the toughest cops on the force—the kind who spares neither his men nor himself.

A smart cop, even if he is a homicide detective, first grade, doesn't go around standing on his technical rights with men like Inspector Flood. Not if he wants to stay a homicide detective, first grade.

Pete used a word which I was glad didn't reach the Inspector's ears.

There was a private elevator which went to the third floor, which apparently contained a living room, a dining room, and a kitchen. We had to walk up to the fourth floor.

"Bedroom at the end of the hallway," the uniformed patrolman on duty said.

There was another uniformed patrolman in the bedroom, and he stepped aside when we entered. He pointed down and said, "Enough lead in him to sink a ship. They better bring a basket. A stretcher would be wasted. He'll never make it."

Pete stepped over to the man lying on his back on the floor. He leaned down and stared at the chalk-white face. He didn't touch him. When he got up, his eyes went around the room. He shook his head.

"This boy's in the wrong place," he said.

"He sure is," the cop began, but Pete stared at him, and he closed his mouth.

"The wrong place, Pete?"

"Yeah, the wrong place. He should have been downstairs in the doc's office."

"It's too late now for any doc," the cop began again and Pete said, "Please shut up."

Pete turned to me. "His name's Phil Kenny and he's a junkie. I remember the face. He must have been after dope; can't figure what he was doing up here."

"Well, I don't think he's about to tell us," I said. "He looks as though he's had it."

"He's still breathing," Pete said. He shrugged and took out a notebook.

We started to work. Routine. I handled the boys who had first arrived on the scene and talked with Dr. Pantell. Pete accompanied the remnants of Phil Kenny downtown to Bellevue. He was back at headquarters, drinking a cup of tea, when I returned.

We cleaned it up fast and I had the report written and in by four o'clock. Then we went out, got into my car, and started uptown.

It was Pete's suggestion that we stop off at the cafeteria and have a bite to eat.

I was so late by then that a few more minutes wouldn't matter.

Chapter 7

It was a grim weekend. A weekend of shattering emotional experiences. A weekend which marked a turning point in my life.

Who can tell what really started it? Maybe it was nothing more than those six bottles of Scotch which Carol asked me to get. Maybe it was because even then I was losing my perspective.

But about Pete.

We sat in the front seat of the car, talking, watching the dawn break.

Saturday morning. We had had it all out and by the time he stepped to the pavement to go up to his two-room apartment, I was sure it was over and done with.

"So we are just going to forget it, Pete," I ended up saying. "Forget it ever happened. Maybe your theory is right and maybe it isn't. In any case, there is just one course you leave open to me. It's too late to do anything about the report, but Monday morning I am making an anonymous call to the local office of the Treasury Department.

"If you are right in your guess, if Dr. Pantell actually has that cash and it is hot money, they are going to know about it. Maybe it does come from drugs; I wouldn't know, but I'll go along on the theory. Maybe the doc is head of some high-class abortion ring. But you and I are going to forget all about it. It's too late as far as the department goes, far too late. But there is one way to clear my conscience and one way to clear yours, whether you want yours clear or not. That's by tipping off the Federals and letting them take over."

Pete shrugged. "You're the boss, Joe," he said.

"Whatever insane idea you may have entertained," I said, "forget it. It doesn't matter if Pantell is a cold-blooded murderer, it doesn't matter if the money is the end product of junk or some other illegal activity. It is not our money and it isn't going to be. So far as you and I are concerned, I am just going to assume that you're tired and maybe temporarily out of your mind. I think you should apply for a leave and take a long rest. Maybe by the time you get back, I'll have forgotten what you've told me."

Pete leaned on the door of the car and half smiled.

"My three-week vacation starts next Saturday," he said. "Did you forget, Joe?"

I didn't say anything.

"We'll do as you say, Joe," he said, "but I'd like to ask you just one question."

"Ask away."

"Tell me, Joe. Tell me the truth. I know you're moral and honest and decent and everything else a good cop should be. But tell me the truth. While we've been talking about it, somewhere in the back of your mind haven't you been thinking just the tiniest bit about whether or not we could really get away with it?"

The remark made me feel just a little bit like throwing up. "Pete, Pete," I said, "you're sick, kid. Really sick."

He stepped back and smiled and shook his head. "You know, Joe," he said, "ever since you and Carol have been married, I've envied you.

Some day I'd like to get a girl like Carol. I'd like to live the kind of life you live with a girl like Carol. I'll never do it on a detective's salary. I'll leave you with another thought." His mouth twisted in a sardonic smile. "You're not going to keep a girl like Carol on a detective's salary. Give it a thought, Joe, while you are making that anonymous call to the Treasury Department."

It was then, as he started for the entrance to the apartment house where he lived, and I started to push down on the gas pedal to pull away from the curb that I realized I had never really known or understood Pete Delanos.

To say that I was tired, both emotionally and physically exhausted, as I drove up the Saw Mill River Parkway and cut over through Armonk on my way home that Saturday morning, would be the understatement of all time. All I wanted to do was climb into a soft bed and sleep for about twenty hours straight.

I'd take a few minutes to have breakfast with Carol and then ...

I remembered about the Scotch, and because I was just entering Armonk, I cut over and stopped in front of the liquor store.

Al Horsey was on duty and he made some sort of lousy joke about starting the weekend early when I ordered the six bottles.

He took the bottles off a shelf and found an empty carton and then added it up, slapped on the tax, and said, "That will be fifty dollars and fifty-two cents. Why don't you just buy a full case? I can give it to you at a discount...."

I didn't bother to explain that no matter what the discount was, I was having enough trouble swinging six bottles, let alone twelve.

I had my wallet out and I was counting my money. There was a twenty, a ten, and a five and three ones. "Damn," I said. "I seem to be ..."

"Would you like a blank check, Mr. Baron?" Al asked.

I started to say yes and suddenly remembered the notice I had received in the mail on Thursday from the Country Trust Company, where I banked. My account was overdrawn by seven dollars and some odd cents. I also remembered that my next payday was a week off.

"Suppose I just stop by later and give you the rest of it," I said, sliding the bills across the counter.

Al shrugged and pushed the money back. "Hell," he said, "don't let it bother you, Mr. Baron. I'll just put it on Mrs. Baron's account."

Perhaps he was just trying to make it easy, just doing it the simplest, most pleasant way. I'm not sure. But at the time there seemed something patronizing about the way he said it; he seemed to have a knowing sneer on his face. I couldn't control my blush.

Reaching down, I picked up my bills, stuffed them back in my wallet. I reached for the carton holding the whisky. "You do that, Al," I said. "You just do that. And I'll be back here Monday morning and I'll ram every goddamned one of these empty bottles down your throat. I told you I'll stop by later with the money and I will."

I turned and stalked out of the store. He was staring at me as though I had suddenly gone completely out of my mind.

Chapter 8

Our place is seven miles northeast of Armonk, and by the time I had turned into the quarter-mile drive leading off the country road which marked the boundary, I was already suffering remorse. I had made the worst sort of fool out of myself and was wondering how I could straighten it out with Al the next time I saw him.

For some reason or other, I have never had the knack of getting along with people who have worked for us nor the merchants and storekeepers with whom we have traded. Perhaps it is because I realize subconsciously that there is something essentially fraudulent about my own position, that I am not really the gentleman that I pretend to be.

Carol, of course, is a sheer genius. Everybody loves her. She can ask people to perform the most impossible tasks, go far out of their way to do some little extra thing for her, and they adore her for it. She is always treated as though she is some sort of royalty bestowing a favor when she makes an outrageous request.

The trouble is, most of the people we know and have made friends of around where we live also seem to get this type of noblesse-oblige reception. When I tip a caddie a couple of bucks for carrying a bag around nine holes, I have the feeling he thinks I'm showing off. I don't even get a polite thanks. Friends of mine, men who have ten times my money, will give the same caddie a buck for eighteen holes, and you would think from the way the kid acts that he'd been knighted or had a papal blessing bestowed on him.

It may be that because I'm a cop, because the people I deal with in my work are always kept at arm's length, I have developed a formidable façade. But I don't think so. I think it is probably because, somewhere in the back of my mind, is the sneaking feeling that I am masquerading under false colors. That, for the grace of God, I should be the one doing the waiting on, rather than the other way around.

In any case, I was wondering just how to straighten things out with Al, and feeling like a complete heel, when I pulled the car up in front of the open doors of the three-car garage.

The MG was not there and it was not parked in the circle in front of the house.

I looked at my wrist watch. It read a quarter to ten.

I found the note on the kitchen table when I lugged the whisky into the house.

"Gone riding with Jack."

It was signed with a sprawling C.

There were two things missing. Always when Carol left me a note, she would mention when she'd be back. And always she would sign it "love."

I didn't have to be a mind reader to know that Carol was sore about something, and I didn't have to think very long about it to realize what was eating her.

I had promised, earlier in the week, to take her horseback riding on Saturday morning. She had every right to be sore.

By the time I had stripped and taken a shower and crawled into bed, I was feeling misused. Carol should have realized that if I was late, I must have been legitimately tied up. She should have known that it must have been pretty important, if I had failed to call. She could have waited. She could have ...

I suddenly realized that I was kidding myself. What I was sore about was the fact that of all the people in Westchester County she could have selected to go riding with, she'd had to pick the one man whom I disliked the most.

Jack and Paula Archer live about two miles down the road, in a fifteen-room, ultra modern stone and glass house which was designed by a world-famous Swedish architect, who probably makes more money in a month than I do in ten years. Jack Archer, a psychiatrist with a nationwide reputation, is no slouch himself. He once told Carol and me that his income is around two hundred and fifty thousand a year, and although he is a notorious liar and braggart, he probably wasn't exaggerating by more than fifty percent.

Jack is a slender, medium-sized man, in his late forties. He is, without doubt, the vainest person I have ever encountered. And not entirely without reason. He has one of those fine, extremely good-looking faces which almost verges on the feminine. He has a quick wit, a caustic tongue, and a capacity for alcohol which is phenomenal. There is no question that he is good in his profession; the fact that he can behave the way he does, drink the amount he does, and still make the income which he does, proves he is good.

Women take one look at Archer and are ready to desert their husbands and babies. He has the sort of glamour and charm which seems to make fools of even the most stable of females, irrespective of whether they are fifteen or fifty. He is well aware of this and has no hesitancy in letting the world in on the secret. He is the sort of man that another man instinctively dislikes and distrusts.

He knows this; it couldn't disturb him less.

Archer makes a fetish of sports, maintaining a couple of jumpers, playing an almost professional game of tennis, shooting golf in the seventies, and, in fact, doing very well in almost anything he tries. He also makes a fetish of breaking up other people's marriages, although as far as has ever been proved, he never goes past the stage of a one-night stand with the various women he enchants.

Paula Archer sees to that. Paula, whom I like, is a couple of years older than Jack, a fine-boned, large woman who has a good deal of basic common sense. They have two children, who are away at private schools.

There are two things about Archer which have always irritated me. From the first day I met him, and he found out what I do for a living, he has called me Dick Tracy. It is probably silly to let this bother me, but for some reason it always has. I think probably it is the condescending way in which he pronounces the words.

The second thing is his attitude toward Carol. I can't say that he even flirts with her, at least overtly. It is something more subtle. It is as though he were letting me know that any time he really wants her, all he has to do is wiggle his little finger.

I don't believe that I'm a jealous man. Oh, I won't deny there have been times I have had pangs, but in general, feeling the way I do about Carol, trusting her and loving her, it wouldn't be possible for me to be really jealous. On the other hand, when a man whom one sees constantly has that sort of attitude or rather conveys the idea that he has it—well, it does something to you.

With me the thing it does is make me want to knock the smirk off his face and change his profile. The fact that Carol herself considers Jack her best friend and confidant certainly doesn't improve my own attitude toward him. The added fact that he encourages her to drink a lot more than she should whenever the four of us are together is another thing which hardly endears him to me.

Not that Carol is a heavy drinker. Anything but. When we were first married, she never had more than a couple of drinks in any twenty-four-hour period. But in the last couple of years, especially since we have been running around with the crowd with whom we have surrounded ourselves, there have been a number of occasions when Carol, if not actually tight, certainly has had too many drinks to be considered a safe bet behind the wheel of a car.

Archer has a neat way of assuring Carol, when she is drinking, that one or two more can't make the slightest difference.

"And why shouldn't you, my dear?" he will say. "Why shouldn't you? You're the most beautiful woman I know and whisky is the elixir of life. Now take me for example ..."

It wasn't until we met the Archers that Carol had ever had a drink before five in the afternoon. More frequently than not, during the last couple of years, the four of us start on milk punches or Martinis within an hour after breakfast, on weekends.

Paula Archer drinks as much as her husband, up to the point when she falls asleep. This is usually about halfway through a party. It gives Jack a certain amount of freedom and is probably one of the reasons he and someone else's wife are usually missing during the later hours of the evenings.

Instead of falling asleep, I lay in bed thinking about how much I disliked the man. Thinking about him and Carol, riding along one of the trails somewhere in the neighborhood. Archer, in his reasonable, logical way, would be explaining to Carol that it was really a shame a man with her husband's brains didn't quit playing cops and robbers and settle down to making some important money.

Carol had let slip, not long back, that it was Archer who had first put the idea into her head that I was destined for better things than being a mere detective. He explained to her that the only reason I liked the work was because I had a basic inferiority complex and a sense of insecurity so that I was attracted by a job which gave me authority.

She had laughed when she told me about it. But I knew she had also taken it seriously. She considered Jack Archer the brightest man she had ever known. She was impressed by his reputation.

Had Carol had the advantage of knowing the psychiatrists I have known, around Bellevue and in police work, she would have realized exactly why Archer was good at his job. I am firmly convinced that to be a really first-rate psychiatrist it is necessary to be just a little bit nuttier than the person you are treating. The Alcoholics Anonymous theory. It takes one to cure one.

Takes one to cure one? Takes one to catch one.

I stopped thinking about my wife and Archer. I began to think again about Pete Delanos. I began to think about Pete and myself. And another doctor. A man named Horace Pantell. And a dead man named Phil Kenny—who had been a heroin addict and a safecracker.

Chapter 9

I couldn't have been sleeping more than an hour at the most.

When I picked up the receiver, it was a man's voice, a harsh, demanding voice.

"This Baron?"

I didn't know who it was, but I knew why. Not Mr. Baron and not Joe.

It had to be the department.

For the first time since I had been on the force, I ducked. "This is Mr. Baron's brother," I said. "Mr. and Mrs. Baron are away for the weekend."

"Can you reach him?"

"I'm not sure. Who's calling, please?"

There was a moment's hesitation and then the voice said, "Just tell him to call Inspector Flood's office if he returns or you can get hold of him."

I hung up. My hunch had been right. I was afraid my second hunch was also right. Trouble.

I had ducked for only one reason. It wasn't because I was dead tired and had had about an hour's sleep out of the last thirty-some hours. Cops aren't supposed to sleep like other human beings. No, it wasn't that. It was because of Carol. I knew what would happen if I were to let her down again.

It was the first time I had let Carol interfere with my job. I felt bad enough about that. I felt worse when I began to speculate about why the Inspector had called. It had to be connected with the Pantell case. It couldn't be anything else.

There was no point in worrying about it.

When trouble comes, meet it halfway. I could call back and say I'd received the message. Or I could call Pete. If they hadn't been able to reach me, he'd be next on the list.

Pete didn't answer the first several rings and I was about to hang up, really worried, when he finally came on.

"Yeah," he said. "Geez, I was in the can. Did they try and get you first, Joe?"

I said they had. "What's it all about, Pete?"

"We goofed," Pete said. "Seems someone down at the morgue was going over Phil Kenny's clothes. They found something—a slip of paper and it had a series of numbers written on it. Somehow or other it escaped us. The Inspector must have been reading the report when he got the information. God, that man must never sleep. Anyway, he started putting two and two together: He finally figured that those numbers might just possibly be the combination to that walk-in safe in Doc Pantell's bedroom. So he wants me to go over and check it."

"Why the hell doesn't he send one of his own boys?"

"His own boys are still all tied up and he said as long as we were on the thing, we might just as well close it. He seemed a little upset because we missed that slip of paper."

"O.K., Pete," I said. "I'll be in ..."

"Don't be a dope, Joe," Pete said. "Why bother? If he can't get you, you're in the clear. I'm in town and I can handle it."

I hesitated. I still didn't want to leave. There really was no reason I should. If only it were the old Pete ...

"I know what you're thinking, Joe," Pete said. "Listen, pal, I'm not crazy, you know. I'll pick up the uniformed man on the beat and take him up with me. You don't have to worry."

I took a long breath and exhaled it. "Good, Pete," I said. "You do that. And, Pete ..."

"I said not to worry. Have a pleasant weekend. Get lost and enjoy yourself. I'll see you Monday morning."

I started to say something but he'd already hung up.

That was the first phone call. The second came before I had a chance to get back to sleep. It was Paula Archer.

"This is Paula," she said, as soon as I answered. "Is Jack there, Joe?"

"Jack?"

"Yes. You see, after he and Carol came back and put the horses up, they called out something. I didn't quite hear because I was in the greenhouse with the door shut. They got in Carol's car and took off. I just wondered if Jack had stopped by ..."

"How long ago was that, Paula?" I asked.

She hesitated a minute or so and then said about two hours. I looked over at the clock radio. It read four o'clock. "I just wanted to ask Jack to pick up ..."

I knew from the tone of her voice that she didn't want to ask Jack to pick up anything. She was checking up.

"They'll probably be along any second, Paula," I said, trying to keep my voice neutral. "I wouldn't worry about them. They probably stopped by the club for a drink...."

"Oh, I'm not worried, Joe," Paula said. "But I did call the club. Well, anyway, as you say, they should be along any time. I'll see you tonight, Joe."

She hung up. I guess she'd forgot what it was she wanted Jack to pick up—just in case he stopped by.

I figured I was through sleeping for the day and so I got up and went downstairs and put the coffeepot on. I didn't wait for it to start percolating. Instead I went to the bar we had built in the butler's pantry and found an open bottle of bourbon and filled a highball glass half full and drank it straight.

I gagged. Then I did it over again and this time I didn't gag. I took the bottle out to the kitchen to spike the coffee.

I was having my second cup when I heard the purr of the MG as it pulled into the driveway. I smiled in what I suppose was a rather sardonic manner. I was just about half loaded.

For some reason, I started feeling pretty good. I'd been thinking about Pete and where Pete was. At first I had thought I was feeling relieved because I knew, once Pete and some uniformed officer walked into that fourth-floor room and opened the safe, whether there was a million dollars or not, the problem would be over. If the dough wasn't there, then Kenny had been lying. If the dough was there, nothing could be done about it.

That's what I first thought. But some small quiet voice told me I was kidding myself.

It wasn't about Pete I'd been thinking. It was myself. It would be over as far as I was concerned and that was the important thing.

Carol walked into the room.

"Hi, stranger," she said. She looked like six million dollars. She was wearing whipcord jodhpurs, a cambric shirt with a blue foulard which matched her eyes. Her short, blonde hair was disheveled and I knew that the top on the MG had been down.

"My gawd, Joe," she said, looking over at the bourbon bottle. "I didn't think I'd live to see the day. Booze and black coffee for breakfast. I suppose this *is* your breakfast?"

"Where the hell have you been?" I asked. "Paula has been trying to trace Jack down and ..."

She stopped smiling. "What does that one mean?" she said. She crossed over and took a cup from the shelf and poured herself some coffee.

"It means I'm damned tired of having women call up and ask where you have taken their husbands."

I felt like a fool when I said it, but I couldn't help myself.

Carol looked as though I had slapped her. "Joe," she said, "you must be drunk. What in the world has gotten into you? Jack and I ..."

"I'm damned sick of hearing about you and Jack," I said. "When I come home expecting breakfast ..."

She carefully put the cup down and stood with her hands on her hips. "See here, chum," she said, and the last trace of a smile had disappeared. "See here. You wake me out of a sound sleep to tell me you'll be along in an hour, and then I wait more than four hours ..."

"Listen," I said, "you know damned well that something came up. Pete ..."

"I'm a little tired of hearing about Pete," Carol said. "The Bell telephone system is very efficient and I'm sure you had a dime ..."

She shouldn't have mentioned money.

I took another drink.

"I'm going to tell you something," I began, but that's as far as I got.

"You're drunk," Carol said. "I might have guessed it. "Whatever made you light into Al?"

"Al?"

"Al—at the liquor store. We stopped by to get some brandy and ..."

"What do you mean you stopped by to get brandy? Goddamn it, I picked up the Scotch ..."

"I heard about it," Carol said. "Jack happens to be on a brandy kick and we stopped by so that I'd have brandy in the house for the party and Al said that you ..."

She shouldn't have mentioned money and she shouldn't have mentioned Jack.

"If that two-bit quack shows up at this house tonight," I yelled, "I'll ..."

Carol turned and walked out of the room.

The two cups of black coffee I forced down my throat didn't do any good at all. I still felt half drunk. What was a lot worse, I felt like a complete, unmitigated heel.

Chapter 10

I finally managed to get in three and a half hours' sleep. Min, the colored girl who comes in three days a week and also stands by for weekend parties, showed up ten minutes after Carol walked out of the kitchen. By this time I was really beginning to feel remorse.

I went upstairs and Carol was in the bedroom changing clothes. For the first few minutes neither of us said a word. Finally, after wandering around the room aimlessly, turning over the pages of a magazine and picking some lint off of the bedspread and doing anything but saying what I wanted to say, I turned to Carol.

"Baby," I said, "I'm sorry. I'm behaving like a first-class idiot. It's been a tough day, or rather a tough day and night and day, and I guess I'm just not myself. Can't we just ..."

"You better climb in bed and get a nap," Carol said. "We've asked these people and there's no reason to spoil ..."

"I said I'm sorry, Carol," I repeated. "I guess I was acting like a cop again. You know, honey ..."

She crossed the room and looked up at me for a moment. But she didn't smile.

"Get some sleep, Joe," she said. "I'll wake you up when people start coming."

I reached out and put my arms around her and I kissed her. It was like kissing an iceberg.

It was the first time in six years that we had seriously squabbled.

Nobody bothered to wake me up, but I guess Carol must have set the clock radio for eight-thirty. I thought at first it was morning when I heard the music. And then I heard the noise coming from below. The stereo was going full blast. I looked at the clock and then I got out of bed. I felt like hell.

It was shortly after nine when I got downstairs. I'd managed a cold shower and a shave and I'd put on clean clothes and I was famished.

It was the usual crowd.

Tina Marble was standing at the bottom of the steps. Tina is a dark-haired, middle-aged fading beauty whose greatest claim to distinction lies in the fact that she inherited five million dollars and has had five husbands, all of whom were wealthier than herself.

She drinks like a fish and spends summers sailing on the Sound. She winters in France. In between times she stops by her place in

Bedford Village where she manages to remain stoned twenty-four hours a day.

Tina was holding two glasses, both filled with something amber which, from the color, was undiluted.

She smiled at me and handed me a glass and I hesitated long enough to empty it.

A mistake. I lost my appetite.

Three or four couples were dancing, the rug rolled back along one wall. I looked around but didn't see Carol.

I wandered through the living room and out into the kitchen, which was crowded. Paula Archer was fooling with a tray of anchovies and nodded at me. I went on into the pantry, which is divided by a shoulder-high wall from the kitchen.

There was a tall stool in front of the service counter and as I settled on the stool a slender hand reached over the counter and it held a Martini glass. There was a diamond bracelet on the wrist and three of the fingers were weighted down with rings. It was a nice hand. It could have belonged to anyone.

I took the Martini.

I thought to myself, what the hell is wrong with me? Here I am, in my own house, entertaining some of the very best people that you can find. Brains, money, talent, social grace. You name it, they got it. I've got a young, attractive, and very beautiful wife whom I love and who, at least up until a very short time ago, loved me. I've got it made. And I hated it. I didn't like the people; I didn't particularly admire either their brains or accomplishments; I was not impressed by their social standing. But there wasn't a thing wrong with these people. Oh, of course there's the usual amount of cheating and adultery, but no worse than you can find in any middle-class suburb. The usual number of lushes, but no more than you'd see at any PTA meeting. The usual number of broken marriages and marriages about to be broken, but no more than the national average.

It must be me.

I wasn't one of them, and there was no point in kidding myself about that. I was a self-made cop, to coin a rather silly phrase. There were a lot of self-made guys here.

Of course there was one difference. The self-made boys who were our guests had really made it. With the exception of Paul Miller, the local high-school English teacher whom everybody likes and who makes about two thousand a year less than I make, there wasn't one of them who didn't make me look like a pauper and a failure.

These are the people Carol likes. These are her friends and companions. Well, I love Carol, so why don't I love them?

I didn't have to think about it too long.

Jealousy. Jealousy and a sense of inferiority.

I was beginning to feel like a second-class citizen. There was no point in kidding myself. I was a second-class citizen. A dumb cop.

I was getting maudlin.

Suddenly I laughed. I was being a plain god-damned fool. I started to get up, to go back to the kitchen to find something to eat. It was the sound of someone entering the room which stopped me. I don't know why, but I just sat back and waited behind the partition in the pantry. Maybe it was because I knew I was drunk and wanted to get some food in me before seeing anyone.

The minute the voice started speaking, I recognized it. "He really gets away with murder."

It was a low, nasal voice, affected and bored. It belonged to Mitzi Harper, who is Darell Harper's wife and has been cheating on the old boy from the first year of their marriage.

"This time he may get murdered. That is, of course, if the exception to the rule proves out and the husband isn't the last one to know."

That voice was easy too. Mary Gildersleeve. Her husband had put a shotgun into his mouth and pulled both triggers, less than a year ago. She proudly and justifiably had the reputation of being the happiest widow as well as the most malicious gossip north of the Harlem River.

"I don't know why Paula takes it," Mitzi said. "It's an even bigger mystery how he managed to seduce our little friend. That man has magic."

"Don't be a damned fool," Mary answered. "You should know more about women than that. No man ever seduces a woman. Men like to think that they do, but the theory is a lot of hogwash. The woman doesn't live who can be made if she doesn't want to be made. You should know, darling. God knows you've been had by everything with pants on in this country."

"There's no point in being snotty, darling," Mitzi said. "You're hardly a virgin yourself. Anyway the thing still mystifies me. If there was one gal in this neighborhood that I didn't think Jack could make, it's our Dick Tracy's wife."

In thinking about it later, I understood that even then I didn't for one second actually doubt Carol or question her faithfulness. I understood that these women were malicious gossips, ready to crucify anyone on the slightest evidence or no evidence at all. I am not even sure if it was actual jealousy which I felt. It was a far more subtle thing.

I was drunk of course. There can be no doubt of that. I was not thinking clearly and I was in no position, emotionally or physically, to think clearly.

But I felt a blind fury. Not only at Jack Archer but at Carol herself.

I heard the two women leave the kitchen and I stood up, staggering a little. I not only hated Carol and Jack Archer; I hated every one of our so-called friends.

It was my house and I was master of my own castle. I'd be goddamned if I was going to entertain a collection of rich bums, phonies, and scandalmongers. Bitches, drunks, adulterers.

Passing through the kitchen, I picked up a half-filled bottle of whisky in one hand and a full one in the other. I walked into the living room. There were perhaps fifteen or twenty people sitting and standing around. They were a blur.

But in the center of the floor a couple were dancing. There was a lot of noise and laughter.

I guess they must have been doing the twist, because, when the music suddenly stopped, they moved close to each other, laughing. The man put his arms around his partner, pulling her to him, and kissed her.

For a moment everything was crystal clear.

Archer stood there holding my wife, kissing her.

I lifted the partly filled bottle to my lips and then I threw it across the room. It crashed against the fireplace. I threw the second bottle.

They were still there in the center of the floor when I reached them. Still in each other's arms. I think Archer was still laughing when my fist smashed into his face. I only hit him once because he was not there a second later.

Carol's mouth was open and her eyes were wide. It is all I remember before my hand lashed out and I struck her.

"Get out," I said. "All of you—out!"

Chapter 11

Pete Delanos poured the coffee from the quart container into a glass and carried it over and sat on the chair at the side of the bed.

"It's hot, Joe," he said, handing it to me. "Be careful."

I took the glass, hunching myself up in the bed. I didn't think I would be able to get it down, but I'd try. Nothing could make me feel any worse. I had nowhere to go but up.

Pete looked at me closely. He wasn't smiling.

"And you mean, Joe, that you honestly don't remember a thing? You don't remember leaving the house, getting into the car, and driving all the way into town? Passing the toll booths—nothing?"

I shook my head. "Nothing."

"You remember hitting ..."

"I've told you, Pete," I said. "Yes, I remember hitting Carol. And not one other thing until I woke up here an hour ago. Oh God. What did I say? Did I ..."

"I've told you, Joe," Pete said. "You rang the bell downstairs, and I pressed the button and you got up here under your own power. When I opened the door you were just standing there—mumbling and about to fall down. I got you inside and at first I thought you'd been hurt. And then I got a whiff of your breath. You were drunk—as drunk as I have ever seen you—just about as drunk as I've ever seen anyone."

I didn't say anything. I tried the coffee, but it was too hot to drink. The glass was burning my hand, and I sat it on the table next to the bed.

I groaned.

"You mumbled and then you were sick and I finally got you to bed. You didn't say anything that made any sense at all. Just mumbled. And then you passed out. You were out for a good five hours."

Pete looked at his watch. "It's six-thirty now—Sunday," he said. "You got here around four this morning."

"Oh Christ. Carol. I've got to ..."

"Take it easy, Joe," Pete said. "I just talked to her. I called your house when I went out to get the coffee."

I looked at him, afraid of what he might say next.

"You didn't hurt her. At least nothing serious. You got a pretty heavy hand and from what she says, she's got a beautiful black eye and a sore face, but you didn't really injure her. The guy you hit—well, he didn't do so well. You broke his nose."

I didn't even want to hear it, but I had to. "And Carol?"

"She was worried sick, Joe. And she was glad to know that you were here and that you are all right."

"Did she ..."

"She asked me to bring you home. She didn't sound exactly

overwhelmed with affection or love, Joe, but I guess you could hardly expect her to be. But she did ask me to bring you home. I think she figures you must be sick, must have temporarily blown your top. Frankly, I think maybe she's right. Tell me, Joe, what did set you off?"

I groaned again. "It's a long story, Pete," I said. "Listen, I don't want to talk about it. I don't even want to think about it. I know what the trouble is. Believe me, I do know. I'm in love with Carol, Pete, I guess I don't have to tell you that. But it just isn't working. It can never work."

"I've been telling you that since the day you got married, kid," Pete said. "Someday you've got to face things as they are and not as you would like them to be. If you want to live a certain kind of life, have certain things, love certain people, then you have to take it on their terms and not on your own."

"Yeah," I said. "Yeah. I know. I'm beginning to understand."

"You have to pay the price for what you get—if you want it bad enough."

"I'm beginning to understand," I said.

For several minutes we didn't talk. And then I turned and looked at Pete.

He was watching me, noncommittal.

"Pete, what happened when you went over to Pantell's place last night?"

"What I expected," Pete said, standing up and lighting a cigarette. "The Inspector's hunch was right. That slip of paper they found on Phil Kenny did have the combination to the safe written on it."

"Yes?"

"Yeah, it was the combination to the walk-in safe in the bedroom. I opened the safe. The uniformed cop from the beat was with me. Dr. Pantell didn't even bother to come up with us after giving us permission to examine the safe again."

"And?"

"And the safe was empty. Nothing at all. Clean as whistle."

"Got some more coffee in the container, Pete?" I asked.

I drew a long sigh. I guess it was a sign of relief.

"Well, that winds that up," I said, at last.

Pete shook his head. "Not exactly."

I looked up at him quickly. "What do you mean, not exactly? If there was no dough, then Kenny was taking you for a ride. Or he may have thought there was money and been confused and believed he had seen it. After all, the guy was dying. Or he may have just been lying...."

"He wasn't lying, Joe."

I moved, twisting around and putting my bare feet on the floor and sitting on the side of the bed.

"He wasn't lying?"

"No, Joe. Phil Kenny wasn't lying. When we opened the safe and found it empty, I sent the uniformed cop—his name by the way is Barsky—down to call the Inspector's office and let him know. While Barsky was gone, I took a flashlight and really went over that strong box."

"What were you looking for?"

"I wasn't sure at the time," Pete said. "But I can tell you what I found."

As he was speaking, he reached into his pocket and took out his wallet. He opened it and extracted a slender band of yellow paper, which he unfolded. It was about twelve inches long and an inch wide and the ends were ragged, as though they had been torn. He handed it to me, wordlessly.

One side was a blank. I turned it over.

There was a printed legend.

It read: "Fifty thousand dollars. Fifties."

I could feel the blood drain out of my face as I slowly raised my eyes.

Pete stood in front of me, his legs spread and his hands on his hips. He was slowly nodding his head up and down.

"That's right, Joe," he said. "One of the bands from one of those stacks of bills Phil Kenny saw before Dr. Pantell gunned him down. Probably torn off accidentally while the doctor was removing the money. He must have figured there was a chance we might return and check the safe."

It took me a little time to digest it.

"And what will he do now?" I asked at last.

"Why, I should imagine that once he knows the department checked the safe and found it empty, he'll probably put it back."

Again I sat there for a few long minutes, thinking. And then finally again I looked up at Pete.

He hadn't moved; he was still watching me.

"How come you happen to have the band, Pete?" I asked, looking down at the slip of paper in my hand. "Is this just another little thing you have left out of a report?"

It was Pete's turn to stare at me and not answer.

"Just another little oversight ..."

"That's right, Joe," Pete said at last. "Just another little oversight.

Maybe," he hesitated a long moment and then continued, "maybe you can give this information to the U.S. Treasury Department when you call them in the morning, along with the ..."

I stood up and reached for the container. But it was empty.

"Go out and get some more coffee, Pete," I said. "Get some more coffee and get a couple of sandwiches."

He nodded, reaching for his hat which he had thrown on the end of the bed.

I stopped him just as he was reaching for the doorknob.

"Pete," I said. "Pete—I don't think I'll be calling the Treasury Department in the morning."

It was Pete's turn to take a long breath and slowly expel it.

I nodded my head very slowly. "There's an awful lot we still don't know," I said. "A lot. Maybe it's legitimate dough. Maybe he won't put it back. Maybe Dr. Pantell ..."

"We're detectives, aren't we, Joe?" Pete said. "We're detectives. Detectives are supposed to find things out."

He opened the door and closed it quietly behind him, and I heard his hard heels as he walked down the hallway toward the elevator.

It took him a long time to get the coffee and the sandwiches. At least it seemed like a long time.

You can do one hell of a lot of thinking about a million dollars or more in cold hard cash in a reasonably short time, so maybe it didn't take him quite as long as I thought it took him.

Chapter 12

A cop, and especially a detective, is forced in the course of his career to sit in on and be a witness to a thousand domestic brawls of one kind or another. Some come out all right in the long run, some lead to violence, and now and then some lead to murder. I have had my share of them, and, almost without exception, my sympathies lay with the injured party. But I had often heard that old bromide that goes "it's a lot easier on you to be the victim than it is to be the guilty person."

That's the way it was when I returned home late Sunday evening.

If Carol had said anything, if she had been nasty or sullen or bitter or almost any way except the way she was, it would have been easier. She could have bawled me out, threatened to leave, even lost her temper and taken a swing at me or thrown an ash tray, and I wouldn't have minded a bit. I would almost have welcomed it.

But she did none of these things. She acted exactly as though Saturday night had never occurred. She acted as though I had not got cockeyed drunk, not lost my temper, not made a complete fool of myself. Not given her that vicious black and purple right eye which she had carefully attempted to conceal behind the dark lens of her sunglasses and carefully applied make-up.

We had dinner in silence and after dinner she put on a sport jacket and tied a scarf around her neck.

"I'm going out for a while," she said.

I didn't ask her where she was going and she didn't volunteer any information. I heard the sound of the MG's engine as she raced the motor and shifted into gear, and then I went into the living room and turned on television. But I couldn't concentrate on it and so I turned it off and tried to read. At ten o'clock Carol still hadn't returned and so I went up and got into bed.

She got home shortly before midnight, and when she came into the bedroom and started to undress, I kept my eyes closed and pretended to be asleep.

When she crawled into bed, she was wearing a heavy flannel nightgown. It was the first time since we had been married that she hadn't slept raw.

I reached over and touched her and she made no response. Finally she turned her back to me.

"Good night, Joe," she said.

"Listen, darling ..."

But she cut me short. "I'm tired, Joe, and I want to go to sleep."

"But..."

She half turned and her hand reached over and held mine for a moment. "Go to sleep, Joe," she said. "I'm not mad and I still love you. But right now I'm tired and I just want to be left alone. There are a few things I have to think out and I want to be left alone for a while. I'm tired and you should be pretty tired yourself. Try and get some sleep."

Chapter 13

I guess Pete and I have known each other so long that it really isn't necessary for one of us to say anything to know what the other is thinking. When I picked him up on Monday morning, he asked how I was feeling and when I grunted, noncommittally, he shrugged and said, "I understand."

It wasn't until we were almost at Centre Street that he turned toward me, one eyebrow raised and a slightly quizzical expression on his face.

"So you've thought it over?" he said. I knew what he was talking about.

"I've thought it over."

"And ..."

"And when we get upstairs," I said, "I'm going to call the captain and tell him I'd like a couple of days to do a little running around on the Pantell-Kenny case. After all, it was a homicide, even if a justifiable homicide. I'll just explain that there are a couple of loose ends we would like to tie up. Sort of hint that perhaps Kenny might have been mixed up in a couple of other jobs—where a gun was used. If we are lucky, if nothing much is breaking, we'll get the time. We don't want to be sticking our noses into anything without the department knowing about it."

Pete smiled.

"That's what I've been wanting you to say, Joe," he said. "So you do see it my way...."

"I don't see it any way yet," I said shortly. "I just said we will pursue it a little bit farther. Find out a few things. We can talk about it after we know a little more."

"That's good enough for me, chum," Pete said. "And believe me, there's plenty more to find out. I'll bet you ..."

"We won't talk about it, Pete," I said.

Pete nodded. He was satisfied. We understood each other.

The captain thought it was a little foolish to waste any more time on it. Thought that the precinct boys should clean up their own back yard. But it had been a slow weekend, nothing much was breaking, and he let us have it our way. We could work on it if we insisted, but he warned us to clear it with Inspector Flood over at the precinct. And he added that we should keep in touch; if anything important came up, we were to drop it back in the laps of Flood's men.

While I waited to have the file of Phil Kenny sent up from downstairs, I spoke to Pete.

"You take Dr. Pantell," I said, "and I'll work on Kenny. Find out everything you can about him. Everything. I don't have to explain it to you. But be careful. Stay away from the doc himself and be careful when you talk with anyone who knows him. I don't want him to get any idea that we are curious. I don't want him going back to Flood with a squawk. But I want everything there is on him, from the time he started kindergarten, through school, medical school, his internship, and right up to today. I want to know what kind of friends he has, what kind of a practice, what are his hobbies. Everything there is. But as I say, be careful."

"Don't worry, Joe," Pete said. "You don't have to draw a diagram."

"And keep in touch," I said as he reached for his hat. "Call in every hour."

He nodded, punched me lightly in the ribs, and left. He was whistling, half under his breath. I knew what he was thinking about. He was thinking about a million dollars. And so was I.

Phil Kenny had an older brother named Francis Xavier, who was midway in a ten-to-twenty stretch in Dannemora, having taken a second fall on an armed larceny rap. I'd get around to him, but there was no hurry. He'd keep.

Phil had a widowed mother, with a Flatbush address and she was in her late seventies. She'd keep too.

He had an address, 716 East Eighteenth Street, Manhattan. The file said that he rented an apartment there and at the time it was written up, some two years back, he'd been paying eighty-five dollars a month rent. Two rooms, a kitchenette, and a bath, on the third floor, and there was a front entrance and a fire escape in the rear. They put that sort of information in the reports; it sometimes comes in handy.

I decided that maybe the address wouldn't keep. I knew that someone had undoubtedly been there from the precinct, but I figured I would give it a tumble. I had to start somewhere.

I wrote down a few more notes, things like who his friends had been, where he hung out, how he spent his time. That sort of thing. And then I sent the folder back to the file room and reached for my hat.

The telephone on the desk rang.

"Lady says she's your wife," the sergeant said and a moment later Carol's voice came over the wire.

"Joe?" she said.

I started to answer but she interrupted.

"I forgot something before you left this morning," Carol said.

Her voice was noncommittal.

"Yes?"

"I forgot to kiss you good-by."

I tried to say something then, but that lump in my throat got in the way and I guess I just mumbled. She went on talking before I could find my voice.

"If it will make you feel any better," she said, "I just want to say that I am still mad as blazes. And I don't want to listen to any apologies. But I did forget to kiss you good-by and tell you that I still love you. That's all."

I was still trying to say something when the line went dead.

I looked up and Lieutenant Goldrick was standing next to the desk and looking down at me, smiling.

"What's the matter, kid?" he said. "You're gulping like a damned goldfish. You hit the numbers or something?"

I nodded. "I hit the jackpot," I said.

If there had been any lingering doubts in my mind about playing along with Pete, they disappeared as I went downstairs and walked over to where I had parked my car. If money lay at the root of the trouble between Carol and myself, if money was the problem, then I would get money. And I no longer cared how I got it.

I drove through the heavy early morning traffic, going uptown.

It was a six-story tenement house, almost all the way over to the East River. Some smart operator had probably picked it up for a song at a tax sale and spent a few bucks cleaning it up a little on the outside, adding a new doorway and front steps, and painting the ancient rose bricks white. It hadn't helped much.

I parked in front of the place and crossed the sidewalk. There was an iron grilled gate at the street level, next to the stairway and I rang the bell. My hunch was right. It was the janitor's basement apartment.

She was an old lady with white hair and an Italian accent and she was smart. She knew at once I was a cop. She even knew what I had come about. She must have been psychic.

"You'll be coming about Mista Kenny," she said, before I could reach for my badge. "He'sa on third, in rear."

Well, of course I knew he wasn't, but I understood what she meant.

"If you have a key," I began, and by now I had unfolded my wallet and exposed my shield. But she didn't even look at it.

"Justa knock," she said.

"Justa knock?"

"Justa knock."

I started to say something, to ask her... But she turned and went back down the several steps leading to her basement rooms.

I walked around the iron rail and went to the front door and entered a dingy lobby. A dozen broken mailboxes lined one wall and there were several almost illegible names in their slots. The bells had long ago ceased to work and the front door was ajar. I walked through it and started up the stairs. A drunk was sitting at the foot of the first flight, an empty bottle in his listless hand and an emptier look in his rheumy eyes. He didn't look up as I passed him. Somewhere down the hallway a man cursed and a woman cried out.

I went up to the third floor. There were two doors, one in the front and one in the rear. I remembered that the report had mentioned a rear fire escape so I went to the rear door and I knocked. I don't know exactly why I knocked; I certainly didn't expect anyone to answer. But the old lady downstairs had said knock, so I knocked. Maybe Kenny's mother had come in from Flatbush to clean out the place. It's a sure thing the brother up in Dannemora wouldn't be there doing it.

Nothing happened and I knocked again, louder. I waited. And then I reached for the knob, and as I did, the door suddenly opened.

Chapter 14

It wasn't his mother.

She didn't look like anybody's mother. She didn't talk like one either.

She said, "Well—what the hell do you want?"

She stood about five foot even in her stocking feet, and I know because that was what she was wearing. Stockings, black silk. There was a very short red pleated skirt above the stockings, and it was a nice match for her hair which was also short and also red but of a far deeper shade. She wore a man's white shirt, which was open at the throat and had the sleeves rolled up to her elbows. It was about six sizes too big for her, except where it crossed her breasts and there it fitted just nicely.

She had on a red leather belt, which made three shades of red if you didn't allow for the petulant, wide mouth which was a slash of lipstick and open enough to show the twin rows of small, white teeth.

She had high cheekbones and her eyes were very large and just a trifle slanted, but it may have been the effect of the eyebrows, which were black, and the eyelashes, which, if they were real, were the longest I had ever seen on a woman.

She was rather slight, and I doubted if she scaled more than a hundred. I could have put my two hands around her slender waist and they would have met, but there was nothing at all fragile or childish about her superb figure. She was tiny but she was every inch woman. She had a complexion that made you know at once that her skin would be softer than the finest silk. But she had a voice like a foghorn, and she was using it again.

"I said, what the hell do you want?"

She started to shut the door.

I put my foot forward, started to reach for my wallet again.

The words were tough and the voice was harsh. But I didn't get the impression that she was tough. I suddenly understood what it was. She was frightened. Very, very frightened.

I had my wallet out now and flashed the badge, and I saw the color slowly come back into her face. She shrugged, stepped back.

"Another one," she said, resignedly. "Well, come on in."

I guess she must have been sleeping in the front room, which was the living room, because there were several disarrayed blankets and a pillow on the long, wide couch. Next to it was an ash tray and it was overflowing with cigarette butts. It was a small, rectangular room and oddly enough it wasn't unattractive. The furniture was fairly new—clean, modern, and in good taste. There was wall-to-wall carpeting, a pleasantly patterned pastel paper on the far wall and clean matching paint on the others. An expensive combination stereo and television stood in one corner, and there was a small service bar facing it. The bar had been opened and a couple of bottles stood on it, half filled and uncorked. There was only one glass. An ice bucket still held several cubes. There was a partly used up case of club soda on the floor.

Venetian blinds covered the two windows and were closed; the light came from three floor lamps.

A one-armed bandit, which took quarters, stood over in the far corner. Somehow, in that pleasantly furnished apartment, it looked almost obscene. Like a carnival barker at a church supper.

She crossed the room and put a quarter in the slot machine and pulled the lever and a moment later a small cascade of coins dangled in the payoff box. She left them untouched, moved to the couch and sat down, crossing her legs.

"Pour yourself a drink, cop," she said. "There's gin and there's rye and there's Scotch."

"It's a little early in the day," I said.

"Well, then, pour me one," she said. "It's never too early for me."

I went to the bar and found two clean glasses and I poured from the Scotch bottle, about two fingers in each glass.

"Mine on the rocks," she said.

I put some ice in one glass and handed it to her and then filled the other half full of soda. I crossed to the armchair facing the couch, but

I didn't sit down. I put the glass on the table next to it.

"And you are?" I began.

"Rosalie," she said. "Phil's girl."

"Alone?"

"Alone."

I turned toward the door which I figured led to the bedroom.

"Do you mind?"

"Be my guest," she said, and lifted the glass to her mouth. She looked bored.

But she wasn't. She was wide awake and very alert.

I looked into the bedroom and then entered and opened a door into a tile bath. I closed it and looked into the closet, which was filled with men's clothes. A second closet must have belonged to her. There were no other rooms, so I went back to the living room and opened the draw curtains which concealed a kitchenette.

She was alone all right.

I returned to the chair and sat down and picked up the drink.

"What are you frightened of?" I said.

She looked up quickly then. "Cops always scare me a little," she said. The voice no longer a foghorn.

"Not so," I said. "You stopped being scared the very second I showed you the tin. Cops put you at your ease."

"All right, officer," she said, "cops put me at ease. Now just what is it you want, now that you have put me at my ease? I've already told your comrades everything I know."

"Tell me," I said. "Who are you, what ..."

She sighed, took another sip of whisky.

"Again?" she said. "I've already been checked out about five times in the last twenty-four hours. Oh well, you might as well join the group."

She crossed her legs the other way, and I suddenly realized that I had been selling Phil Kenny a little short. He might have been a junkie and a small-time punk, but he had a certain element of taste.

"I'm Rosalie Carver. Twenty-two years old. The late Phil Kenny's girl—or common-law wife, if you want to put it that way. We have been living together since I was nineteen. I don't work, but when I did I was in a chorus line. No record and I'm not on the junk. As soon as the funeral is over, I'm going to see that Phil's things get sent to his mother. And then I'm going to blow."

"Blow where?"

"Back home. To the Middle West. Where I came from. And where I came from is my own business."

She stood up then and walked to the bar.

"Ready?"

"Not quite," I said. "Maybe you better take it a little slow yourself...."

"Maybe you better just mind your own business," she said. "So I've told you who I am. Who are you?"

"Joe Baron, detective first grade. Homicide. Working out of headquarters," I said.

"You look like a Joe," she said. "What do you want from me? Kenny's dead. Killed, they tell me, while performing an armed robbery. No mystery."

"No mystery," I said. "I guess you knew a lot about Phil Kenny...."

"I knew everything and I knew nothing," she said. She made a slightly stiffer drink than I had given her and returned to the couch. This time she tucked her legs up under her. I had a little difficulty keeping my mind on my job.

"I knew that he was a junkie. But he didn't peddle it, in spite of what the cops may think. And anyway, some of our best people are users. Hell, if they clamped down on junkies, they would be putting half of the medical profession in the country out of business. Also, I guess he did a few other things that weren't too legal. But I wouldn't know anything about that. All I know is that he was good to me. He gave me everything he could and he didn't ask a damned thing in return. He picked me up when I was broke and on the town. He treated me decent and he didn't push me around. He didn't even insist that I love him. I didn't love him and I didn't particularly admire him. But I liked him and I appreciated him. I'm sorry he's dead, sorry he had to go out the way he did. But I don't know a thing about his business, I don't know any of his friends, and I haven't a thing to say about him to the police or anyone else, except that he was good to me and kind to me. And that is that."

"That is that," I said. "So now tell me what it is you are afraid of."

"I'm afraid of cops like you, who come around asking a lot of questions and looking to make trouble."

"I'm not looking to make trouble," I said. "In fact, I'm going to take you at your face value. I believe everything you have said. You're not a junkie, you have no criminal record, you don't want any trouble."

"O.K. Then what is it you want? I've already gone through the song and dance with the police. They've checked me out. What do you want?"

"I want to know a few things about Phil Kenny."

She slowly shook her head. "You've come to the wrong place," she said. "Let me explain something to you. You probably won't believe me, but I know almost nothing at all about Phil. Sure, I've been living with him. As man and wife. But do you know something? We didn't even sleep together. That's right. Didn't even sleep together. Phil treated me like he would have treated a daughter. He liked me the way he liked good music, and nice things. He liked to have me dress up and go out with him. To the track and to restaurants and to the theater. And then he would come back home and he'd give himself a shot in the arm and he'd pour me a drink and we'd sit and look at television or play records and later on he'd take another jolt and he'd go off somewhere into his private dream world.

"I cooked his meals, took care of his clothes; looked after him. He supplied the money. Where and how he got it was his business and I didn't know, didn't want to know, and still don't.

"Along the line, he managed to build up a bank account for me. It comes to something like three thousand bucks. I'm sending a grand of it over to his mother, sending another thousand to that brother of his in prison, and the other thousand I'm taking as a stake for a new start. The rest of his stuff goes to his mother. That's it. Finis."

"No friends?" I asked.

She looked up sharply.

"I mean Kenny. Didn't he have some old buddies? ..."

"He knew guys out at the track. He was away a lot during the daytime and I guess he saw people, around pool halls or wherever he hung out. But not around here. We didn't have friends. I've been taking dancing and singing lessons and I kept busy. We were satisfied with each other's company."

She started to get up and the telephone on the small mahogany table next to the couch suddenly pealed. She stopped in her tracks. Her hand shook a little as she reached for the receiver.

I couldn't hear the voice at the other end, but she spoke hurriedly after a moment.

"You have the wrong number," she said and hung up. She went to the bar and began pouring a third drink.

"Do you drink so much because you're frightened?" I asked.

She swung toward me so quickly that the glass in her hand spilled half of its contents on the floor.

"Why don't you get out, Joe?" she said. "Your name is Joe, isn't it?"

"It's Joe," I said. "I don't want to get out. I want to talk to you. You interest me. In fact I even like you."

She half smiled. "If you like me, have another drink with me. And talk to me all you want to. I like to be talked to. But don't ask me any more questions. Don't talk to me about Phil Kenny. And for God's sake, stop acting like a cop. I could stand to see a human being for a change. So make like a human being if you can. I suppose even cops can be human if they really try, can't they?"

"Cops are human as well as anyone else," I said.

I got up and went over beside her and reached for the Scotch. She turned toward me and her hand came out and she took the bottle and put the cap on it. She poured the contents of her own drink into the ice bucket.

"Listen," she said. "You are right about my drinking too much. At least without food. So why don't we go out and get something to eat some place? And then later we can have a few more drinks and you can talk to me all you want to. Just so you obey the rules."

"The rules?"

"Yeah, about Phil Kenny. Subject is out of bounds."

"Anything else out of bounds?"

She cocked her head and looked up at me. "Just what might you have in mind?"

I felt the blush coming in spite of myself.

She didn't wait for me to answer. "I'll get into some clothes," she said, and a moment later she was out of the room and I heard drawers opening in the bedroom.

I called through the door. "I'll wait downstairs. The car's in front of the place," I said.

I walked down the first flight and ran down the rest of the steps. I had remembered the small candy store across the street. There was a phone booth.

I left the message to be given Pete when he called in. He was to get up to Eighteenth Street as fast as he could. Keep out of sight but watch the building. Check anyone who came and went to the third-floor rear apartment.

I understood why Rosalie Carver had suddenly decided it was a good idea to eat before doing any more drinking. She wasn't being smart about the drinking. That phone call had not been any wrong number.

She was anxious to get me out of the place as soon as possible. To get me out before whoever had been on the end of that line showed up to see why she had answered the way she had.

Chapter 15

She had wanted a glass of milk, laced with brandy, because she said that she hadn't had any breakfast. We made a deal: I'd stop at the Vanderbilt Hotel and get her the drink if she would promise to eat something. She promised and we each had a milk punch, but then we didn't have breakfast after all.

"Listen," she said, "I don't know why you want to be with me. I have already told you I haven't anything to say."

"Maybe I just like you."

She laughed. "All right then, you like me. So I'll tell you what I'll do. I feel a little low and when I feel a little low the only thing that cheers me up is getting my hair done. Suppose I go into the beauty parlor and spend an hour building up my spirits and making myself beautiful. You pick me up then, and instead of having breakfast, we can have lunch."

"What beauty parlor?" I asked.

"Oh, I'm not going to run out on you," she said. "I suppose there's one here in the hotel. You can come in and wait or else you can do whatever cops are supposed to be doing to earn a living. I'll be no more than an hour."

Her hair looked great the way it was, but I didn't argue. I walked to the beauty salon with her and I left her at the door. After she had gone inside, I waited around for a few minutes. She didn't come out.

I went to the lobby and found a telephone booth. I called headquarters and there were no messages. Then I tried my house again. I wanted to talk to Carol.

I could hear the phone ringing at the other end and it rang several times and no one answered. I was about to hang up when Min came on. She told me that Mrs. Baron had left the house. In case anyone called, she would be at the Archers'.

I know it didn't make any sense, but I was sore all over again. I tried to tell myself that she had only gone over to smooth things out. And then when I thought of her apologizing for me, it made me see red. No one had to apologize for me—certainly not to Jack Archer. For a moment I was tempted to call her, but then I decided against it. The hell with Archer and the hell with Carol.

I looked at my wrist watch. Rosalie had said she would be about an hour. I had a little more than a half hour to kill. I went back to the bar and ordered a drink. When twenty-five minutes were up I returned to the telephone booth and called headquarters.

Pete had phoned in and left a number for me to call back.

The number was the phone booth in the candy store across the street from Phil Kenny's apartment house. Pete picked up the phone on the second ring.

"I got your message," Pete said, "but only after I already came down here to Eighteenth Street. I was up on the East Side, talking to the doorman in the apartment house next door to Dr. Pantell's, when the doc suddenly came out. He seemed in an awful hurry and on a hunch I followed him. He drove down here to Eighteenth Street and he's across the street now. Been there for half an hour. I guess he ..."

"Did anyone else show up over there?"

"Could be. A few people have walked in and out of the building. But they looked pretty much like they lived there. Should I try and see what's happening?"

"Nothing is happening, Pete," I said. "Phil was living with a girl. She got a phone call while I was talking with her and got out in a hurry. Seemed frightened. If Pantell is up there, he's probably waiting for her to come back."

"Well, should I wait around? What does the girl look like? Is she ..."

"She's with me," I said. "Stay around for a while longer. Try and check whether anyone shows up to meet Pantell. The chances are he'll give up and leave. If he does, you might find out where he goes. Unless you have something better in mind."

"I have a couple of things," Pete said. "That doorman gave me several leads. Anyway ..." He hesitated a moment and then spoke quickly. "The doc's leaving the building now. He looks mad about something."

"O.K., Pete," I said. "Take it from there."

He started to ask me something about the girl, but I hung up. I went back and was standing outside of the beauty parlor when she came out. Rosalie Carver had looked pretty good when she went into the place; she looked like a million dollars as she left it.

"I'm hungry now," she said and smiled.

"You're hungry—and you're lovely," I said. "What will it be—Toots Shor's or Twenty-One?"

She looked at me quickly, her head cocked. "Do cops go to Twenty-One?"

"This cop does."

"Take me."

We were early, which was just as well because we had no trouble getting a table. She skipped a drink when I suggested one, and ordered a kidney pie and rye toast and black coffee. I tried the same. She seemed contented just to sit and eat. She was very relaxed. Once she said, "You're a sort of funny cop."

"You're a sort of funny gangster's moll," I said.

For a moment I thought she was going to get mad, but she smiled and said, "Touché."

After she had ordered a second cup of coffee, I looked at her and said, "I have some advice for you."

She frowned.

"You had a visitor after I left. Dr. Pantell. I understand he looked a little upset when he didn't find you in."

She stared at me, her face losing color. "What is this, a game?" she asked.

"No game," I said. "We had a man watching the place. I called in while you were in the beauty shop. I just thought I would tell you."

She didn't say anything for several minutes and then she again gave me that half quizzical look. "You said something about advice."

"Well, so I did. The advice is that it might be a good idea to call him if he wants to see you. Don't duck him. And you have nothing to be frightened about. If you feel like talking, I'm ready to listen. It's part of my job."

Her voice was cold when she answered. "I have nothing to be frightened about. I have nothing to say to Dr. Pantell. I have nothing to talk to you about—at least so far as your job is concerned. It's been a nice lunch."

She started to get up.

"Listen," I said, "don't go off mad. I'm just trying to be friendly. I like to be with you."

She hesitated a moment and then sat down again.

"All right," she said. "But don't ask questions. Anyway, we've eaten. What do we do now?"

I shrugged. "Anything you'd like to do," I said. "I'm an unusual cop. I would rather play than work."

She laughed suddenly. "Got plenty of time?" she asked.

"My time is your time."

"All right then," she said. "I'll tell you what I'd like to do. I'd like to take a ferry ride—to Staten Island."

I thought she must be kidding, but I went along. "And?"

"We can stop somewhere and buy a wastepaper basket."

I began to think that the food hadn't done much good. I waited for her to go on.

"We will fill it up with ice cubes and then we will get a couple of bottles of champagne and when we get on the ferry, we can put the bottle on ice."

"It sounds great," I said. "I'll get some paper cups."

"No," she said. "Not paper cups. We'll stop at a department store and buy two champagne glasses."

"Anything else?"

She thought for a minute. "Well, you can buy me a harmonica. I can play one, but not very well. While we are drinking champagne on the ferry, I'll play for you. Would you like that?"

"I'd love it," I said.

"And when we get to Staten Island, we can buy a bottle of brandy and drink it on the way back. I think I would like to get just slightly high. In a nice way, of course."

"Of course," I said. I beckoned to the waiter.

"I want to stop in the john for a second," she said. "Do you happen to have a dime?"

"You don't need dimes in places like this," I said.

"The tip," she said, making a fast recovery.

I handed her a half dollar from the loose change in my pocket. And then I selected a dime and gave that to her also.

"For the phone call," I said.

She hesitated and started to pout. And then she quickly laughed.

"Once a cop always a cop," she said. "Oh well, maybe I'm just taking your advice. But don't let it go to your head."

I paid the check while she was gone and the waiter brought a telephone to the table and I put in another call for Carol. She answered almost at once.

I didn't say anything about Archer. I just told her that I was working on a job and that I might be a little late getting in.

"Try and get home early," Carol said. "You must be feeling a little lousy today."

"I'll try," I told her.

Rosalie was back waiting when I hung up.

"Damn," she said. "The nice ones are always married."

"Let's get that wastebasket," I said, standing up. "And the ice cubes."

Chapter 16

It wouldn't have happened at all if it hadn't been for the combination of events. I try to tell myself this, but in my heart I know that it isn't quite true.

I try to tell myself that Carol was partly to blame. But that isn't true either. What was to blame was several things, but mostly myself. My vulnerability so far as Carol is concerned. Perhaps my pride. Or, if I am being completely honest, perhaps it is just that I am a little more human, a little less strong, than I have always thought I was. Of course, if I want to make alibis for myself, say it was all in the line of duty, I can say that the ends justify the means and it had to happen if I was to find out what I wanted and needed to find out.

Or perhaps I can be really honest, at least with myself, and admit that I succumbed to an age-old desire. In any case it happened.

I had known all afternoon that it might.

We hadn't been on the ferry ten minutes, opening the bottle of champagne surreptitiously, before I realized I was having one hell of a good time.

There was something infectious about her, something unbelievably gay and enchanting. And of course before the ferry docked at Staten Island, I was just a little bit tight and she was a little bit tight and the whole day had taken on a rosy glow.

She played a half dozen old sentimental songs on the harmonica, off key and a little crazy, and they sounded great. We sang a couple of duets and we didn't carry the tunes very well and had to hum half of the words. We finished one bottle of champagne and then the second bottle and tossed the wastebasket and melting ice cubes overboard and followed them with the glasses.

A deck hand passing by, watched us with sour eyes and this seemed very funny.

"The man is shocked at the antics of the idle rich," Rosalie said. "We must not disappoint him."

She turned toward me suddenly, leaned forward, and putting her arms around my neck, lifted her face and kissed me fully on the lips.

She pulled away as I instinctively pressed toward her. Turned and thumbed her nose at the deck hand and he muttered something under his breath and moved off.

We called a cab when the ferry landed and asked to be taken to a bar. On the way we passed a small motion picture theater and the marquee said that *Never on Sunday* was playing.

"I've seen it three times," she said. "Instead of the bar, let's buy a bottle of cognac—and this time we can use paper cups—and we will go in and see it again."

She snuggled down next to me in the back row of the darkened movie and her right hand held my left, except when I poured the paper cups full of cognac and we drank out of them. I think we must have sat through the picture twice. It was already dark when we left the theater and we had discarded the empty cognac bottle on the floor beneath the seats.

I told her I had to make a phone call.

Pete had left a message to call him at his apartment, but that it wasn't important.

There was no answer when I called my own home.

I checked my watch and saw that it was a little after seven. Carol should have been home. I had told her I would be a little late. Well, perhaps she had been shopping and hadn't hurried back. She would plan a late dinner.

Rosalie wanted some seafood and we found a small restaurant near the waterfront and she ordered triple portions of steamed clams for each of us.

We had a double Scotch and soda while we waited for them.

At eight o'clock I tried phoning my house again. There was still no answer.

I wasn't worried. I was annoyed. On a hunch, I called the Archers. Their maid answered, and when I asked for Mrs. Archer, she told me that the Archers were dining with the Barons. I didn't think I heard her right and she repeated it.

I banged down the receiver. I was too damned mad to thank her and say good-by.

Rosalie must have noticed from my expression that something was wrong when I got back to the table. Her mouth turned down at the corners and she made a long face.

"What have I done now?" she said.

I stared at her for a moment and then I shrugged. "You've seduced me," I said. "Come on, let's leave this place. Get back to America. Get drunk."

"Great," she said. "Any particular plans?" She was mumbling her words a little. She was tight. I was tight myself.

"Wherever you want to go," I said.

"I want to go where I can kick off my shoes and be comfortable. How about my place?"

"Your place will be fine," I said.

"All right then, stop frowning. Gather yourself and let's get a couple of jugs. I have the records and the etchings—you get the booze."

An hour and a half later we were sprawled on the couch in her living room, the hi-fi going full blast. I had taken off my coat and loosened my tie. My shoulder holster hung on a chair next to the stereo outfit. I'd kicked off my shoes because she had wanted to dance and she liked to dance in her bare feet and wasn't taking any chances on my size elevens, even if she was pretty stoned.

She'd changed and was wearing a pair of shorts and a thin, orlon sweater and no stockings. She didn't have anything on under the sweater.

The hi-fi was on an FM station and it was signing off with the National Anthem when we staggered into the bedroom. She was laughing, a little crazily, and was almost helpless. I had to take the shorts and the sweater off as she couldn't manage them. She could manage other things though. She was a genius. She may have been a little tipsy and unsure on her feet, but she knew what to do when she was on her back.

I don't remember falling asleep.

Chapter 17

It was still dark when I woke up. I woke up because I heard her crying as she lay folded in my arms. I knew at once where I was and how I happened to be there. I had a headache, and I ached in every bone and muscle of my body.

She was clinging to me desperately, her slender arms around my neck, her small face pressed into my shoulder, and her beautiful legs twined around my legs.

"You're married, aren't you?" she said.

"Yes, I'm married."

"And you love your wife, don't you?" She said it not in an accusing tone, but as though she knew and was sure.

I answered without thinking.

"I know," she said. She didn't pull away. "That's the kind of luck I have," she said. "You probably don't believe it, but what I told you about Phil Kenny was true. We didn't sleep together. You're the first man I've been with in two years."

She moved closer and her arms tightened and she kissed me. Then suddenly she pushed me away and snapped on the light at the side of the bed.

"Oh God," she said. "I should mix my drinks! Get me something. In the kitchen. A bromo or a headache pill or a drink or anything. But something."

I staggered out of bed and I found the kitchen and there was a bottle of Alka-Seltzer and I poured two glasses, with triple doses. She had the sheets up and around her neck when I came back and made a face but got it down.

"You know something?" she said.

"No, baby," I told her. "I don't know a damned thing."

She ignored the answer. "You know, because of what you told me—that you love your wife—I'm going to do what you wanted me to do. I'm going to answer all those questions which you didn't ask me. I'm going to tell you what you came here to find out."

I looked at her, shaking my head. "And why...."

"Like I told you," she said. "Because you told me you loved your wife. You see, when you told me that, you were telling me the truth. You didn't snow me, didn't lie to me. So I want to do what you want me to do. Because you are nice and because I think you're a good man and because you didn't hurt me."

She hesitated a moment, staring into my eyes.

"Do you suppose I could get a drink down?" she asked.

"If you really want one," I said.

"Not too strong," she said. "And maybe you better put it in some black coffee. This may take a little time."

I started to turn away and she spoke in a low voice.

"Put your shorts on, Joe," she said. "You have a very nice body, but somehow it seems a little nicer to be served in bed by a man wearing shorts than by a nude Apollo."

She started to laugh hysterically. "I don't know why," she said, "but a naked man is really the silliest-looking thing."

I made the coffee strong, but the drinks weak. I sat at the side of the bed and I held her hands in mine as she talked.

"What I say," she began, "is off the record. I am not going to repeat it; it can't be used as testimony in court, and once I've said it, I will deny it to my dying day. But it is the truth. And maybe it is what you really came here to find out. I can start with this. You were right about one thing. I was frightened. I'm still frightened. And not by the police."

"What are you frightened of?" I said.

"I'm frightened of the man who murdered Phil."

I guess she expected me to be shocked or surprised. She was watching me very closely as she said it.

"The police reports show that Phil was shot while performing an armed burglary," I said.

"He wasn't armed," she said. "But let me tell it from the beginning. I think you know about some of it; some you don't."

She stopped talking and was silent for a long time and I began to wonder if she'd changed her mind. But then suddenly she leaned forward and asked me to kiss her and I did. I started to pull her toward me, but she pushed me away and said, "Later—when I get through."

She wanted more coffee and I brought it to her. I still had a headache, but I was feeling better.

She started at last.

"You have to understand about Phil Kenny—and about me," she said. "When Phil first picked me up, I was on the stuff myself. Just getting started. And do you know why I stuck with him, why I liked him? I'll tell you. Phil got me off the stuff. He literally held my hand and talked me off of it. Over a long period of time. It worked—I guess something like the Alcoholics Anonymous theory maybe. Phil liked me, but he thought of me as a kid. Phil didn't go for women.

"Maybe there was something wrong with him. I don't know. But he just didn't have any sex at all. What he liked was money and easy living. Good food, good clothes, the track, the theater, and comfort. And he had the habit and didn't want to kick it. He was moral as hell about other people when it came to junk, but he wasn't quitting the stuff himself. Maybe he substituted it for sex, I couldn't say. But that was his weakness. Junk and liking nice things. And because he was lazy and didn't have any particular way to support his luxuries, he was crooked."

"How crooked?" I asked.

"Well, he wasn't a thug or a gunman or anything like that. And because of the way he felt, he wasn't a pusher. He wasn't a stoolie either. Although I guess as a cop you know that. But he was a damned good accountant and bookkeeper, and although in his own way he worked for his money, he was still a crook because he worked for a crook. About the biggest one that there is."

"He had a record," I said. "Larceny, a couple of little things in that line."

"Not recently," she said. "For the last couple of years, since I had been with him, he had this job. He worked for Dr. Pantell. The man who murdered him."

"And why did Pantell want to murder Phil Kenny?"

"He wanted to murder him because Phil was trying to steal a million dollars from him."

"But then ..."

"Only it wasn't quite like that. Because you see, Dr. Pantell arranged that Phil would try and steal that money. You see, Phil knew too much. Way too much. And Phil was a junkie. It was Pantell himself who kept Phil in the stuff. And Dr. Pantell is a very clever and vicious man. He knows that in the long run no junkie can really be trusted. And when Phil, who worked for him, began to learn too much about him, he realized that Phil would always present a possible danger.

"So he decided that he would have to get rid of him. But he never does anything the simple way. He arranged it so that Phil would virtually commit suicide. He arranged it so that Phil would try and take that million. Because you see Phil understood himself as well as Pantell understood him. He knew also that he represented a possible danger. He knew that his only out would be to get his hands on enough cash at one time so that he could completely disappear. It was a case of two clever men, but Pantell was more clever.

"He set Phil up for it. He let Phil know about a million dollars he kept in that safe in his home. Phil was there when the doctor put the money in the safe. He told me about it. And then Pantell arranged it so that he would be away on Saturday night and give Phil every possible chance to get the money. He understood Phil all right. Phil thought he was being smart, that he'd get the money and blow. And he walked into a murder trap."

She stopped talking and indicated she wanted more coffee. I heated up a couple of more cups and this time skipped the booze. She was right, of course. She had to be right. She wouldn't have known about the money if she wasn't right.

"Maybe you should tell me a little more about Dr. Pantell," I said.

She shrugged. "I can't tell you much. I don't know much. Even Phil didn't know much. On the surface, Dr. Pantell is a completely reputable, high-class physician. I don't think even now anyone can pin a thing on him. On the other hand, from what Phil has told me and from what I can put together, Dr. Pantell is either the front man for or the brains behind the biggest dope syndicate operating out of

New York. He isn't a pusher, isn't even a user. He probably never sees a middle man. But he's the brains. Because he is beyond suspicion himself, he is the perfect man for the part. He probably sees no more than two or three persons who know who he is and how he operates. It's a sort of chain of command thing."

"Then how did Phil ..."

"Phil was originally a legitimate patient, or so he told me. Pantell needed someone to do accounting work for him. He needed someone that he would have a hold over. He recognized Phil as a user at once. In the beginning Phil knew very little. But after a while it was inevitable that he would begin to put two and two together. That was when he became dangerous, at least in Pantell's eyes."

"If," I said, "Pantell is this sinister figure you make him out to be, why didn't he just put a contract out? Have Phil taken care of?"

She shook her head. "It could have been any of a number of reasons. Maybe he has enemies in his own organization. Maybe he was afraid that Phil had information that his own people might want. Maybe he just doesn't trust anyone. He certainly didn't trust Phil. In any case, he did it his way and he did it safely. You know the story now but do you think you could prove a word of it? Even if I were willing to talk, which I'm not."

I thought it over for a minute or so. "No, I don't think I could prove it," I said.

"I want to show you something," she said. She stood up and crossed the room and pulled open a dresser drawer. When she came back she had an envelope in her hand. She opened it and took out a sheaf of hundred-dollar bills.

"Five thousand," she said. "You didn't happen to notice when you came in last night. The envelope was on my dresser. It wasn't there when we left yesterday morning."

She reached in the envelope and took out a folded piece of paper and handed it to me. The message was typed, unsigned. It read: "Stay healthy. Leave New York for good. You are suffering from amnesia and need a long long rest."

"Do you think I am right in being just a little frightened?" she asked.

I didn't answer her. "What are you going to do?"

She cocked her head again. "One thing for sure," she said. "I am sending this money back to Dr. Pantell. I don't need it. I don't want it. Phil left me enough."

"A second thing you are going to do," I said. "You are going to get out of town. As far away as you can get. Change your name, get in touch with no one. Men like Pantell don't fool."

"I know," she said. "I'll be staying just long enough for Phil's funeral."

"No," I said. "No, you are leaving right now. As soon as I can get some clothes on you and get you packed."

"I'm not going to spend my life running away," she said.

"You won't have to," I said. "I'll promise you that. But for the next few days you simply have to disappear. I'll be in touch with you and as soon as it's safe, I'll let you know."

She stared at me curiously for several moments. "Is this Joe the cop talking or Joe the man?"

"Just Joe," I said.

I leaned over and kissed her. "Get dressed," I said.

She started to put her arms around me, and then quickly moved away. "That's right," she said in a small voice. "I remember you said something about being in love with your wife."

I didn't have any answer.

I dropped her off at Grand Central. She was getting a train as far as Philly and from there she was switching to a plane and going out to Cleveland. She didn't want to tell me where she was going from there, but she promised that she'd be in touch with me by phone within three days. I paid off the cab and she stood on tiptoes and brushed my lips gently and her eyes were a little misty. I waved when she turned a few hundred yards away and lifted her hand. I watched until she was out of sight.

I don't believe that anyone had followed us from her apartment.

And then I went into a phone booth and dialed the number up in Westchester. It wasn't going to be an easy telephone call to make and I wanted to do it quick, before I had a chance to think about it too long.

Carol answered on the first ring.

Chapter 18

It was Thursday afternoon before Pete and I really got to talk to each other. Tuesday morning, about a half hour before I reported in, a young mother over on Gramercy Park had taken her six-months-old baby for an airing and then returned to her apartment and placed a pillow over the infant's face and smothered it. She had cut both her wrists with a dull kitchen knife and, apparently believing she had no more than a few minutes to live, called her husband who was an airlines engineer out at International Airport.

Some misguided gynecologist had told her he suspected she had cancer of the womb, and she'd gone home and thought it over and decided that no one but herself should bring up her child.

Pete had not showed and I went out on it alone, arriving a little after the ambulance doctor had discovered the baby was past any hope but that the mother suffered only superficial wounds, making it a real tragedy.

The young husband arrived before I left and I had a word with him in private. I suggested he keep back the information that cancer of the womb is not necessarily a fatal thing, at least for a while. His wife had enough on her mind for the time being. I checked her in at the prison at Bellevue, and before I could get back to headquarters, I was on my way uptown to investigate a gang shooting at an East Side playground. It kept me going the rest of the day. Somewhere along the line I reached Pete. He was out on sick leave.

"Damndest thing that ever happened," he said over the phone. "There I was, outside of Pantell's, talking to his chauffeur, when who comes out the door but the doc himself. It was late on Monday afternoon. Well, I had to think pretty quick because of course he recognized me at once. So I told him I was just stopping by to see him for a second, to sort of clean up an odd and end of the Kenny case. He invited me back in the house and that's when it happened."

"What happened?"

"I slipped and fell, going up the front steps. Must have been a pebble or some kid's marble or something. Anyway, I thought I broke my damned ankle. "Brother, the pain ..."

"Never mind the pain."

"Never mind, hell," Pete said. "It was agonizing. Anyway, to cut it short, the doc took me inside. Made an X-ray and fortunately there was no fracture. But he said I pulled a ligament. He put on a bandage and said I should take a day or so off and stay off my feet. I spent an hour or better with him. I don't want to go into it over the phone...."

"I'll stop by on my way home tonight," I said.

"Do that, Joe," Pete said. "I'll be taking sick leave for the next couple of days."

But I didn't get a chance to stop by because by the time I cleaned up the schoolyard thing, it was already after nine o'clock. And I just didn't dare get home late again. Or at least not later than this. Things were not going exactly smoothly at home.

Wednesday was like Tuesday. Going from morning to night, but I did manage to get to the house in time for dinner and things were a little more pleasant. Thursday started out with a bang, but it was one of those days when everything seemed to break just right and so, by four o'clock, I was checked out and on my way uptown. I would give Pete a few minutes.

He was drinking tea and watching television when I pushed the door open after he'd called to me to come in. He held his leg up on a chair in front of him and when he stood up, winced a little when he came down on the foot. But he said it felt O.K. and that he'd be back to work the following morning.

"Want to collect my salary before the vacation starts, kid," he said. "But don't expect me to be doing any hundred-yard dashes. This thing is still sore."

"You shouldn't have let Pantell see you hanging around," I said.

"Sit down, Joe," Pete said. "I've got things to tell you. Plenty of things. And it's a very good thing I did see Pantell. Pour yourself a drink, by the way. You have a small celebration coming."

"I do?"

"Yes, you do."

"Why?"

"Why because within ten days you will be the proud possessor of a half a million dollars," Pete said.

"You're going too fast, Pete," I said. "But before you start, I'll tell you a couple of things I've found out while you've been laid up. I won't go into detail—" there were a lot of details I would never tell Pete or anyone else as far as that went—"but I'll give you a general rundown. I'm satisfied that Pantell is some sort of large-scale illegal drug operator. I'm satisfied that he had a lot of money in that safe and that it is possible it is back in the safe again. I am also satisfied that he deliberately murdered Phil Kenny."

"I was sure of that all along," Pete said. "But that is all beside the point."

"Not quite, Pete," I said. "I may go along with you on your scheme. I will go along if it looks right. But one thing I am going to do. Sooner or later I'm going to see to it that the Federals get the dope on Pantell. I don't think he can be nailed for the Kenny murder, but they are going to know what he does and how he operates. Once they have the tipoff, they'll get him. They have the men and they have the technique."

"Listen, Joe," Pete said, "try and remember I'm a cop, too. I want him nailed just as much as you do. I don't like the idea of anyone getting away with murder and I'd go out on the limb to see that anyone mixed up in dope is picked up and that the book is tossed at him. But feeling that way and still liking the idea of grabbing onto a million bucks— a million criminally obtained bucks—are two different things. We are not planning on sticking up a bank, Joe. Or taking it away from widows and orphans."

"I know, Pete," I said. "I just wanted it clear about Pantell."

"All right. We understand each other. Now here's the dope on the doc himself. Like you, I won't go into detail. But I haven't been just sitting here with my foot on a stool for two days. I've been on the phone and I've been running around.

"To begin with, the doc's background is straight. A naturalized citizen, he studied in Europe and got his degree in Switzerland. When he came to this country, he interned in New York City hospitals and passed his med exams. Been practicing for some twenty-five years and from all I can find out is a good, competent doctor. Belongs to a number of reputable medical associations and all that sort of thing. But there are two odd bits about him. First his friends and his hobbies. He doesn't have any. Goes to the theater now and then, but usually alone. Almost never entertains, rarely goes out. Doesn't go in for sports or any sort of social life. Except once a year he takes a vacation. Supposedly he travels for two or three months in Europe.

"The second odd thing is his clientele. He handles a lot of show-biz people. Big names. And he handles the very top-flight gangsters in the country. The boys who are mixed up in the syndicates. Guys like Costello, Goldman, Ziegler. He's their personal doctor. They come from all over the country to see him."

I nodded. "It figures," I said. "Show-business people and gangsters have a way of hanging around the same places, patronizing the same shops. It would be a perfect front, give him a completely legitimate reason for keeping in touch with his contacts."

Pete nodded. "There has never been the slightest suspicion that he's mixed up in anything. On the other hand, he lives anything but the normal life of a prosperous Park Avenue doctor. The cover-up is too good, too perfect. He's just a little bit too respectable. Believe me, Joe, I hadn't talked with him for ten minutes before I knew. I could actually smell it. He has racket written all over him. Only it isn't movie-style or television-style racket. It's modern, streamlined, big-business, organized racket. Dr. Pantell is a very dangerous man."

"Why would he still keep the money in his safe, Pete?" I asked. "A guy with the connections you say you think he has ..."

"It's simple," Pete said. "Because it means just what the word says.

Safe. Nobody—that is no one in the rackets—keeps money in a bank's safe-deposit box any more. Not with the courts going out of their way to issue injunctions permitting district attorneys to open them any time they want to. And where can you keep money? Brokerage firms report all purchases and sales to the tax people. You can't invest it legitimately without explaining its source. It has to pass through some sort of institution. So where else but in a private safe? Don't forget that Pantell usually has two or three people on the premises. And certainly no one knows that he keeps that sort of money around. As you say, Kenny found out only by accident and because he had been working as an accountant for the doc. The run-of-the-mill mobster or hoodlum wouldn't know. And if Pantell is what we think he is, he wouldn't have to be worrying about protection from the run-of-the-mill stick-up artist. He has better protection from his own organization than the cops themselves could give him."

I nodded. I couldn't have agreed more.

"In that case," I asked, "what makes you think you and I have a chance to move in on it?"

"Two things make me think so, Joe," Pete said quickly. "The first is that you and I are probably two of the very few people who know he has the dough stashed there. And he doesn't know that we know. He doesn't know that Kenny lived long enough to tell us about it."

"The second reason is even better. This Sunday night he is leaving for a ten-day vacation in Bermuda. The house is going to be deserted except for the butler. The doctor told me that he felt he needed a rest. That business the other night seemed to upset him. Or so he says. Maybe it did. I guess even murderers need a rest after finishing off a job."

"And you think then, Pete ..."

Pete pulled a folded paper from his pocket and started to spread it out on the arm of his chair. "Move around and take a look, kid," he said. "The plans of the house. And they aren't guesswork. I got them through the architect who redesigned it for the doc. I told the architect I was an inspector from the City Department of Plants and Structures and we were checking for possible building code violations. He was indignant and whipped out the blueprints. Two Cub Scouts could knock that place over as an exercise for their merit badge."

Chapter 19

Carol crossed the room slowly; she hesitated a moment as she stood in front of me and then suddenly she swooped down and landed in my lap. She turned and, taking my face between her hands, stared into my eyes for a moment. And then she kissed me.

It lasted for a long time.

"Joe," she said. "What is it, Joe? What's happened to us? What's happened to you? For a week now, since that awful Saturday night, you've been going around like a man who is half dead."

I didn't say anything. There wasn't anything I could say. She snuggled closer.

"I still love you, Joe," she said, her voice barely audible. "There's no one else. There never was and there never will be."

"I love you, Carol," I said. I wanted to go on, tell her the same things she was telling me. But my voice choked up and I couldn't. I was remembering what had happened with Rosalie Carver.

"You have to believe me; have faith in me," Carol said.

"I believe you," I said. "And I love you, Carol. I don't know what comes over me. It's just that ..."

She put her fingers across my lips. "It's that job of yours, Joe," Carol said. "Oh, can't you understand? Don't you see it? I know you like the work. I know that you are a good cop. But, darling, it isn't for you. You think that it's only the money I'm interested in, but that isn't true. It's that I think there are other things, more important things which you could be doing. I want to be proud of you. I want ..."

I pulled her closer and this time I put my fingers across her lips and when she stopped talking, I sealed her lips with my own. After a long time I spoke.

"All right, honey," I said. "I'm going to do what you want me to do. I'll quit the job. But you just have to give me a little time. Say six months. Six months from today, I promise you that I'll quit. I'll hand in my resignation."

She leaned back so that she could look into my eyes. She started to say something, but I didn't let her talk.

"There will be no regrets," I said quickly. "I'm doing it because I want to do it. You're a lot more important to me than any job. And I haven't been fair. I know that. I shouldn't ask you to live on what a cop makes, not when you don't have to. And I just can't see myself living off your

money. So there is only one thing to do. I'll get into something where
I can make the kind of money I have to have."

"What ..."

"Law," I said. "I'll start now, while I'm still on the force. I can get into
night school for a refresher course. You see ..."

"Oh, darling," she said. "Darling, couldn't you just go in now, right
away, and quit? Couldn't you ..."

I shook my head. "No—no, you see, I've been thinking about this. All
week now. I've talked to several people about it. As a matter of fact
..."

I was playing it off the cuff now. Making it up as I went along. I hated
to lie but I had to. I was going to have to get used to telling a good
many lies before it was over and done with. Lies would be a part of
it from now on.

"As a matter of fact," I said, "I've talked with a law firm downtown.
They told me that if I would get in six months of night school first,
then quit the force, they would take me on."

"Why, Joe," she said. "Joe, that's marvelous."

"Yes," I said, "yes, it will work out. Actually, I will start out making
more money, just working with them, than I've been making as a cop."

I was beginning to set it up, beginning to alibi for the money I was
now counting on getting.

I felt like hell, telling her this. But then, when I saw how happy it
was making her, I shrugged it off. Maybe she was right after all.
Maybe money was that important.

And it wouldn't be a complete lie. I would give them notice down at
the department. I would go to law school at nights. I'd even try and
line up a job with a law firm. I didn't think I'd have much trouble with
that part of it. The experience I had would be valuable. Later on, once
I was through with the department, I could start using some of the
money. It would be easy enough to make Carol think I was getting it
as salary.

But I would have to be careful. Carol would not be too easy to fool.
The fact that it was known that she had a private income would make
it easy as far as my friends in the department were concerned. But I
would still have to be very cautious. I wouldn't be able to flash around
any important money for a long while.

The best way would probably be to set up a brokerage account. I
could start getting lucky in the market. A lot of people were.

One thing was sure. Once it was over and done with, I would be
through with Pete Delanos for once and all. It would be the end of the

friendship which has lasted most of my lifetime. I never wanted to see him again. It wasn't that I couldn't trust Pete; I knew he would never double-cross me. But I just didn't want him around anymore.

And I'd get out of the department as soon as I reasonably could. Not only because I had promised Carol—that was the least of it. I knew, even then, that every day I spent as a cop I would be reminding myself that I was a damned hypocrite and liar. I wasn't a real cop anymore. I was a man planning to commit a robbery.

That night Carol and I slept locked in each other's arms. I lay awake for hours after she'd gone to sleep. I kept trying to tell myself that it wasn't really a robbery, that I would be merely taking money from a vicious criminal who had himself obtained the money by dealing in the lowest racket of them all. I tried to tell myself that actually all I was doing was penalizing a man who deserved a great deal worse than merely losing his ill-gotten profits.

I tried to tell myself I was doing the only thing I could do to save my marriage and save my pride. That I would be making the woman I loved happy.

But I was kidding myself and I knew it.

If I was doing it just for Carol, just to make her happy, I should be able to tell her what I was planning. And I knew how she would take that. Carol wanted money and an easy life, but Carol would have rather seen me dead than doing what I was going to do.

No, I was doing it for myself. To make myself happy. I was doing it because I had too much pride to live on my wife's money. Because I didn't quite have the courage and the guts to quit my job and take the chance on going into something, even if I had to use her capital, and try and make a success of it. I was doing it because it was the easy way out.

I had a lot of trouble getting to sleep; I had a lot of trouble with my conscience. But I would have to get used to that. I'd have to get used to a lot of things.

In the meantime, well, I pulled her closer to me and she moaned in her sleep and her face moved and her lips found mine and she kissed me but she didn't wake up.

Chapter 20

Inspector Flood reached me on the phone late Friday afternoon. He sounded grumpy.

"I know it isn't your baby," he said, "but we are all tied up here in the precinct. Anyway, you handled the early part of it and he particularly asked for you by name. He said you were the one he wanted to see, you and your partner."

"But I don't understand. It's all cleaned up and ..."

"Sure it's all cleaned up. I know that. But this guy's a taxpayer and he's entitled to a little courtesy. Anyway, he said it would only take a minute or so. He just wants to see you."

"You wouldn't know what the doctor has on his mind?"

"How in hell would I know? Just drop in and talk to him. He said he was going to be going away this weekend, and if you could come by sometime later today ... anyway, stop by."

The Inspector hung up.

Pete was watching me, curiously.

"That was Inspector Flood," I said. "It seems that Dr. Pantell called. Said he wanted to see us!"

Pete raised his eyebrows. "So ..."

I looked around the squad room. There were half a dozen detectives sitting around.

"So," I said, carefully keeping my voice down and without expression, "so we'll stop by."

I looked at my watch. It was almost four.

"Let's go," I said and reached for my hat which was on the desk. Pete followed me out, still limping a little.

"I don't like it," Pete said, while we were weaving through traffic on the way uptown. "I just don't like it. I wonder ..."

"No use wondering," I said shortly. "But it's too bad you went back. Too bad he had to find you asking questions...."

"I know," Pete said. "But what the hell, he didn't seem suspicious or anything. I just hope ..."

"We'll know soon enough," I said.

The outside door had a small copper plate and the engraved letters said "Waiting Room." The door was unlocked and we pushed it open and entered the well-furnished small chamber. I noticed the lock on the door as we entered. It looked sturdy.

There was a small room off the waiting room, separated from it by a shoulder-high glass partition. Behind the partition I noticed a desk, a typewriter, and several file cases. It was probably where his nurse sat during visiting hours. No one was in the room.

There was a small pushbutton next to the partition and under it was a sign which said "Ring."

I rang.

A moment later and the door at the end of the room, which I remembered led into the doctor's private office, opened. Dr. Pantell stood there for a moment, looking at us. He smiled and stepped into the room. He walked up to Pete and extended his hand.

"The ankle," he said. "How's the ankle?"

Pete shrugged. "Why ..."

He had Pete lift his leg and put his foot on a chair. He pulled up the trouser leg and unrolled the elastic bandage and felt around and Pete winced.

"It'll hurt for quite a while," he said. He stood up and turned to me.

"Detective Baron, I believe," he said. He extended his hand and smiled. But his eyes didn't smile at all. "Come in," he said. "Come into the office. Work's over for the day."

He turned, but instead of going toward his office, he crossed over and snapped the lock on the outside door. And then he herded us into his private office. He went to a small icebox and opened it, taking out a tray of cubes, a bottle of Scotch, and some soda. He made three drinks and handed each of us one and kept one for himself.

He waited until he'd lifted his glass and sort of half smiled before he spoke.

"You've probably wondered why I wanted to see you," he said.

I nodded, but said nothing.

He put the glass down and I noticed that he had barely touched its contents.

"Well, you see," he said. "I have been a little concerned about that man who was killed here last week. Quite concerned. So I looked him up. I even attended his funeral."

"Yes?"

"Yes. I'm afraid that my conscience began to bother me just a little bit. In any case I discovered that he had a mother who was still living. Somewhere out in Brooklyn. I have arranged for a small sum of money to be sent her to sort of tide her over."

I nodded again. "That was very kind of you," I said.

"No, merely my duty," he said. "I also discovered that the man had been living with a woman; I guess you might say that she was his common-law wife. I understand that her name is Carver. A Miss Rosalie Carver."

Neither Pete nor I said anything.

"Again," the doctor said, "I felt a sense of responsibility. I wanted to do something for the girl."

He hesitated, watching our faces. No one spoke for several moments.

"The trouble," he said, "was that when I looked her up I learned that she had disappeared. No one seems to know what has happened to her. The shock ..."

"I doubt, Doctor," I said, "that you have to worry about the girl. I should imagine that she has merely taken off—now that Kenny is no longer around to take care of the bills."

He looked up at me sharply for a moment. "Oh," he said. "Oh—you know Miss Carver then?"

I shrugged. "We know about her," I said.

"Well, I thought if I could find her, I might be able to help her. Perhaps find a job for her, let her have enough money to see her through until ..."

"Girls like the Carver girl—well, they manage," I said. "It isn't quite as though she was his wife, or the mother of his children or anything like that. I'm sure that she will be all right."

The doctor indicated our glasses, and Pete held his out. I declined a second drink and the doctor rushed over a box of cigars. I told him I used cigarettes only and took a crumpled pack from my pocket.

"I'm going away for a week or so on a much-needed vacation," he said. "I shall be leaving Sunday. I just thought that I would like to see if I couldn't help the girl before I left. It was an unfortunate tragedy, and I would like to do anything possible to see that innocent persons ..."

"Broads who shack up with criminals aren't usually quite so innocent," Pete said. "I wouldn't let her worry you, Dr. Pantell."

"A good many things worry me. My conscience would rest a lot easier if I knew where the girl was and that she was all right. I just thought perhaps the police ..."

I stood up. "The case is closed, Doctor," I said. "We have investigated and the girl was in no way involved. She has a clean record."

Dr. Pantell stood up and gave that odd smile which never seemed to reach the upper half of his face. "Well," he said, "if she turns up, if you run across her tracks, I would certainly appreciate knowing where she is. I should like to do something for her. Incidentally, you have been most kind going out of your way to come and see me. I am sure that you are infringing on your own free time to do so."

He was taking his wallet out of his pocket as he spoke. "I would like to see that ..."

I put up my hand. "That isn't necessary, Doctor," I said. "It's all a part of the job. Anyway, it's been a pleasure and—thanks for the drinks."

I started for the door but before I reached it, I hesitated and swung back. "By the way," I said, "while you are gone on this vacation, be sure that the place is locked up tight. You wouldn't want a second ..."

"Oh I hardly think lightning is likely to strike in the same place twice," he said. He smiled and shrugged, lifting his heavy eyebrows. "Anyway, the quarters will hardly be deserted. Jeffers—he's the butler—will stay on. He lives here and he'll be around to see to things. I'm giving my nurse a couple of weeks' vacation and an answering service will handle my calls. Jeffers is in his seventies, but he's still pretty spry. Besides, my chauffeur will be around most of the time. He doesn't actually live on the premises, but I've arranged for him to stay in the house while I'm gone. No, I don't think I'll have anything to worry about."

"I'm sure you won't, Doctor," Pete said.

"You take care of that ankle," he said. "Bathe it in warm water and stay off of it as much as possible."

"I'll do that," Pete said. "As a matter of fact, I'm starting on my own vacation. Won't be going away, but I'll be taking it easy."

"Yes—yes, take it easy," Dr. Pantell said. He saw us to the door. "Could I have my man drop you off?"

"We have our own car," I said. "But thanks."

He shook hands again. "You won't forget to let me know if you dig up the Carver girl," he said, as we started toward the street. "Just phone and leave the message and it will reach me."

Pete waited until we were in the car and had pulled away from the curb. "Well," he said, "what do you think?"

"I think he's damned anxious to get his hands on Rosalie Carver," I said. "I think the healthiest thing she ever did was to disappear."

I met Carol shortly before seven-thirty at the country club and we had dinner. There was a dance later in the evening, and I'd had time to stop at the house and change to a black tie.

The dance was crowded and at one time during the evening I spotted Dr. Jack Archer across the room. He was wearing dark glasses and had a piece of adhesive tape on his nose. He looked as though he had been drinking a good deal.

He may have seen us or may not. But he didn't speak or nod. A number of other people did nod to us and several stopped by the table to say hello. But I noticed that no one asked Carol to dance.

It couldn't have bothered me less. I was glad to have her to myself for a change.

But I would have to see that I went out of my way to be polite and make people feel at ease around me. I didn't want to get the reputation of being a jealous husband. I didn't want Carol to feel that other men were afraid to dance with her.

We went home fairly early. I had explained to Carol that I was going to have to go into town on Sunday. That I had some work to clean up on a case. She looked at me a little curiously, and I knew what was on her mind.

"I'm going to hand in my notice next week," I said.

She smiled and squeezed my hand. "You won't be sorry, Joe," she said. "You won't be sorry."

She was wrong of course. I'd be damned sorry—for the rest of my life.

On Sunday afternoon, just after one o'clock, Pete and I stood on the mezzanine platform at International Airport and looked through the observation window. We had our eyes on the Pan Am plane which was loading at the finger ramp a hundred yards away. More than half of the passengers were already aboard.

We were taking no chances. We were going to be absolutely sure that Dr. Pantell made that plane. Kenny had made the mistake of underselling the doctor, and we had no intention of following in his footsteps.

I could see that Pete was getting a little nervous. He started to say something, and as he did I suddenly spotted them. I quickly nudged him and pointed.

Dr. Pantell was walking ahead and he was carrying nothing but a brief case. He was followed by a uniformed chauffeur who held a light overcoat over one arm and carried a small airline bag in his other. The doctor was bareheaded and his white hair was blowing in the wind.

They reached the door of the plane and the doctor hesitated and held out his hand for the airline bag. The chauffeur said something and then in a moment turned away. He was a big man, standing at least six feet two, and he had broad square shoulders. His nose had been broken at some time in the past and he had an ugly, scarred face. The visor of his uniform cap covered and shadowed his eyes.

"Name's Bellows," Pete said. "Maurice Bellows. Thirty-two, and a record. Assault and battery. Used to be a prize fighter. He's supposed to be a little punchy. But he could be dangerous. Been with the doctor for several years now. I sort of have a hunch he is more of a bodyguard than a chauffeur...."

I nodded. "Could be," I said.

The portable ramp was wheeled away from the plane's door and the pilot began to warm up the engines. We stood and watched until the plane began slowly to move away from the finger platform.

"That chauffeur," I said, as we turned and started for the parking lot. "Do you have any idea if he carries a gun?"

"If he does," Pete said, "it's illegal. He had no license for one. But I don't worry about him too much. He's a beer drinker and when he stays at the house, he hangs out in the kitchen. With the doc away, he'll be hitting the beer. It makes him sleepy and as near as I can learn, he usually hits the bed around nine o'clock when he isn't on duty. He'll be sleeping in a small bedroom on the ground floor, in the rear of the building."

"And the butler?"

"His bedroom is on the first floor also. He doesn't sleep much, but he likes to watch television. Has a set in his room and he sits in front of it by the hour. He's a little deaf so he keeps it turned up high. The old man won't be any trouble at all. Just have to be quiet and cautious when we get in. Bellows might be a problem if he was awake, but you can be sure he won't be. The tape and the ether, that's all we need."

I nodded. "Sure," I said. "All we need. But we are going to be damned careful, especially with the ether. And especially with the old man. That stuff can be tricky."

"If it will make you feel any better," Pete said, "we can just tie up the old one and gag him."

"It will make me feel a lot better," I said.

"You'll feel a lot better after next Friday night," Pete said. "A million bucks can make anybody feel a lot better."

Chapter 21

They assigned a young third-grade detective named Karl Wolski to take Pete's place while Pete was on vacation. He was only a little over a year out of the Police Academy, but he had stopped a holdup in a booze shop and taken a couple of forty-five slugs in the right leg doing it. He had killed the two men who were sticking up the place, and when he got out of the hospital they jumped him a couple of grades and transferred him to brains. He was a bright kid and very polite. It was he who got the telephone call on Thursday morning.

He spoke for a moment or so into the mouthpiece and then turned to me. "Some dame for you," he said. "The sergeant downstairs says she sounds stoned to the gills." He held out the phone.

"The hell with her, whoever it is," I said.

He shrugged and spoke into the mouthpiece again. But he didn't hang it up.

"Sergeant says it's a long-distance call that's paid for. She still wants to talk to you."

I reached for the instrument.

It was Rosalie Carver and the sergeant had been right. She sounded as drunk as anyone I had ever heard over the phone.

"Gotta see you, Joe, gotta see you," she said. "Important. Gotta see you right away."

I asked her where she was.

"Listen," she said. "Ain't important. But I gotta see you. Right away. Love you, boy, and have to see you." Her voice suddenly got foggy and I couldn't understand her. I didn't dare say too much, but I told her to sober up. I asked her to give me her phone number and I would call her back.

But the line went dead suddenly and I guess she hung up. I called the desk and asked the man on duty where the call had originated.

"Albany," he said. "And was that babe drunk! You sure pick 'em, kid."

I sure did.

It bothered me, but then something happened almost immediately which captured my attention. We, my new partner and myself, were on our way over to the East River where some barge captain had spotted a man floating in the water on his stomach. He was dead but that wasn't what made him interesting. What made him interesting was that his hands were clasped behind his back as he floated and the wrists had been neatly wired together. That made it murder, of course.

Sometime during the afternoon while we were still trying to wrap up the evidence, I talked with Pete on the phone. He was holed up in his apartment, taking it easy. Marking time. Waiting for Friday. He didn't have much to say. Just, "Everything is set. I have ..."

I cut it short. I didn't mention the call from the Carver girl.

On Friday morning, before I left the house and as I was kissing Carol good-by, she pushed back from me and looked into my face.

"A girl," she said. "called you last night before you got home. About three times. She sounded very odd."

"A girl? What girl?"

Carol shrugged. "She didn't give any name," she said. "But she did say that it was very important and that she would try you again. She sounded as though she might have been drinking."

"Oh just another one of my drunken women," I said lightly. "You know how it is with a devastatingly handsome devil like ..."

Carol laughed and kissed me. She walked with me out to the car. "Darling," she said. "You are sure you don't mind?"

"Don't mind?"

"About my going away. You know, leaving you here all alone. I don't think ..."

"Don't be silly, honey," I said. "I want you to go. It was my suggestion anyway, wasn't it? I want you to go and have a good time. I'm just sorry I can't get away to come with you. But ..."

It had been one of those lucky breaks. The Hadleys, who lived a mile down the road and were crazy about horses, had invited Carol down to their Virginia farm for a hunt meeting. I had at once insisted that she go. It couldn't have worked out better. I didn't want her around on Friday night. I wasn't worried about anything going wrong, but I just felt better knowing that she wouldn't be at the house. And so she had agreed that she would leave that afternoon, drive down in her car, and return the first of the week.

She had wanted to keep Min on to look after me, but I told her that I would be happier alone.

"Pete will come out and stay for a couple of days," I'd explained. "We'll enjoy doing a little batching. You know, booze, dancing girls, gambling, sinning it up."

"Yeah—yeah." She laughed. "I know. But I still think I ought ..."

"No Min," I said. "We don't want witnesses to our sinning."

And so it had been arranged and now I was kissing her good-by and telling her to be a good girl and to take care of herself. I would miss her. I always missed her.

"I'll call you tonight as soon as we arrive," Carol said.

"No, honey," I said. "I'll call you. I don't know what time, exactly, I'll be home. I'm picking up Pete when I get off work and we're going to hit a steak house in town and have dinner and go to a show afterward. Pete is getting tickets to a musical. So we'll drive out after the show and it might be late. I'll call you. You should be there shortly after dark so I'll call at seven. If I miss you, I'll try again in a half hour and call each half hour until I get you."

We kissed good-by then, and she stood waving after me as I drove off.

I hadn't lied to her about the steak dinner and the show. The musical would let out at around eleven o'clock. We were going to hit Dr. Pantell's at exactly twelve-thirty. It would give us time to stop off at Pete's apartment and pick up the stuff we had to pick up.

Things were pretty quiet all morning and I never left headquarters. I had a little paper work to catch up with. At twelve-fifteen I sent out for sandwiches and coffee and at one o'clock the phone rang and Wolski signaled to me.

It was Rosalie Carver. She still sounded drunk.

"I wanna see you, Joe," she said. "I'm lonely and I want to see you. Back in town—in a bar over at Forty-first and Third. Can you come on over?"

"Listen, kid," I said. "You're being foolish. Very foolish. I told you to stay away. And you should sober up."

"But, Joe," she said, "I'm scared. I don't want to be alone. I need someone with me."

For a moment I hesitated. I was on duty and it would be difficult to get away. She had every right to be frightened, and I knew that she shouldn't have come back. On the other hand, I also knew that Pete had called Bermuda less than an hour ago and that he'd been able to verify that Dr. Pantell had checked in at the Bermuda Plaza and was still there. She'd be safe for a day or two in any case. Her voice interrupted my thoughts.

"You still there, Joe?"

I said I was.

"I've taken a room," she said. "You come over here as soon as you can. If I'm not still here, I'll leave an envelope with your name on it with the bartender. It will give you the name I am using and the address. Will you promise to come as soon as you can?"

The other phone was ringing and I spoke hurriedly. "Sure," I said. "Sure. As soon as I can. But lay off the sauce. Get sober. This is no time to crack up."

"I'll wait for you, Joe," she said. "Try and make it soon."

At ten minutes to two there was a call from downstairs and we were told to go over to a rooming house on Canal Street. A Chinese had been found there with a hatchet buried in his head.

We never did get back. I left Karl Wolski down at Bellevue, some time shortly after five-thirty. He was cleaning up the case and would report back in. I had him make the call in because I didn't want to talk to anyone downtown. I didn't want to get any new assignments.

Before going uptown, I stopped at the bar on Forty-first Street. There was no envelope for me.

I questioned the bartender and I described Rosalie Carver. I said she might have been a little tight.

"The dames who come in here usually are a little tight," he said. "That's no description. Anyway, I just came on duty a few minutes ago. If you say she was here around noontime, well, she'd be long gone before I came on. We don't let 'em hang around when they are getting stoned."

I had him check again, but there was no envelope.

It worried me, but there was nothing I could do about it. I tried to put it out of my mind. I had other things to think about. In any case, I figured she'd just got tired waiting. Probably decided to go to her room and sleep it off and she'd get in touch with me in the morning.

I telephoned the Hadleys' farm down in Virginia at seven on the dot from Pete's apartment. Carol had not arrived yet but a maid said that the Hadleys had called and said they would be a little late. They were stopping along the road and were going to have dinner.

I told her to tell Mrs. Baron that I had called and that I would call back again in an hour.

And then Pete and I left and took a subway down to Times Square. It was quicker than driving. We went to a steak house on Forty-fifth Street and had double sirloins. For some reason, I had a terrific appetite. We had imported German beer, mixed with bass ale, hash-browned potatoes, and garlic bread on the side. Pete had a tossed green salad, and I skipped the salad and ordered artichokes, with a drawn butter sauce. We didn't discuss our plans for later in the evening and barely spoke during the dinner.

I tried the Virginia call again at eight, while the waiter was clearing off the table and getting ready to bring the coffee and brandy. She answered on the second ring. She wanted to know if I had lined up the dancing girls yet and sent me a half a dozen kisses over the telephone.

Pete and I left the musical during the intermission. It was a lousy show; we decided we'd get back to the apartment and do our waiting there.

The telephone rang a few minutes after we had sat down. It was the department downtown. They said that they were trying to find me and thought Pete might know where I was.

Pete looked over at me and shook his head.

"Saw him earlier this evening," he said. "I guess he's on his way home. If it's important ..."

He held the receiver for a minute or two more and then shrugged and hung up.

"Didn't say what it was," he said turning to me. "Just said they were looking for you but that it would keep until morning."

At twelve o'clock Pete picked up the suitcase and opened it. He took out the two guns, short-nosed .38 specials, and handed one to me. Then he stripped off his service revolver and I did the same. He closed the suitcase and we left the apartment.

I noticed a pile of early morning tabloids on the floor of the elevator as we rode downstairs to the lobby. My eye caught the headline. It said something about the nude, beaten body of a chorus girl being found in a hotel room.

I didn't pick up a copy of the paper. Nude, beaten bodies of chorus girls were always being found in hotel rooms.

I was off duty. I was very definitely off duty.

I drove down Broadway and when we came to Sixty-first Street I turned. The Ford sedan which Pete had arranged for was standing at the curb midway in the block. Pete got out, taking the suitcase. He didn't say anything.

I pulled away from the curb and ten minutes later I was parking in front of the night club on East Fifty-second Street. The doorman hurried over, a belligerent look on his face. I spoke before he could say anything. I had my wallet in my hand, exposing the shield.

"Take care of it for me, son," I said. "I'll be maybe a couple of hours."

He looked at the shield, looked up at me, no longer belligerent, but not exactly happy. I opened the wallet and took out the five-dollar bill and pressed it into his hand.

He still didn't look happy but he looked surprised. I guess he wasn't used to having cops hand him money. He looked at me closely and nodded. He would remember me. I wanted him to remember me.

I went into the night club and handed the check girl my hat. She gave me a check and a smile and I started for the main room. The place was jumping.

But instead of going inside, I stood at the bar and ordered a drink. I left two dollars under the half empty glass and went back into the lobby and to the men's room. I came out a minute or two later and walked over to the door.

The doorman was opening the door of a cab which was pulled up in front of the place and double parked.

I slipped outside and started up the street. Pete picked me up a half block away.

We drove directly to East Sixty-eighth Street.

There were no lights showing in Dr. Pantell's house. The place looked deserted.

Pete parked the car a half block away, finding a spot where he had to crowd the fireplug. He'd probably get a ticket. It wouldn't matter. His cousin would pay it. The car belonged to his cousin. It had Jersey plates and so he'd probably just tear up the ticket.

We carried the suitcase when we walked back to the house.

Pete stood in the shadows, in the doorway of a private brownstone a couple of doors down the street. He had the bag with him. There was a taxi just leaving the apartment house across the street, and I waited until the doorman had returned inside. Then I mounted the steps of Dr. Pantell's residence.

I didn't use a skeleton key. The door was locked, but a jimmy inserted in the jam sprang it at once. I stepped inside, into complete blackness. For a second I stood dead still and listened. I thought I heard the sound of music coming from somewhere in the rear.

I had the pencil flash in my right hand, the .38 special in my left, when the door nudged open a moment later. I could feel the suitcase rub against my leg as Pete set it on the floor. He must have crossed the room because a moment later a flash went on for an instant. A second later and he had jammed the back of the chair under the doorknob.

We didn't use our lights again until we had entered the doctor's private office and closed the door behind us. There were no outside windows.

It was not necessary to say a word. We both knew what we had to do; we had memorized every detail.

Pete opened the bag and took out the tape and the bottle of ether.

There was a door at the end of the office and it led into a hallway. At the far end of that hallway, some twenty-two feet away, was the door leading down the eight steps which would bring us to the apartment in which the butler had his quarters. We spotted the light under the crack of his doorway as we hit the top of the steps. We didn't need the flashlights.

We had pulled the gloves on our hands, the masks over our faces, and the heavy wool socks over our shoes as we had stood in the doctor's private office.

The television was going full blast, and the noise drowned out any sound we made as we opened the door.

He was sitting with his back to us, facing the set. His head was on his chest, and he must have fallen asleep as he watched the picture. He didn't make a move as we stepped over to him.

I probably had the tape over his mouth before he woke up. Pete had his hands behind him and was taping them when he made a movement and then quickly struggled. The struggle lasted only a moment or so. He never did see us. We left him still in the chair, hands taped behind him, arms taped to the chair itself, eyes and mouth both covered with tape. He was breathing heavily and I hesitated for a moment. But he had plenty of air.

Neither of us had said a word.

We left him there and slowly started for the hallway again.

The house was completely dark and we risked the pencil flash several times as we made our way through the kitchen. We waited several moments outside of the door of the room where we knew that Bellows, the chauffeur, would be sleeping. We put our ears to the door and listened but there wasn't a sound. I reached for the knob and slowly turned it. I nudged Pete when I felt the click.

And then we threw the door open and rushed into the room, each with a pencil flash in his hand.

The room was completely empty.

A chauffeur's cap and uniform was neatly hanging on a peg behind the door. There was a movie magazine opened on a chair beside the made-up bed, a crumpled package of cigarettes. A half-filled ash tray lay next to them.

The private garage was just off the bedroom and connected to it by a door with glass in its upper half. A quick look showed us the car was gone.

Pete shrugged and spoke for the first time.

"It figures," he said. "The boss away so he just took off with the car for a date or something."

I made a quick examination of the room. There were a few clothes in the dresser, a couple of sport coats and slacks in the clothes closet.

He could return at any time. I didn't like it but there was nothing we could do about it. If we were reasonably quiet, we should be all right. The chances are that he would enter his room from the garage and go directly to bed. He certainly wouldn't be wandering around upstairs.

On the other hand, there was just the remotest chance that he might look in on the butler if he returned, before going to bed.

Pete read my mind.

We carefully closed the door and went back to the butler's apartment. Pete flicked off the television set and lifted the old man and laid him on the bed. He taped his legs together and then pulled the covers over him. We turned off the overhead light as we left the room.

He'd be safe enough until morning. I'd make a telephone call sometime the next day, find out if the chauffeur had returned and discovered him. If he hadn't, I'd have to put in an anonymous call to the precinct station. I didn't want to do it. I didn't want the burglary discovered, and I was sure that Pantell himself would not report it.

On the other hand I didn't want the old man to die in case the chauffeur failed to return for any reason.

We started up the back stairs using our pencil flashes cautiously. Pete had retrieved the suitcase and was carrying it. It was an easy trip. We had been all through that house just two weeks before. And we had studied the plans of the building which Pete had dug up.

The door to the fourth-floor bedroom was ajar, and as soon as we entered we closed it. I kept a tiny beam from the flash on the floor as Pete went to the windows and checked them. The heavy curtains were already drawn.

A look at my wrist watch showed me that it was ten minutes after one.

I held the light as Pete took what he needed from the suitcase. It didn't take him long.

We weren't going to attempt to try the combination. Pantell would have changed it for sure. We were going to blow it. It didn't present any tremendous problem.

I started taking the mattress off the bed as Pete plugged in the high-speed steel drill. He knew exactly what he was doing. He should. He'd been on the safe and loft squad two years, and he'd had plenty of experience with explosives when he was in the Army.

The drill made a high, shrill whining sound and I found the heavy machine oil in the suitcase and squirted it on the drill as Pete pressed it home. It didn't completely stop the noise, but it helped.

Pete made the three holes around the combination and put in the napalm. He rigged the fuses and when they were set, we put the mattress in front of the safe, piled blankets around it. We used an electric detonator which worked from flashlight cells. When Pete pushed home the plunger, we were standing in back of the closet door.

It hardly made any noise at all, but there was a large flash and smoke began to fill the room. Pete coughed and we put on the pencil flashes.

It took a crowbar to get the door all of the way open. The inside door was easy; a heavy jimmy handled it. There were two large suitcases in the safe. Pete took a knife from his pocket and used it to jimmy open the one nearest him. I held the light.

I guess we both whistled under our breath as the lock snapped.

The suitcase was jammed with bills, neatly stacked and banded.

"Holy Jesus!" I said.

I cut the flash and as I did the room was suddenly bright with light. It caught us so completely unexpectedly that for the briefest of seconds we just stood there, completely paralyzed.

Chapter 22

"Don't make a move!"

I knew that voice. I had heard it only a few days before, downstairs in the office when we had been talking with Dr. Pantell.

There was a sudden odd little plinking sound and I felt something tear at my sleeve.

I knew what it was and I guess Pete knew too.

We were standing together, just at the opening of the safe, and it was Pete who moved first. As he swung he shoved me and I went to my knees, and I guess that is what saved me. Because again I was conscious of that strange little plinking sound and I knew that there must have been a silencer on Pantell's gun, and he was shooting directly at us from where he stood in the doorway.

I was just dimly aware of the gun in Pete's hand when I heard it crash out. By now I was on the floor, rolling, and my own gun was in my hand. I fired blindly, aiming at the doorway as I turned.

The big one, who had been standing next to Dr. Pantell, grunted and the gun fell with a thud from his hand, hitting the floor at the same time that he did. I saw the gun in Dr. Pantell's hand leap away as though it were alive. There was a third man, but he was behind the other two, and he was trying to get his gun around them so that he could use it, but before he was able to do so, I sent a shot at his knees and he screamed and fell forward.

Pete's own gun was silent now and I saw that he was staggering. I figured at first that his ankle had given away under him. But I didn't have any time for thinking. All I could do was act.

I was on my feet now and I didn't fire again. Instead I was across the room in two leaps and the barrel of my gun caught Dr. Pantell across the forehead and he grunted and fell. The man who had been behind him was on his knees and groping for a gun which lay several feet away from him.

I brought the barrel of my revolver down across his head.

When I looked up and back toward the safe, I saw that Pete had straightened up. He had dropped his gun on the rug and he was pulling out one of the suitcases. He was leaning over in an odd way and having trouble with the bag.

"Take them," he said. "Take them, kid."

I knew that he was hit but I didn't know how bad. I looked back and saw that Pantell was out cold. The big man wasn't moving and the other one was on his hands and knees, slowly weaving back and forth.

I reached Pete and put my arm around him, but he brushed it away. "The suitcases, goddamn it!" he said. "Get the suitcases."

He stared at me like a madman. He was holding his hands to his stomach. His face was dead white.

"You've been hit," I said. "We have to get out of here."

He looked at me with fury. "Get those bags," he said. "I can make it downstairs."

I put one bag under my right arm and held the other in my hand. I shoved the gun in my belt and I reached for Pete, but he shook my hand loose. He staggered toward the doorway and I had to help him shove Pantell out of the way.

The light from the room outlined the hallway.

We made the third floor and the elevator was standing there with the door open. I pushed Pete in and he sagged against the wall. I threw the suitcases inside and closed the door and pushed the down button. I had my gun back in my hand when we reached the first floor.

The lights were on, but no one was there.

I got Pete as far as the doorway and then turned off the lights.

"I'll bring the car to the front of the house and come in and get you," I said. Pete grunted and said, "Hurry."

Looking out the door, I saw a cab standing in front of the apartment across the street. I pulled my mask off and waited a moment but the driver was in no hurry to move. So I opened the door all of the way and walked down the street. I had to take the chance. Time had run out. I had to drive around the block, and it was a couple of minutes before I was back in front of the apartment house. I left the engine running at the curb as I ran up the steps.

Pete was still leaning against the doorjamb. I started to take him by the arm to support him, but he cursed and pulled away.

"The suitcases, damn it," he said.

I hesitated just a second and then I reached for the two bags.

A man and a woman were getting into the cab across the street as I threw the bags into the car.

I went back again to the doorway and when I opened the door, Pete fell out, crashing into me. He was unconscious as I carried him to the car and put him in the front seat.

I heard a window open somewhere above and a moment later there was the crash of gunfire. Whoever was shooting wasn't bothering with a silencer any more.

The glass in the windshield suddenly shattered and fell in on me. But by now I had the car in gear and was pulling away from the curb. I heard several more shots as I raced down the street.

Pete must have come to when the cold air from the shattered windshield hit his face. He groaned as I turned into Second Avenue. I looked in the rear-vision mirror. No one was following us.

Pete tried to say something and then gave it up and just sighed.

"How bad is it, Pete?" I asked. "Can you tell me where ...?"

"Bad enough," Pete said. "Bad enough."

"I'm going to get you to a doctor," I said. "We'll ..."

He reached over and took my arm. "No," he said. His voice was suddenly strong. "No—no doctor. I can make it. But we have to dump this car. We can't do it in this car."

I started to protest but again he said he could make it. "Probably just grazed my guts," he said. "But get rid of the car. We can't ..."

We were passing under an overhead light and I looked over at him quickly. He seemed to have a little more color and he was sitting straighter and his eyes were wide open.

"Parking lot," he said. "Over on First Avenue. In the Seventies. Closed at night but we can dump the car there. You leave me in the car and go get your own. I can hold out until you get back."

"You can't hold out," I said. "Hell, you're bleeding and ..."

"I can hold out. It's our only hope. Dump this car and get the other one. Then pick me up." He hesitated and then spoke in a low voice. "I think the bleeding has stopped," he said.

"I found the parking lot and there were half a hundred cars in it. It was one of those lots which was used for overnight parking, and the people who used it probably paid by the month. There was no watchman, no lights.

I found an empty spot far over by a brick wall. I just hoped the owner of the spot would not be returning until I could get back.

I got Pete into the back of the car and stretched out on the seat. I tried to examine him but he wouldn't let me.

"Just hurry," he said.

So I left him and started walking and a block away I flashed down a cruising cab. When I got back to the night club on Fifty-second Street, I had to wait around for almost ten minutes before the doorman disappeared inside. And then I went in and went to the men's room and I quickly checked and saw that there was no blood on me. My sleeve was torn and I knew that that first bullet had gone through, missing my elbow by a fraction of an inch. I came out and this time the doorman was outside when I went out.

He remembered me. He reached in his pocket and handed me my keys.

"About five cars down," he said.

I thanked him and wished him good night.

There was a car pulling into the parking lot when I got back so I circled the block slowly. When I returned, a man and a woman were walking up the street. I pulled into the lot and got as close to Pete's car as I could.

Pete made me move the two suitcases before he would let me help him into my car. Again I suggested a doctor, but he wouldn't hear of it.

"Take me to your place," he said. "I'll be all right. Just get me up to your place."

Chapter 23

We had passed the last Parkway tollgate and were approaching Hawthorne Circle. I felt Pete move beside me. He spoke, his voice sounding muffled.

"Light me a cigarette, Joe," he said.

I lit two cigarettes and handed him one. He groaned under his breath, but then quickly said, "Don't worry about me. I'm all right. I'll make it."

"All right. Maybe you will, Pete. But it won't do you any good. There's that car of your cousin's. It will be found before morning, and the minute the man at the parking lot sees it, with its windshield shattered and blood all over the seats, he'll call the police. They'll trace the license and ..."

"It's all right, Joe," Pete interrupted. "It wasn't my cousin's car. I stole it but I didn't want you worrying and so ..."

"You stole it! Goddamn it, Pete ..."

"It was safer that way," Pete said. "Look what happened."

"Sure—safe," I said. "So safe that it has our fingerprints all over it."

"No," Pete said. "No, while you were gone, I moved around enough to take care of that. They'll find the car all right, but there won't be any connection."

We drove a few minutes more in silence, and Pete's cigarette fell to the floor and I took my foot off the throttle to stamp on it.

"I'm glad that Carol won't be home," Pete said.

"You should be," I said, bitterly. "If she was home you'd be in a prison ward at Bellevue and I'd be in the interrogation room. Carol isn't going to get mixed up in this."

"Look, Joe," Pete said. "Just get me to a bed and give me a couple of days. I'll be all right. But if you are really worried, pal, drop me off at some motel. I can take care of myself. I don't want to crap you up anymore."

I began to feel like a heel. Sure, Pete had gotten me into it, but I wasn't exactly a child. My eyes had been wide open.

"We started it together, kid," I said, "and we'll see it through together. You're going to be all right, Pete. We'll manage something. But you better not talk anymore. Just take it easy until I can get you into a bed and see how bad it is."

Pete grunted. A few minutes later he spoke again.

"Son of a bitch," he said. "He was using a silencer. And it was just like it was with Kenny—he was going to cut us down without giving us a chance. Do you suppose he knew who ..."

"Don't talk," I said. "He couldn't have recognized us, but he certainly must have suspected something. The thing was a frame—except the money was in the safe. But he couldn't have known it would be us. Maybe he just suspected ..."

But there was no use speculating. Dr. Pantell had been there, had caught us in the act. That's all that counted.

When the automatic overhead garage doors dropped behind the car, my eye went to the dashboard clock as I started to turn off the ignition key. It was twenty minutes to four. I opened the car door, and I heard a telephone ringing inside the house.

Pete had either fainted or fallen asleep. He was out cold. I didn't touch him but went at once and opened the door leading into the kitchen. When I reached the phone and lifted the receiver, I heard nothing for a moment and then thought I detected a gentle click. It could have been someone checking to see if I was home; on the other hand, whoever it was might have given up just before I answered.

I didn't have the time to worry about it.

Pete came to and moaned as I carried him upstairs. I put him down on the bed and went into the bathroom and returned with a pair of scissors, bandages, and iodine. I didn't try to get his jacket off but opened it as he lay on his back. The center of his shirt was soaked with blood.

It took me a good fifteen minutes and toward the end of it the telephone again rang, but I was busy and let it ring.

The bullet had caught Pete in the side and apparently had plowed in at a downward angle. It was still in him. I knew that he must have bled internally and I thought it would be a miracle if it had escaped any vital organs. I couldn't, in fact, understand how it could have.

The blood had coagulated around the wound and was no longer flowing.

I managed to cut his clothing away before I went to work on the wound itself. The medicine chest yielded up some sulfa powder, which was a couple of years old at least and very likely inactive, but I used it after washing out the torn flesh with a weak solution of iodine and water. I put bandages over the place where the bullet had entered and that was about the best I could do. I took his pulse and it was fast. He was breathing very heavily and I thought he was still passed out until his eyes suddenly opened and he spoke.

"Jesus, it hurts."

I stood up. "I'm getting a doctor," I said.

"Get me a drink," Pete said. "No doctor."

"A drink would kill you."

"Damn it, Joe," Pete said, his voice suddenly strong, "get me a drink."

So I went down to the kitchen and poured a shot of bourbon into a glass and mixed it with water and brought it up and put it to his lips. He drank it all and suddenly there was color in his face. When he spoke, his voice was clear and strong.

"I saw plenty of guys in the front lines get lead in their guts and pull through—without a doctor," Pete said. "I'm tough. Just have to rest up for a while. Did you bring the dough in?"

"I will," I said.

"I'd like to see it—right now."

"You take it easy," I said. "Just take it easy. I'll go down and get ..."
The phone was ringing again and I reached for the instrument
beside the bed. "Baron," I said.

It was young Wolski and he was calling from headquarters.

He apologized for getting me up. He said, "I've been trying to get you
since early this evening. I tried everywhere." His voice sounded tired.

"Well ..."

"That case you and Delanos were working on," he said.

I felt myself going a little pale. "Yes?"

"Well, things have been happening. Inspector Flood wanted to get
a hold of you but he got me instead. Because they told him down here
that I was working with you now."

"Get to it," I said. "What's happening? What case that Delanos and
I were working on?"

"That Dr. Pantell thing. It seems that the guy the doctor shot
robbing his place had a girl friend. Girl named Rosalie Carver."

I didn't say anything. I waited for what he would say.

"They found her early last evening. In a hotel room over on the
Upper East Side. Someone had stripped her and beaten her to death.
Or more likely tortured her to death. The inspector said he thought
you should know about it."

It was so long before I could find anything to say that he must have
thought I'd hung up.

"Are you still there?" he said at last.

"Yes—yes, I'm still here." I shook my head, trying to gather myself.
Pete was staring at me questioningly, but I ignored him.

"Do you know who did it?" I asked at last.

"Nothing yet," Wolski said.

"Well—I'll get down right away."

"You won't have to," he said. "The precinct, Flood's boys, are handling
it. They called me in for a while but when they couldn't get you and
realized I hadn't been on the thing originally, they took it all over by
themselves. I just thought you should know what's going on so I called.
You don't have to get down now. Flood said to tell you if I reached you
that he'd like you to contact him."

"I'm glad you called," I said. "I appreciate it." I hesitated a second,
and then I said, "By the way, do you know if anyone has been up to
talk to Dr. Pantell about it? Of course it couldn't concern him but ..."

"That's a funny thing," Wolski said. "It seems that Dr. Pantell was
having his own little troubles last night. I heard about it from one of

Flood's boys. Someone reported hearing gunfire from in front of his house. When the precinct car got there to investigate, they discovered the front door jimmied open."

"And?"

"But that was all. The butler was home and he said nobody had entered because he had been there all evening. And he didn't know anything about the gunfire. Nothing actually had happened except the door being jimmied and broken in, but it was kind of a coincidence."

"What did Dr. Pantell have to say?"

"Why, he wasn't there himself," Wolski said. "The butler said he was vacationing in Bermuda."

I thanked him again and told him to try and get a little sleep. He'd had a long day.

I'd had a long day myself. And it wasn't over yet.

Chapter 24

Pete closed his eyes while I was telling him about the phone call. He was breathing regularly and deeply and by the time I'd finished he was sound asleep. I pulled the sheet over him and turned off the light.

The curtain was drawn at the window, but I could see daylight just beginning to show around the edges.

There was surprisingly little blood on the seat where Pete had sat. I did the best I could with soap and water and at least removed any visible traces. And then I took the two suitcases and carried them down into the basement. They were identical, large Gladstones made of quarter-grain leather. I looked first into the one Pete had opened. There was a table next to the deep freeze, and I laid the bag open on it.

I didn't count the actual money. There was too much of it. But I made a quick estimate after going through four or five of the stacks. It would come to well over half a million dollars. The bills were all relatively new, all in large denominations. There was nothing under a twenty-dollar bill.

I put the money back in the bag and started on the other one. The lock yielded to a little pressure, and I spread the bag excepting to see a duplication of the contents of the previous suitcase. It wasn't disappointment that I sensed; it was shock.

The suitcase was filled with small paper parcels, some two inches by four inches by six. They were uniform. I guess I knew what to expect when I tore open the first one.

The second suitcase was filled to the brim with raw heroin. I am no expert on drugs, but I would have guessed that on the retail market, it would have brought a couple of million dollars after cutting.

I suddenly understood why Dr. Pantell and his gunmen had started shooting without warning; I understood why someone had taken a chance of blasting away from that upstairs window in the hope of stopping us.

And as I stood there looking down at that suitcase full of drugs, I thought, God, there's enough here to ruin a dozen lives, a hundred lives, a thousand lives. Enough to motivate and be responsible for untold robberies, assaults, rapes, murders.

My eyes went slowly to the suitcase holding the money.

I determined at that moment to do one thing: no matter what else happened I would see that the suitcase containing the heroin reached the hands of the Federal Narcotics people.

Twenty minutes later and I had brought down the remains of the large roll of wrapping paper which we had purchased the previous December to wrap up Christmas presents before mailing them. I discarded the suitcase and made four individual bundles of drugs. I used my fountain pen and carefully printed an address down in Foley Square.

In the upper left hand corner of each package, I printed the name and address of Dr. Horace Pantell. I wanted to be quite sure that the Federal people would make the connection.

The money presented a little more of a problem, but at least I had a temporary answer. At the bottom of the deep freeze, Carol and I had stored a couple of dozen bluefish which we had caught during a trip off Brielle some weeks before. Neither of us cared a great deal for fish, but rather than let them go to waste, we had decided to wrap them in aluminum foil and put them in the freezer.

I opened the box and removed the packages on top until I reached the fish. I took out approximately enough of them to fill the suitcase. And then I removed the stacks of money from the suitcase and starting wrapping them in foil. It took quite a while, and oddly enough the money took up almost exactly the same amount of space as the fish had occupied.

I then divided the fish between the two suitcases and took them out and put them in the trunk of the car in the garage. I knew a nice deserted spot, a locally infamous lovers' lane down near Dobbs Ferry and just off the Parkway, where I would be able to drop them off. In a day or so after they had thawed, those bluefish should be pretty ripe. I didn't much care whom they would disturb.

Pete was still sleeping when I got back upstairs. I went into the bathroom and had a cold shower and toweled off and then shaved and put on fresh clothes. It was Saturday and my day off, but Inspector Flood would be expecting to hear from me. I could call him on the phone, but I thought it was a lot better idea to go into town and see him. He wanted information from me, but I wanted a lot more information from him.

I hated to leave Pete alone. I realized that there was every chance that Dr. Pantell would have put two and two together and come up with the right answer. I knew he hadn't recognized us, but he had known that his place might be robbed and he was smart. Very smart.

But there was nothing I could do. I was afraid to move Pete, and even if I hadn't been, there was no safe place to take him. I would have to take a calculated risk.

The doctor couldn't possibly go to the police, and any move he made would have to be direct. He wouldn't know how badly Pete might be wounded, and even if he did suspect us, I was sure that he would not move in on a couple of armed cops in full daylight. He would be bound to take time to reconnoiter. And time was what I needed.

I left Pete a note, propped up on the night table next to his bed. I told him I'd be back early in the afternoon and to try not to move or do anything if he woke up.

The story was all over the front pages of the newspapers, but I didn't bother to give more than a glance to the headlines as I sat in the Automat and had coffee and toast. I wanted to know what was happening, but I didn't want the newspaper version. I wanted to get it straight from headquarters—or rather straight from the precinct house.

Rosalie Carver's pictures, both before her death and after, filled the front pages. The one taken after death was probably retouched. Even at that it was pretty grim fare for the public at large.

Chapter 25

The Sergeant on the desk sent me into the Inspector's office at once. He was alone and he came to the point fast.

"You talked with her, Baron," he said. "A few days ago. She must have said something, given some hint ..."

"I made out my report sir, and ..."

"Damn it, I've read your report," Flood said. "I know what's in it. But you spent some time with this girl. You must have caught things, meaningless at the time, which now, now that this has happened, could mean something."

I nodded. "I gather," I said, stalling for time, "that there isn't any doubt about murder? ..."

"Doubt?" The Inspector laughed bitterly and pulled a folder over and opened it. He reached in and took out an eight-by-ten glossy print and sailed it across the desk at me.

"Take a look," he said.

It was the official police body picture—as Rosalie Carver had been found. One look was plenty.

"See that? Does it look like suicide? Let me tell you something, mister. They went to work on her with knives and fists and cigar butts and God only knows what else. But they were careful. They took a long time doing what they did. Take another look at that picture. Notice something? Look at the lips and the mouth, and the throat. No injuries. The only parts of her body that weren't violated. They wanted to keep her talking. They broke most of the bones in her body, and they did it slowly, one by one. Her stomach was full of alcohol— but it was also full of black coffee. They gave it to her to bring her to, probably. She had something they wanted—information I suppose— and they were out to get it. We don't know if they did or didn't, but if she had anything to say, you can bet she said it. It probably took a couple of hours or more to kill her."

I felt like throwing up.

"It happened on the fourth floor of a flea bag up on Third Avenue. The maid went in to leave towels about seven o'clock last night and this is what she found. She screamed and is still probably screaming.

"There was only one other person on the floor all afternoon. A drunk and he says he heard nothing. The girl had checked in around four o'clock using a phony name. Paid in advance. It wasn't robbery. She had four hundred and some dollars in her purse when we found her. A couple of things we do know. Whoever did this must have been a junkie. No normal human being could have stomached it. Now you tell me about her."

I told him—told him as much as I could. I didn't explain about spending all afternoon and evening with her. I didn't tell him what had taken place between us. I just said I'd had a few drinks with her, taken her to lunch. Questioned her. I told him what she'd told me about her relationship with Kenny. I said that Kenny was a user and a small-time operator. But I didn't mention Dr. Pantell. I had my own ideas about the doctor and as I talked with the Inspector, I knew that I was going to have to do something about those ideas. But I couldn't do it officially.

It was the Inspector himself who brought up Dr. Pantell.

"We have tried to contact that doctor who killed Kenny," he said. "He's supposed to be in Bermuda, but we haven't been able to reach him. The hotel where he's staying says he is away on a three-day fishing trip."

"Do you make any connection ..."

"No, at least not yet. There probably is no connection. But we aren't going to miss anything on this one. This girl was probably nothing but another small-time bum, but we are going to get the maniac who killed her. The guy was a sadist, but there is more to it than that. She wasn't raped, wasn't sexually violated. Just tortured to death. It wasn't a crime of passion, committed by the run-of-the-mill psycho. This was a deliberate, organized murder. So if you have any ideas, any slightest hint of an idea, start working on it."

I nodded. There was nothing I could say.

"This one," the Inspector said, standing, "I am not going to hand back to headquarters. This one I take care of myself. No human being should have to die this way—and, by God, nobody is going to get away with it—not in my precinct."

I told him I would go over the notes I'd made after talking with the girl and see if I could figure out anything. I said I'd be glad to do anything I could to help. And then I left.

I knew there was nothing more I could do for Rosalie Carver, nothing I would be able to do for Inspector Flood. But there were a few things I could do about the person or persons who had been responsible for her death. And I intended to do them.

Leaving the precinct house, I began to think of those telephone calls yesterday afternoon. She had wanted to see me.

She had been drunk, had sounded drunk. But she had also been frightened and maybe she had been more frightened than drunk.

And now she was dead.

Alive she would always have been a threat to the doctor.

Had Pantell found out what the girl had told me? Was that how he happened to return from Bermuda in time to interrupt Pete and myself as we were breaking into his strong box?

If this were true, then there would be no mystery in his mind as to who had robbed him. He would know who had his money, who had the suitcase full of heroin.

I pulled the car sharply over to the curb and got out and went into a drugstore on the corner. I got change at the counter and then I entered the phone booth and put in the long-distance call to Virginia.

The Hadley maid called Carol to the phone and her voice sounded sleepy.

I don't know why, but I felt a terrible sense of relief the moment she said, "Darling, how nice of you. But it's so early."

I said like a fool, "Are you all right?"

"Of course I'm all right. Why shouldn't I be all right? I only had two cocktails before dinner last night and ..."

I guess I must have sighed audibly in my sudden sense of relief.

"What's the matter, Joe?" Carol said. "You sound so odd. And it's such a funny time to call. And ..."

"Listen, honey," I said. "Listen a moment. How long are the Hadleys planning to stay? I know you said you would be coming back the first of the week, but I had the impression they were going to stay on for a while and ..."

"They're staying for two weeks, Joe," Carol said. "I'm coming back Tuesday. Remember, I told you all about it?"

"Well," I said, hurriedly, "I can't explain it over the phone, but I wish you'd stay a little longer yourself. A good rest, a real vacation ..."

"Joe! I think you must have found that dancing girl!"

"I'm serious, honey," I said. "I really can't explain it, but I want you to stay there for a little longer. It's terribly important to me and I'll tell you all about it when you get back. I want you to be careful and ..."

"Joe, something's the matter. What is it? What's happening?"

I knew that I had played it badly, hadn't been smart at all. But I went on desperately.

"Carol, do what I ask you. Don't ask any questions—just do what I ask. Stay there for a few days. I'll keep in touch and there's nothing to worry about. But just stay there."

There was a long silence and finally she spoke in a barely audible voice. "All right, Joe," she said. "Whatever you want."

She sounded hurt. I was telling her how much I loved her as she hung up.

I found a dime in my trouser pocket, checked my notebook, and made my second call. The phone rang several times and then a woman's voice spoke.

"This is a recording. I repeat, this is a recording. Dr. Pantell is out of town and will not return until the end of the week. As soon as you hear a buzz you may speak for two minutes and it will be recorded and the message given to Dr. Pantell upon his return. Thank you. This is a recording. I repeat, this is a ..."

I replaced the receiver.

I knew I must get back as soon as possible, but I made one other stop on the way back to Westchester. It was at a postal substation in the Bronx.

I didn't have the packages weighed or registered or insured. I just purchased a couple of dollars' worth of stamps and pasted them on the faces of the packages and dropped them on the parcel post counter while the clerk was busy at another window. I had a lot of confidence in the U.S. mails. I had a lot of confidence in the Federal Narcotics Bureau. If I was a few cents short in postage, they would be glad to pay the extra money. It would be worth it to them.

Chapter 26

Pete was sitting up in bed when I got back. His face was very pale and his eyes were sunken into his head, but he was fully awake. The first thing he said was, "For God's sake, get me some water. And a shot of booze. And I'm hungry."

"If you feel like eating, you can't be too bad," I said. "But no booze."

"I feel like hell," he said. "I held that whisky before, so I guess there aren't any holes where they shouldn't be. But I don't feel any too great. What's been happening?"

"After you eat," I said.

I heated up a can of chicken soup and buttered some toast. Then I went back and while Pete sipped the soup I told him about Rosalie Carver.

Pete was quiet for a long time after I finished speaking. Finally he looked up.

"Joe," he said, "something happened between you and that girl when you saw her. Something you didn't tell me about."

"Nothing that meant anything," I said.

"Pantell knew that you'd seen her," Pete said. "That's why he wanted to talk to us."

I shrugged.

"He knew."

"Yes. He knew. And he also knew that we—or at least someone—was going to knock over that safe."

"What are you getting at, Pete?"

"Just this. Did the girl tell you about the dough in that safe and then did you tell her what we planned to do?"

I shook my head. "No, Pete, I didn't tell her. She told me about Pantell, all right. I've already explained that. But I told her nothing. Nothing at all."

"You didn't get tight and let slip ..."

"I've told you. I told her nothing."

Pete tossed his hands out and then groaned from the sudden effort.

"All right. There's only one way to figure it. Pantell saw me nosing around trying to find out something. He put two and two together. And he probably figured the girl had tipped us off about the dough in the safe and that we were planning to do just what we did do. I think he must have figured it right from the beginning, when we started taking an interest in the safe. And he set it up for us. Only it backfired on him."

"Not completely, Pete," I said. "You're lying there with a bullet in your guts. Rosalie Carver is dead."

"That's right," Pete said. "She's dead and nothing can be done about that. But we have the million bucks. That's what we went out for and that's what we have."

"About a half a million, Pete," I said. "The second bag was filled with something else. Heroin. Raw heroin."

Pete looked at me and whistled. He didn't even question the half million.

"Heroin?"

"Yeah. And don't get any ideas ..."

Pete looked at me and slowly shook his head, a hurt expression in his eyes.

"For God's sake, Joe, come off it. What do you really think I am, anyway? Do you think that for one second I'd touch that filthy stuff? Why ..."

I felt a little like a heel.

"What have you done with the dough?" Pete said.

"It's down in the basement, wrapped up in the freezer," I said. "But if Pantell really suspects us ..."

Pete shook his head. "I've got to get out of here," he said. "Yeah, I have to get up and get out. I got you into this and I can get you out of it.

We'll split the dough and then I'll take that dope and move out. I'll leave a trail so wide he can't miss it, and at least it will get him off your back."

"You're crazy," I said. "You got a piece of lead in your guts and you're going nowhere. Anyway, I'm in this and ..."

"You have Carol to think of," Pete said. "I'm alone. In a day or so, I'll be fine again and I ..."

He'd reached the edge of the bed and his feet were on the floor and that's when he fell.

He was unconscious when I managed to get him back under the covers. I saw that the wound in his side was bleeding again and I changed the dressing. I knew that he couldn't stay around much longer. I'd have to get a doctor.

By five o'clock I had made up my mind. Pete was conscious again, but he was running a high temperature. Part of the time he was coherent and then his voice would begin to fade and he'd start mumbling, and I knew that something would have to be done. I wracked my brains to think of some possible person I might trust, but there was no one.

I could take him and leave him in the emergency ward in a hospital with some cock and bull story, but I knew it wouldn't work. Nothing would work but the truth.

Pete's voice interrupted my thoughts as I sat beside his bed.

"Joe," he said.

I turned to him. "Yes, Pete?"

"You've got to do something, Joe," Pete said. His voice was very weak, but I could see that he was fully conscious and in his right mind. "You got to get this bullet out of me."

"I know, Pete," I said. "And that's just what I'm going to do. I am going to call an ambulance right now and ..."

His eyes became furious and he struggled to speak. "No! No ambulance and no doctor!"

I started to protest but he kept on.

"You've got to try it my way first," he said. "It's my life and my responsibility and it's going to be my way."

"There is no way, Pete," I said. "Just ..."

"Listen to me," Pete said. "I did a hitch in the medics while I was in the service. Remember? I don't know much but I do know a little. Now you go to a drugstore. Get ether. Get plenty of pure alcohol, cotton, medical scissors, probes. Tweezers. Something to sterilize things in. That lead is somewhere in me and it isn't in my stomach or intestines or I couldn't have eaten. You have to find it and get it out."

"God, Pete!" I said. "I can't. I don't know ..."

"You're a cop. You've taken first aid courses. You can give me ether and keep me under. You can try and stop the bleeding. You can probe. If I can lie here and take it, you can do it."

"But a real doctor ..."

"I haven't gone this far to quit now," Pete said. "Go on. Get the stuff you need. Do it now while I still have some strength. And no doctor. If I have to die, I die, but I'm not giving up and tossing in the sponge. Now promise me, Joe."

I looked at him for a long time. I understood what he meant. I understood about giving himself up.

"All right, Pete," I said. "I'll do what I can."

"Then get moving," he said. "One thing the Army taught me about medicine—time is important and I've been waiting too long already."

I got up and straightened his pillow and then I walked downstairs. I was trying to remember everything I'd ever learned about first aid work, everything I'd ever learned about anatomy. I was trying to think what I would want at the drugstore. I was trying to get up my courage.

I was still trying to think clearly when I opened the garage doors to drive out.

It was then I remembered Dr. Carlo Effenshez.

I met Effenshez some six months before, met him officially while Pete and I were investigating the death of a girl up in the East Bronx. The girl had been found at four o'clock in the morning in the street outside of the doctor's office and the coroner's report established that she had been dead something less than an hour when her body was discovered. It had also established septic poisoning, complicated by extreme loss of blood, as the cause of death. The autopsy showed that she had had an abortion very shortly before she had died.

It was one of those infuriating cases which homicide detectives all too frequently encounter. We had every possible bit of circumstantial evidence to involve the doctor. We even had a witness who had seen her enter his office. We had his background and reputation which was unsavory to say the least. We discovered the girl's fingerprints both in his office and in his examination room.

We had our own impressions of the doctor himself and we had a thorough conviction that he was guilty. But we had nothing at all that we could bring into court. Before we were through, we knew beyond any reasonable doubt that Effenshez was a part of a large abortion ring and we had dug up enough evidence to get a conviction on two of his associates. But we couldn't pin him. At one stage in the long investigation we had gone so far as to hint to the doctor that if he would talk, would let us know who had sent the girl to him and who else was involved, we might be able to see that he himself was kept out of it.

But he didn't bite. He took a chance that the district attorney wouldn't seek an indictment on circumstantial evidence and he was right.

I remembered at the time that I had several distinct impressions of Dr. Effenshez. I remembered thinking that it was a shame that a man who was considered a really first-class gynecologist and surgeon by a number of his associates should be involved in illegal medicine. I remembered that he gave the impression of being a man who would do anything for money.

I knew that I would have to take a chance on Effenshez. Money would reach him and we had the money.

I turned and went down into the cellar. It took me the best part of ten minutes to get at the money at the bottom of the freezer. I took out one package of fifties. The band read ten thousand dollars. It should be enough to deal with Dr. Effenshez. We had figured from an examination of his bank accounts that his price for an abortion was around five hundred to seven fifty. For ten thousand he should be willing to take the bullet out of a policeman—and keep quiet about it.

It took me several minutes to repack the deep freeze and I thought at one time I heard footsteps overhead. I hurried. I just hoped that Pete hadn't tried to get out of bed. I would check on him before I left.

And I made up my mind that if Effenshez told me that it was essential to get Pete to a hospital, I would do so, no matter what happened.

The package of money was too large to get into a single pocket and I tore the band off and began stuffing sheaves of bills in various pockets as I walked up the cellar stairs. I entered the kitchen and started to cross it. That is when I saw her.

Chapter 27

She was standing in the opened door, between the kitchen and the garage. Her mouth was half open and her eyes were staring at me wildly. She was watching as I put the last of the bills into my side coat pocket.

Paula Archer said, "Why, Joe! What in the world ..."

I stopped as though I had been hit by a bullet. "What in the hell are you ..." I began. And then before she could say anything, I came to.

"Paula," I said, "you surprised me. How did you get here?"

The color came back to her face. "You surprised me, too," she said, "coming up out of the cellar like that and looking as though you had ..." She hesitated, took a step forward, and regained her poise.

"We stopped by to see you and Carol and saw your car in the garage. All the doors were open so we came in looking for you. After all, we decided life is too short for good friends to spend it feuding and Jack wanted to get things straightened out and ..."

"Jack," I said suddenly. "What do you mean, Jack? Where in the hell ..."

She took a sudden step back, her hand going to her mouth in a little gesture of fear.

"Joe," she said. "Joe, what's gotten into you? I'm just explaining to you. Jack and I stopped by because Jack felt that that silly business last week ..."

"Where is Jack?" I repeated. "Tell me—where is Jack?"

She looked a little lost for a moment and then spoke in a weak voice. "He—why we thought we heard someone moaning upstairs and he thought perhaps someone was hurt and he ..."

I didn't wait for her to finish. I turned and ran for the stairs.

"Stay right where you are," I half yelled. "Stay ..."

"Joe," she yelled, calling after me almost hysterically. "Joe, Jack is trying to be friendly and make up and ..."

But I was halfway upstairs and didn't hear the rest of it.

Jack Archer, immaculate in riding breeches, polished leather boots, sports coat and tan foulard scarf, stood at the side of the bed holding Pete's wrist in his hand and looking at the watch on his own wrist.

He looked up as I tore into the room. His face, still showing black and blue bruises and with the plaster on his nose, was completely without expression.

"This man," he said, "is dying."

There was a small scream behind me. Paula, who had followed me upstairs, stood there, leaning against the doorjamb with her right hand half covering her mouth.

"Paula," Archer said, "go down to the car and get my bag. Hurry."

He turned back to Pete, who lay on the bed breathing heavily and with his eyes closed. He didn't as much as look at me as I approached and stood at his side. The odor of brandy was on his breath, enough to asphyxiate a horse, and I knew without even thinking about it that he was very likely more than half drunk, as he usually was at this time of day on a weekend.

But you would have never guessed it from his actions during the next three quarters of an hour. Dr. Jack Archer must have been one hell of a brilliant medical student before he had decided to specialize in psychiatry.

Not once during that entire time did he speak to me or question me with the exception of his one remark before he started working on Pete. He made that while Paula was down getting his satchel.

"It will help," he said, "if you can give me an idea of what happened and how long ago it happened."

"He was shot," I said. "About fourteen hours ago. The bullet is still in him."

Paula Archer had once been a nurse—that's how Archer met her—and she went back to being one the moment she returned to the room with the bag. She had completely recovered herself, and if there were questions in her mind as to what it was all about, she, like her husband, held them in abeyance.

As Archer was stripping away the bandage over the wound, Paula turned to me.

"I don't believe you can help, Joe," she said. "Maybe it would be better if you waited outside."

I closed the door after myself and went downstairs and found the bourbon bottle and poured myself a drink. The perspiration was rolling off of my forehead.

Sometime later, perhaps twenty or twenty-five minutes, I heard Paula's voice calling and I went to the bottom of the steps. She asked if I could find some absorbent cotton and I went up to the bathroom and found a half a roll and brought it into the room.

Pete was stretched on the bed, covered completely with sheets except for a small area around the wound. Archer was leaning over him with a pair of narrow forceps in his hand and didn't look up. Pete's face was drained of color and Paula stood at his head with chloroform and a sponge in her hand. I gave her the cotton and then crossed the room but didn't leave. I didn't leave until it was all over.

When he finally finished after putting on a dressing and a loose bandage, Archer pulled the sheet over the operating area and turned to Paula.

"Stay with him," he said.

He looked over at me then and sort of nodded his head toward the door. I followed him out and he went into the spare bathroom and spent several minutes scrubbing his hands and arms. At last he rolled down his sleeves and sighed. He spoke for the first time.

"I could use a drink," he said.

He followed me downstairs to the kitchen and I found a half-filled bottle of brandy and put it on the table with two glasses. Archer filled them halfway to the brim and emptied his in a single gulp. Then he sat down and looked at me.

"Will he ..." I began.

Archer reached into his pocket and took out a small lead slug and laid it on the table.

"I've done everything I can do," he said. "I'd say send him to a hospital if I thought it would do any good, but right now he shouldn't be moved. He shouldn't be moved for at least forty-eight hours and by that time he'll either be dead or he'll very likely pull through. It can be either way. By the way ..." He hesitated and his face assumed that supercilious expression which used to annoy me so much. Except right at the moment nothing Jack Archer could possibly do would any longer annoy me.

"... by the way, did you shoot him?"

"No," I said. "I didn't shoot him. Pete ..."

Archer held up his hand. "Don't tell me about it," he said. "I don't want to know. Oh, I recognized him all right—at least I recognized him as another cop whom you've had out at the house here now and then and who is supposed to be an old buddy or something. But I don't remember his name and I don't want to know it now. In fact, if my guess is right, I don't think I want to know anything about it at all."

"But, Jack ..."

Again he held up a hand in protest. "You said he was shot more than twelve hours ago," he said. "Well, he wasn't in a hospital, he hadn't had any medical attention—unless you consider that Boy Scout bandage I found on him medical attention—and from all appearances he was going to just lie there until he died. I don't know what it is all about, but I do know that you're a policeman and know the rules."

"Yes," I said. "I know the rules."

I knew what was going to come next. I knew.

"I'm a damned sight better psychiatrist than you think I am," he said. "And a lot smarter. In a lot of ways you are a stupid son of a bitch and you are also pretty much of a bore. But oddly enough I half like you and I know that you are honest. In any case, your wife is a friend of mine and so are you if you only knew it. So I am going to assume that whatever this is all about is strictly your business. I am going to assume that you know what you are doing. And I am going to ask you only one thing. Either go to the phone right now and call the police department and explain that I have just performed an emergency operation because I had no chance to report it without risking the patient's life—or else tell me that no matter what happens my name will never be mixed up with his nor will Paula become involved."

I stared at him for a second or two unbelievingly.

Here was the man whom I had beaten in a drunken jealous rage only a week ago, telling me that he was willing to risk his reputation—even more, risk a criminal charge and the loss of his license—because he considered himself a friend.

"My God, Jack," I began, "I don't know what to say ..."

"Don't say anything," he said. "Just forget that Paula and I stopped by here this afternoon. You can be sure we will forget it."

"But ..."

"I don't want to know a thing," he said. He poured his glass full of brandy again and this time took only half at the first gulp. He got to his feet.

"I'm going up to Paula and we are leaving. Unless of course you want to make that phone call."

I shook my head.

"All right, but remember—keep us out of it," he said. "Watch him closely and be sure and check his temperature. Right now he's sleeping and he'll be out for several hours. I've got him filled up with morphine. I'm going to leave you a few pills and if everything works out all right, and he's still alive, that dressing should be changed in a couple of days. Someone will have to take out the stitches sooner or later. He can be fed if he wakes up and he's hungry, but only very lightly.

"He lost some blood, but he's a husky guy and I don't think it will bother him. The big danger is septic poisoning from that bullet I took out of him. And that's a straight gamble. It will happen or it won't. If his temperature starts to go up very suddenly—well, it will be up to you. From now on he's your baby. Now go up and ask Paula if she's ready."

"Jack." I said, "Jack, I don't know how to thank you. Honestly."

"Don't try," he said. "Just give my love to Carol." He smiled at me and reached for the rest of the brandy. "And get over the idea I'm trying to make your wife," he added. "I don't go around chasing the wives of guys whose guests end up with bullets in their guts."

It wasn't much of a joke but I forced a smile. I owed him that much.

A moment later Paula walked into the kitchen. She looked at us curiously for a moment but didn't say anything.

"We'll be going now," Archer said.

Paula hesitated in the doorway as they left and half turning said, "Tell Carol to give me a ring."

"She's away for a few days," I said, automatically.

Paula looked at me oddly and then shrugged.

"Oh?"

Chapter 28

It was midnight before I finally got to sleep. It had been the worst evening of my life. For the first few hours after Jack Archer and Paula had left, I sat upstairs next to the bed which held Pete, waiting for him to regain consciousness.

Each time my eyes went to his white, bloodless face I would go over what had happened and each time I would start wondering about Archer. Why had he acted the way he had? Would he really keep quiet and not make a report? Or was it just another of his vicious jokes and had he reassured me only so that he could safely get out of the house? What had Paula meant by that cryptic "Oh?" when I had told her Carol was away for a few days?

Was it possible that they might believe I had found Carol and Pete together, done something to Carol, and then shot Pete? And had Archer helped me to stall for time until he could get out of the house?

But as the hours passed and nothing happened I began to regain my confidence. Certainly, if Archer were going to do anything, I would know by now. But even as I began to develop confidence in Archer and cease to worry about him, other problems edged in to worry me.

Dr. Pantell. Where was Pantell and what was he planning? Had he actually guessed our identities? And most important of all—what about Pete?

I looked at my watch and saw that it was nine o'clock and then I looked over again at the bed. Pete opened his eyes and was staring at me.

"The money?" he said. "You started to show me the money."

I realized that he hadn't understood what had happened. Hadn't realized that Archer had been there and operated on him.

Quickly I told him, explaining that the bullet had been removed. He asked again about the money and I told him that I would show it to him in the morning. That he must rest and try to sleep. I asked if he wanted something to eat, but he shook his head. His only interest was the money.

I gave him three of the pills Archer had left and soon he was again sleeping, moaning now and then, but not moving.

I found a folding cot in a downstairs closet and brought it upstairs and spread a blanket on it. I didn't take off my clothes but merely removed my shoes and necktie and jacket and turned all the lights but the nightlight off. I remember hearing the clock chimes at midnight and at half past twelve, and then I remembered nothing more. The cot was uncomfortable, and the service revolver which was strapped under my shoulder didn't help matters, but I was so utterly exhausted that I finally passed out.

It was the sound of the telephone which awakened me.

It was a collect long-distance call and the operator asked if I would accept the charges. For a moment or so, as I tried to shake the sleep out of my eyes, I didn't quite understand. I started to turn to Carol to tell her someone was calling collect and in the half light of the shaded room I saw that I wasn't lying in the bed and then my mind cleared and I realized that the operator was saying that Mrs. Baron was calling and she wanted to know if I would accept the charges.

I pulled the telephone closer and told the operator to put her on.

She sounded a long way off.

"Joe?"

"Yes. Is this ..."

"It's Carol, darling," she said. "I hope I didn't wake you. But I've had a miserable night. I've been worrying and I couldn't sleep. You sounded so funny yesterday. And, darling ..."

"I'm fine, Carol," I said. "Everything is all right. Now you ..."

"But I've been thinking," Carol said. "I just wanted to call you and tell you I've been thinking about everything and that I ..."

There was a sudden strange, rattling sound from the bed and I saw a shadowy movement. I spoke into the phone quickly.

"Hold the line a second, honey," I said. "Hold on. I'll be right back."

I quickly dropped the receiver and stood up. I flicked on the light on the night table next to the bed and as I did, there was another weird coughing sound. As I looked down at Pete, he suddenly half rose up, his eyes wild and staring, his mouth half open as a thin trickle of saliva started down the side of his chin. Again that macabre sound came and even as I reached out to him, he fell back.

I said, "Oh my God!"

Pete had died as I watched him. I stood paralyzed for several seconds and then I turned back to the telephone.

"Carol," I said, "I'll call you back in a few minutes. Please, dear, I'll call you back...."

I replaced the receiver as she started to say something.

I didn't need to feel his pulse, didn't have to hold a glass in front of his opened mouth to find out if he still breathed. Pete Delanos was dead and nothing I could ever do would change it.

It must have been at least twenty minutes later, and I was still standing there, staring down at his lifeless form, when the sound of the ringing of the telephone again brought me to. I shook my head sharply to clear it and again lifted the receiver.

"What is it, Joe?" Carol said. "What's happening? I know something is wrong, Joe. Please ..."

"Carol, darling," I said. I struggled for words and for a moment nothing came.

"Oh, Joe," she said, "I've been so wrong. I know it now and that's what I wanted to call you and tell you. I've been wrong all along. About the house and about the money and about your work and everything. I want you to do what you want to do and if you want to be a cop that's fine and I love you and ..."

"Baby," I said. "Baby, please. Don't say anything and don't ..."

"But I wanted to tell you, Joe. And I'm coming home and I'm going to be a real wife and ..."

"No—no," I said and I almost yelled the words. "No, Carol, you can't...."

"What *is* the matter, Joe? What ..."

I forced myself to control my voice. I knew I would have to keep control, make sense.

"Listen, honey," I said. "Don't worry. Don't worry about a thing. We can talk it over when you get back. Everything will work out—just fine. But you must promise to do what I ask you. Stay where you are for a few more days. Wait until you hear from me. There's nothing to worry about and I'll explain everything when you get back. We'll work everything out. But you must promise to do what I ask you. You must promise me ..."

"Are you sure, Joe? ..."

"I'm sure, honey," I said. "I'm sure I love you and I'm sure everything will be fine. Just do this one thing for me. Without questions."

She was silent for a long time and at last spoke in a small voice. "I love you too, Joe," she said. I heard the receiver drop down as she hung up.

Chapter 29

I was still in the room, still looking at Pete Delanos as he lay dead on the bed which Carol and I had shared since the day we had moved into the house, when the telephone again rang. I turned and looked at the instrument as though it were a snake. I didn't know whether to answer or not. It occurred to me that it might be Carol again and so I crossed the room and picked up the receiver.

"Baron?"

I said yes. I didn't recognize the voice.

"Listen close, Baron," the voice said. It was a low, husky voice and it could have belonged to anyone. "Listen closely. You are not going to get away with it. Understand? You are not going to get away with it. I want the money back. I want everything back. I am going to get it back. Just think it over."

I started to say something, but before I could, I was cut off.

If my mysterious caller had believed his message would throw me into a panic, he was only partly right. I was already in a panic.

I staggered across and into the bathroom and turned on the cold water in the shower. I stayed under it for a long time, and finally, when I came out and started to towel myself, I was thinking a little more clearly.

I thanked God under my breath that Carol was safe. I knew that I could give myself up and confess to everything which had happened. But would that insure her continued safety? I doubted it very much. My testimony against Pantell would be worthless in itself, especially now that Pete was dead. I had nothing but my word, and it would be the word of a confessed burglar and thief against a reputable physician who would have had plenty of time to cover his traces.

No, surrendering now would gain nothing, even should I turn over the money. They would pick up Pantell and question him, certainly, but he would deny everything and I'd have no way of proving my story. In the meantime, I would be in prison and he would be free to seek vengeance. I had already seen one example of his vengeance, and when I remembered that official police photo of Rosalie Carver, I shuddered and knew that the only thing I could do was play for time.

I would have to do something about Pete and at once. I would have to make sure that Carol stayed away until ...

It was the telephone again and I reached for it hurriedly. If it was just that voice again I could have a chance to stall. But it wasn't.

It was the Captain down at headquarters.

"Looks like you've got yourself into something, Joe," he said.

"Yes?" My voice was thin.

"Yeah. Just had a request from Inspector Flood. He's all keyed up about that Rosalie Carver murder. He's asked that you be reassigned to the case. Feels that you might be able to help...."

"I thought the precinct boys were handling ..."

"Flood wants you," the Captain said. "He's got some kind of bug up his fanny and he thinks you're the man for it. He wanted Delanos, also, but I told him Pete was on vacation. Anyway, like it or not, it's your baby. So report into the precinct. I told him I'd have you show as soon as I could get a hold of you."

"For God's sake, Captain," I said. "I was in Saturday and was supposed to have today off and I ..."

"Can't be helped. He wants you now."

"But I'm all tied up."

"O.K. We'll compromise. You can have until noon but he'll be calling me back by then and I'll have to tell him I reached you. Finish what you have to finish but be sure to be there by noon."

I looked over at the clock as he signed off. It said ten-fifteen.

It would take me a good hour to get into town.

That gave me just about forty-five minutes to do what I had to do. And there was nothing I could do in forty-five minutes. Nothing safe.

I needed time. I had to have time. And I didn't dare to fail to show up. Inspector Flood was already acting a little strange and I couldn't take a chance on not showing.

I went back to the bedroom and stared down at Pete for several minutes and then I reached and pulled the sheet over his face.

I hated to leave without doing something about him but in the short time I had there was nothing I could do. Dr. Pantell might show up, but if he did, it wouldn't matter now. Pete was safe. The money was still down in the freezer, but the way I was feeling at the moment, I would almost have been glad if I never saw it again. And Carol was safe, at least for the time being.

I went back downstairs and put on my jacket and reached for my hat. I walked through the kitchen and into the garage.

It was while I was reaching for the door of the car that I heard the sound of a car as it came to a stop outside.

I needed time and now, perhaps, time had run out.

An engine stopped and then there was no sound at all. Finally a car door slammed and my hand moved until it rested on the butt of the gun strapped under my left armpit.

I heard the crunch of gravel outside. My eye went to the window of the garage door. I saw a face staring at me.

I had my service revolver in my hand as I swung up the overhead door.

Jack Archer stood there looking at me, a quizzical expression on his face.

I blushed and put the revolver back in its holster.

"Some greeting," he said, casually. He shrugged, raising his eyebrows. "I just thought I'd stop by. See how the patient might be doing."

I was unable to say a word.

His expression suddenly changed and he looked at me seriously.

"Actually," he said, "I just wanted to tell you something. If anything happens—I guess you know what I mean—well, if anything happens I thought I'd tell you that it wouldn't have mattered. That is to say it probably wouldn't have mattered whether he'd gone to a hospital immediately or not. If he was going to die, he would have died anyway."

He started to turn away.

"Thanks, Jack," I said. "Thanks for telling me."

"Take care of yourself," he said carelessly. A moment later he was in his car and gunning the engine.

Chapter 30

Inspector Flood wasn't in when I showed at the precinct but he had left a message for me. It was a typed sheet of yellow lined paper, in a sealed envelope. He instructed me to co-operate with the precinct brains assigned to the case, but suggested I might do better if I took off on a tack of my own.

"One piece of information which you should know about," he had written. "We have established a peculiar link between the girl's death and Dr. Horace Pantell. It appears that a man named Bellows, who is supposed to be employed by Dr. Pantell, was seen in the lobby of the hotel where the girl was murdered a short time before the body was found. So far we have failed to turn him up. You can get details from the reports. You might try and follow up this angle."

I went upstairs but none of the men assigned to the case was around. I studied all the reports so far filed.

The day clerk at the hotel had been questioned about anyone either making inquiries for the Carver girl or anyone hanging around the place. He had described several persons.

Taken downtown, he had been shown a number of mug shots and when he had come across a photograph of Maurice Bellows, Dr. Pantell's chauffeur, had at once recognized him as a man who had been hanging around the lobby on Friday afternoon. He remembered that the man had bought a newspaper and sat reading it for some time. He couldn't remember whether he had left the lobby and gone upstairs or not. But he was positive of his identification.

There was a wanted out on Bellows, but he had apparently gone into hiding.

Efforts had been made to contact Dr. Pantell, but the latest report, sent in less than two hours ago, said that he was still registered in Bermuda but off on a fishing trip and unable to be reached.

I went through the rest of it and there was nothing of any value. A detailed autopsy report had failed to develop any new clues and detectives assigned to the case were running down leads on the dead girl's friends and acquaintances.

A number of Kenny's associates had been picked up and questioned, but again detectives had run up against a blank wall.

The inspector had instructed me to work on the case, and he would expect results. I knew that I would at least have to make a pretense of doing something.

Two things I wanted to do. I wanted to find Maurice Bellows, and I wanted to find Dr. Pantell. I wanted to find him before he found me.

I tried the phone and again I reached the tape recording. So I got into my car and drove up to his place. I knew that if he were there, it would be a lot safer if I went in with someone else, but I was afraid to have anyone with me if by chance I should find him home. I knew that sooner or later I would have to face him alone, and the sooner, the better.

There was a uniformed patrolman standing in front of the house, and when I questioned him, he told me that he didn't know why he had been assigned to be there, but that he had been instructed to get the names and addresses of anyone leaving or entering and inform his sergeant at once. He said he had been there for four hours and no one had entered or left. I thanked him and rang the bell for a long time, but no one answered.

I had a list of addresses where Bellows was said to have had friends. I knew that most of them would already have been covered, but I had to start somewhere.

By eight o'clock that night I had been in a dozen assorted bars and poolrooms, gymnasiums and horse parlors. I had talked with a half a hundred characters of one sort or another; had paid off a half-dozen stool pigeons.

From each of them I learned the same thing. They knew Bellows and they'd seen him around, but just when they weren't sure. One thing they all were sure about. It hadn't been during the last week or ten days.

Some were lying, I knew. But not the stool pigeons. They would have talked if they had known anything. I could only reach the conclusion that Bellows was either lying low, well hidden, or that he had already blown town.

At eight-thirty I called the precinct. I had enough to file a reasonable report and I was desperately anxious to call it a day. I wanted to get back to the house in Westchester. I had things to do. A lot of things.

There was a message for me from the Inspector. A report had come in that Bellows had a sister living out in Long Island City.

It was a two-story stucco house and it looked like a strong wind would knock it over. A young colored man answered the door when I rang. He said his name was Jackson and that he and his wife had been renting the place for the last three months. He had no idea where the previous tenant was.

I tried the houses on each side and I got the same story from both of them. Bellows' sister, a woman named Ida Fennelly, had lived in the house alone up until some few months back. She had moved away and no one knew where. The postman had mail for her and had tried to find out when she had failed to leave a forwarding address. I got the same story at a candy store down on the corner. They had never heard of her in the tavern across the street.

I showed a picture of Bellows to everyone I questioned and no one ever remembered seeing him.

I gave it up and headed back toward Manhattan. It took me a good three quarters of an hour to type out the report at the precinct house and it was well after midnight when I finally signed out. An hour later I was turning into the lane leading to my house.

Chapter 31

I saw the reflection of the lights in the living room window as I made the last bend.

My heart jumped and I started automatically to jam on the brake. I was beginning to skid when I spotted the outline of the small car. It looked familiar—too familiar. A moment later and I recognized it as Carol's MG.

I maneuvered out of the spin and pushed down on the accelerator. Moments later and I pulled up behind her car. I was half out of the Chevie before it had come to a complete stop. And then I looked through the window and saw her. The Venetian blinds were down, but open, and I could see through them plainly.

She was sitting on the couch and she must have just arrived. She had on her jacket and a small cloth hat. She was just sitting there looking down at the floor. Her hands were crossed in her lap. There was something odd about the way she sat and again my heart began to thump.

She looked as though she were in a state of shock.

I thought, "Oh God—she's been upstairs, been in the bedroom."

But I didn't waste any time thinking. I ran up the steps and I reached for the doorknob. The door slammed open and I ran through the hallway and into the living room.

I said, "Darling—oh, darling!"

She looked up at me slowly. Almost without expression.

"Carol," I said, "Carol, I ..."

It was then that he hit me.

Chapter 32

The one who used the blackjack was an expert. The blow was placed exactly right. And just hard enough. It staggered me and I stumbled and fell to my knees. It didn't quite knock me out but it dazed me just long enough so that the other one could reach over and take my gun.

They took me then, one on each side, and they tossed me on the couch next to Carol. A third man was at the windows pulling the blinds shut and drawing the curtains.

I recognized the white hair as I came to. Dr. Pantell had found me before I had found him.

He turned and spoke. "Just relax, officer," he said. "It's going to be a long evening."

The door slammed and Maurice Bellows entered.

"I would have warned you but he was outside ready to kill you at once if I did," Carol said. She looked at me and the tears were filling her eyes.

"Shut up, lady," Pantell said. "And keep shut up."

He walked over so that he stood in front of me.

"We can make it nice or we can make it nasty. It's going to be up to you. Of course, you know what we have to do. You haven't left me any choice. And the only choice you have is the way we do it. So I'll ask you once and that is all. Where is it?"

Bellows crowded alongside him and the small man, the one who must have used the blackjack, stood at his other side. The fourth man, a thin redhead with bad teeth, walked over and stood behind the couch in back of Carol. He held an open switch-blade knife in his hand.

I knew what Pantell meant. I knew only too well. And I knew what they were going to do. What they had to do. They were going to kill both of us.

For myself, I no longer cared. But I would have died a thousand times over to have saved Carol. And yet I understood that I couldn't save her. I had nothing, nothing at all to bargain with. The only hope was to play for time.

"The money," I began, but I got no farther.

Bellows reached out and the barrel of the gun in his hand slashed across my forehead. Carol screamed.

"Get used to it, lady," Dr. Pantell said. "And no more yelling. The next time you yell, Red there in back of you will fix your mouth so you'll never again be able to open it."

I could see her slump in her seat and for a moment I thought she was going to faint. But her small white teeth buried themselves in her upper lip and she sat suddenly straight. Her hands clenched until her knuckles were white.

"Don't touch her," I said. "I'll tell you everything you want to know. Just don't touch her."

"I know you will tell us," Dr. Pantell said. "I'm sure you will. So start telling."

"It's downstairs. In the freezer," I said.

Dr. Pantell smiled, that cold smile that never quite reached the upper part of his face.

"We know what's downstairs in the freezer," he said. "I should have explained to you. We've been here all evening. We were here when the little lady arrived. Sort of a welcome home party you might say. But I haven't any time for jokes. You know what I want—now where is it?"

I knew I would have no time. I had to answer. But I had to think. I had to have time to think. But there would be no time.

They were going to kill us; of that I didn't have the slightest doubt. But I had to stall. It was hopeless, but it was the only alternative.

The truth? I couldn't tell them the truth. They wouldn't believe the truth.

I knew that there was only one thing I could do—I had to make them concentrate on me. I had to make them kill me and do it at once, before they could start on Carol. There was just a chance that if they killed me, and quickly, they would realize she couldn't know anything about the heroin. Just one slender chance that instead of torturing her they would kill her at once.

"I'll get it," I said. I started to stand up and Dr. Pantell stepped back. I didn't wait until I was fully erect. I started halfway up and I dove from a squatting position. I'm fast but I wasn't fast enough.

This time the little one with the blackjack didn't catch me across the forehead or on the side of the skull. He caught me full in the face. I could feel the cartilage of my nose give way. I dropped to the floor and I stayed there, but not because I wanted to. Because I couldn't move.

It was the glass of raw whisky which they threw in my face which brought me to.

Dr. Pantell was talking in his insanely reasonable voice.

"All cops are stubborn—and stupid," he said. "Take your pal upstairs in the bedroom. He was stupid and he tried to rob me and now he's dead. This gun killed him—" he took the snub-nosed pistol from his pocket and held it in front of him—"and eventually this gun will also kill you. But not until I have gotten what I came to get. Maybe you don't believe me, eh? Well, as I say, cops are stupid."

He half turned, nodding at Bellows. "Teach him," he said.

I saw Carol about to open her mouth and I could hear the scream coming. She must have seen the desperate expression in my eyes. Must have read the warning. Again her teeth clamped down over her lip. But this time I didn't see the thin line of blood. This time I was being kept busy.

Bellows, the big one, held me by one arm and the tall thin redhead came around from the couch and held me by the other. The little man with the blackjack did the work. He started on my face and he gradually worked down to my throat and on down my body. He never missed a vital organ or a tender spot. He knew his business.

He never hit quite hard enough to knock me out. But he knew how to hit so that it hurt. He spent a lot of time on my kidneys and was moving down when I finally passed out. The last thing I remember was seeing Dr. Pantell standing behind Carol with his hand over her face. He was a doctor and I guess he realized at just what point she would no longer have the will power to resist screaming.

It probably took them quite a while, but they finally brought me to. Someone had taken a towel and wiped the blood off my face so that I could see. I couldn't see well, but I could see.

Dr. Pantell was again standing in front of me. My throat was raw and felt filled with knives and I vaguely guessed they had poured liquor or brandy into me.

Dr. Pantell said, "Can you hear me?"

I think I must have nodded.

"I'm going to explain it to you for one final last time. To begin with I have already explained to you that I have the money. The money that your partner upstairs and either you or someone else took from me.

"Now I want the rest of it. The heroin. Because you see, if I don't get it, then I am going to have Red here go to work on the little lady. I am going to have him and the boys do exactly to her what they did to the Carver girl. Only slower this time. Harder. Understand? I know that you are tough and that we could probably kill you before you'd crack. But are you really so tough? Are you so tough that you'll sit there while we ..."

His voice faded and I guess I must have passed out again, because the next thing I knew someone was holding my lower jaw and something warm was being poured into my mouth. Dr. Pantell held my wrist in his hand and he was taking a hypodermic needle away. "This should bring you around for a few minutes at least," he said. "Now. To repeat, in just one half a minute we are going to start ..."

It was hard to see him, hard to hear him, but I was concentrating on him as though my very life, or what flickering flame was left of my life, depended on each syllable. I was aware of his sudden hesitation, aware of his eyes suddenly lifting from my face and opening wide. I may or may not have heard the shout—I am not sure. But I saw the quick movement as he started to raise the gun he held in his hand.

I must have heard the sound of the first blast. But I am not sure. I am sure that I saw the sudden splash of red where the white hair met his forehead. Aware that I watched him as he slowly crumbled.

And then all hell seemed to break loose in the room and I don't remember the rest of it.

Chapter 33

I had no sense of time at all. I don't even know when I first actually began to be aware of the fact that I was alive, that my name was Joe Baron, and that I was a man who was married to a girl named Carol and that I was a cop, a detective, first grade, attached to Homicide.

I only know that there was a room and it gradually began to take shape. That everything was white and without definition or outline. That gradually I became aware of a body and that the body was mine although I seemed incapable of moving any part of it.

There was no pain, just a vast nothingness. And then the room took on vague definition and I understood that I was a person and that I lived.

There were forms moving around and they became people. But still white. I felt a sense of touch—it must have been when they were changing bandages and dressings. And then I was able to detect odors. I think it was about at this period that the idea gradually grew on me that I must be in some sort of hospital because that was the first conscious thought I had.

The rest came slower.

It was almost like being born all over again.

There was the day when I knew that someone was holding one of my hands and that someone had a hand on my forehead.

By this time I was learning very rapidly about pain.

It was very slow but it finally came. All of it. And when it came, it came in a rush. The memory.

I think I must have screamed because a door opened and someone came in. A bandage was removed from my eyes and I made out the outlines of a face above me. I felt something in my arm and it must have been a needle because for a long time there was nothing again.

The next time I started right in where I had left off, remembering. But this time I didn't scream.

Carol was the first one. Suddenly I looked up and there she was.

I tried to say something and I felt tears in my eyes, but I couldn't talk and she quickly put slender fingers to my lips and said, "Don't, darling. Don't say anything. You aren't to try and talk."

I was satisfied that day just to have her with me.

I must have recovered very swiftly then. I remember thinking how odd it was that she would come and go, and the doctor and intern would come and go, but there was never anyone in the room at other times. There should have been a uniformed policeman in the room.

Or perhaps they had him stationed outside of the door.

And then there was the day the doctor came in and took my pulse and said, "Don't talk. Just let me know if you are strong enough to see someone for ten minutes. Nod your head if you are."

I nodded, trying to convey a yes.

"Are you able to understand me?"

I nodded again.

"And you remember your wife?"

I nodded quickly.

"And what happened to you?"

Again I nodded.

"All right," he said. "Ten minutes."

Carol came in first and she quickly walked to the bed and leaned over and her lips brushed my lips. She sat in the chair next to the bed.

"You are not to say anything, darling," she said.

The door opened and a very straight-backed, slender man, somewhere in his fifties and with shot-gray hair and wearing gold-rimmed glasses, entered. He was immaculately dressed. He looked as if he might be a banker or lawyer.

But I knew different. I knew he was a law officer. I don't know how I knew, but I did.

He closed the door carefully after himself and then moved over so that he was in my line of vision.

He took a billfold out of his pocket and flapped it open and held it out.

"Are you able to read?" he asked.

I nodded.

I was right. He was a law officer. Federal. Treasury Department. Narcotics Division.

"I am going to tell you, very briefly, what happened," he said. "You were there, but I think you missed most of it. You probably don't realize it, but you have been here for about three weeks. For a while we didn't think they were going to pull you through. But they have and you are going to be all right. Anyway, here's the way it was. Can you remember the Monday night when you returned to your house, found your wife there waiting for you? Do you remember Dr. Pantell and the three men with him?"

I nodded.

"And you remember everything that happened up until that time?"

Again I nodded.

"You remember being beaten?"

I nodded again.

"Well," he said. "We were there when it happened."

I saw Carol give him a startled look.

"Yes." he said. "We were there. Two other operators and I. You see, we had followed Dr. Pantell to your house. While he and his men were in the basement, searching the place, we got inside and concealed ourselves. The reason we had followed him is quite simple. Someone sent us a number of packages of heroin, through the mails. They had the doctor's name and return address on them."

He stopped talking for a moment and took an unlighted pipe from his pocket.

"It wasn't a complete surprise," he said. "We had actually been on Pantell's trail for some time. But we had never been able to get the goods on him. We knew that he was supposed to be in Bermuda and we had had a man tailing him. We knew when he left by private plane and returned to the States. We picked him up when he landed, but then we lost him for a couple of days."

He stopped again and started to fill the pipe.

"But when that stuff reached us in the mails, we made an all-out effort. We were lucky. We picked up his trail again and made a contact as he was leaving New York. He was on his way up to your place."

He was watching me very closely as he talked. It was neither a friendly nor unfriendly look.

"We were in the house when he discovered the body of your partner. We knew when he found the money. By the way, the money helped to tie it up. Some of those bills were marked, although he didn't know it. We recognized them. You see they had been passed to him by one of our own operators—a man who was murdered before he could get back to us. It made the tie-up we needed to get convictions against the doctor and the other three men we picked up. Because you see, we were there listening when he admitted that it was his money.

"We were there when he admitted killing Delanos, but I guess you knew all about that because we found the bullet which killed your partner in your pocket. A ballistics test showed it came from the gun which was in Dr. Pantell's hand when we shot him in your house.

"We also heard him admit the murder of the Carver girl."

This time he took a moment out to light the pipe.

"You see," he said, "I am a Federal officer. I am not particularly interested in local crimes, except, of course, as any conscientious citizen is interested in seeing justice done. But in a sense my interest stopped once we had nailed Pantell and his gang. Once we had tied that up."

Again he stopped talking for quite a while. He turned to Carol. "Will you excuse the pipe?" he said.

Carol nodded, staring at him as though she hardly understood what he was saying.

"The rest," he said, "is unofficial. I don't really know who mailed the heroin to us. But I do know it belonged to Dr. Pantell. I don't know how that money actually got into your freezer. But I do know it also belonged to Dr. Pantell. Maybe Delanos put it there before he died. I wouldn't know.

"It is possible that Delanos took the money and was planning to keep it and was merely using you and your friendship as a shield to cover himself. It is fully possible you were an innocent victim in the plot. If you were, you have taken quite a beating."

He hesitated a moment and then turned to Carol.

"I can't ask your husband any questions because he shouldn't talk. I really don't need to ask him anything. And I don't suppose he wants to ask me anything. But do you have any questions to ask, Mrs. Baron?"

For several seconds Carol stared at him, then she spoke.

"Tell me," she said at last, "please tell me one thing. You say you and your men were in that house all the time. You were there while they were beating Joe. Why didn't you stop them? Why did you let them? ..."

"We stopped them when we felt that they were going to hurt you, Mrs. Baron," he said. "Before that, we needed to overhear what they had to say in order to get the evidence which was essential. I am sorry we waited as long as we did, but I will tell you something, Mrs. Baron. It is just possible that your husband is lucky to get out of this with no more than a beating. It is even possible he deserved that beating."

There was a knock on the door and a moment later a nurse put her head in.

"Right away," he said. "I'm almost through."

The door closed and he moved toward it, turning with his hand on the knob.

"Oh," he said, "one more thing, Pantell was killed in the gunfight at your house. The other three are going to be tried for the Carver murder and it's open and shut. They'll get the chair. And I have a message for you. From an Inspector Flood. He said to tell you that the department is happy to accept your resignation. He also said he will be wanting to have a few words with you as soon as you are well enough to talk."

When he left, Carol leaned over me. Her lips again brushed mine.

"It will be all right, Joe," she said. "It's going to be all right. We'll start over, darling—start right this time."

THE END

LOVE TRAP
- - - - - - -
Lionel White

For Jimmy and Fran

Chapter 1

A man can leave the house for a quiet walk on a summer's Sunday afternoon and after a while he will come to an intersection. For a moment he may hesitate, not having any particular destination, and then, perhaps, he will walk straight ahead and nothing at all will happen except he enjoys the peace of the day and tires himself sufficiently to return home and lie down for an hour before supper.

Or he might take the left turn at this same intersection, pass on for a block or two and then, crossing another street, find death under the wheels of a speeding car. The driver of this car will likely enough be a complete stranger, a second man whose orbit of life would never have crossed that of the first man's—if this first man had not turned left at that particular intersection at that particular moment.

Once again, this man who is out for a Sunday afternoon stroll, could just as easily take the right-hand turn at the intersection and a moment or two later some little, easily forgotten incident could take place which might change the entire course of his life. Might indeed change the intricate and secret pattern of his essential character.

The incident itself could be of complete insignificance; a thing so remote and inconsequential that the man would pass on utterly unaware of it.

It could very easily happen this way.

II

I have always loved the city in the summertime. The quiet of the deserted streets, the absence of the usual traffic clamor, the very clarity of the atmosphere itself, temporarily free of the usual gas fumes from the hurrying taxis and trucks and cars—all of these are negative things, but they are a part of it. Especially I like the city right after it has rained and when there is still that damp freshness which seems to penetrate into one's very body and soul, to cleanse and wash away the dust and debris of the years.

This—the desertion of the city on the long summer weekends—is one of the principal reasons why I take my yearly vacations in the winter. This, and of course the fact that by taking a winter vacation, the office gives me an added week. The office is always very busy during the summer months, being an office which is engaged in a seasonal business, and they appreciate that I am willing to stay on and work on those hot, sultry days when I am most needed.

I was thinking again of the office as I walked down the south side of East Fifty-fourth Street and approached Third Avenue.

I was thinking that I, Harold Granville Wilkenson, thirty-six years of age, had spent exactly one quarter of my life as an employee of the McKenny-Fleckner Construction Company.

It was with considerable bitterness that my mind went back over the past nine years, since the day I graduated from Harvard, an architect, and with a degree to prove it. Within the month I'd gone to work for the firm.

Nine years. Lord, it doesn't seem possible that the time can have passed so swiftly. Of course, many things have happened during these years; good things and bad things.

Things like my marriage to Marian and things like the death of my mother.

That was one of the bad things, when mother died. I guess, to me, it was worse than it would have been to most men. My mother, a Granville, was widowed by the time I was a six-year-old.

Although she came from a fine New England family and a family which at one time had been very wealthy, as well as prominent in the arts and industry, everything had been lost save the heritage of culture and refinement by the time my father unfortuitously died, leaving us virtually penniless. It will be only charitable to say nothing of my improvident father and his family.

In any case, it was fortunate that my mother had brains as well as breeding. She was able to turn a talent for gardening and designing to good stead and she became a landscape architect, managing to make enough money to see me through Groton and Harvard, as well as to assure us a comfortable if not luxurious living. Yes, among the things which had happened in those nine years was mother's death shortly after my marriage.

Many things happened during the span of the years, but compared to the things which didn't happen, they were as nothing.

Certainly, however, a lot of things had happened as far as the McKenny-Fleckner Construction Company was concerned.

Tom McKenny became a millionaire during the nine years. A millionaire! And he was an uneducated, shoestring contractor, little better than a free-lance carpenter, when I designed the first low-cost house for his firm.

Sam Fleckner has also become a millionaire, which is even more surprising. A millionaire and a man with a national reputation as a creator of large, lower middle-class housing developments.

In a sense I feel even more bitter about Sam than I do about McKenny. In fact, I hate Sam Fleckner. Sam, two years older than I am, is, strangely enough, also a Harvard man. Or at least that is to say he attended Harvard, taking a course in business administration. He matriculated three years before I myself graduated. Not of course that we ever travelled with the same set or had been intimate during those school years. We knew each other slightly, but Sam, whose father had a tailor shop in the Bronx and who had attended the New York public schools, was completely unknown at Cambridge; merely another member of that vast, nameless morass which comprised the general student body.

Contrary to the general belief, not more than five percent of the men who go to Harvard have the type of family and educational backgrounds which are essential in order to have their university mean something in a truly significant social and business sense.

It is ironic in view of this that it was Sam Fleckner, Sam the son of a tailor and with neither money nor family nor background, and with an absolutely undistinguished university record, who was responsible for hiring me and for my nine years with the firm of McKenny-Fleckner.

I was trying to remember what Fleckner had been like on those few occasions when I had known him back in the Cambridge days as I came to Park Avenue and was forced to stand at the curb and wait for the traffic light to change. As usual on Sunday afternoons there was almost no traffic, but I always make it a point to wait for the light. I believe in taking no unnecessary risks; I also believe in obeying the law, even if it's only a city ordinance.

Usually when I walk on Sundays, I follow the same route. I start from our three-room apartment on East Fifty-fourth and go east as far as Second Avenue. Then I turn right and go down to Forty-second Street and make a second turn, walking to Fifth Avenue and end up going back uptown to make a complete circuit. On this particular Sunday, for no reason at all, I turned right on Third Avenue. Why I did, I can't imagine, although often when I walked by myself on the weekday evenings, I would make this turn in order to stop by at a certain Third Avenue bar for a glass or two of beer.

This would happen only on those evenings when Marian was not at home. Marian had signed up for some evening courses at the Columbia University Extension summer session and was away two or three nights each week. I never, however, went to this bar on Sunday and in fact I wasn't even sure that bars were allowed to open on the Sabbath.

In any case, as I say, on this particular Sunday afternoon, I turned right on Third Avenue and started south, walking on the west side of the street in order to keep in the shade.

I was still thinking of Sam Fleckner and not paying much attention to where I was going when it happened.

He was a small, undernourished child, barefooted, dressed in a pair of faded overalls and a sweater, not more than five or six years old, and apparently he had just emerged from the hole-in-the-wall candy and ice cream store. He hit me head on and he was carrying a chocolate ice cream cone in his dirt-encrusted hand.

Apparently he was running with the cone to his mouth because, as he crashed into me, most of the ice cream splashed to the sidewalk, but a certain portion of it smeared across the front of my white linen coat and down onto my trousers.

Even before I had fully realized what had happened, the child was screaming obscenities and his eyes were filled with tears. He suddenly stood back a foot or so and opening his mouth, spat, aiming at either my face or chest. The spittle hit the front of my coat.

He turned and fled.

I looked at the child's fleeing form and then down at my clothes. For some inexplicable reason the entire thing struck me as hilarious and I began to laugh. It was all so ridiculous—that urchin's tear-stained face and my own soiled clothes. I really don't know why I should have laughed as I am careful with my clothes and like to appear neat. Also, Marian herself presses my garments and only this morning she had put the creases in my Oxford-gray trousers.

Taking out a folded handkerchief, I tried to wipe off the worst of the mess, but quickly I saw that I was only making matters worse. It was then that I became conscious of my surroundings; I decided to go on down the Avenue for another block and stop in at Howie's Bar and Grill, in case the place was open.

I would borrow a rag and some soap and water. I might even have a drink. Marian wouldn't be too happy about the drink, as by a sort of tacit agreement we never take anything until sundown; on the other hand, she wasn't going to be too happy about the condition of my clothes either.

Howie's Bar and Grill is a typical unpretentious East Side saloon, the sort of establishment which just escapes being a real dive. I don't know why the place seemed to attract me, unless it is some hidden facet of my character which I have inherited from my father's side of the family. There is sawdust on the floor and the black mahogany bar is old and scarred. There is always the smell of stale beer about the dimly lighted, long, narrow room, a smell which I don't find particularly offensive.

The clientele—well the clientele is about what you would expect to find in a Third Avenue Irish saloon. Workmen, a few white collar people from the newspaper offices in the neighborhood, men and women who live in the nearby tenements. Few women, however, except in the afternoons.

Now and then I would see other types, broad-shouldered, surly men who drank alone and rarely spoke and looked like policemen on their days off. Also cab drivers. And other small, too-well-dressed little men who, I suppose, were some sort of racketeers or gamblers or who followed those odd, almost fictional occupations which I have never been fully able to comprehend, but have to do with traffic in women or drugs.

But I liked the place and I also liked Howie, who owned it. Howie was at one time a policeman, or so he had told me, and I gathered that he had lost his job over some sort of scandal in the Department. But he was pleasant and liked to pass the time of day with him. He was a great follower of sports and we'd talk baseball, if it was the summer, or football and boxing in the winter.

In spite of his heterogeneous clientele, Howie ran a very strict place and he didn't tolerate rough language. He served no food, although I understand that he was supposed to do so because of his license. He would, if asked, sometimes make up a sandwich or two. There was no free lunch, so frequently found in such places, and Howie one time explained it to me by saying that he didn't give away pretzels and so forth as the practice attracted bums and panhandlers. He did have a television set, but he was the only one who was allowed to turn it on and he kept the audio low. There was no jukebox.

I entered Howie's and walked to the end of the long bar to where Howie himself stood, with his elbows on the mahogany, bent over and reading the Sunday comic strips from the *Daily News*. He looked up at me over the steel rims of his reading glasses and at once his eyes went to the front of my coat.

"Accident, Mr. Wilkenson?" he asked. He grinned.

I told him about it.

"Go on out into the kitchen," he said. "You'll find a towel or something on the sink. Try some soap and water and if that doesn't work, well, then we'll try something else."

He motioned with his right hand, over his shoulder, to a door at the end of the hallway leading from the rear of the room.

I nodded.

It was necessary for me to pass the entrance to the twin rest rooms, which were off the right side of the hallway, to reach the kitchen. One of two doors, the first one, led into the women's rest room and the other into the men's. As I started down the hallway, I was aware that someone was following close at my heels. Entering Howie's, I had observed that there were several persons standing at the bar, but I had noticed none in particular.

For some reason, as I came to the swinging door leading into the kitchen, I half turned and, out of the corner of my eye, I saw that it was a man who had followed me down the hallway. He was reaching for the knob of the men's room door.

Having just come in from the bright sunlight of the streets, it was difficult for me to see clearly in the dim shadows of the hallway. The figure seemed vaguely familiar, but I was not able to distinguish the features of the man's face.

In any case, I was a lot more interested in trying to clean my clothes than I was in the identifying of what was without doubt a complete stranger, and I paid the matter no further attention.

A quick look at Howie's kitchen made me regret that I had ever eaten a sandwich prepared in the place. I did, however, find a clean towel lying on the edge of the galvanized double sink. It took quite a while to get the brown stains out and I was wet through by the time I finished.

I was rinsing out the rag, preparing to put it back, when I first became aware of the voices. Voices coming through the thin building-board partition next to the sink. It is possible that I had been hearing them for some time without being fully aware of it. It was only when I heard the name McKenny that I stopped what I was doing and made a real effort to overhear the conversation.

Apparently there were two of them, both men, and they were standing not more than two or three feet away, on the other side of the wall. That would mean that they were in the men's washroom. As I leaned closer to hear, the sound of their voices dropped but I could sense that they were having some sort of argument.

I listened for a moment more and then shrugged and started to turn away. McKenny is, after all, a rather common name. It was at that moment that one of the voices was suddenly raised and the words came to me sharply and clearly.

"I tell you," the voice said, "Tom McKenny doesn't even carry a gun."

I was still holding the wet rag in my hand as I leaned close and put my ear against the thin partition.

I could almost feel the blood leave my face. Five minutes later, as I heard the slam of the door which led into the men's room, I was shaking like a leaf.

III

I think it was shock more than any sense of fear or cowardice. Shock at what I had overheard.

I dare say that anyone, overhearing the plans for an armed robbery—a robbery which might also involve murder—would be shocked. Especially so if the crime was to involve the firm for which he worked.

The door to the men's room had slammed and I thought for a moment that both men had left. And then I heard the sound of water running in a bowl and I knew that one of those whom I had overheard was still there. As I say, I was shocked, and to be quite honest about it, I guess I was a little frightened also. My first inclination was to go out into the barroom and see who came from the men's room. But at once I began to understand that I didn't want to know who these men were, that to know might well be dangerous. And yet, at the last moment, as I stood there trying to get my thoughts into some sort of coherent order, my sense of curiosity came to the fore and proved too powerful a sensation to be denied.

I threw the wet towel onto the sink and left the kitchen. Howie was still standing at the end of the bar buried in the comic sheet.

Bartenders seem to have some sixth psychic sense or perhaps it is just the result of years of experience in dealing with all sorts of people—drinking people who constitute, apparently, potential problems. Howie once more looked up at me. He pushed his glasses up on his forehead and let the paper slide to the floor behind the bar.

"You look a little upset, Mr. Wilkenson," he said. "Better have yourself a drink. You don't want to let those stains bother you. The cleaner can get them out."

"It isn't the stains," I said. "It's ... it's just ... well, I had a sort of rough night."

He nodded sympathetically.

"I know how it is," he said. "I'll fix you something."

I didn't notice what he fixed. I stood facing the bar, but out of the corner of my eye I was watching the hallway which led to the men's room.

He was a small-boned little man with a parchment complexion and I doubt if he weighed more than a hundred and twenty-five pounds. His eyes were russet-brown, long-lashed and set deep-socketed over a large, fleshy nose. The jaw line was fine and his pointed chin gave him the look of an alert bird. He wore a narrow-brimmed hat, but I could see that his hair was dark. The hat itself, with its red and yellow feather, was a complement to the pinstriped suit with the padded shoulders and the too-wide lapels.

I looked for black silk socks and patent-leather shoes, but his socks were a conservative gray and his shoes were in good taste—the only part of his sartorial travesty which was.

He walked with a hurried, almost mincing step and his hands were busy as his fingers opened and closed incessantly. I would have taken him for a bookmaker's runner or possibly a seller of filthy postcards.

When he came opposite me, he looked directly into my eyes, his face expressionless, and I turned away at once.

I mumbled something to Howie about it being unusual for me to take a drink in the middle of the day, although, actually, it was almost three o'clock.

"Be good for you," Howie said. "My own remedy. Scotch Perfect."

It was good for me. It even tasted good. Later Howie told me what it was and I can certainly recommend it. An ounce of good imported Scotch, an ounce of the best dry vermouth and an ounce of an imported sweet vermouth. Over cracked ice and with a twist of lemon peel.

But I wasn't thinking of the drink.

The little man in the pinstriped suit came up and leaned against the bar a few feet from where I stood. I watched his face in the mirror.

There was a tall, heavy-chested man standing next to him and they each ordered drinks. The little man downed his in a hurry, half turned and sort of patted the big man on the shoulder.

"O.K.," he said. "Here—tomorrow night."

He didn't pay for his drink but turned and left. His companion had another drink while I was finishing mine.

I wanted to leave. I knew I should leave at once. I should go to the nearest police station and find an officer and tell him what I had overheard. Or perhaps I should call Tom McKenny or Sam Fleckner. But the thought of Fleckner seemed to act almost as a cataleptic agent and to paralyze my thinking. Call Fleckner? Why should I?

But again, in all probability, it was curiosity which inspired my next move. I myself ordered another drink. I had decided to wait until this second man left the bar and then ask Howie who they were.

A third drink, and then a fourth, and still he hadn't left. The place was filling up now and Howie was increasingly busy. I'd have little chance now to talk to him. And that large, thick-chested man was showing no signs of leaving. He'd switched his drinks and was working on beer. He'd probably stay for hours.

Already the drinks were affecting me. I almost never take more than two drinks at the most at one time and I knew that the four I already had consumed were probably clouding my thinking.

The idea crossed my mind that it was a sort of a shame I hadn't gained a little more experience in the drinking department while I had been in college, as so many of my friends had done. Yes, I should have learned to drink instead of learning to design houses and buildings. After all, what good had becoming an architect done me?

I smiled and observed my own face in the mirror behind the bar. It wasn't a pleasant smile.

Architect indeed. All I had ever designed were the first four low-price houses which McKenny and Fleckner had used as the models for their widespread development projects. Sure enough, those designs were responsible for getting me my job. For getting the job and keeping me on it for nine long, deadly dull years. A splendid reward! A hundred and fifty dollars a week, and the company was still using those basic designs to pile up new millions.

Oh, they'd been good to me all right. They only needed the four designs and then there was no longer the necessity for an architect. But they'd been more than generous about it. They'd continued my pay check, only now, instead of designing houses, I was sort of an office manager. Nice, year-around work. Lovely work. It even took me out of doors—when I'd go to the bank for the money to make up the payrolls. Or now and then drive out to Long Island where McKenny and Fleckner kept a thousand workmen busy on one project or another.

They'd been fair all right. Except being a high-class bookkeeper wasn't quite what I had gone through Harvard to do. I didn't need a degree for that. No, and it wasn't what my mother had had in mind when she'd struggled and humiliated herself to put me through

Groton and the University.

I wanted to order another drink, but then I thought twice about it. I was already a little drunk. I'd never be able to outlast that other one, the big man who must have been in the washroom with bird face.

I decided to leave. I wouldn't go to the police. The thing to do was to call Tom McKenny. I didn't want to talk with policemen with liquor on my breath. Yes, Tom McKenny, not Sam. Why should I do Sam any favors?

Howie was back at my end of the bar and I beckoned to him. I gave him a ten-dollar bill when he came over and he rang it up in the cash register and handed me my change. He looked at me rather closely for a second.

"You all right, Mr. Wilkenson?" he asked.

"Of course I'm all right," I said shortly. I turned, prepared to leave.

It must have been the heat, or possibly, the emotional excitement of the last half hour. But for some reason I had a sense of dizziness and I know that I swayed a little. And almost at once my stomach felt like it had on that one occasion, some years ago during our honeymoon, when I had become seasick while taking the boat trip between Boston and Provincetown.

I swung on my heel and half ran for the men's room.

Ten minutes later and a little paler, I left Howie's Bar. I must have looked about as bad as I felt.

Once more coincidence played a part in the drama which was soon to be unfolded. Had I not been sick there in the men's room, I would have missed seeing her.

She was seated behind the wheel of a silver Buick convertible, directly in front of Howie's Bar and Grill. The car was stunning, but even its gleaming splendor was a poor setting for the girl who was its mistress. A slender, golden girl with flaming hair worn long and curled under at her shoulders. A girl with large azure eyes smudged on her perfect oval face. A girl with a glittering smile showing all of her perfect white teeth.

The smile was not for me. It was for that large, heavy-bodied man who had stood next to me at the bar. The man whom bird face was to meet on Monday night. He was climbing into the car as she held the door open.

Her voice was low and husky.

"Well, was Katz all set?"

I didn't hear his answer for she was gunning the motor as she finished the question. And then, in a moment, the silver car swept past me and on south down Third Avenue.

I started for home. At least I knew who one of them was. Katz.

All the way back to the apartment I planned how I would do it. How I would call Tom McKenny and tell him what I had heard. Yes, McKenny was the one to tell. After all, McKenny might be the one most involved. For Tom McKenny invariably drove out to the construction locations on Fridays with the payroll.

It was then that for the first time the realization suddenly came to me that I didn't know where they planned to commit the crime. Suppose it was to be in the office! I myself, Harold Granville Wilkenson, could be a part of it!

I went limp then at the thought of what might have happened if I hadn't overheard that conversation. For I knew something that neither Katz nor his criminal partner knew. I know that Tom McKenny did carry a gun—and that he would use it.

I hurried faster. I had to get home and tell Marian and then call McKenny. I was no longer worrying about the way my coat and trousers had been stained. If it hadn't been for a small boy rushing blindly out of a store with a dripping ice cream cone, I might well be a candidate for murder.

Marian and I live on the third floor of an old brownstone house, one of the thousands which are rapidly fading from the New York scene. This house, like so many others in that section of Manhattan, had been built during the lush mid-eighties and was one of the sort which my own grandfather had at one time owned and used as a town residence. Along in the early nineteen hundreds the neighborhood, as well as the house itself, had already begun to deteriorate.

The onetime mansions gradually were redesigned and altered and became rooming houses. And then some twenty-five or thirty years later, when the neighborhood once more regained respectability, the owners again redesigned them, installed new plumbing and fixtures and made them into small apartment houses, each one containing a single or double apartment to the floor.

The old families were gone for good, however, and the apartments were rented to small upper-middle-class families or working couples, mostly without children. The neighborhood, that part of it which had not been absorbed by commercial enterprises, was residential and respectable, but it never regained its original exclusiveness.

But I wasn't thinking of that. I was only thinking about getting home. I had been gone for more than two hours and Marian would be wondering what had happened to me. Well, plenty had and I could hardly wait to tell her about it.

The downstairs door is always left unlocked as it leads into a small foyer in which are the individual mailboxes of the four tenants of the building as well as the doorbells. I pushed my way through and hurried up two flights of stairs. I knocked on the door of our apartment.

When Marian failed to answer at once, I knocked a second time. It took me several moments to realize that she wasn't going to answer. Puzzled, I took my key from my pocket and inserted it in the lock. I entered and was not at once aware that I was alone in the place. I called, not dreaming that Marian could have gone out.

But I was alone. I don't know why, but I experienced a momentary sense of annoyance. Where could she have gone?

When I had left, Marian had been leafing through the Sunday papers. She was still in her housecoat and we had just finished a late combination breakfast and lunch. Usually, when I go for my Sunday afternoon walks, Marian stays home and, after finishing the papers, cleans up the place and then bathes and gets dressed. She rarely goes out.

At once I noticed the newspapers, lying half on the table and half on the floor, in the dining alcove off the living room. It wasn't like Marian not to clean up after herself.

Marian's not being home didn't worry me; it merely gave me a sense of irritation. I couldn't imagine where she had gone, unless possibly around the corner to the delicatessen for something she might have forgotten. We always had Sunday-night supper in the apartment, but it was usually a light meal. After, we would either go out to a movie or stay home and watch television.

I went on into the bedroom and noticed, as I was changing my clothes, that Marian had taken off the housecoat and left it lying over the back of a chair. I knew I should call McKenny at once, but I felt very uncomfortable in my soiled coat and trousers and wanted to change. Also, for some reason, the knowledge which I possessed and would soon share gave me an odd secret sense of power. I couldn't help thinking of the position in which I found myself.

By accident I had learned something of vital importance. Something which, if I were to keep quiet about it, might well cost my firm thousands and thousands of dollars. Thousands of dollars? Why not only that, but if I were to say nothing and permit an armed robbery to take place, it might well cost a man his life!

It was an intoxicating thought.

Having changed my clothes, I went into the bathroom and brushed my teeth and took an aspirin tablet. I had a slight headache. I returned to the living room and, looking over at the mantel, noticed that the clock read ten minutes to six. Good Lord, where had the afternoon gone?

And where was Marian?

I became more and more irritated as the hand of the clock moved on toward seven. It was damned inconsiderate of her to have gone out without as much as leaving me a note of any kind. Thinking about it, the idea suddenly crossed my mind that Marian had been showing less and less consideration for my feelings within recent months. Not that she wasn't a good wife and not that she didn't fulfill her wifely duties. It was just that lately it seemed she had become discontented and critical. The change had started along about the time I had come home several months back and told her about the ridiculous thing which Sam Fleckner had suggested.

It had happened one evening just as we were about to leave the office for the day. Sam had asked me to have a drink with him. At first I had hesitated, but he had insisted. We'd gone to a cocktail lounge not far from where I live.

It had been the most unusual conversation. I'd known at once that Fleckner had wanted to tell me something, but his opening remark, after we'd found a table and ordered drinks, took me by complete surprise.

"Harold," he said, "why the hell don't you quit?"

I stared at him.

"Quit?" I was completely amazed. "Quit. Why I ..."

But he'd interrupted me at once.

"Don't misunderstand me," he'd said, hurriedly. "It isn't that I *want* you to quit, or that we are in any way dissatisfied with you. But you're an architect and, I think, a damned good one. The trouble is, we just don't have any use for an architect. And ..."

"Have you found my work unsatisfactory? ..."

He quickly lifted his hand in protest and again interrupted me.

"Your work is fine," he'd said. "We couldn't be more satisfied. The only thing is, the way we're geared, there just is no place to put your real talent and brains to use."

I'm afraid I laughed a little bitterly then.

"You found a use for them when I came to work for you nine years ago," I'd reminded him.

At least he had the decency to blush.

"But things have changed in nine years," he said. "Things have changed."

They certainly had, I reflected. Changed for McKenny and Fleckner. But hardly for me.

"Yes, things have changed. We hoped, in the beginning, to become general contractors. Only it seems that we found a certain pattern, a certain formula, and now we just go on repeating ourselves. But you, well, you should get back into the designing end of the game. You should break loose and start out for yourself."

"On what I have saved on my salary?" I asked.

At least he had the grace to look embarrassed.

"Well, Harold," he said, "I know you can't have put aside a great deal. But the thing is, I think you'd make a damned good man in your own field. Think it over. And if you'd like to give it a crack, well, I think I could see my way to helping you out while you get started."

He went on talking but I wasn't listening to him. I was thinking instead of how much I hated this tall, lean, too-good-looking man with his too-expensive clothes, his jewelry and his smug assumption that money was important and that it could make up for the qualities he so obviously lacked. Finally, I held up my hand and shook my head.

"If either you or Mr. McKenny are dissatisfied ..." I started. Once again, with his usual lack of breeding, he interrupted.

"Hell, Harold," he said, "Tom would be sore as hell if he thought I was trying to talk you into quitting. He knows how valuable you are to us. You know that your work is ..."

This time I interrupted him.

"In that case," I said, "I think we'd better just forget this conversation. I'm quite contented the way things are."

I left shortly afterward. God, I was furious. That arrogant fool! He thought the reason I wasn't interested in quitting and starting out on my own was solely because I was satisfied with my job. Couldn't he understand that I would have given anything, anything in the world, to quit and start out on my own? I know I am a good architect. I know I could make a success of it.

But to have him, Sam Fleckner, make such a thing possible? The idea was poison to me. Apparently he couldn't understand how I felt about him. I resented everything about the man. His handsome— handsome in a sort of flashy Semitic way—good looks, his white teeth which he was forever showing in a broad smile, his black, patent-leather hair. Everything that he was and stood for I hated. Particularly I hated his attitude of hail-fellow-well-met. He acted as though we were friends of long standing, as though we were old boyhood pals.

The man must have been blind not to sense how I felt about him.

I must try to be fair and in so doing, I will have to admit that I resented his success; not only his success, but the money which he had made and which was the very obvious reward of that success. Oh, no doubt he had a shrewd mind and he was a hard worker. But it seems hardly just that his rewards should have been so out of proportion to my own.

When I had come home that night, Marian knew I was upset about something and she kept after me until I finally told her of the conversation. It was the first time that I can recall when Marian seemed signally stupid.

"But what's wrong with his helping you get started?" she'd asked. "After all, he gave you the job you have now. And anyway, it just means that he has confidence in you and thinks you'll really go places."

Women are so stupid about such things.

I didn't bother to labor the point.

But several times since then, Marian has brought it up and each time I've tried to explain my attitude to her. She has even gone so far as to suggest that I am snobbish about the thing and tell me that irrespective of what I think of Sam Fleckner, money is money and I shouldn't be so particular where I get it.

I can't seem to make her understand that it is one thing to work for a man like Fleckner, but that it is something else altogether to accept favors from him or join him in a partnership venture.

But, as I say, women seem to have a peculiarly blind spot when it comes to the relationships of one man with another.

I was thinking about this as I walked over to the telephone. I sat down at the small deal table, under the front windows, and opened the phone book. I started looking for Tom McKenny's number and then closed the book in annoyance. I remembered that McKenny lived out in Westchester and I had only the Manhattan directory.

McKenny was married and had three children. Marian and I had been out to his place several times—a large, rambling ranch house which he had had designed by a firm of famous architects and had built himself—and I must say that he had excellent taste as far as the house and grounds were concerned. I have always resented the fact, however, that he had not asked me to design the place for him. I am quite sure I could have done a better job of it.

The operator told me to dial information and I did. I gave her

McKenny's name and address and, while I was waiting to get the number, I pulled the drape to one side and looked out the window.

For a moment I watched a girl walking on the other side of the street, and then my eye was attracted by a long, low sports car drawing up to the curb in front of my own house.

Suddenly I stood up and leaned forward. Slowly I reached down and put the telephone instrument back in the cradle.

Marian was stepping out of the sports car. I couldn't see the driver, as the canvas top was raised, but I didn't have to see him. I knew that car very well. It was Sam Fleckner's Allard, a special job which he had imported from England not three months back.

Even as I watched, she leaned forward into the car and said something and then she stood back, smiling, and waved as the car slowly moved off.

I believe it was at this precise moment that it first occurred to me to say nothing to anyone of the conversation I had overheard in Howie's Bar and Grill.

Chapter 2

In a way, I hold Marian directly responsible for what I did on Monday evening.

After Sam Fleckner had dropped her off in front of our apartment and she had come upstairs, we had the first real argument of our nine years of marriage. It was so serious that I ended up sleeping on the convertible couch in the living room.

Her explanation of the thing seemed simple enough and certainly the argument was not a result of what she had done. It was because of the way I felt about why she had done it.

Fleckner had come to the apartment soon after I had left for my Sunday afternoon walk. According to Marian, he had stopped by to talk with me once more about quitting my job and opening offices as an architect. Not finding me home, he had stayed on and talked with Marian about it. Apparently he had found her a sympathetic audience.

After talking a while, Marian had suggested a cocktail and then, when she had gone out to the kitchen to prepare the drink, she'd discovered we were out of liquor. He had insisted they go out to one of the cocktail lounges in the neighborhood.

This itself, I thought, was in bad taste. But the fact she had gone out with him wasn't the thing which infuriated me. What made me see red was Marian's willingness to sit and talk to the man about me and about what he felt I should do with my career. Not only had she been willing to talk with him about it, she had actually agreed with his ideas about coming in with me as a silent partner and financing the venture.

She was grateful!

Fleckner himself, a bachelor, may possibly be forgiven for not understanding, but certainly for Marian to have sided with another man against her husband was unforgivable.

I don't like to think of that evening and the things we said to each other. I do remember that at one point I completely lost my head. I think it was when Marian accused me of harboring a jealousy for Fleckner. Either that, or when she told me that I was a hopeless snob. In any case, there was a point in our discussion when I was unable to control myself and I slapped her. It was a silly thing to have done and I regretted it at once. I probably would have apologized, but I didn't have the chance.

Marian was holding a glass of milk in her hand and even as my open hand struck the side of her face, she threw the glass at me. Fortunately, the glass struck my shoulder and fell to the floor and broke. But the milk spilled down the front of my clothes. A moment later and she whirled and left the room, going into the bedroom and locking the door behind herself.

It made it twice in a single day that I had had my clothes soiled, first by a careless child and now by my own wife.

We barely spoke to each other in the morning while we had breakfast. I left for work without kissing Marian goodbye. I'd had a sleepless night.

But two things I had decided. I would never, under any circumstance, go into any sort of private venture with Sam Fleckner. And before telling either him or Tom McKenny about what I had heard, I would go back to Howie's Bar and Grill that night and see if I couldn't obtain some additional information. I had a vague idea in the back of my mind that the story might be of some value to the company which insured the payroll of McKenny-Fleckner.

I wasn't sure about such things, but it seemed to me that they might be willing to pay a reward for such information.

I waited all Monday morning for Marian to telephone, but she didn't. Once or twice I was on the verge of calling her, but each time I would start thinking over what had happened and I hesitated. After all, the argument was not my fault. I figured in any case that she herself had thought it over and was embarrassed about the attitude she had taken. I would see her later that evening, after she returned from her classes at Columbia, and no doubt we would straighten everything out.

Fortunately, Marian left early for her classes on Monday nights and I ate out, alone.

Monday afternoon passed almost before I realized it. The time seemed to fly.

Along about four o'clock, Tom McKenny stopped by my office. McKenny and Fleckner's main offices are located in a rebuilt structure on the Upper East Side, near the East River. The building at one time had been a warehouse and when the firm took it over, they renovated the entire four floors.

The ground floor is used as a place to store machinery and as a garage for the firm's trucks and cars. The second and third floors are also used for storage, as we keep a large inventory of such things as cement and lumber, window frames and plumbing fixtures and so forth. Fleckner, who does most of the buying, is always snapping up odd lots at discount prices and at government surplus sales, and the company needs considerable space to hold these inventories.

On the fourth floor are the offices. We employ a couple of dozen clerks and bookkeepers, a few draftsmen, and there are offices for Sam Fleckner as well as for Tom McKenny. Tom is infrequently in as his end of the business takes him out in the field where he oversees the actual construction work. Fleckner handles the office and business end of it, although I myself am, in everything but title, the actual office manager.

When Tom McKenny does come in, he rarely uses his own office, but spends most of his time in the storerooms or in my office. He even has a small desk in the corner of my office and uses my secretary.

McKenny is a large, jovial, red-faced Boston Irishman in his early fifties. We are not friends, in the real sense of the word, but I believe that Tom McKenny has respect for me and likes me. Certainly he depends on me. We have never been intimate, and we have always used the word "mister" in addressing each other. Nevertheless, we understand each other and Tom McKenny knows that I consider him a good man in his field and a good man to work for.

I was busy with some estimates on sewage piping when he came in and nodded, saying hello. He went at once to his small desk, opened the bottom right-hand drawer and took out a pint flask of whiskey.

He called over to Miss Minor, my secretary, and asked her to bring him a couple of paper cups and some water. While he was waiting, he peeled off his coat and I noticed the sweat circles under his arms. His face was very red and there was a thin layer of perspiration on his brow.

"Jesus," he said, "it's hot out. The middle of Long Island on a day like this just ain't fit ..."

Miss Minor handed him two cups, one filled with water, and he stopped in mid sentence while he poured himself a drink. He didn't offer me one and I certainly wouldn't have taken it if he had. Not in office hours and not straight like that, out of a bottle.

Miss Minor left the room on some errand or other and I looked up at him. For a second I was tempted to tell him. But even as I was thinking about it, he corked the bottle and stood up, making a small belch.

"I'd hate to be one of you slaves working under this hot roof," he said, and laughed. He started to leave the room.

Perhaps he meant it as a joke, but that word "slaves" irritated me. If we were slaves, then, he, certainly, was the slave driver. He and his whiskey during working hours, his coarse jokes and fabulous profits from other men's work and sweat.

No, I wouldn't tell him. Neither him nor Sam Fleckner. Let them protect their own payroll if they could. Why should I intervene?

II

Howie was busy, but he took a minute or two to stop and talk when he brought the Scotch and soda. He asked how I felt and if I'd taken the suit to the cleaners.

"Feeling fine," I said. "The suit will be all right."

We discussed the baseball scores for a bit and Howie told me the Giants were playing in a night game and that he'd get it on television.

"Drop back after dinner and watch it," he suggested.

I told him that I'd had an early dinner, but that I'd probably stay on. And then I walked over to one of the six booths lining the wall opposite the bar. I sat down in the booth, facing the corner where the television squatted like some ugly Cyclops. In the booth directly behind me were two people. I'd noticed them when I came in.

One was the girl who'd been driving the silver Buick convertible. The other was the dapper little man known as Katz.

They were sitting on the same seat in the booth, directly back of me, and their heads were close together as they talked in a subdued, almost secretive fashion. I could hear their voices from where I sat, could tell when it was the man and when it was the girl speaking, but I was unable to distinguish the words.

I was pretty sure that they hadn't observed me when I left the bar and approached the next booth.

He came in during the first inning of the ball game. The big, heavy-set one. He didn't stop at the bar, but went directly to the booth behind me.

The girl called him Roy.

By this time Howie's was crowded and I had to move over in the booth which I occupied to make room for a second man, who also wished to sit and watch the game. When he had asked if I minded if he sat next to me, I couldn't very well complain. I was nursing my drinks, trying to make them last as long as possible, and I knew that seats were at a premium.

Fortunately, my companion was engrossed in the game—the Giants were playing the Dodgers out at the Polo Grounds and it was a crucial game of the series. Howie had turned the set a little louder than usual as he had a full bar and most of his customers were baseball fans. Because of this, the three people in the booth behind me were forced to raise their voices in order to make themselves heard.

Watching the game, but concentrating on their conversation, I strained to hear every word.

A great deal of it I missed completely. Actually, if it hadn't been for the telecasting of the ball game, I should probably have heard nothing at all. As it was, the announcer would now and then lower his own voice and I would catch a fragment or two from the booth behind me.

It was only by putting these few casual phrases together with what I had learned the previous night, as well as with what I myself knew of McKenny-Fleckner Construction Company business, that I was able to piece the thing out.

Many of the details were lacking, of course, but I can tell you that what I did discover left me breathless.

As I suspected, they were planning a stickup. It was to be on the following Friday afternoon, out on the big Glenwillow project on the northern shore of Long Island. Katz, the big fellow, and one other man would do the job. The third man was the driver and the girl was to be planted in a second car to which the mob would switch after ditching the first car, which would be stolen just before the robbery.

They planned to get Tom McKenny when he drove up to the project. Apparently they knew that it was the first of the company's jobs he would visit and that he'd have the payroll for the workers on that project as well as for the other three big developments with him when he arrived. They figured he would be carrying fifty thousand dollars.

They were wrong about that. I know. I make up the payrolls. Tom McKenny would be carrying better than one hundred and twenty thousand dollars!

There was one thing which I was unable to learn whether they knew or didn't know.

Tom McKinney always drove alone in his car with the money. But directly behind him were two armed private detectives in a second car. This is, in a way, a very important fact. Because if it hadn't been that I, myself, had this knowledge, I would have acted a great deal differently than I did and several lives might have been saved.

It was around the time of the seventh inning—I distinctly remember that the Dodgers were leading—when there was a movement in the next booth and a moment later Katz, the small, bird-faced man, pushed his way out and started over toward the bar, carrying a couple of glasses. Howie was very busy and I guess Katz wanted service without waiting to catch the attention of the waiter who came in to help Howie out in the evenings.

It was while he was on his way back that he saw me sitting in the booth. For a brief moment his eyes met mine. He seemed to hesitate just the fraction of a second. I could tell that he had half recognized me from somewhere and was trying to remember where it could have been.

I wanted to get up. To run.

It was the most unusual sensation. Fear possibly, but something else as well. A sense of terrific excitement. But even as one half of my mind told me that the sooner I left the place the better off I would be, something else kept me sitting there. The subtle sense of danger was almost like an intoxicant.

After Katz returned to the booth, I heard no more. Either they kept their voices to a whisper, or else they stopped talking. However, less than fifteen minutes passed before the broad-shouldered one also got up. He went to the men's room.

He, too, stared at me on his way back.

I kept my eyes on the television screen and a little later I was aware that the booth behind me was emptying.

I felt real fear then. I wondered if Katz had recognized me as the man whom he had followed down the hallway that previous afternoon. I wondered if they realized how much I had overheard that very evening. And, also, I wondered if it were possible that they knew who I was—that I worked for McKenny and Fleckner.

The last was quite possible. After all, they apparently knew Tom McKenny. And certainly they had a great deal of inside information about the firm.

I know I must have gone a little pale thinking about it. I began to regret not having gone to the police at once.

Would they be outside there, somewhere on the street, waiting for me, when I left?

It seemed now that Katz's deep-socketed, russet eyes had been full of significance as he had stared into my face. And the big, thick-chested man? Hadn't there been something threatening in the way he had looked me up and down?

I was truly frightened then and I almost cried out. I must have made some sort of noise, because the man sitting next to me and watching the ball game turned suddenly and stared at me for a moment and then spoke.

"Is anything wrong?" he asked.

I realized that I must be very pale and at once I became aware of holding my glass in my hand and of my hand shaking so that the liquor was spilling over the edge of its rim.

I smiled a sickly smile.

"It's the game," I said. "I always get excited when I watch these two teams play."

"Giant fan?" he asked.

"Dodger," I said.

I left Howie's at ten-thirty. There was an empty taxi standing in front of the door and I quickly climbed into it. Taxis are an extravagance I rarely allow myself, but on this night I was in such a state of nervousness and excitement that the added luxury seemed well worth the expense.

An odd thing happened as the cab driver pulled up in front of my house.

A silver Buick convertible slowly passed as I was getting out and handing the driver his money. I noticed it just too late to see the occupants. It could have been a coincidence, but after all there aren't too many silver convertibles around.

The sight of that car almost made me change my mind once again. It almost convinced me that I should call the police and stop this dangerous game I was playing. If it hadn't been for Marian, I undoubtedly would have done so.

III

It doesn't seem possible that after nine years of marriage I shouldn't know my own wife. Apparently, however, there is a fine difference between knowing all about a person and really knowing that same person—knowing in the sense of understanding the subtle depths of mentality and emotional reasoning.

Certainly I had always thought that I understood Marian completely. Although we had had a rather short engagement—knowing each other less than a year prior to our marriage—there was little that I didn't know about Marian and her background when we were married.

In many ways Marian's life had paralleled my own. Her mother, Helen Fairless Wintrop, had, like my own mother, been widowed. Marian was still in her teens when this happened. The only difference was that Mrs. Wintrop had been left a small trust fund, enough to make ends meet. Marian had gone to the right schools and I had first met her the year she graduated from college. At the time she was taking a postgraduate course in decorative art.

Marian is several years younger than I am and I cannot say that ours was one of those intense love matches which you read about. But we soon discovered that we liked pretty much the same things, that we had the same background and shared many mutual friends. I suppose, in a sense, our marriage was pretty much engineered by our respective mothers.

Because of a lack of money, I had never had much of a social life. My previous contact with girls had been slight. With the exception of two dismal experiences with professional prostitutes while I was still in college—unsuccessful experiences of which I was ashamed and had been bitterly disillusioned by—I had had no sexual relations with women. I had been led to believe that being with a woman was the normal thing to do at that age, but the two times I tried had merely left me with a strong sense of revulsion.

The first couple of years of our marriage had been difficult. Marian had wanted to work and, although I was making a very meager salary, I had insisted that she stay home and take care of the apartment. I didn't object to her pursuing a hobby if she wished, but my pride forbade me permitting my wife to contribute to our joint support. Actually, there was no reason that she should, as her own mother had died immediately after our marriage and Marian had inherited the small trust fund. She used this money to purchase her own clothes and to help with the household bills.

Our differences, however, didn't arise over money, or even a lack of common interests. The thing which came between us was our individual attitude concerning a sexual relationship.

Marian is a handsome woman, slender and graceful and standing five feet seven, exactly the same height as myself.

She has always been athletic and has a fine strong body. But there was, and still is, something almost too vital, too animalistic about her, which, in a subtle way, offends me.

I pride myself on being completely normal, but I still feel a reticence when it comes to sex and emotional manifestations. I can't believe that sex in a marital relationship is as supremely important as a lot of persons prefer to believe.

Even after nine years, I am still embarrassed when I see Marian's naked body.

It is strange that this very fact was responsible for my taking the action I did when I entered our apartment after leaving Howie's Bar and Grill on that Monday night.

I paid the cab driver and I noticed the silver Buick. And then I started upstairs. Seeing that Buick revived all of my fears. I was sure, now, that Katz and the one called Roy knew who I was and had realized that I must have overheard their conversation. On my way upstairs, complete sanity returned to me. I decided that I would call the police the very moment I entered the apartment.

She must have heard my footsteps as I approached the door. It opened as I was reaching for the knob.

"Hal," she said. "Darling. I've been worried about you."

Her arms went around my neck and she pressed her body against me and her lips searched for mine. I was at once aware that she had undressed and was ready for bed. She had nothing on but a thin negligee.

She had called me Hal. It was her nickname for me, but a nickname which she never used except during those moments of personal intimacy we infrequently shared.

I started to say something then, started to draw away from her. But she leaned back and put her fingers over my mouth.

"Darling," she said, "I'm so ashamed of myself. Ashamed about our argument. And letting you sleep on the couch and ..."

"It was partly my fault," I said. "There's something I must tell you. Something ..."

"Not now," she said. "Not now. I won't hear anything now. I just want you to come to bed. We can talk later."

I tried to protest, tried to explain. But she would have none of it. She insisted that I come into the bedroom and take off my clothes and get ready for bed.

"Don't say anything," she said, kissing me again and imprisoning me with her arms. "Not now. Not until later."

Well, it could wait. It was more important that we made up our fight, more important that we smoothed over our differences.

But I was still thinking about Katz and the other man and the silver Buick convertible, an hour later, as I fell asleep. The last thing I remember was Marian going into the bathroom and my waiting and planning to tell her everything before deciding what to do. But I fell into an exhausted sleep and didn't awaken until after daylight the next morning.

I was up and shaved and ready for breakfast and Marian was in the kitchen preparing the coffee. I had thought the whole thing over and I was determined that the first thing I would do would be to see Tom McKenny and tell him the entire story and then he could get in touch with the proper authorities. I was thinking very clearly, even wondering what momentary insanity had made me even consider withholding my information, when I walked into the living room. Marian came out of the kitchenette carrying a steaming pot of coffee. She put it on the table, and then turned to me and smiled and said good morning.

"Darling," she said, "we are friends again, aren't we?"

I smiled back at her.

"We're friends," I said.

"Well, then," she said, walking over to me and standing in front of me and looking into my face, "Well then, I want you to do one thing for me."

"I'll do anything for you," I said. I reached for the morning paper which was lying on the table next to my coffee cup.

"You won't be mad if I ask?"

"I won't be mad."

"Then darling, I want you to see Sam Fleckner and at least listen to what he has to say."

I dropped the paper and stared at her.

"Marian!" I said. "Marian, I thought we had gone all over ..."

But it got me nowhere. She still insisted. She tried to reason with me, with a woman's usual illogical reasoning. Tried to explain that it wouldn't hurt to at least listen to Fleckner.

She seemed incapable of understanding the humiliating position which such a course would put me in. But I controlled my temper. I told her, at last, that I would think it over. But even as I told her, I felt a blind hatred for this man who had interfered in my life and who was trying to turn my own wife against me.

Thinking of Sam Fleckner brought back to my mind that other thing. It also made me remember that if it hadn't been for both Sam Fleckner and Tom McKenny failing to give me the breaks I had deserved, I would never be in this position.

Once more I changed my mind. I would tell Fleckner and McKenny nothing about the planned robbery. Let them protect themselves. Let them protect their own money. Their own money? The phrase itself brought a bitter smile to my mouth. The hundreds of thousands, possibly millions, which they had made were largely windfall profits which in actual truth belonged to the taxpayers and which they had obtained if not actually through fraud, certainly in a highly unethical fashion.

Certainly by keeping my mouth closed about the robbery I would be guilty of nothing.

Another thought had also suddenly occurred to me. If I were to talk, to tell what I knew, what actually could the police accomplish? All Katz and that other man had to do was deny the entire thing. Deny it and what *could* the police do to them?

It would be my word against theirs.

But what would they be liable to do to me if I talked?

Yes, wasn't I actually putting myself in greater danger by talking than I would by staying quiet? And why should I endanger my own life in order to do a favor for either Sam Fleckner or Tom McKenny? Why indeed?

IV

It was the worst week that I had ever spent in my life. The worst, but on the other hand, the most exciting. The strange thing was the sense of power I felt. The power which the information I possessed gave me.

The time literally flew by. Before I knew it, it was already Friday morning.

Leaving the apartment, I reflected that within another five hours the McKenny-Fleckner Construction Company would be out a hundred and twenty thousand dollars. Only I could stop it; only I had the power to sidetrack the robbery. But I would not use that power.

My first stop was at the bank, where I had left the payroll lists the previous day. The money was delivered in bulk and two men from the bank brought it to our offices. I always accompanied them. Once in the office, a half-dozen clerks whom I supervised began at once placing the various sums in individual envelopes.

It was all done before eleven-thirty. At exactly twelve o'clock, Tom McKenny would come into my office carrying the black satchel which he had used from as early as I could remember. The money was placed in the bag and then McKenny would start out to make his rounds to the various jobs which were underway in the field.

Why McKenny himself always insisted on doing this, no one knew. Sam Fleckner had frequently joked with him about it and suggested someone else take care of the task.

I think, actually, it was a hangover from McKenny's early days when he had started out, employing only two or three carpenters. Paying the men off himself gave him a subtle sense of power, of being the boss. He still did it, and I believe that in some odd way it was a symbol which reassured him once each week of his success and how far he had come during the last decade.

The idea I got, the thing which was to make such a difference, not only in my own life, but in the lives of a number of other persons, came to me at eleven o'clock, right after we had finished making up the payroll and after the others had left the office. Ellen Minor, my secretary, and I were alone in the room.

I think seeing Tom McKenny coming in and taking a drink out of the private bottle he kept in that bottom desk drawer is what gave me the thought.

The germ of it came when, watching McKenny, I suddenly realized he wasn't the type of man to stand still while he was being relieved of the payroll. No, Tom McKenny would put up a fight. And I knew that he'd be carrying a gun—the loaded revolver that he kept in that same desk drawer with the whiskey.

Thinking about it, and watching him, I started to get up from my chair. I would have to warn him. But then I got my idea. If the gun were not loaded....

I sat back. Yes, if Tom McKenny's gun was empty, there was every chance that he wouldn't be hurt. I didn't know just exactly how they planned to handle the holdup, but I could visualize it. McKenny would drive up to the job and the gangsters' car would pull alongside of him. He might or might not attempt to reach for his gun. But even if he did, and pulled the trigger and nothing happened, they'd merely disarm him and take the satchel containing the payroll money.

There was, of course, the other car which followed McKenny. I didn't believe Katz and Roy knew about that car. Certainly, the detectives in that car, seeing what was taking place, would interfere and when they did the bandits' attention would be taken from McKenny. McKenny himself wouldn't be hurt so long as he didn't start using a gun. And if the gun was empty, then obviously he couldn't use it.

I reached across my desk and took some papers from my workbasket.

"Miss Minor," I said, "would you do me a favor? Take these estimates down to the third floor and see if you can find Mr. McKenny. Ask him to look them over."

I knew that she would be gone for several minutes. McKenny had just left the room and I happened to know that he had gone down to the garage on the ground floor.

She was no sooner out of the room than I got up and went over to McKenny's desk.

I didn't have to search for it. I'd seen the revolver lying there, next to the whiskey flask, a hundred times. I opened the drawer and I reached in and took out the gun. It was a .38 caliber police special. I was familiar with guns, having grown accustomed to them during the two years I spent in the National Guard.

It took me only a second to break it and take out the shells. I was putting them into my pocket when the voice spoke from behind me.

"Sneaking a drink, Harold? I'm ashamed."

I stopped as though I had been shot.

It was Sam Fleckner. I didn't have to turn and see. I knew the deep, sardonic, half-amused tone of his voice only too well. How long he had been standing there watching me I had no way of knowing. For a split second, as my hand still held the revolver, I was tempted to turn and make some excuse for handling the gun. And then I realized, that from where he stood in the doorway, he would not have been able to see the gun itself. And he had suggested I was taking a drink.

Of course, Fleckner meant the remark as a joke. He knows me better than to think I would ever take a drink in the middle of the day. For another second I racked my brain for some excuse for having my hand in Tom McKenny's private desk drawer.

And then I carefully laid the revolver down and picked up the flask. I swung around with it in my hand. I forced a smile.

"You're right," I said. "Believe it or not, I am. I've got a very sore throat and I thought I would take a small drink. Don't want to catch a summer cold."

"Hell," he said, "you are taking a slug! Well ... I'll be."

"I'm sure Mr. Kenny wouldn't ..."

He laughed again.

"By God," he said, "Tom would be delighted to see you—or anyone—take a drink. Anytime. I'm even delighted myself."

He laughed again.

At ten minutes to twelve Tom McKenny came back into the office. He went at once to his desk and opened the drawer and took out the pistol, tucking it into his rear pocket.

"Mr. Wilkenson," he said, "I wish you'd get your hat. Want you to come on out to the island with me this afternoon. Want you to figure a concrete estimate on these new basements on the Parkway project."

I stared at him, the blood leaving my face.

"Don't you feel well," he asked, suddenly, his voice solicitous. "Sam just told me that you had a sore throat ..."

"The fact is, I'm not feeling very well, Mr. McKenny," I said. "I thought that perhaps I'd go home early and get to bed."

"Nonsense," he said. "What you need is a little fresh air. You come on out with me. We'll be all through by two thirty or three and then we'll stop at Belmont on the way back and catch the last three or four races. Do you good."

Arguing with him was futile. Tom McKenny was not the man to respect anyone else's wishes.

I was lucky to find the opportunity for dropping the .38 shells in my wastebasket before we left.

Chapter 3

Tom McKenny wheeled his Cadillac sedan out of the garage at exactly twelve o'clock. I was sitting at his side. The black satchel containing the money lay between us. As we turned the corner of the building, a dark sedan which had been idling at the curb, pulled in behind us. I knew that the two men in its front seat were the private detectives McKenny hired to follow him.

I cursed the vanity of the man. Why couldn't he have done the normal thing and had them deliver the payroll? Why, if he insisted on doing it himself, didn't he at least have them ride in the car with us?

But I knew the answers without asking. It was a part of the man's personality that he would want to carry the money himself. A sop to his sense of power. It was his basic vanity which made him carry the satchel in his own car. But vanity or not, he was still cautious enough to want the protection of those others. He wanted it, but he didn't want to have to admit it. So this was the childish way in which he compromised.

Thinking about it made me suddenly hate him. He had insisted that I come with him, that I put myself in this terrible position of jeopardy. What right had he to endanger my life? Yes, thinking about it brought tears of frustration and hatred into my eyes. I could have killed the man myself.

We drove over to the East River Drive and then up to the Triborough Bridge. I must have shown my nervousness and probably McKenny saw me looking now and then into the rear-vision mirror. He noticed it and said, "Try and relax. It's a lovely day. Enjoy it."

I was tense with fear. I wanted to tell him then. Tell him everything. Warn him what was to take place.

But how could I? How could I explain why I hadn't spoken before? How could I explain about that empty gun?

If I talked now, I would go to jail for sure. The least that would happen would be that I'd lose my job. No, I couldn't talk. I could do nothing but sit there and wait. Wait and pray.

Traffic was heavy as we swung into the Northern State Parkway. Hundreds of cars were leaving the city early for a long weekend. I began silently to hope that Katz and Roy and that other one had changed their plans, had decided to postpone the stickup to some other time. After all, I wasn't sure. I wasn't positive. I had only overheard fragments of the conversation.

God, I'd never dreamed that I would find myself in this position.

But there was nothing I could do without giving myself away. The die had been irrevocably cast when I had kept my own counsel.

We turned off the parkway at last, and as we did I swung around in my seat and looked behind. My heart dropped when at first I no longer saw the car with the armed guards. But then, a moment later, its nose ducked out of the long line of cars and it swung in behind us once more.

I drew a deep breath of relief.

McKenny looked over at me curiously.

We took a lateral road, heading north, and passed through two small towns. The development project lay a couple of miles ahead.

We had to cross Route 25A and our destination was not more than a mile further on. There was a green light at the intersection. As we approached, the light changed to red and Tom McKenny pulled up to a stop. The car following came alongside.

The light changed, and our car shot ahead. We couldn't have gone more than a quarter of a mile when we came to the next intersection, a narrow, hardtop road, just beyond a sharp turn.

McKenny slowed for the turn and just as we passed, the truck shot out. It didn't miss us by a hairsbreadth. And the next second we heard the crash.

Tom McKenny instinctively pushed in his brake pedal.

At first I didn't fully realize what had happened. The crash was so close that for a second I thought it was our car which had been struck. But then, as the Cadillac skidded to a short stop that almost threw me through the windshield, I realized it was the car which had been following us that had been hit.

I was on my knees on the floor and I started to get up. I had just raised my head level with the doorjamb when the other car, the one coming from the opposite direction, screeched to a stop at our side.

The men who leaped from it were masked. One held a submachine gun under his arm; the other had an automatic in his hand.

I heard the harsh order as I started to duck back down under the dashboard. The order to "stick 'em up."

Tom McKenny committed suicide.

Yes, there is no doubt in my mind about it at all. He must have known he wouldn't have a chance.

He committed suicide and but for the grace of God, he almost caused my own death.

The second that order came, I saw him deliberately reach for his gun. He jerked it from his side coat pocket. I distinctly heard the click as he pulled the trigger.

I was staring into a pair of russet eyes as the gunman pressed the trigger of his own weapon.

The last thing I remember was the staccato sound of the submachine gun. And then it seems as though the very sky fell and I was crushed.

II

"He's coming to now, Lieutenant. Any minute ..."

And then the voice faded out. Next I became conscious of a sharp stabbing pain in my arm. There was a soft murmur of other voices. I tried to open my eyes. I felt a hand on my forehead and then, very clearly, I heard Marian's voice.

"But I want to stay," she said. "I want to be here when he ..."

The other voice, that first one, interrupted.

"You can come back in as soon as he is fully awake," the voice said. "But right now you must leave."

I heard the sound of a door quietly closing. And then I did open my eyes. It took me a brief moment to remember. But as the white walls of the room came into focus and my head cleared, it all came back to me.

A thin, dark man in a white coat was leaning over me. I was lying on a bed and I knew at once that this man was a doctor and that I was in a hospital.

"Can you hear me?" he asked.

I started to nod and it was then I became conscious of the terrible, splitting ache in my head.

"Just take it easy," the dark man said. "Don't try to strain yourself."

I searched his face. I knew that I had been hurt and for a moment I wondered if I were dying.

"It's nothing," he said, looking down at me, but apparently speaking for the benefit of those others in the room as well. "Nothing. Bullet merely grazed the side of the cranium. There's a concussion, of course, but I don't believe there's a fracture. I'm amazed that he's been unconscious as long as he has."

"He'll be able to talk?"

It was a soft voice with a faint burr which reminded me somehow of Boston. A voice I had never before heard.

I turned my eyes and the owner of the voice was standing at the side of my bed, looking down at me. He seemed very tall. It was only later that I learned my first impressions of him were completely wrong. Actually he was not more than five foot ten; he had narrow, sloping shoulders which gave him an oddly studious appearance. But the thing which always impressed me most was the expression on his wide, obviously Irish face. A face under an unruly mop of faded red hair with the lightest blue eyes I had ever seen, wide eyebrows and a line of freckles across the nose which had been left over from his boyhood. A face with a very human, understanding expression which never changed. The eyes, which by all rights should have been cold and uncompromising, were actually warm with sympathy.

He was a man in whom you instinctively wanted to confide. He was Detective Lieutenant Shawn O'Malley of the Nassau County Police, assigned to the district attorney's office as a special investigator.

"Any minute now," the doctor said. "I'll leave you alone with him. But try and make it short. He should rest."

The doctor, followed by a middle-aged woman in a white uniform, left the room and the man with the soft Irish voice pulled a chair up beside the bed.

"How do you feel?" he asked.

"Terrible," I said.

"It could have been much worse," he said. "Yes, much worse. One of the bullets which got McKenny passed on and grazed the side of your head. It was already spent, otherwise you might have been dead too."

I stared at him.

"Mr. McKenny's dead?"

"Yes. McKenny, he and one of the guards who were following in the other car. The second guard was knocked unconscious in the crash. He'll live."

I stared at him. "It all happened so fast ..."

"Yes, it happened fast. I guess you realize what happened?"

"I just remember a crash," I said. "And then a man sticking a gun into the side of our car."

"Fine," he said. "That's what I was hoping. What did this man look like?"

It came to me then. The realization that I was getting myself into a trap. What did he look like? I didn't dare say what he looked like. I didn't want to even remember what he looked like. I must think. I must have time to get my story together. Time to plan ...

I closed my eyes and expelled my breath, sinking back into the bed. I didn't want to talk anymore. I didn't dare talk. I must learn first just what the police knew. Learn if any of those who had committed the robbery had been picked up. Learn exactly what had happened.

He reached over and gently shook my arm. I pretended that I had again lapsed into unconsciousness.

"Can you hear me?" he asked. I felt him lean across the bed.

He waited a moment or two and then gently shook me. I made no move.

"Mr. Wilkenson," he said. "Try and hear me, Mr. Wilkenson."

I made no move.

And then, the thing he did next, gave me one of the greatest surprises of my life. It also gave me my first insight into the vicious character of the man whom I would be seeing so much of in the days to come.

He did it deliberately.

He reached out with one hand and using his forefinger and his thumb, snapped his finger across the bridge of my nose.

The pain was so intense that it brought tears to my eyes. Instinctively and without even thinking about it, I cried out. At the same time, my eyes opened wide and I stared up at him.

They must have heard my cry outside the door.

It flew open even as Detective Lieutenant O'Malley stood up from his chair. His eyes were watching me and he was smiling in a soft, sympathetic way. He turned as the others entered the room.

"Lapsed into unconsciousness," he said. "Something must have happened in his subconscious mind to frighten him and he cried out."

The doctor quickly reached my side. Behind him was Marian, and in the crowd of people who had suddenly entered the room, I thought I detected the tall form of Sam Fleckner.

"He must rest now," the doctor said hurriedly. "I'll give him a sedative and everyone must clear out."

Marian was trying to say something but I quickly closed my eyes again. I didn't want to hear anything, didn't want to say anything. I had to have time to think.

III

The headache was completely gone and I was alone in the darkened room the next time I gained consciousness. I had no idea of the time, or in fact, even the day. There was a dim night light on the table by my side.

I fumbled around until I found the button which summoned the nurse.

She didn't want to talk, but I finally prevailed upon her. It was Saturday evening, just after eight o'clock. I had been in the hospital for more than thirty hours.

Marian had stayed on until the doctor had finally sent her home to get some rest. The nurse, a middle-aged woman with a stern and uncompromising manner, refused to discuss the robbery; she would only tell me that I was going to be all right and that I was not seriously hurt.

"You'll need your rest," she said. "The doctor says you may be released tomorrow if there are no complications."

I asked to see a newspaper, but this she refused me. She also said that I could not use the telephone.

"You may have something to eat," she told me, "but you may see no one. Doctor's orders."

I had no appetite, but I was able to force down some weak soup.

The place was very quiet and from my room I could hear no outside noises. Once I attempted to get out of bed; I wanted to look around for my clothes. But immediately the headache returned and I lay back again. I felt half doped.

My mind remained very clear. I was trying to remember as much as I could of what happened.

I was also beginning to realize what might still happen. The detective would be back. He'd be back to question me. I began to understand what he would want. He'd want a description of the men who had waylaid us. He'd want to take me down to police headquarters and have me go through pictures files. There wouldn't, of course, be the slightest chance that they could suspect me of having anything to do with the thing, but still they would figure I would be their best hope of getting a lead. They would want me to tell them about the man with the russet-brown eyes.

Tell them? It could only lead to my own undoing.

I began to wonder if they had discovered that McKenny's revolver had not been loaded. I began to wonder …

But then, suddenly, I had no time left to wonder about anything. My eyes, wandering at random around the room, had stopped at the door. I became aware of the fact that the knob was slowly turning. At first I merely thought it was the nurse coming back to check up on me. But there was something strange about it, something too quiet. Something which brought the sudden terrible lump of fear into my throat and wanted to make me scream out.

Even as I opened my mouth to yell, the door opened and I think it was only the quick surprise of seeing her which kept the sound locked in my throat.

The shadowy figure was unmistakable. I recognized the husky whisper at once.

She glided toward my bed, the golden girl with the azure eyes of the silver Buick convertible. "Be quiet."

She reached out toward me and once more I opened my mouth to scream. I knew the depth of fear.

Her hand went swiftly to my lips then as she leaned over me. I could smell the odor of her and her long golden hair brushed my face.

"I've brought this for you," she said. Something dropped on the bed at my side.

A moment later the door closed softly behind her and she was gone. It was several minutes before I recovered sufficiently to breathe normally—to begin to think.

The odd thing was that the thought uppermost in my mind wasn't curiosity as to how or why she had come; it was a quick fury at the police for leaving me exposed. Anyone could have entered that room. Anyone could have come in and silenced me forever.

Minutes later I reached over and turned on the desk light at the side of my bed. My hand found the medium-sized, oblong box which she had laid at my side. I was trembling as I picked it up. For a flashing second I had the rather dramatic thought that it could be a bomb. But at once I recognized the striped paper and knew it was a box of candy.

I think I must have laughed then, a little hysterically. But almost as quickly I stopped laughing.

Candy: Could it be poisoned?

Curiosity finally got the best of me. Carefully I removed the silver string binding it and removed the paper. It was a two-pound box in which was usually packed one of the better-known commercial brands of chocolates.

Slowly I opened the box.

And then I just lay there staring at the contents. It must have been a full fifteen minutes before I counted the bills. There were fifty of them. Fifty one-hundred-dollar bills.

I didn't need a diagram. I didn't have to be told. This was to be my payoff for keeping my mouth shut.

IV

I left the hospital at eight-thirty on Sunday morning.

I left with Detective Lieutenant Shawn O'Malley walking on one side of me and with Sam Fleckner walking on the other.

Since before six I had been awake and the nurse had permitted a telephone call to come through from Marian at seven fifteen. She told me that she had already talked with the doctor and that I could expect to come home sometime before noon on Sunday. She would come to the hospital for me herself. But it didn't work out that way.

They brought me my clothes and a very early breakfast. The nurse offered to help me dress but I insisted I could handle it myself. I still had the traces of a headache, but I wasn't feeling bad. The moment I was left alone, I climbed out of bed and began putting on my clothes. Almost at once I was faced with a serious problem. What to do with the contents of the candy box?

At first I thought I might be able to conceal the money in my various pockets. I tried this, but the very obvious bulges would certainly create curiosity. Quickly I repacked the bills in the candy box. For a moment the idea occurred to me that I might mail the package to myself, but then I realized that such a course would seem very suspicious. I finally decided that the best thing to do was merely to carry the box out under my arm. Should Marian herself ask about it, I would tell her that I had purchased a box of candy for her while driving out to Long Island.

The nurse had brought a Sunday paper in with my breakfast and I rapidly went through it, reading the follow-up stories of the robbery. It was as I had expected.

The criminals had made a clean break, taking the payroll and leaving behind the wrecked truck. There had been no witnesses. Tom McKenny had been killed instantly. The detective who had been hit by the machine gun bullets had died on the way to the hospital. The second detective, a man named Farrell, was still in a critical condition. Police had talked with him, however, but he had been able to give them almost no information.

He'd only remembered that a truck had collided with their car and that a moment later, as he was pulling himself out of the wrecked machine, he'd been dimly aware of hearing gunfire. He'd lapsed into unconsciousness and had not come to until hours later.

The truck, of course, had been left at the scene. It turned out to have been stolen from a warehouse depot in Long Island City some hours before the stickup.

The story went on to say that I, too, had been shot and that my condition was fair. Several details of the story were completely wrong, whether on purpose or not, I do not know. The paper had the payroll figured at $140,000 instead of $120,000. They had Tom McKenny's age wrong and said that he left a widow and two children instead of three children. They listed me as a vice president of the firm.

There was a picture taken at the scene, showing the wrecked truck and guard's car, along with the Cadillac sedan in which McKenny and myself had been riding. One odd thing about the story was the fact that there was nothing about the bandits' second car, the one which had come from the opposite direction and from which the gunmen had alighted. In fact, the story seemed to overlook completely this facet of the case, and the reader was left to assume that the gunmen must have arrived in the truck itself. I thought this was unusual, as newspapers usually give a more accurate coverage of details, and lacking the actual facts, they make them up.

I was still reading the story when the door abruptly opened.

I looked up, nervously.

Detective O'Malley, closely followed by Sam Fleckner, entered the room.

O'Malley stood at the side of the door and Sam walked quickly across the room. He put his arm over my shoulder and leaned down. "How are you, old man?" he asked. He looked into my face, his expression solicitous.

I am afraid my voice was a little petulant when I answered him. Somehow or other I disliked that expression, "old man." And I have a distinct distaste for people who put their hands on me.

I stood up quickly.

"As well as could be expected," I said. "I'm waiting for Marian—Mrs. Wilkenson."

"Fine—fine," Fleckner said. "Knew you'd pull through all right. But I'm afraid ..."

O'Malley stepped forward.

"You'll have to see Mrs. Wilkenson later," he said, his voice soft and sympathetic. "Sorry, but we really haven't had a chance to talk with you yet and ..."

"Talk with me?" I stared at him. "There's nothing to talk about. I've been shot at and wounded and now I want to go home. It seems to me ..."

Both of them interrupted me at once. Sam started to say something about the police wanting some additional information, but the detective's voice cut him off.

"Want you to come down to headquarters," he said. "Look over some mug shots. May just be a chance that you can identify ..."

"I can identify no one," I said quickly. "It all happened too fast. I never had a chance to see anything."

"That's just it," O'Malley said. "You see, we still haven't had a statement from you and ..."

"A statement." I was indignant. "What possible statement could I make? After all, haven't I gone through enough as it is? Haven't I?"

"Don't misunderstand the Lieutenant," Sam said quickly. "After all, Harold, you were there and you're about the only one left. He has to know."

"Yes, we have to know," the detective said. "Certainly you'll be wanting to cooperate."

"Of course I want to cooperate," I said, tersely. "But after all, I have gone through a great deal and it would seem that I could be permitted to go home and rest."

"The doctor says you're fine," Sam said. "No danger at all and that in another day or so, you'll be just as good as new."

"Well, I won't feel as good as new."

"We better get started," O'Malley said.

I could see that arguing would be of little avail. There was something else which suddenly occurred to me. I didn't want to antagonize the police. I knew that sooner or later I would have to give my version of the entire affair and I had my story ready. The sooner I got it out of my system the better.

I reached down and put out my cigarette, and my eye fell on the wrapped-up candy box lying beside my plate on the small table on which my breakfast had been served.

"I'll be glad to tell you all I know of what happened," I said then. "I can tell you everything right now."

O'Malley nodded. "Fine," he said. "That will be fine. But I'm afraid that we'll still have to go down to headquarters. We have to take a formal statement and we'll need a stenographer."

We left the hospital a few minutes later.

I guess I expected to see a police car waiting at the curb and I was a little surprised when we walked over to the side of a five-year-old Dodge sedan and Lieutenant O'Malley opened the door, inviting us to climb in. Sam Fleckner got into the back and I sat beside the policeman.

"We found the getaway car," he remarked, casually, as he started the motor. "About a half a mile away. Apparently there was a second car planted and waiting for them. The car which they had abandoned was stolen."

Sam Fleckner leaned forward.

"Tom's funeral is set for early tomorrow morning," he said. "If you like, I'll be glad to pick you and Marian up."

I didn't answer him. It annoyed me having him refer to Mrs. Wilkenson as Marian.

V

I had always thought of police stations as rather drab, old-fashioned buildings, housing bare and dismal high-ceilinged rooms, decorated with spittoons and scarred oak desks. The room in which I eventually found myself surprised me. It could have been the office of any well-organized modern business. With the exception of several uniformed police officers, I might have thought myself in a bank or insurance company.

Fleckner sat in a chair at one side of the room while I dictated a formal statement. A neat, middle-aged woman with graying hair took it down in shorthand and Lieutenant O'Malley asked the questions, interrupted me frequently in order to clear up one detail or another.

My story was short and simple. With one exception, I told him exactly what had happened and exactly as I have written it here. The exception was that I hadn't the faintest idea how many men were involved in the robbery and that I was completely unable to remember what they had looked like. I knew it would be a mistake to give false descriptions of the men and so I compromised by giving none at all.

"Only a voice," I told him. "Nothing else. A voice saying 'stick 'em up,' and then I was aware of gunfire and I knew nothing else until I came to in the hospital."

"And you didn't see the truck at all?"

"I heard the crash," I said.

"But you didn't see the truck?"

"I didn't see the truck. I saw nothing. After the crash—and I thought at first that it was our car which had been struck—I went to my knees on the floor when Mr. McKenny pushed on his brakes. And then the next thing I knew was when I heard the voice."

O'Malley nodded slowly.

He waited a moment and then told the woman to type up the statement.

"Want you to look over some mug shots," he said at last.

I shrugged.

"It will be a waste of time," I said.

"Yes, it probably will," he agreed. "But it's one of those things we have to do." He reached out and offered me an opened pack of cigarettes.

He smiled then and his eye went to the candy box lying on the desk at my side.

"Reach for a sweet instead?" he said. "Well, they're probably better for you." He hesitated for a moment.

"By the way, did you have the candy with you during the holdup?"

The question caught me completely off guard.

Thank God, Sam Fleckner for once in his life said the right thing and came to my rescue. I know that in another second I should have given myself away if he hadn't spoken just when he did.

"I guess that Marian will be a lot happier getting you back than getting a box of candy," he said.

It was a bad moment.

I stood up, reaching down for the box and just then a uniformed officer put his head through the opened doorway.

"Ready for you in the file room, Lieutenant," he said.

Five minutes later I was seated at a long oak table, looking over stacks of official police photos. I must have gone through literally hundreds and thousands of them and I was getting very tired when it suddenly occurred to me Marian would be expecting to pick me up at the hospital and that she was probably already there, wondering what had happened to me. Quickly I dropped the picture which was in my hand and swung to Lieutenant O'Malley, who had been sitting patiently at my side.

"Good Lord," I said. "Mrs. Wilkenson was expecting to ..."

"I know," he said. "We called her. She'd already left, but Mr. Fleckner has gone to the hospital to intercept her. They'll come back and pick you up here. Probably downstairs now waiting."

Once more I was annoyed. I was getting a little tired of Sam Fleckner interfering in my life and my plans.

I felt something else—a sensation which never before in my life had I experienced. It was jealousy, a definite jealousy of Sam Fleckner. It was almost a physical thing, a physical pain. I didn't want Fleckner being with Marian. I didn't want him putting his hand on her and holding her arm or being close to her.

Understand, at this point I certainly had no real reason to be jealous and certainly I had no defined suspicions which might justify it. But there it was anyway. The image of Fleckner and Marian together was sufficient to arouse in me that bitter sensation which must, in all truth, have been harboring itself like a fugitive in my heart and mind for a long, long time.

It must have been about fifteen minutes later when I came across the picture. In spite of the fact I had been prepared from the very beginning to see either Katz's face or that of the big man called Roy, I never really expected that I would find their photos in that vast file of mug shots. It is odd, also, that at the very moment I recognized the photograph I was holding in my hand, I should have been thinking of Detective Lieutenant O'Malley himself. I was thinking that he was, actually, a rather stupid man after all and that I should certainly have nothing to worry about as far as he was concerned.

Here he had a spectacular payroll stickup on his hands and he was very obviously wasting his time—as well as my own—instead of being out somewhere trying to do something about it. I was thinking that, after all, unless a policeman is able to use a blackjack or some other method of illegal interrogation, he really is pretty helpless.

Then that photo came up on top of the pile which I was inspecting. The photograph of "Roy."

I recognized it the moment my eye fell on it. A picture which must have been taken some years before, the identification, however, was very clear and obvious. The face was a little thinner and there was a blank, almost somnolent expression which was so typical of all the other mug shots. But the wide apart gray eyes, under dark heavy brows, the slightly concave nose over full wide lips, were unmistakable. In spite of myself I must have hesitated just the fraction of a second before laying the picture in the pile of discards.

The next moment I was forced to change completely my opinion concerning Lieutenant O'Malley's intelligence and alertness.

Quickly his hand reached out and he picked up the photograph. For a moment he said nothing as he stared at it and I made a controlled effort not to obviously observe what he was doing.

"This one," he said suddenly. "Was there something familiar about this one?"

He thrust the photograph back at me.

I was forced to take it.

This time I looked at the legend under the picture. I pretended to study the face for a moment or two.

It was a regular police identification photograph of a man named Roy Anders, thirty-nine years old and identified as a bank robber and suspected murderer. The picture had been taken some five years previously. There was a set of fingerprints beside the picture as well as a very accurate description of the man. He was described, also, as extremely dangerous.

I stared at it for a moment or so and then again laid it down.

"No," I said. "No, it means nothing to me at all."

O'Malley nodded slowly.

"Just thought you hesitated for a second," he said. "Perhaps—well, perhaps he's someone you may have seen somewhere or other recently."

"No," I said. I was careful not to speak too quickly, not to show the excitement I felt. "No, I've never seen the man before."

He nodded again. But I noticed that he was careful to keep the picture separate from the other discards.

I decided that I should not again make the mistake of underestimating this soft-spoken, oddly deceptive man.

And I began to worry. I knew that a thorough checkup of my own movements would bring out the fact that I frequently went to Howie's Bar and Grill. I knew that a checkup of Howie's might well establish the fact that Roy Anders was also a customer of the place.

I felt very ill at ease.

The idea came to me that my own safety lay, somehow, in getting word to Roy Anders that he was a possible suspect.

Chapter 4

The most horrible thing has happened.

It is now Monday morning and I am sitting in the living room of our apartment with the shades drawn and the door double-locked. I have just finished reading the morning newspapers.

I am convinced that Detective Lieutenant O'Malley is trying to get me murdered. Not only that, but Sam Fleckner is helping him and I believe that my own wife is a willing participant, if not an active one, to the scheme. Even the press, which I have always believed to be at least ethical, if not thoroughly honest and above board, seems to be cooperating.

It is difficult for me to understand how anyone can be so completely unscrupulous and callous as certain members of the police department.

Marian is back in the bedroom and has slammed the door. I have gone over the newspaper story twice, hoping against hope that I had read it wrong. But I haven't. It is all here.

All down in black and white.

The newspaper says that I have positively identified two of the men who took part in the payroll stickup! The article quotes both Lieutenant Shawn O'Malley and Sam Fleckner.

My God, can't they understand what they are doing to me? Don't they see that they are signing my death warrant?

Not more than five minutes ago I spoke to O'Malley on the telephone. The man is completely incredible.

He told me that Fleckner had told him I would be willing to fall in with the scheme. If Fleckner did tell him, then Sam Fleckner himself is trying to get me killed.

Is it possible that my feelings of jealousy concerning Fleckner can be based on logic and reason? Is it possible that the man is purposely putting my life in danger in hopes that something may happen to me? Is it even possible that Marian herself can be falling in with some subtle, vicious plan of his?

O'Malley is now on his way here and foolishly enough I told him I would wait until he arrived before I myself called the press.

Sam Fleckner is on his way up to the apartment. He is under the impression that Marian and I are going to attend Tom McKenny's funeral out in Scarsdale. The man must be mad. I would no longer think of showing myself in public than I would of cutting my throat after what has happened.

I simply can't understand Marian. This last twenty-four hours has been about the worst I have ever spent and Marian is largely responsible for it.

It started yesterday, shortly after noontime, when I left the police station after that ridiculous procedure of going through those reams of photographs.

O'Malley finally tired and permitted me to leave. He thanked me for the trouble he had put me to and I had gotten up and stretched and found my hat. Marian and Sam Fleckner were waiting downstairs.

The moment I entered the room, she rushed over to me and put her arms around me, staring into my face.

"Oh, Harold," she said.

I have always disliked any demonstrations of affection in public and this time was certainly no exception, particularly with Sam Fleckner standing there and half smiling.

"I'm tired," I told her, quickly, "and I don't feel well. I should like to go home at once."

"Sam's going to take us home," she said.

"That won't be necessary," I told her, speaking in a low voice so that Sam himself would not hear my words. "I'd much prefer to take a cab."

She stood back, still holding my arms.

"But Harold," she said, making no effort to keep her own voice low, "but Harold, Sam has his car out in front. Now don't be silly. He wants to drive us back."

"But I still would prefer ..."

I got no further.

Fleckner walked across the room and took me by my arm as Marian stood back.

"Now old man," he said, "you've had a tough time of it. You just come on along and we'll get you right home. You should be taking it easy. Doctor says you want to rest up, particularly as you'll have to face Tom's funeral tomorrow."

Protesting did no good.

We were no sooner in the car, not the Allard this time, but Sam's big Chrysler sedan, and crowded in the front seat, where Sam had insisted we all sit together, when the business came up about the candy.

"Imagine the guy," Sam said, turning to Marian, who was seated between the two of us. "Imagine—thought so much of you that while he was still in the hospital he managed to find a box of candy to bring home."

Marian looked down at the two-pound candy box I was holding on my lap.

"Why Harold!"

Her hand at once reached out for it.

Quickly I shifted the box, holding it tightly.

"Later," I said, my lips thin. I could feel my face go white with anger. "Later. I should like, if possible, to be taken home now. As soon as possible."

God, how I hated Fleckner at that moment. I blamed him for everything. If he hadn't been taking Marian out for a drink on that last Sunday afternoon, when I had returned home from Howie's after overhearing that fatal conversation, none of this would have happened. If it hadn't been for his trying to argue Marian into my making a deal with him, it still wouldn't have happened.

Everywhere I had turned, his interfering had cropped up. He'd even walked in while I'd been taking the bullets out of Tom McKenny's gun. The man had a positive evil genius for intruding where he wasn't wanted.

And now, here he was, once more creating confusion and trouble.

No one spoke again until we had passed through the Midtown Tunnel and were on our way up the East River Drive. And then, as usual, Fleckner was the first to break the silence.

"I've got to go up and see Claire this afternoon," he said. "Promised her I'd see to all the arrangements for poor Tom's funeral."

"If there's anything we can do ..." Marian began.

"We can go home and let me have some rest," I interrupted. "After all, I have been shot and it would seem to me ..."

"Of course," Marian said, reaching over and putting her hand over mine. "Of course, dear."

Sam looked over at me peculiarly for a moment and then turned back to his driving.

"You need a little rest, Harold," he said.

I didn't answer him and when we pulled up in front of the apartment house on East Fifty-fourth Street, I stepped gingerly out of the car. He shut off the engine and for a moment I really believe that he had the audacity to consider coming upstairs with us.

"Coming Marian?" I said, and turned toward the steps.

She stepped through the door as I opened it. I didn't turn as I heard Fleckner gun the motor to pull away from the curb.

We were no more than in the place when Marian began. "At least you could have been courteous," she said. "He was only trying to be helpful."

"He's too goddamned helpful," I snapped, walking across the living room and throwing my hat on a chair. "Too goddamned helpful altogether."

"Why Harold Wilkenson," Marian said. "What in the world has gotten into you lately?"

I swung to her.

"Gotten into me? Gotten into *me*? I'll tell you what's gotten into me. I'm tired and sick of that sonofabitch. I don't like anything about him and I don't like his calling you Marian and telling you what he thinks I should do and we should do."

Quickly she crossed the room and once more she put her arms around me.

"We won't talk about it now," she said. "I want you to go in at once and lie down."

I started to protest, to say something. But then I stopped as I felt her hand touch the candy box I was still holding tightly.

"Oh," she exclaimed. "The candy. How in the world were you able to get me candy while you were in the hospital?"

I had to think quickly. I knew at once that it would be dangerous to say that I'd bought her the candy before I went to the hospital. The only time I would have been able to have done so would have been while Tom McKenny was driving us out to the island. And that car with Farrell and the other detective had been following us all the way.

Farrell was still alive and Farrell knew full well that we had not made any stops.

It meant that I would have to account for the candy some other way. Have to say that I'd sent out of the hospital room for it. And it was very obvious that if anything should ever come up, the nurse would say that I hadn't.

There was no way I *could* account for the box. And both Sam Fleckner and Lieutenant O'Malley had seen the box and knew I'd had it at the hospital.

"Marian," I said. "Please sit down. There is something I must say to you."

She looked at me for a moment, curiously, but then turned and went to the large red leather chair which I usually use myself.

"Yes."

"This is very serious, Marian," I said.

She started to get up.

"Wouldn't it be better for you to rest now," she said. "And then later, perhaps ..."

"I must talk with you now," I said quickly. "At once."

She sat back again in the seat. She wasn't relaxed.

"It's about this box. I must ask that you trust me completely and ask me no questions."

I could see the puzzled expression come to her face and I hurried on.

"I want you to say, if anyone should ask you, that you brought me this candy when you first came to the hospital on Friday to see me. Say that you brought it and left it."

She stared at me speechlessly for several seconds, her mouth half opened.

"But that's silly, Harold," she said at last. "I didn't bring you the candy. Goodness, I was so worried and everything when they called and told me about the robbery and your being injured ..."

"Of course you didn't bring it," I interrupted. "That's just the point. You didn't bring it, but I want you to say that you did."

"But why in the world do you want me to? ... Harold, what's this all about, anyway? What is there about this particular box of candy?" She started to get up.

I wanted to scream at her, to strike her. But I knew that I would have to control myself. It was essential that Marian should fall in with my plans. I couldn't take any chances.

Exerting supreme control, I started in again and explained to her. I told her that she must not question me and that sometime I would explain everything to her. But that she must do as I asked about the candy box.

Sometime later, when I got up and went into the bedroom to lie down, she had agreed to do what I asked. But she looked at me very oddly and I could tell that she probably thought the blow to my head had slightly addled my brains. She decided, in any case, to pamper me for the time being.

An hour later, when she left the apartment to go down the street and do a little shopping at the delicatessen, I quickly got out of bed and started to find a place to hide the money.

I had been able to get her out of the apartment by asking her to buy something for my dinner which I knew she didn't have in the house at the time.

Removing the bills from the candy box, I dug out my overnight one-suiter which I kept stored on the top shelf of the bedroom closet. I put the money inside and carefully locked the bag. And then I tore the candy box and the wrapper in which it came into tiny fragments and ran them down the toilet. I was all through and back in bed when Marian returned to the apartment.

II

At eight o'clock the telephone rang and Marian answered it. It was Fleckner and he wanted to talk with me. I refused to speak with him and had Marian say that I was asleep and that she didn't wish to disturb me. She returned to the living room to tell me that it was very important and I told her I still didn't wish to be disturbed.

She was on the phone for some time and was just returning after hanging up when it rang for the second time.

It was Detective Lieutenant O'Malley and he too wished to talk with me. I point blank refused to talk with anyone.

Once more Marian talked for some time. When she finally came back to the bedroom, I pretended I was actually asleep. But she insisted on sitting on the side of the bed. She shook me gently.

Marian wanted to talk with me about the robbery. She wanted to tell me what both Fleckner and O'Malley had called about. I forbade her to as much as mention the subject.

At eleven o'clock the doorbell rang. Marian was already in the bathroom, preparing for bed.

I was furious. Leaping out of bed, I put on a dressing gown and went to the door. I swung it open, fully expecting to see Sam Fleckner or possibly Lieutenant O'Malley himself. I was determined to tell whoever it was just what I thought about being constantly disturbed and pestered.

It was a uniformed patrolman. He spoke while I stood in the doorway, preparing what I had to say.

"Don't want you to worry, Mr. Wilkenson," he said, "but there's going to be a man stationed down in the hallway tonight. He's a detective and he'll be on watch."

My mouth opened in surprise.

"A detective!" I exclaimed. "What in the world for? On watch for what?"

"Couldn't say," the policeman said. "All I know is that I received word from the precinct that a detective was to be stationed here. Just thought I'd let you know."

He turned and left as I stood staring after him.

I was so furious that when I returned to the bedroom I said nothing at all to Marian.

It was eight-thirty the next morning when I read the papers and found out. I learned that Sam Fleckner and Lieutenant O'Malley had cooked up a story about me having seen and being able to identify the men who had murdered Torn McKenny and hijacked the payroll. I knew that Marian must have known about the plan—a plan to use me as bait for a trap to catch the killers.

And she had told me nothing at all of it.

Five minutes ago I had point-blank accused her of as much.

The only answer she had given was that she had tried to tell me about it the night before and that I had not let her speak.

No wonder they had stationed a detective to watch downstairs.

I wondered what Roy and Katz would think after they read that story in the morning papers. I wondered how they'd feel about the five thousand dollars they had spent for my silence.

It was when Marian had sarcastically asked me if I was afraid and if I didn't want to help find Tom McKenny's killers that I had completely lost my temper. That's when I struck her in the face.

And now she was in the bedroom crying and I was sitting waiting for Lieutenant O'Malley to make an appearance.

Lieutenant O'Malley—yes, and Sam Fleckner himself as well—they were as evil as the men who murdered Tom McKenny. They were ready to sacrifice my life in their search for vengeance. My life—the life of an innocent man!

III

Well, Marian finally seems to have come to her senses. I am the last person in the world to believe in violence, but I must say that the scene we had this morning was not without its ultimate benefit.

The thought of striking a woman—in fact physical violence in any form—has always been extremely repulsive to me. Perhaps I have been wrong. All I can say is that since losing my temper and hitting her, Marian's attitude has certainly changed for the better.

I was alone in the room when Lieutenant O'Malley arrived and I wasted no time in letting him know exactly what I thought. He had, of course, understood at once that I was burning with fury at his underhanded tactics.

The man actually had the audacity to attempt putting me on the defensive.

"You want to help, don't you?" he'd asked. "You want to see this thing cleared up and the men who shot you and killed McKenny brought to justice?"

I stared him coldly in the face when I answered.

"Not," I said, "at the cost of my own life. Not if I have to put myself in further jeopardy. Understand me clearly. I feel that it is the duty of the police to solve the crime; I feel that if the police had been alert, such a crime would never have happened in the first place. And I certainly see no reason for you to endanger my life in order to make up for your own lack of ability."

Marian must have entered the room without my hearing her and listened while I was talking. I became aware of her presence when her voice interrupted.

"My husband is right," she said. "He has gone through enough. He wasn't hired as a payroll messenger and it is not a part of his job to risk his life. I said it last night and I will say it again. I don't think you have any right to give the impression that he would be able to identify the bandits."

O'Malley turned to her at once. I could see that he was embarrassed.

"The police will see that he is not molested," he said. "We will ..."

"The police were unable to protect Mr. McKenny," I cut in quickly. "The police were not able to keep me from being attacked ..."

"That is hardly fair, Mr. Wilkenson," O'Malley interrupted. "We may not be able to anticipate a crime, but certainly we are able to prevent one when we know it might take place."

Marian started to say something, but I cut her off.

"I'll handle this," I told her. "The fact remains you have released a story to the newspapers which is not true. You have publicly stated that I could identify the criminals. Well, I can't. And I intend to inform the press ..."

The harsh ring of the doorbell interrupted me and O'Malley stepped lightly across the room to open the door. Sam Fleckner entered.

I think it was something about the way he was dressed—a dark Oxford-gray suit, white linen and black tie, with black highly polished shoes and black silk socks—which inspired the sudden idea which came to me.

It is amazing the number of thoughts which are able to pass through a man's mind in less than the fraction of a minute, the capacity of a man's mind to put them together and to come up with a plan fully formed and logical.

Looking at Sam, I realized at once what there was which struck an odd note in his appearance. He was always a very neat person in his dress and showed unusually good taste in his selection of clothes. But I knew at once that the ensemble he had selected for this day was something special. He was ready to attend the funeral services for Tom McKenny.

At the same time my mind was analyzing a completely separate collection of thoughts.

I knew that nothing I could do now would be of any help as far as negating the vicious story which Lieutenant O'Malley had released to the press. I might deny the story and say that I hadn't actually recognized those men in the car who had shot me down and killed McKenny, but what good would it do? What possible good? Would Roy Anders and his partner, Katz, believe my statement? I doubted it very much.

There was only one possible way I could convince them that I hadn't talked to the police, that I hadn't attempted to double-cross them. That was by personally making a contact with them.

To do so I must have freedom of movement.

I must have freedom to find them before they found me.

Quickly I spoke.

"The damage is done," I said. "I am referring," I went on, turning to Fleckner in order to bring him up to date, "referring to the fact the police have put my life in jeopardy. Understand me—I do want to see these criminals captured. I want to help in any way I can. But I don't want to be killed doing it.

"In any case, what has been done has been done. There is only one further thing which I can see to do. I must not be asked to go out in public until such a time as these men have been apprehended. The police must keep a constant guard on this house. I would like to go to the funeral this morning, for instance, but I think to do so would be foolhardy. I am sure that Marian's being present will serve the purpose just as well as though we were both to go."

"I'll stay here with you Harold," Marian said quickly.

"No," I said, "I would much prefer that you go. I think it is only proper."

"In that case," Lieutenant O'Malley said, "I'll be glad to have one of our men come up and stay with you."

"That won't be necessary. I would much prefer to be alone. Keep a man in front of the house if you like. But I will be all right here so long as no strangers are permitted to enter the building."

Twenty minutes later, as I stood beside the front window and looked down into the street, watching Sam Fleckner help my wife into his car, I was thinking of only one thing. I was thinking about how I would go about finding a slender, golden girl with flaming hair and azure eyes.

IV

Contacting Howie, getting in touch with him, was a lot easier than I had thought it would be. But getting him to meet me was something else.

I knew that Howie probably didn't come to work until sometime in the afternoons as he was on duty fairly late in the evenings. But I called the bar and grill anyway. It was a disadvantage not knowing his last name and I assumed, correctly, that Howie was a contraction of Howard, his given name.

I didn't hesitate when a man's voice answered the phone.

"This is Pendergast," I said, my own voice terse and businesslike. "Sergeant Pendergast of the Fourteenth Precinct. Like to talk to Howie."

"Howie isn't here."

"Didn't expect he would be," I said. "Let me have his home phone number."

The voice at the other end hesitated.

"Or you can have him call me back at the station," I said. It worked. He gave me the number.

"You can get him up until one-thirty."

I thanked him and hung up.

I called the number at once, before the man at the bar had a chance to get hold of Howie.

Howie answered on the first ring and I recognized his voice at once. I told him who was calling and it took him several moments to get the idea through his head. Once he understood it was me on the other end of the wire, his voice assumed at once a sort of guarded and yet curious note.

"Read you got shot up a little in that stickup, Mr. Wilkenson," he said. "How are you?"

"Fine," I said. "I'm fine. It was only a surface wound."

He waited for me to go on, merely mumbling "fine" a couple of more times.

"The fact is," I said, "I'm home resting up. Have to stay around the house for a few days."

"Yes?"

"Yes. The trouble is, though, that I'd like very much to see you."

"To see me?" His voice was suddenly cautious.

"Yes. You see, I have to ask you about something and I'm unable to leave the house at present. I'd like ..."

"Go ahead and ask," Howie said. He no longer sounded friendly.

"Well," I stumbled for a moment, finding it difficult to explain. I could tell that he was highly suspicious. And I guess by now he was beginning to wonder how I'd found his telephone number.

"The fact is," I went on, "I don't want to talk about this over the telephone. I was wondering if you wouldn't be kind enough to stop by at my apartment for a few minutes."

"Stop by at your place?"

"Yes, you see ..."

"Why don't you come by the bar tonight?"

I told him again that I wasn't able to leave the house for a few days. He kept on demurring for a few more minutes and then at last he grudgingly asked me if I was alone.

I told him that I was.

"Well," he said at last, "I guess I can do it all right. Only thing is, I haven't had my breakfast yet. Not dressed."

I gave him my address and said that I'd be alone for the next two hours. He said at last that he'd try and make it. I was having a cup of coffee myself, some hour and ten minutes later, when the knock came on the door. I put the cup down at once and went to answer it.

I didn't open the door, however.

"Who is it?" I asked.

"Detective Penelli," a muffled voice answered through the paneled wood. "May I see you for a moment, Mr. Wilkenson?"

Cautiously I opened the door a couple of inches, keeping the burglar chain on.

"Fellow here says he's a friend of yours," the detective said. "Mr. McCracken. Know him?"

I started to say no, to say that I'd never even heard of a McCracken, and then just as I opened my mouth to speak I was able to make out the dim figure of the man standing behind and to one side of the detective. It was Howie.

"Yes—yes," I said. "Yes, I know him. You may let him in, please." I opened the door all the way.

"Just wanted to be sure, Mr. Wilkenson," the detective said, smiling slightly. Howie pushed past him and entered the apartment. He didn't look happy.

I thanked the man and closed the door.

"What the hell is this anyway?" Howie asked. "Why, you'd think ..."

I apologized to him at once. I explained that the police were just taking normal precautions.

"Yeah, I know," Howie said. "Used to be a cop myself. Guess you must have tagged those guys that knocked off the payroll."

I shook my head. I explained that I really hadn't seen the men at all, but that the police said I did in the hopes of developing a lead. The news didn't seem to surprise Howie at all.

He stood there in the center of the living room, not bothering to take off his hat. He refused a cup of coffee when I offered him one. I could see that he was both uneasy and slightly annoyed. I knew I'd better start right in, before he decided to leave.

"This is going to sound very funny," I said. "But the fact is, I want you to help me if you can."

"Help you?"

"Yes. You see, it's like this. I saw someone in your tavern the other day. Someone I'd like to get a hold of. The only trouble is, I don't happen to know the name."

He looked at me coldly for a moment or so.

"Yeah? Would this someone have anything to do with that stickup you were in?"

"No." I went on to reassure him on this point. "The thing is, however," I said, "that this someone is a girl. I, well ..."

His expression didn't change, but I detected sudden interest.

"Well, it's like this. The girl fascinated me. I want to find out who she is."

For several seconds he stared at me. Then he laughed and it wasn't a pleasant laugh.

"Why?"

"Because," I said. "Just because I want to find out. And I thought that possibly you might be willing to help me."

He sat down then.

"Jesus Christ," he said. "You get me to come all the way up here to find out who some broad is? What the hell is this anyway? Are you trying to kid me, Mr. Wilkenson?" He had me over a barrel and I knew it. It was then I got my brilliant idea.

"Excuse me just a moment," I said.

I went into the bedroom and closed the door. When I returned a couple of minutes later, I held two hundred dollars in fifties in my hand. I had remembered something about Howie. He'd been on the police force and been ousted as a result of some scandal or other. Scandals usually involve money.

I held out the money.

He didn't offer to take it.

"Maybe I can't help you," he said. "Maybe I don't know who the girl is."

"Take the money anyway," I said. "For your trouble in coming up here, even if you can't help me."

He hesitated a second or two longer and then took the bills. Unblushingly he counted them and then neatly folded them and put them into his inside breast coat pocket.

"The girl," I said, "drives a silver Buick convertible. She has blonde hair, worn long, and very blue eyes, almost green. She was in the bar Monday night, sitting in the booth behind the one in which I was sitting, watching the ball game. She ..."

But I knew that I didn't have to go any further. I knew that Howie remembered—remembered and knew to whom I was referring. I waited for him to speak.

For a long time he said nothing. I began to fear that he wasn't going to say anything. He reached into his pocket and took out the bills. Carefully he recounted them.

"And supposing I don't remember and don't know?"

"I was hoping you would remember and would know," I said. "But you may keep the money anyway."

He nodded and put the bills back.

"I hope you are not going to make a fool out of yourself, Mr. Wilkenson," he said at last. He turned half toward the door and spoke out of the side of his mouth.

"Sari," he said. "Don't know her other name. But the last time I heard, she was hatcheck girl down at the Middleton House. In the cocktail lounge."

I started to thank him but he cut me off.

"She was also," he said, speaking very softly, "Roy Anders' private property. I don't want to be offensive, Mr. Wilkenson, but Roy Anders eats guys like you for breakfast."

And then he was gone.

V

I suddenly found myself in a very ridiculous position. Lieutenant O'Malley had arranged things so that no one could get in to see me, or at least, no one I didn't want to see. On the other hand, it was equally impossible for me to get out to see someone whom I might not want the police to see. Undoubtedly I would be able to come and go as I wished, but by the same token, I would be followed by my "bodyguard."

The thought had been comforting—up until the point where I had learned the name of the girl and decided to see her. That would be one rendezvous during which I would certainly not want to be accompanied by a police officer.

But I worked it out. Sometimes I think I must have a natural criminal mind. Either that or the police are not quite as bright as they are cracked up to be.

I waited until two o'clock. I would have waited even longer but I was afraid that Marian would be returning and then getting away would present an additional problem. And so, just before two, I dashed off a hurried note to Marian, telling her that I was going out for a while and not to worry. I left it stuck in the corner of the mirror, opposite the entranceway, where she couldn't possibly miss it.

By this time I had determined that Penelli, my guard, was stationed downstairs in the hallway, where he was able to observe both the front door as well as the rear door which led out to the courtyard.

I put on a conservative business suit, a white shirt and a striped tie. I carried a light felt hat and in my breast pocket was a pair of dark sunglasses.

Then I went to the front window and opened it a few inches. In my hands I had three electric light bulbs. I waited until the street was completely deserted. And then I tossed first one bulb down to the cement sidewalk and a second later, the second two bulbs. They sounded like pistol shots as they burst.

I didn't wait. I knew what would happen.

When I reached the hallway downstairs, it was deserted. Through the glass front door I could see the figure of Penelli, obviously looking up and down the street. A moment later and I was out the rear door of the house. I went quickly through the small courtyard and it took me but a moment to vault the six-foot fence. I was in the courtyard of the apartment house backing up to our own place, a yard I had frequently observed from out of my own rear window. Fortunately the door leading into the ground floor of the building was open. Another moment and I was through the lobby walking casually down East Fifty-third Street.

I caught the first passing taxi.

I told the driver to take me to the Middleton House. He knew the address, on East Fortieth Street, just off Park Avenue.

As the car weaved its way through the heavy midtown traffic, I sat back with a sense of satisfaction. I seemed to have a positive knack for this sort of thing. I even forgot to be frightened and worried—at least for the moment.

Chapter 5

Several times during our marriage, Marian has told me that I really don't understand women. She has, in fact, as much as hinted that I don't have the normal man's attitude toward sex or toward females in general. I have always felt that this attitude on Marian's part is an indication of a subtle weakness in her own character. Or, at worse, possibly a throwback to some generic lack of morality in her family line.

It is quite true that my standards are high, even perhaps a little old-fashioned. Having succumbed twice to temptation in my youth and having found those experiences both disenchanting as well as unrewarding, I have a natural disinclination to repeat the experiences. As far as my marital arrangement itself is concerned, I feel very strongly that sex in a marriage relationship can be a highly overrated factor.

Don't misunderstand me. Marian is an attractive woman; I am sure that other men find her so. She is well built, is pretty in the popular sense of the phrase and has always shown an over willingness to cooperate. In coldly analyzing my relationships with my wife, I must admit frankly that I have never been in love with her in the more sensational meaning of that elusive phrase.

Certainly we have found a lot in common; we come from the same sort of backgrounds and have always liked pretty much the same things and the same people. I have felt that, whereas I have never experienced the overpowering sexual urges which seem to drive so many other men, my attitude toward my wife is healthy and normal and on a cultural basis which complements the general tone of my personality.

I feel confident that there has never been any other man in Marian's life and, up until the time when Sam Fleckner began interfering in our affairs, it was inconceivable that Marian didn't give to me her complete loyalty and understanding.

Certainly, since the day of our wedding, I have never looked at another woman with anything but the most casual interest. Certainly I have never felt the slightest physical desire for another woman.

I have taken time to establish these facts for a definite and important reason. The reason has to do with Sari Mizner. That was her name—Sari Mizner.

As the taxi in which I was riding slowly progressed toward the Middleton House I was suddenly aware of a very strange and shocking thing.

This golden girl with the azure eyes whom I was going to see had affected me in a way in which no other woman I had ever met had touched me.

Yes, it is true. The realization was swift and sudden. From the very moment I had first seen her sitting in the silver convertible in front of Howie's saloon, she had done something to me. I had to admit it.

True enough, I was trying to find her in order to get word to the others that I was on their side and that I hadn't double-crossed them. It was essential that I make the contact through the girl. I certainly had reason enough to want to find her.

But there was something else. Some odd, strange sense of excitement and expectancy which drove the blood swiftly through my veins and brought the breath sharp and fast into my throat. That gave me a feeling of exhilaration, the like of which I had never before experienced.

The really amazing part of the whole thing was that even as I sat back in the taxi and thought of the girl, a separate part of my mind kept returning to my wife, Marian. And this part of my mind was playing a strange and evil trick on me. I thought of Marian and I felt a completely foreign lustful passion for her. I thought of her with strange and unfamiliar images of desire. The very ideas which were swiftly passing through my mind left me with a sense which was a contradictory combination of uncontrollable passion and at the same time a sense of utter revulsion.

II

You would really have to know New York to understand the Middleton House. It is a small residential hotel in the Murray Hill section, peculiar to that city. At once respectable and rather exclusive, the Middleton has, at the same time, a peculiarity fugitive air of licentiousness. It is a subtle thing and difficult to explain. Understand, the place, though small by comparison to the large commercial hostelries of the metropolis, is well appointed and certainly, on the surface, well managed and expensive in both appointments and atmosphere.

Perhaps it is that fact that the Middleton, like so many of those midtown residential hotels, had installed a cocktail lounge. There was no entertainment in the accepted terms of the phrase, but there was subdued piped-in music and in the late afternoons and evenings a piano player came in and played rather risqué songs from old Noël Coward scores.

It was one of the hotels which appears inhabited by the upper crust of celebrities, but there always seem to be too many really beautiful girls in the bar and cocktail room. Too-well-dressed men with slick hair and over-pressed clothes found the leisure to spend their afternoons in the place. Certainly all of them cannot be residents.

Possibly I am naive and certainly I have not had a great deal of experience with such things, but it seemed to me that the Middleton House permitted itself to be used as a sort of rendezvous for people whose motives in meeting each other certainly couldn't stand the light of publicity.

The cocktail lounge had not opened when I arrived and I had no desire to be seen idling in public places. On a sudden impulse I decided to check into the establishment.

I went over to the desk and asked if I might have a single room and bath. The clerk had all of the quiet dignity in appearance of a bank vice president. He explained, however, that they had very few rooms allocated for transient trade and that he was filled up. As I was turning away, embarrassed, he spoke again.

"I do have," he said, "one very small room with an inside exposure, if that would be satisfactory for the time being. How long are you planning to stay, sir?"

Up until that very moment I had thought only of taking a room for a few hours. But on a sudden whim, I said, "Why, for possibly a week or ten days. My luggage is checked in at the airport and will arrive later."

He offered to show me the room, but I told him that that wouldn't be necessary. I was a little surprised when he failed to ask me to pay in advance. But he didn't; he merely pushed a card over for me to sign. I'll never know why I did it, but the name I signed was Sam Fleckner. I knew of course, better than to sign my own name. But why I should have chosen Fleckner's I simply cannot say. In any case, that was the name I used.

Once upstairs and in the very small, but well-furnished room, I was considerably shocked to see by the card attached to the back of the door that the rent was fifteen dollars a day. It was a high price for the accommodations. The thought struck me that there was probably a reason for the stiff tariff. The clerk had not been surprised at my lack of luggage; he would undoubtedly not be surprised if I were to have visitors—female visitors.

I don't know why, but the idea gave me a peculiar thrill.

The desk clerk told me the cocktail lounge opened at four o'clock and so I waited until four-thirty until I put in the call. Then, I picked up the receiver and asked if I could be connected with the checkroom. A girl's voice answered almost at once. I should like to say I recognized her voice, but I am afraid that all voices sound pretty much the same to me over the telephone, at least until I get to really know their owners.

"This is the checkroom."

"Is this Sari?" I asked.

For a moment there was a silence and then the girl spoke again.

"Who's calling please?" It was very noncommittal.

"The man who received the two-pound box of candy a couple of days ago in the hospital. Is this Sari?"

I could almost hear the gasp at the other end of the wire. She hesitated for several moments before speaking.

"It could be Sari."

"If you are Sari," I said, "I want you to come to Room 1002. You will have to be here within three minutes or else I will have left."

I didn't want her making any telephone calls. I didn't want her to have an opportunity to get in touch with those others before I saw her.

Again there was a silence for several long minutes at the end of the wire. I didn't think she was going to answer at all, but at last she did. Her voice was very low and guarded.

"I am on duty," she said. "I won't be able to get away—not for at least ten minutes."

"I will be here for exactly three minutes—no more." I was very precise—definite.

She hung up the receiver without saying another thing.

I was looking at my wrist watch, sitting in the chair facing the door to the hallway, which I had left slightly ajar.

She arrived in exactly one minute and four seconds.

I guess I had expected some sort of uniform. In any case I was surprised and just a little shocked at her appearance. She slid into the room without knocking.

I guess you would call it some sort of afternoon tea frock. It was strapless and crossed the front of her body very low on her breasts so that the dark inviting hollow between them was deep and seductive. Her back was naked to the waist. She had soft, almost translucent skin, peach tinted and without the slightest blemish or imperfection. She wore a minimum of makeup and actually needed none. The long dark lashes, which served to give her startling eyes that smudged look, had to be natural. Her hair was simple and unaffected but for a trace of short bangs across her wide forehead.

She stood slightly less than five feet three and she had the most beautiful figure I have ever seen. She was a gangster's girl and I knew it. She was probably his kept woman. She patronized Third Avenue saloons and she worked as a hat check girl in a rather dubious hotel. And yet, with it all, she seemed as fresh as a young girl just out of Vassar and there was an air of culture and refinement about her. Even her voice, when she spoke, was subdued and without accent.

But her eyes were anything but friendly as she stood there just inside the still opened door.

"Come in," I said, "and please shut the door."

She hesitated for only a moment, her eyes making a quiet search of the room. And then she stepped forward and closed the door behind herself.

"You'll do all the talking," she said. She made no move to sit down.

"You remember me?" I said, making a question out of it.

She said nothing and there was no expression on her face. It suddenly occurred to me that she may have suspected a police plant of some sort. I tried to reassure her.

"Please," I said. "We are completely alone. No one knows I am here. No one at all. I have not registered under my own name."

She still made no move, just stood there looking at me.

"I have gotten in touch with you," I said, "for a very important reason. I want you to take a message to someone for me."

I waited again for her to say something, but she remained silent.

"You can talk, can't you," I said.

"You will do all of the talking," she said then.

"As you wish. I want you to see a certain man, or possibly two or three men. I want you to tell them that the story the police have given out, the story about me being able to identify certain people who were involved in something which took place this last week out on Long Island, is a complete lie. That I have told the police nothing of the sort. That I haven't the faintest idea what happened. That from the very first, until I recovered in the hospital, I was unconscious."

I stopped, waited again for her to speak or for some sign that she was following me.

"Go on," she said at last.

"Tell them," I said, "that I received the candy and that I am duly grateful."

She did a surprising thing then. She walked across the room and opened the bathroom door. She looked into the closet, which was vacant of clothes. She looked around the telephone and behind several pictures. She was still suspicious; she was seeking for a hidden microphone.

She came back at last and this time she sat on the couch opposite me. She placed her pocketbook on the small coffee table between us. It was one of those large, open types. Along with a small packet of Kleenex, a wallet, a compact, lipstick, and various unidentifiable objects I noticed the butt of a small gun. It looked like a .25 automatic but I was not sure. I am not very familiar with firearms. Her expression was still noncommittal, but this time there was a slightly more friendly quality in her rather husky voice when she spoke.

"I haven't, of course, the slightest idea of what you are talking about," she said. "But go right ahead, if you wish."

"There is no one here, Sari," I said. The sound of her name on my

tongue gave me a very odd thrill. "No one here and no hidden
microphones. Don't you understand? I am trying to cooperate. I am
not trying to trap anyone; I am trying to protect people."

"How do you know my name?"

For a moment it occurred to me to lie to her. But as quickly as the
thought came to me, I changed my mind. I would be utterly frank. It
was the only thing to do. I must convince her, and through her those
others, that I was being completely honest. I could take no possible
chance of increasing their suspicions. I told her about calling Howie.

At last she stood up.

"I have to get back downstairs," she said.

I also stood up.

"But will you do as I ask? Will you see ..."

She turned to me and for the first time she smiled. "Listen," she said.
"I haven't the faintest idea of what you have been talking about. I
don't know who you are and I've never seen you before."

I knew a moment of panic then and I started to protest; but she was
swift to interrupt me.

"However," she said, "you seem like a nice man and I wouldn't
want you to worry. Perhaps, just perhaps, if you would care to be in
the cocktail room around eleven this evening, I might be able to see
you for a moment. So that you wouldn't worry, of course."

And then she was gone.

III

Twenty minutes after the girl had left my room, I also was out of it
and in a department store on West Forty-second Street. I purchased
an inexpensive leather suitcase and had the initials "SF" stamped on
it. I then went into the men's department and bought a pair of
summer slacks, three shirts and some underwear and socks. From the
department store I went to a nearby messenger service and arranged
to have the bag sent to my room at the Middleton House.

And then I returned home.

I must say that Lieutenant O'Malley is a dangerously inquisitive
and insolent man, although I do not have much consideration for his
ability as a detective.

It seems that he discovered my absence from the apartment almost
the moment he himself returned to the place, accompanied by Marian
and Sam Fleckner. For some reason which I am unable to fathom, he
went to Tom McKenny's funeral with them.

The moment they returned, and even before Marian was upstairs and reading the note I had left for her, O'Malley talked with Detective Penelli, whom I had outwitted in leaving the apartment. Penelli told him the story about the light bulbs exploding on the sidewalk and apparently O'Malley saw through the thing at once. He rushed upstairs and immediately verified his suspicion that I had left.

The three of them were sitting in the living room, waiting, when I returned. Penelli himself met me in the lower hallway. He looked at me reproachfully, but said nothing.

Lieutenant O'Malley's opening remark was unfortunate.

"Just where in the hell have you been?" he snapped as I opened the door.

"We were worried about you, dear," Marian said quickly.

I swung to the police officer.

"I dislike your tone," I said. "Am I under arrest or something? Just what ..."

Fleckner saw fit to interfere at this point.

"Take it easy, old man," he said. "The Lieutenant only has your best interests at heart."

"Yes?" I was sarcastic. "If you people have my best interests at heart, you'd hardly be putting me in this dangerous position."

Marian quickly got to her feet. She suggested a drink and then, without waiting for an answer, went into the kitchen to prepare it.

"You shouldn't be walking around without a bodyguard," O'Malley said. He still spoke in that deceptively soft, sympathetic voice. But it no longer fooled me. The man was a bundle of hypocrisy under his cloak of gentle understanding.

"My life is my own," I said. "In fact"—and it was here I had my sudden inspiration—"in fact, I have decided that the safest thing I could possibly do would be to go away for a few days. To take a short vacation and just disappear until you either collar the criminals or this thing blows over."

Marian was re-entering the room and she heard the last of my remark.

"We could go together," she said. "Perhaps—that is of course if it is all right with Mr. Fleckner if you take the time off—perhaps we could take a short cruise up to the Cape."

Sam was quick to reassure us that it would be all right.

I must say that is the least he could have offered after what I had been through in his firm's services.

The detective cut in at once.

"A very bad idea," he said. "I don't think you should be leaving town just at this time. I think it would be much better if you stayed where we can keep an eye on you."

I turned to him, furious.

"An eye on me indeed! Good Lord, I had no trouble at all in getting away from you while your man was supposedly keeping an eye on me this morning. And by the same token, I can safely assume that no one would have a great deal of trouble getting to me. I think I also may safely assume that I can probably do a better job of protecting myself than the police can do."

Marian started to say something but I kept on.

"And another thing. I don't wish to put my wife into jeopardy. I want her to stay here while I am gone. You might leave your men here to be sure that she at least is safe."

They argued with me, all three of them. But I was adamant. I insisted on having my own way. And this is how it happened, that at six o'clock that evening, I was at the airport, stepping into a plane bound for Montreal. I had been taken to the station by Lieutenant O'Malley himself.

I carried only my overnight bag and a change of clothes and my toilet articles. I had packed the bag myself. Packed it—careful not to disturb the large envelope containing the fifty-dollar bills.

It's the damnedest thing about O'Malley. At times he seems absolutely psychic. And he has the memory of an elephant. All the way out to the airport he bombarded me with a series of questions. Once I had convinced him that I wasn't even sure myself where I was going or where I planned to stay, he made me reassure him that I would be in contact with him at all times. And then he took to asking a lot of irrelevant questions about my personal life and habits. I tried to avoid the conversation, tried to maintain a silence, but it was almost impossible. He wanted to know all sorts of things, impertinent things such as how long I had been married and how I liked my job. He even asked me if I was happy with my wife. There was no shutting the man up.

I think it was right after I had coldly informed him that Marian and I were very happy together, if it was any of his business, that he made the remark which upset me so much.

"Yes," he said, "I imagine that you must be. I thought so when I saw that you had bought a box of candy for her while you were still in the hospital."

The remark, coming as it did, almost threw me. Good God, the man simply couldn't have known about that box; couldn't possibly have guessed its significance. But he did mention it.

I'm afraid I fumbled a little, but at last I explained to him that the candy had been brought by Marian *for* me.

"Odd I didn't notice that she had it with her when she came to the hospital," he said, musingly.

"Odd?" I stared at him. "Why odd? Do you notice everything about everyone?"

He smiled at me.

"Why yes. I do," he said.

He stayed at my side even after I found my seat on the plane and right up until the pilot began to warm up the engines.

I thought about him during the entire trip to Montreal. Certainly he could not suspect me of being involved in the robbery. Certainly he couldn't believe that I had anything to conceal or was in any way connected. And yet he certainly had seemed unduly curious.

I realized that I would have to be very, very careful.

IV

I had less than a twenty-minute wait in Montreal before the plane returning to New York was ready to take off. I went no further than the coffee shop in the waiting room after buying my ticket back to Manhattan.

One rather strange thing took place, however, while I was sitting there reading a late edition of the local paper. A tall, extremely slender man in a black suit and wearing a derby, which was shockingly out of place in the heat of the summer evening, took the stool beside me, although there were a number of other vacant places at the counter. I thought that he was looking at me rather curiously and I turned and stared at him for a moment. He smiled.

"Smooth trip up?" he said, his voice very friendly.

"Quite," I said, turning back at once to the newspaper.

"New York's pretty hot these days," he said, pursuing the one-sided conversation.

I tried to ignore him, but there was something a little frightening about the man. It was almost as though he were trying to establish an acquaintanceship.

For a brief moment I wondered if he could possibly be connected with Katz or Roy Anders. I couldn't remember him as having been on the plane and he certainly was not a New Yorker from the tone of his voice and diction. But the man was amazingly persistent. He wanted to know if I planned to stay in Montreal and he completely ignored the fact I refused to answer him or give him the slightest heed.

I didn't finish my coffee. Instead, I paid my check and went out to the gate to await the take-off of the plane. For a moment I thought he was going to follow me, but what he actually did was pay his own check and trail my steps through the waiting room and then stand nearby and watch as I finally climbed aboard.

He made me very nervous.

All of this cloak and dagger sort of thing gave me a very strange feeling while I was flying back to New York. In a way, I suppose the sensation was somewhat similar to that which a criminal must undergo. Not, understand, that I considered myself criminal in any possible sense of the word.

But I had very deliberately deceived the police, I had lied to my wife and I had lied to the head of my firm. I had with me almost five thousand dollars, which, although I felt I had justly earned, I must admit was really not mine in the full legal sense of the phrase. On the other hand, the money had been given me, unsolicited.

I was flying back to New York to go to a hotel where I had checked in under an assumed name. Whether this is illegal or not, I don't really know.

But the thing which gave me the biggest thrill was the fact that I was going there with a definite plan of meeting a very beautiful and glamorous girl. A girl who very definitely did have criminal connections.

I think it was during this plane ride south that certain basic changes in my character began to take place. For a time I tried to think of Marian, but every time my mind dwelt on the subject, I knew only a sense of annoyance. Yes, even bitterness. I began to realize that Marian suffered very definite defects in her character.

And then my mind would go to the girl I was to meet that night. A very lovely girl and a provocative girl. I found it hard to believe that she could really be "Anders' girl," as Howie had referred to her. How in the world could a girl like Sari go for a crude, brutal sort of man like Anders must be? What could she see in him? What could he possibly have to offer her?

And, in fact, was she really his girl after all? Wasn't it just possible that Howie had merely leaped to a conclusion? Or, again, wasn't it just possible that she herself was entrapped in some relationship which she found actually distasteful?

I would soon know.

Yes, I would know.

It was very intoxicating. I had five thousand dollars, more money than I had ever before possessed at one time. I had freedom. I had a hotel room waiting for me and a tentative date with a lovely girl.

I also had a vague feeling of fear.

I wondered if it were possible that she was merely luring me to some rendezvous which would put me at the mercy of the man Anders and his partners in crime. For a moment I thought vaguely of trying to buy a gun to protect myself if necessary. But quickly I shrugged the idea off. I would be no match for those others in a conflict of violence. No, I must depend upon my superior intelligence.

At one point it occurred to me not to see the girl at all. To return home to Marian and the protection which the law might afford.

But once again I thought of the girl Sari.

At twenty minutes to eleven I was back in Room 1002 in the Middleton House. Wrapped up and unopened, in the bathroom, were two bottles of Scotch whiskey and two bottles of soda. The suitcase I had sent to the hotel that afternoon, as well as my other suitcase, were in the closet. In my wallet were the hundred-dollar bills, or at least a number of them. The rest were in the suitcase.

I went down to the cocktail lounge.

I carried my hat. I wanted an excuse to stop at the checkroom.

V

She was alone. The minute I saw her and handed her my hat, I knew something had happened. She was a different girl. Radiant. Her eyes sparkled and her face was smiling and friendly and there was something intimate and lovely about her. Even the husky voice was softer and it was friendly and warm. She seemed very glad to see me.

The cloakroom was a small, oblong space, just outside of the barroom proper. There were very few hats hanging on the hooks, but there was a small, gray miniature poodle standing on the counter. She held one hand on its collar.

"Spooky," she said. "One of my customers checked him in." She smiled and patted the dog affectionately.

"I'd like to trade places with him."

I said the words and even as they left my lips I felt a deep sense of embarrassment. It was the last thing in the world I had intended to say. Not the sort of remark I have ever been guilty of making. Much to my surprise she laughed. She looked at me and laughed.

"I'm afraid the management wouldn't approve," she said. "However"—she hesitated a moment and seemed to look around to insure that she wasn't being overheard—"I'll be off in half an hour. Go in and have a couple of drinks and I'll see you then."

I nodded.

"Are you still upstairs?" she asked.

Again I nodded.

"I'll be up around a quarter to twelve."

I was so startled at both her words and the change in her manner that I started to turn away, my hat still in my and.

She reached over and took my sleeve and leaned toward me.

"Better go in and have a drink. It'll look more natural." She took my hat and told me I wouldn't need a check. So I entered the cocktail lounge and found a seat at a small table under a dim purplish light at the side of the room. I told the waiter to bring me a Scotch and soda. I asked if they served anything to eat and I was told that the kitchen was closed. I wasn't really hungry, although I had missed dinner. I was too excited to be hungry.

I was back upstairs in little less than half an hour. I had ordered two drinks and not finished the last one. In what was almost a frenzy to return, I had even forgotten to retrieve my hat, possibly because, as I passed by the cloakroom, I noticed that Sari was no longer behind the counter.

At once I called downstairs and asked that some cracked ice and glasses be sent up. Like magic, the bellboy arrived with the order; he had no more than left them when the second knock came on my door. I crossed the room and opened it.

She had thrown a powder-blue silk scarf over her shoulders and she was carrying a snakeskin bag under one arm. I wondered if she had the small gun in it. In her hand was my hat. She smiled, entered and laid the hat on the bed.

"You are Harold Wilkenson," she said, "and so I will call you Hal. I'm Sari Mizner and you may call me Sari. My friends do."

It was peculiar, her use of that nickname, Hal. I had always somehow resented it when Marian used the name, although she used it only during our most intimate moments together. But coming from this girl's lips, I found it very appealing. I must admit, however, that I blushed.

"If that's cracked ice," she said, looking over at the silver bucket which had been placed on the dresser, "and you have anything to go with it, I'd appreciate a drink."

She walked over to the small hotel radio set buried in the wall, took a quarter from her bag and put it in the slot. She twisted the dials until she found a jazz program and turned the volume low. She turned and watched me as I mixed two Scotch and sodas.

"Were you able to get in touch ..." I began, handing her one of the glasses.

Quickly she raised her hand, touching my lips.

"We are not going to talk about that," she said. "I'll tell you only one thing and then don't ask me any questions. None at all. Not if you want me to stay."

"I want you to stay very much," I said.

"All right. I can only tell you that you have nothing to worry about. Nothing at all—just so long as you were telling me the truth."

In spite of myself, I started to ask her if she had seen those others, but she silenced me at once. Reaching out, she took one of the glasses from my hand and then walked over and sat on the couch, which was, really, merely the bed made up to resemble a couch. I started for the single large upholstered chair, but she indicated with her hand that she wanted me to sit next to her.

"I'm tired," she said, the moment I sat down. "For a few minutes, can't we just sit here? Listen to the music. Then you can make me another drink."

It only took about three minutes before she was ready for the second drink. I got up to mix it and she told me to take my time and finish my own first. I did.

She watched as I poured the Scotch into the glasses for the second drink and, as I reached for the soda, she quickly stood up and took the Scotch bottle from my hand.

"Have to watch my weight," she said. "So I go easy on the soda." She splashed about two more ounces of liquor into each glass.

VI

I don't think I'll ever take another drink.

My head is splitting wide open, I have trouble focusing my eyes even now and I have spent the last hour hanging over the toilet bowl and throwing up. Nothing comes out of my mouth but a sort of greenish-black bile.

This must be what they mean when they talk about really first-class hangover. I've never been so sick in my life. I can't believe that it was

only the liquor. Undoubtedly the wound in my head has something
to do with it. That, combined with my general state of high nervous
tension and my lack of regular meals these last few days.

Not that I didn't get drunk. Disgustingly, mawkishly, stupidly
drunk, more drunk than I have ever been in my life. The horrible thing
is not so much the physical pain which I am suffering; it is the fact
that for the first time in my life I can't remember what happened.

A lot I can remember and perhaps, the way I feel about some of the
things I did and said, it is better in a way that there are certain
episodes of last night which have faded out forever.

I have just looked into the mirror and my mouth is smeared blood
red with lipstick. There are stains on my neck and on my linen. My
eyes are charred holes in my face and the whites resemble a bad
sunset.

The sight of the lipstick brings part of it back to me. Strange, as I
start to retrace the evening, the way certain things do come back and
I am gradually able to piece fragments together so that my tortured
mind is beginning to form a vague picture.

What a fool I must have made of myself!

She said that she didn't want to talk but just sit and listen to the
music and have a few drinks. I remember that part of it very clearly.
Perhaps we had three or four drinks, but then we did talk. Or at least
I talked.

For a girl of her type, Sari is certainly a terribly sympathetic and
understanding person. A sensitive person.

She asked me about my work and I guess the drinks were really
taking effect because I remember telling her all about myself. About
my mother and then later my school days and my marriage. I told her
about my job with McKenny and Fleckner and even about my
frustrations and my dislike for Sam Fleckner.

She understood. Yes, in spite of the drinks, which for some reason
or other didn't seem to affect her in the slightest she understood.
Sympathized and understood.

She even understood about Marian. I can't understand how I could
have shown such a complete lack of reticence, but I must have told
her a great many things about Marian and myself.

I blush even now as I remember telling her about the business of
the nickname. About Marian's calling me Hal.

That was when she leaned close and kissed me. When I told her that
Marian only used my nickname when we made love.

About that part of it I have the clearest possible memory.

God, it was like nothing which had ever happened to me before. When those soft, half-parted lips found my own and she pressed her warm honeyed mouth against mine. She did it with her eyes wide open, half turned toward me on the couch, and my own eyes were wide too as I leaned over her slender figure. I had never kissed anyone before while I looked at them.

Something happened then and I knew that my hands tore at her clothes.

She was neither angered nor frightened. But she had gotten up and pushed me away. She was nice enough about it. She only said that we had gone far enough and went to pour another drink.

I was limp with passion and I got off of the couch and I staggered into the bathroom. That's when I first threw up.

That's when the period began about which I have only glimpses of memory.

I remembered I brushed my teeth and washed my face with ice-cold water and that I came back into the other room and that we again had drinks. I remember, at some time or another, telling her that I loved her and that she was marvelous and like nothing I had ever known before in my life.

I even remember asking her about Roy Anders and her sudden anger and then my going to my knees and putting my arms around her waist and holding her and begging her to forgive me. I remember crying with my head in her soft lap.

It seems to me that around this time something most unusual and unaccountable happened because Sari was no longer Sari but had become my mother and it was my mother that I was holding in my arms.

Maybe all of this happened after she left and that was a part of a dream I had.

It seems impossible that Sari and my dead mother should have become confused, even in a dream. No two women were ever at further poles; no two women could have been more dissimilar.

I don't remember Sari leaving.

The only thing I have left of her now is the note, scrawled in lipstick on a piece of hotel stationary, which I found this morning on the dresser when I woke up.

"I'll see you tonight."

I love this girl and I know it as I kiss the paper on which she has written the words.

And yet, somehow, in the very center of my brain, is the knowledge that Howie was telling the truth. That she is, actually, Anders' girl.

Are women really like this? That they can belong to one man and permit another man to make love to them?

Is Marian too, like this? Is she really a slut under that smooth, cultured, controlled exterior?

It is possible. Thinking of her and of the way she acts around Sam Fleckner, I know that it is possible.

One thing which is contributing heavily to the way I feel is the thoughts I am having about Marian and about Fleckner. It is odd that the result of my own experience with Sari should be an almost overwhelming suspicion of my own wife.

I can't help but wonder if I have been blind about Marian all of these years. Is it possible that I really have never known her at all?

That almost aggressive sexual passion of hers—isn't it very possible that not finding the same sort of thing in me, she has turned to someone else? Isn't it possible that that someone else can be Sam Fleckner?

Thinking about the two of them together, it seems to me now that of late they have looked at each other with a sort of secret understanding. It is almost impossible for me to understand what Marian might see in the man, and yet, something tells me that he is the sort of person women do find attractive. There is something of the brute animal about him, a singular quality which I have often detected in Marian herself. Yes, the more I think of it, the more I am becoming convinced that there is something between them, something low and vile and carnal.

Chapter 6

It is now early on Friday morning, exactly one week from the day on which the McKenny-Fleckner payroll was hijacked.

I am no longer safe.

The things which have happened during the last few days have been so frightening that I sense danger on every side of me.

For, since I left the Middleton House that Tuesday morning after spending most of the night with Sari, a series of incidents have taken place which have completely shattered my sense of peace and security, which have changed the entire course of my life.

It isn't bad enough that most of the time my mind has been on Sari, that I have been bitterly disappointed and upset at her failure to see me as a result of her failure to show up for our appointment on Tuesday evening. That I have had the vision of her lovely face and body incessantly on my mind. No, it isn't only that which has completely wrecked the peace of my mind.

On top of it are the other things which have happened. The things to do with Sam Fleckner and Lieutenant O'Malley and yes, even with Marian, my own wife.

It would almost seem that there is some sinister conspiracy afoot to drive me insane with worry and fear.

At least I have one faint consolation; I have talked with Sari on the telephone and she has finally agreed at last to see me. She is coming to my room at the Middleton as soon as she finishes her work in the checkroom downstairs.

But these other things. They have been monstrous.

It started on Wednesday morning.

All day Tuesday I lay in bed at the hotel. Each time I would try and get up, the nausea would come back and I was powerless to move. Finally, toward evening, I sent downstairs and ordered a light soup. I slept and some six hours later, I awakened with a ravenous appetite. The headache had disappeared.

I dressed and went downstairs and it was already dark. Looking over toward the cloakroom, I was startled to see a corn-silk blonde behind the counter. I knew a moment of panic then, wondering if Sari had left and some other girl had taken her place. I was almost tempted to ask, but decided that it would not be safe to do so. I comforted myself with the thought that it was probably merely her night off. She had written that she would see me, and I must have faith in her.

And so I went out and bought the evening papers and then went to a nearby restaurant and ordered a large dinner. I ate ravenously.

Returning to my room, I opened the papers. There was nothing at all in them concerning the holdup.

And then I lay back on the couch and I waited.

It wasn't until twelve-thirty that I finally called downstairs and asked the girl at the check counter if Sari had been in. She told me that it was her night off, as I had suspected. Further, she refused to let me have her address or phone number and seemed very suspicious at my questioning her.

I was frantic. Once I was almost tempted to try Howie, but I quickly realized the folly of such a course. I even went to the phone book and looked for her name, but she was unlisted. Hating myself, I looked up

Roy Anders, but he too was not listed in the Manhattan directory.

It wasn't until after two o'clock that I finally gave up. She was not coming. I tried to tell myself that she had gotten tied up, that something had happened to keep her away.

But why hadn't she phoned?

Was it because she didn't want to? Or was it because she was with Anders? The last thought almost drove me out of my mind. I could visualize the two of them together, he with his hog-like barreled chest and his coarse face. Pawing her, doing things ...

I hated him and I was furious that I hadn't tipped the police off to the planned stickup so that he would have been arrested and put some place where he would never be able to see her.

I hated her for being with him.

At last, after the sun had already come up, I fell into an exhausted sleep. I was emotionally and physically exhausted.

II

It was the last real sleep that I had.

When I awakened around midday on Wednesday, I felt strangely refreshed. My mind was very clear. It occurred to me at once that the police would be concerned over my failure to get in touch with them. Marian, too, would be worried. I didn't care so much as far as Marian went. A little worry on her part would do her good. But I didn't want to have the police becoming too curious. I decided to return officially from Montreal. But instead of going to the apartment, I would go directly to the office.

At eleven o'clock I was dressed and ready to leave the hotel. Once downstairs I went to a restaurant for a late breakfast and while I was waiting for it, stepped into a convenient telephone booth.

Marian answered the phone at once.

I gave her no opportunity to talk. I told her that I was back in town and in a hurry. I said that I was on my way to the office and that I would call her later in the afternoon.

Brusquely I cut off her questions, repeated that I would call her, and hung up.

I smiled with a certain amount of self-satisfaction as I returned to eat my breakfast. It wouldn't hurt to let her understand that I was running my own life.

I took a subway uptown and at twelve-thirty I walked into the offices of the McKenny-Fleckner Construction Company. I had timed myself so as to arrive during the lunch hour, while as few persons as possible were around.

Old George Grainger was downstairs in the garage when I entered the building. He was leaning over the opened hood of Sam Fleckner's big Chrysler sedan, working on the engine. I recognized George from the rear without trouble. He was about the widest man I had ever seen and, despite his sixty-five years and three hundred pounds, was still a fine mechanic. It seemed a shame to me that he spent more of his time working over either Fleckner's or McKenny's cars than he did on the company machinery.

I picked my way across the cement floor and stopped for a moment at his side. He looked up, a slightly startled expression on his face.

"Why Mr. Wilkenson," he said. "Didn't expect to see you, sir!"

"Hello George." I said. "What's the trouble? Mr. Fleckner's car broken down again?"

"No. No, not exactly. Just doing a ring job on her. Should have her out by the weekend. She's a fine car, but he drives her just like he does that racing car of his. Runs her right into the ground."

I nodded.

"And how are you feeling, Mr. Wilkenson?" George asked. "Saw in the papers one of those bullets creased your head. Certainly is too bad about Mr. McKenny. Yes sir, sure too bad about him."

"My head is about healed," I said.

"Well, I certainly hope they get the bastards. People like that should be ..."

I left him mumbling to himself.

I walked over to the elevator and I had to wait for a full five minutes. Finally it stopped and Williams, the colored man who operates it as well as acts as janitor, opened the grilled doors. He also asked about my head and told me it was sure too bad about Mr. McKenny.

"Where've you been, Williams?" I asked as he pulled the elevator door shut. "I must have waited more than five minutes."

"Yes sir, I know Mr. Wilkenson," Williams said. "But I got tied up. They delivered a box of dynamite and no one was around and I didn't want to just leave it on the floor. So I had to take it down into the vault in the basement. Sorry I kept you waiting."

I told him that it was all right. He certainly shouldn't have left the dynamite lying around.

Personally, I have complained a number of times to Sam Fleckner about this very thing. I believe that it is against city ordinances to have dynamite delivered to the building in the first place. But both he and Mr. McKenny always laughed it off.

"Safe enough," Sam would say, "just so nobody starts fooling around with it. After all, it's quite a trick to explode dynamite without a cap."

I couldn't see it that way at all, but it really wasn't my department so there was nothing much I could do about it.

I got off at the fourth floor, walked down the long narrow hallway and opened the door to my office.

Sam Fleckner was sitting in the chair behind my desk. Detective Lieutenant O'Malley was sitting across from him, at the desk which Tom McKenny had always used. They were alone in the room.

For a moment, after I had entered and turned and started across the room and then stopped in surprise, there was a dead silence.

O'Malley was the first to break it.

"Well I'll be damned," he said. "So you've turned up at last."

Sam just sat there staring at me. He wasn't smiling; there was absolutely no expression at all on his dark, angular face.

"How was Montreal?"

I knew the second he asked that it was some sort of trap. O'Malley's opening remark had irritated me and I had been about to snap back at him when he asked about Montreal. It really wasn't any of his business where I went or what I did. On the other hand I was in no position to antagonize the man.

"Montreal? Montreal was all right," I said.

"When did you get back, Harold?" For once there was nothing patronizing or even friendly in Fleckner's voice.

I suddenly felt a sense of that old relationship, employee-boss, which has always humiliated me.

I tried to stall for time, but I was given no time at all.

"We've been trying to get in touch with you," O'Malley said. "Things we have to find out. Where have you been?"

"I went to Montreal," I said.

"Yes. I know." O'Malley's voice was still sympathetic and there was the habitual friendly, understanding expression around his eyes. "I know you went to Montreal. I also know that you turned right around and came back to New York."

"What?" My eyes were wide with surprise. How could he know? Was he merely bluffing, attempting to pump me?

"We know because a detective that we had alerted up there to kind of keep an eye on you told us so. Unfortunately, he didn't let us know until too late to pick you up again when you got off the plane back at

LaGuardia."

I remembered the man at the lunch counter at the Montreal airport. "Good God," I said, attempting to conceal my confusion with anger. "Good God Almighty! Do I have to report my every movement to the police. What the ..."

"You are the one who wanted police protection," O'Malley said drily.

"Marian has been very worried about you, Harold," Fleckner cut in. "Have you called her yet?"

"I called her," I said.

The Lieutenant stood up and started to walk over to the window. Fleckner also stood up, indicating that he was giving me my own chair. He had a rather strange, almost antagonistic expression.

"Wilkenson," he said, "I can't understand you. Tom McKenny has been murdered, this firm has been robbed of more than a hundred thousand dollars and you yourself have been shot and wounded. And now, while an investigation is going on, you see fit to just up and disappear. I wish you'd tell me what's bothering you. You're a friend of mine and your wife's a friend of mine. Just what seems ..."

"You are acting very much like a man who might have something he wishes to conceal," O'Malley cut in.

I stared at him.

"Are you trying to say that you think I may have had something to do with what has happened?" I asked. My face was pale and I'm afraid that my voice was rather high-pitched. "Are you by any chance ..."

"Certainly not," Fleckner said. "The Lieutenant doesn't believe that you could possibly be implicated in any way. And you know how we feel about you here, Harold. But we do think that your actions have been a bit odd."

"Let's all sit down and have a little talk," O'Malley interrupted. "I don't want you to feel that anyone is being unfriendly and I certainly don't want you to feel that we have the slightest doubt of your integrity. I am not going to ask you why you wanted to go to Canada and then turned around immediately and returned to New York. I am not going to ask you where you have been or what you have been doing. But there are a few things that I think I should know."

"I'll tell you anything that is in my power to tell," I said.

I was feeling a little relieved. After all, I could ill afford to antagonize the man, even if I did wish to protect my own privacy. His next remark, however, completely disconcerted and frightened me.

"I don't know whether you are aware of it," O'Malley said, "but Mr. McKenny's gun was unloaded at the time of the robbery. It is my understanding that he invariably carried a loaded weapon when he delivered the payroll. I also understand that he kept the revolver in the drawer of his desk here"—he indicated the bottom drawer of the desk Tom McKenny had always used—"and that the gun was always loaded."

I must have shown my surprise and shock. Not, of course, surprise at the information concerning the unloaded gun, but surprise that the point had been established at all. But the detective and Fleckner misunderstood what was behind my expression.

"Yes," Fleckner said, "poor Tom walked into that mess thinking he was carrying a loaded gun."

"Perhaps he had been cleaning it or something," I said, "and forgot to replace the shells."

O'Malley looked at me a little sadly.

"Hardly," he said. "If he'd realized that the gun was unloaded, he certainly wouldn't have pulled it in an attempt to shoot."

Fleckner nodded.

"Someone unloaded the revolver," he said. "Whoever did it is directly responsible for Tom's murder. As guilty as the man who actually shot him."

"What we are trying to find out," O'Malley said, "is who might have taken the shells out of that gun."

"Taken the shells? Good Lord man," I said, "you don't think anyone around here would do a thing like that? How could anyone possibly have known ..."

"Easy," O'Malley said. "Way I got the thing figured, this job must have been fingered from the inside. Almost had to be. The men who pulled it had a great deal of very reliable information. They knew that McKenny delivered the payroll. They also knew that he was followed by two private detectives in a private car. That's why they had the truck ready to cut in and run interference. They probably knew about the gun. Certainly they knew the route McKenny took to get out to Long Island. It almost had to be a job worked from the inside."

This time my surprise was really genuine. It suddenly came to me that everything he said was really so. But he had it in reverse. Instead of the killers knowing everything about the office routine and the gun, I was the one who had known everything about the robbery plans.

And now they knew that the gun had been unloaded and that someone, someone undoubtedly from our own office, had been responsible. At that very moment I remembered back to last Friday morning when I had been standing over Tom McKenny's opened drawer, actually unloading the gun, and Sam Fleckner had walked into the room unexpectedly. I don't know how I was able to keep from fainting. In spite of myself my eyes went to Fleckner.

Thank God he was looking out of the window. I drew a sudden breath of relief. He must have forgotten the incident. I began to feel a little easier about it when O'Malley made his next remark, the one which really threw me.

"There's just one chance we may be able to trace the party responsible," he said. "We've had the gun fingerprinted and we not only found the dead man's prints; we also found another set. A very clear thumb and forefinger."

III

It was a full three hours before I was able to get away. O'Malley insisted on a detailed examination of the records of all current and past employees. He wanted the names and dossiers of every conceivable person who might have access to the office.

It was, all in all, one of the most difficult three hours I had ever spent. I expected that at any moment Sam Fleckner would remember having seen me in Tom McKenny's drawer. Several times I was on the verge of bringing it out myself, merely to beat him to the punch in case he did remember. Certainly, later, I wished I had.

But in the back of my mind was that nagging doubt. Had Fleckner actually seen me handling the gun? Had he watched as I unloaded the shells? There was nothing about his manner or attitude which would tell. Even if he had, certainly he couldn't have suspected me of actually having anything to do with the robbery.

Thinking about it and about all of the trouble and danger into which I had been thrust, I began to resent the fact that Anders and Katz had sent me a measly $5,000. I was the one who was in danger; I was the one who was taking all of the chances. If it hadn't been for me, Tom McKenny could very possibly have forestalled the stickup. At the very least, he would have wounded or killed at least one of the gunmen.

I deserved a lot more than five thousand. A lot more.

O'Malley left some time after three-thirty. My secretary had returned, but Sam Fleckner had sent her out on an errand, obviously to get rid of her. I thought this was a little highhanded on his part, but I said nothing.

Ten minutes after the detective had departed, Sam, who had seen him downstairs, was back in my office. I was seated at my desk, making a pretense of catching up with my work. I can't say that I was displeased when he told me to knock off and go on home.

"Take a few more days, Harold," he said. "I think you should be home resting up. Fact is, I'm driving downtown and I'll drop you off."

I started to say that I'd be all right and that he should go on ahead and that I'd clean up a few things before I left. And then I got this other idea. It occurred to me that perhaps it might be smart to be as friendly with Sam Fleckner as I could. The thought came to me as the result of a remark he made just then.

"Going to be pretty damned busy around here in another few days," he said. "With poor old Tom gone, now, I guess I'll have to be out in the field most of the time. Really should start looking around for someone to take Tom's place, I guess."

Tom's place. Could it be he was thinking of me? Would he offer me a partnership in the firm? Wasn't it possible? After all, the man had wanted to back me in a separate venture as an architect. He'd offered to come in as a partner on that. So why not this? Wasn't it logical? Wasn't I the right man, after my years of experience with the firm?

"I'd appreciate your dropping me off and I *am* rather tired," I said. I tried to sound friendly and grateful. "I guess maybe we could both use a drink. Suppose I call Marian and tell her we'll be by and you can drop up for a cocktail."

Sam looked at me, his expression showing more than a slight trace of surprise.

"Fine," he said. "That'll be fine."

We had to kill another half hour downstairs in the garage while Fleckner talked with George about the work he was doing on the Chrysler.

And then he wheeled the Allard out and I climbed into the bucket seat at his side and we headed downtown. In spite of the no parking regulations, he left the car sitting at the curb in front of my apartment while he came upstairs with me.

I noticed that there was no longer a detective on duty.

Marian was surprised to see us together. I could see at once that she was dying to get me alone and ask me questions. But she had no chance and for once I was glad to have Fleckner around.

Marian made three Manhattans and served them with a plate of cheese and crackers. Sam drank his hurriedly and for the first time since I had known him, seemed in a hurry to get away. However, I insisted that he couldn't go off after a single drink.

"Can't fly on one wing, you know," I said and laughed. Marian looked at me, startled. "Not," I was quick to say, "that I think drinking in the afternoon is a good idea, but we've all had a rather trying time of it and I guess one or two won't hurt at all."

Sam didn't say anything. But I noticed that he and Marian exchanged glances. There was a peculiarly intimate look that passed between them and it annoyed me. But I swallowed my displeasure. I was determined to be pleasant to the man.

"What in the world will you do without Tom?" I asked while Marian was in the next room getting another drink together. "After all, he's going to be mighty tough to replace."

Either he didn't hear me or his mind was on something entirely different.

"God, but I feel sick about Claire and the kids," he said. "Tom was Claire's whole life. They're really going to miss him."

"We'll all miss him," I said. "Especially the firm. I don't know where you'll ever find a partner who has the knowledge of the business that Tom had."

"Oh, that won't be too much of a problem," he said, casually. "I have a nephew, just getting out of M.I.T. Smart youngster. Thinking of bringing him into the firm anyway and I guess we could groom him for the spot. Then Tom's oldest boy will be coming along in another few years. Time we started thinking of young blood. No, don't worry about the firm. We'll never exactly fill Tom's shoes, but we'll manage. There are other ways in which we'll really miss him."

I barely heard the last of it.

The sonofabitch! Young blood! Goddamn him, how about me? I am still young. I was young when I started with the company. What was wrong with me? Why some young squirt just out of school? And waiting for Tom's oldest boy!

I knew then, once and for all, that as far as McKenny and Fleckner was concerned, I was all through and washed up. Sam Fleckner would see to it that I never got anywhere. He'd keep me an office worker for the rest of his life if he had the chance.

When Marian returned with the drinks I had a difficult time not throwing one in his face.

Thank God he left within the next few minutes.

IV

Marian was most difficult. She should have had the intelligence to see that I was very disturbed. She should have understood that the last thing in the world I wanted was to be questioned.

No sooner had Fleckner departed than I asked her to get me another drink.

"But Harold," he said, "you've already had two." She looked at me, startled, almost frightened.

"So I've had two," I said. "What of it? I want a third."

She stood in front of me looking down into my face. "Harold, I want to talk to you. I want ..."

"Talk," I said. "Talk all you damned please. But be good enough to get me a drink while I'm listening."

For a second more she stared at me, her eyes wide. And then she turned, wordlessly, toward the kitchen. In a couple of minutes she was back with the drink which she handed me. I noticed that she hadn't finished her own original one.

"Where in the world have you been?" she asked. "I've been so worried. When that detective and Sam told me that you hadn't stayed in Montreal ..."

"It's none of their damned business where I stayed."

"It isn't necessary to swear, Harold," Marian said.

"It isn't necessary," I said, "but on the other hand it isn't anyone's business but my own no matter what I say."

She reached over suddenly and put her hand on my forehead, looking into my eyes, her own brown eyes worried and her brow wrinkled in a perplexed frown.

"You're not well," she said. "Something's bothering you. Can't you tell me what it is? What's ..."

"Listen, Marian," I said, my voice steady and quiet. "Please listen to me for a moment. I am perfectly well. I have never felt better in my life. But I have just gone through a three-hour session of questioning and I'm not up to any more of it. All I want is to be left alone and allowed to finish this drink in peace."

For the next twenty minutes we just sat there, me sipping at the Manhattan and Marian staring at me. The expression in those worried eyes of hers was worse than the questioning would have been. Finally I couldn't stand it anymore.

"Damn it, Marian," I said, "stop staring at me as though I were some sort of freak or out of my mind or something. If you have to ask me something go ahead and ask it. Ask it and get it over with."

For a moment longer she hesitated and then she spoke.

"There are a lot of things I'd like to ask," she said. "After all, you just walked out and left me and I've had to stay here and answer a hundred and one questions myself. That detective—Lieutenant O'Malley—he and Sam and I don't know how many others ..."

"O'Malley," I said quickly, "O'Malley? What in the world has he been asking? Has he been here?"

"Several times. And he asks all sorts of things. He seemed to think that I knew where you had gone. Oh, he asks every sort of thing. He even wanted to know about the candy."

"The candy?" For a moment I didn't understand.

"You know, the box of candy which you told me about. The one you told me to tell people that I had brought to the hospital for you."

That candy again! What is the matter with that insane detective? The man must be demented. What possible significance could he attach to a box of candy? Why did he constantly harp back to it?

"So he asked about that," I said. "And just what did you tell him?"

"Well, I told him just what you told me to. But somehow ..."

"Somehow what?" I snapped, getting to my feet quickly.

"Well, somehow he got me all mixed up. He wanted to know where I had purchased the candy and for a moment I was so confused that I just couldn't think clearly. He wanted to know what kind of candy it was and all sorts of strange things."

"Strange things?" I was really worried now.

"Oh, you know. Like had I ever bought candy for you before. And if you like candy and what kinds you liked and so on. It was all really very silly."

"So how did it end—this silly questioning?"

"I'm afraid that he just didn't believe anything I told him," Marian said weakly.

I looked at her.

"You are a fool," I said. "Honest, Marian, you are really a very stupid woman."

She looked at me, startled.

"Harold, are you drunk?" she asked. "What in the world has come over you anyway? What ..."

"I'm not drunk," I said, "and nothing has come over me."

For a moment she just looked at me.

"Sam is right," she said at last, "something is wrong with you.

Maybe that wound in your head ..."

"Sam! That ungrateful bastard," I yelled. "Listen, I'm sick of Sam Fleckner, I am sick of you. I'm sick and tired of all of you. The stupid police, everything. I'm going out."

She started across the room toward me, her face very white.

"But Harold, you just got here. Don't you want to lie down and rest? I'll start dinner. I won't ..."

"The hell with dinner," I screamed. "The hell with everything. Make dinner for yourself. I'll be back later."

I grabbed my hat and slammed the door.

I had suddenly decided that I wanted to see Sari. I wanted to see her in the worst possible way. I wanted kindness and understanding and the softness of her arms and lips. I didn't want questions and recriminations.

I found a cab at the corner and climbed in. I gave the driver the address of the Middleton House.

V

I didn't bother to go up to my room.

The corn-silk blonde was still in charge of the check concession outside of the cocktail lounge. I can't tell you the sense of disappointment I had when I saw her.

I left my hat and went into the bar and ordered a drink. It was amazing how much I had been drinking lately.

Not seeing Sari had made me want to cry.

I waited until the girl at the checkroom was alone and then I went out and gave her the check for my hat. When she handed the hat to me I carefully peeled a twenty-dollar bill from the roll I carried in my trouser pocket.

"I want to know where Sari is," I said. "I'm a friend of hers and I have to see her. Can't you ..."

She made no move to take the money.

"She's not here," she said, staring at me with a blank, neither friendly nor unfriendly expression.

I questioned her and I couldn't tell whether she was being evasive or not. The only thing I learned was that Sari hadn't quit her job, but was taking a few days off. The girl either didn't know or wouldn't tell me where she lived or how I could find her. She said that the girls, all of the cloakroom girls, were hired by a man who owned the concession. I might find out there, but she doubted it. She gave me the name of the company.

I gave her the twenty-dollar bill anyway.

And then I started uptown. I would go to Howie's Bar and Grill. Howie's was the first place I had seen her and Howie's was where I had seen those others—Roy Anders and Katz. There was just a possible chance I might find a trace of her there.

The minute I walked into the place I knew that something was wrong.

There were no more than a dozen men standing at the bar and all the booths but one were empty. It was occupied by a sailor and a girl with startlingly black hair, wearing a sweater which was positively indecent.

Howie stood where he usually did when he wasn't busy, at the end of the bar. He was leaning forward on his elbows, talking with a man who had his back to the door.

I know Howie saw me when I entered, but he dropped his eyes at once and gave no sign of recognition.

I looked over the customers carefully. There was no one there who could do me any good.

I waited for all of five minutes and then, growing impatient, I took a half dollar from my pocket and knocked sharply on the surface of the bar with the silver rim of the coin.

Howie looked up at me, annoyed. He seemed to shake his head slightly. I couldn't understand what was the matter with him. A moment later the man talking with him turned and started toward the door. He had to pass almost directly opposite me, so close that I could have reached out and touched him. But he was no more than halfway down the bar when I recognized him.

It was Penelli, the detective who had been guarding my apartment on that day when I had sneaked out.

Quickly I turned my head. I don't know whether he saw me and recognized me or not as he passed. I think that my face, in any case, was suddenly so pale that he might have had difficulty in recognizing me.

If there had been any doubt in my mind as to what he was doing in Howie's bar, it was dispelled a couple of minutes later when Howie walked down and stood in front of me. He spoke in a low, harsh voice and there was no friendliness at all in his tone.

"You are causing me a lot of trouble, Mr. Wilkenson. A lot of trouble and I don't like it. I would be pleased if you would take your business elsewhere."

"Listen Howie," I said, my own voice sharp and clear but low enough so that only he was able to hear me. "Listen, what did he want? What is he doing here? Why ..."

"I can tell you nothing," Howie said. "I just don't want trouble."

"Howie," I said, "Howie, did he ask about why you came to see me?"

"He asked."

"And you told him? You told him that I wanted to know ..."

"I told him nothing. Do you think I'm as damned a fool as you seem to be making of yourself? I told him only that you had left a cigarette lighter laying on the bar and that I came by to bring it to you."

"Thanks, Howie," I said. "Thanks a lot. I want you to know ..."

"All I know is that I don't want any trouble. I don't want any questions from the police. I wish you would go somewhere else."

I thanked him again. I wanted to ask him once more about Sari. I wanted to ask him about Anders or Katz. But I knew that this wouldn't be the right time. No, I'd have to let him cool off first.

So I ordered a drink, which he grudgingly served me, and I handed him a twenty-dollar bill and told him to have a drink on me. I turned away, not waiting for the change.

He didn't say good-bye. But he did accept the twenty.

I returned home to my apartment. The thought of sleeping in the same bed with Marian was repulsive to me. I was thinking of Sari. But the thought of going back to that room at the Middleton House and sitting there alone without her, was impossible.

I needed rest. I needed time to think.

Chapter 7

Thursday was even worse than Wednesday.

By midnight on Thursday I had gotten myself beaten up for the first time in my life. I'd learned that Sam Fleckner had found out enough to convince himself that I had something to do with the robbery of the payroll and with Tom McKenny's murder.

And by Thursday at midnight I already had decided that I was going to kill Marian. I was also going to kill Sam Fleckner.

It started right after breakfast.

I came back to the apartment very late on Wednesday night and I was unable to sleep. I'd spent the few remaining hours, until Marian awakened, in a large chair in the living room, drinking black coffee and smoking one cigarette after another.

Marian had gotten up at seven and had insisted I have some breakfast. Lieutenant O'Malley arrived just as we were finishing.

It started the second he entered the room.

He'd found that the fingerprints on the gun were mine.

He didn't believe the story I told him. What made it even worse, Marian herself had sat there and listened as I talked, and I could tell by the way she looked at me that she too had not believed me. The terrible part of it was that O'Malley was watching her face, rather than my own, as I talked. I could see that he understood the lack of belief in her.

I'd done the best I could. I told him about being in Tom McKenny's desk drawer that morning before we had left to deliver the payroll. I told him that I had looked for Tom's habitual bottle of whiskey and taken a drink from it, and that I undoubtedly moved the gun in order to get at the whiskey.

It was that business about taking a drink of whiskey which had brought the worried look of doubt to Marian's eyes.

No, neither of them had believed me, but on the other hand, no one in the world, with the possible exception of Sam Fleckner, could actually swear that I wasn't telling the truth.

It wasn't that either Marian or the detective thought for a moment that I would actually be implicated in the robbery, or even that I might have had any motive for touching the gun. They just felt that I was lying and that I was concealing something.

Marian kept watching me as I spoke. She watched me as though she believed I wasn't quite in my right senses.

"Well," O'Malley said, when I finished, "at least your story holds together a little bit. We found your fingerprints on the bottle as well as the gun."

He went on to say that it was too bad I hadn't remembered and told him about it in the very beginning.

I think, with him, I might even have gotten away with the story if it hadn't been for Marian's amazing stupidity.

"But Harold," she said, when I finished speaking, "taking a drink! How in the world did you ever happen to be taking a drink at that time in the day? And in the office, too?"

I could have killed her right then and there.

"Damn it," I said, "and why shouldn't I have taken a drink? Certainly, Tom McKenny wouldn't have minded. I had a cold. And so I took a drink. Sam Fleckner himself can tell you about it. He came in while I was doing it and I explained it to him."

"He never mentioned it to me," O'Malley said drily.

"Ask him," I said. "Just ask him. He's bound to remember."

"Had you ever taken a drink out of that bottle before?" O'Malley asked the question casually, as though it really didn't matter.

"Yes," I said, "several times."

Once more I saw the surprised skepticism in Marian's face as she watched me. And once more I was aware that the detective was looking at her and not at me.

He left at last and I could see that Marian was only waiting to start her own series of questions. I didn't give her the chance.

"It's after nine," I said, as soon as the door had closed behind O'Malley. "After nine and I have a stack of work waiting for me at the office. I want to get uptown at once."

I stood up and went to the closet where my coat was hanging. I didn't give her a chance to as much as open her treacherous mouth.

"I'll be home late," I said and swung out of the apartment.

II

I didn't go near the office. I realized now that getting in touch with Sari, and through her, possibly Anders or Katz, was imperative. Lieutenant O'Malley was getting too close to the truth for safety—either their safety or my own.

I had had no experience with this sort of thing, no contact with police and police methods. Certainly Anders or Katz would be able to advise me, to let me know what would be the best method to frustrate O'Malley and his investigation.

For a moment or so, I even considered the idea of contacting a lawyer. I believe that the more notorious criminal attorneys are used to coping with situations of this type. But quickly I changed my mind. How would I know what lawyer to go to, what lawyer would be safe?

There was one further consideration. Here I was, to all intents and purposes an innocent bystander, taking the brunt of the police investigation. And why? Why to protect Anders and his gang. It seemed to me that if I were to be placed in this position, five thousand dollars was a very meager reward.

Yes, I would have to find Sari. God only knows, during the last few days I had wanted to see her badly enough. But up until now the reasons had all been personal. Now it was something else; it might be a matter of actual survival. Survival for all of us.

Walking across town, unconsciously drawn in the direction of Howie's Bar and Grill, it even occurred to me that I might go to the police and make a full confession. I should never have been involved in the first place. After all, I had not taken part in the robbery, and even though I may have emptied Tom McKenny's gun, I had done so with the best of possible motives.

But then I realized that I could expect neither sympathy nor understanding from the police. Also, I would have to give up the five thousand dollars and the very thought of doing so was repellent to me. I had earned the money and it was mine.

I shall never know what possessed me to walk in the direction I took that morning. There seemed to be some fatal attraction about Howie's. In a sense it wasn't too surprising for, after all, had it not been for that fatal Sunday afternoon's visit to the tavern, I never should have become involved in the complicated procession of events which was to lead to the ultimate tragedy of my life.

Some obscure and little understood fate had directed my footsteps that first time and now once again I was retracing those footsteps.

Less than a block from my house, I had a strange feeling that I was being followed and I caught myself stopping and turning swiftly and looking behind me.

But there was no one in sight, nothing but a cruising cab which pulled up to the curb at the corner, even as I started again on my way. It was only when I thought about it later that I remembered that the flag on the cab was down and that someone must have been huddled in the back of it.

I continued on my way, but I still had the feeling that I was being watched. It made me extremely nervous.

I was less than half a block from Howie's when I saw him. Saw Katz.

The little bird-faced man with the large nose was leaving the doorway of a small restaurant. I stopped automatically and stared. Even as I watched, a cab pulled up beside him and he opened the door and entered.

At first I started to run toward the cab, my mouth half opened to call out. But I was not fast enough. Already the driver was pulling away from the curb, headed downtown in the opposite direction.

It was the merest stroke of luck which brought the second taxi alongside of me at that moment. Within a half minute I was in the back of the car and instructing the driver to follow the car in which Katz was riding.

Katz could not have had any idea he was being followed. The driver of his taxi zigzagged across town, taking advantage of lights, and in the normally heavy traffic of the midmorning it was not difficult to keep him in sight. When the cab reached Eighth Avenue and Twentieth Street, it pulled to the curb and Katz got out. While he was paying the driver, my own taxi came to a halt about one hundred yards further on. I gave the man a five-dollar bill and told him to keep the change.

Katz walked a half block down the street and then turned in at the entrance of a new, medium-sized apartment house. I hurried, but by the time I had followed him into the building he had disappeared.

I cursed my luck. I should have intercepted him before he'd entered. There was no doorman and the elevator was self-operated. I walked over to the wall on which were rows of mailboxes. Under each was a name and floor number as well as a bell button.

There was no Katz, no Anders, no Mizner.

An indication of my emotional condition can be understood when I say that as I stood there, the perspiration beading my forehead and my hands shaking with nervousness, I felt the tears of frustration come to my eyes.

Using my forefinger to mark the place, I started all over again to check the names. And then I found it. R. Anderson, Apartment 4B. It could be Anders. At least, it was close enough that I must make sure.

I took the elevator to the fourth floor and then walked down the hallway until I stood in front of 4B. I was standing there, hesitating, trying to make up my mind what to do, what to say if I should knock on the door and it turned out to be the right place, when the decision was taken from me.

I heard no sound on the other side of that door when suddenly it swung inward. His broad shoulders almost totally filling the opening, the man stood there motionless, looking at me. I was still staring at him, openmouthed, when I felt something sharp poke me in the center of my back. And then the words, coming from directly behind me.

"Go right on in, Mr. Wilkenson."

At once I knew what had happened. It had been no piece of blind luck which had made me encounter Katz. The man had been waiting for me all along. Probably outside of my apartment. He must have been in a cab and when I had left he'd followed me. It must have been his cab which I had seen when I'd experienced that sensation of being followed.

Later, once he'd determined the direction of my footsteps, he'd driven on ahead. He'd been very clever about it. He'd made sure I saw him, that I was able to follow him. And then, later, he had led me to the apartment house on Twentieth Street. But once inside of the building, he'd not actually entered the apartment himself, but waited for me somewhere down the hallway and as I stood in front of the door, sneaked up behind me.

Anders made no attempt to step aside to allow me to enter. Instead, one large square hand reached out and took hold of the lapels of my coat. As he stepped back into the room, he jerked and then turned, so that I was thrown halfway across the apartment and landed on my hands and knees.

I looked up to see Sari half lying on the red leather couch, a long cigarette holder in her hand and an amused expression around her eyes. In an instant, the expression changed and her eyes went up and over my head.

"No. Roy," she said, "Please ..."

And then the heavy boot connected with the side of my head and I had less than a fraction of a second to feel the explosive pain before the blackness came over me.

III

She was still in the same position, half lying on the red leather couch, when I opened my eyes. But I was no longer on the floor. I was slouched in a chair with my head resting on my folded arms.

Something warm and sticky seeped through my spread fingers and I held my hand away and saw that it was blood. My shirt was wet through and at first I thought that that also was blood and for a moment I thought I would faint.

I forced my eyes down and saw then that I was soaking wet. Someone had thrown a pitcher of water over me in order to bring me to.

I tried to control the shaking of my body and limbs. Slowly I raised my eyes.

Katz was on the couch, next to her, his felt hat still on the back of his birdlike head, his elbows on his knees and his large russet eyes wide and staring as he watched me. The eyes were oddly disinterested and he looked at me as though I were some strange, but rather repulsive zoological specimen.

Roy Anders stood next to the couch, his legs apart and his hands on his hips. His coat was off and his white shirt opened at the throat, exposing a hirsute chest. His expression was not disinterested. He waited until my own eyes met his and then he spoke. His voice was rather high and thin, coming from that deep chest, and he had a peculiar accent, half Midwestern and half Scandinavian.

"You are a man with bad habits, Mr. Wilkenson," he said. "They can get you into trouble—they have gotten you into trouble."

"I can explain ..."

But he didn't give me a chance.

"No, Mr. Wilkenson, I don't think you can explain," he said. "I don't think you can explain what you were doing eavesdropping on a conversation which was no business of yours, in a barroom a week ago. I don't think you can explain coming back to that barroom to find out other things which were none of your business. I don't think you can explain your willingness to accept money which you knew to be stolen and not report it to the police. I don't think you can explain your anxiety to find a girl who didn't want to see you. And lastly, I don't think you can explain what you are doing here this very minute."

Katz stood up as Anders finished. He looked at the big man with annoyance.

"You talk too much, Roy," he said. "This guy should do the talking. He's got an angle, so let's find out what it is."

"No—no." I spoke quickly. I could tell by the way Anders started toward me that I wasn't going to have much chance to explain anything. He was a man who acted first and asked questions later.

"No," I said, and I'm ashamed to admit that my voice cracked and that the fear I felt must have been all too obvious. "You don't understand. It's the police. They suspect me. They know ..."

He was in front of me and his big paw reached down and he again took me by the front of my shirt and jerked me to my feet.

"Give him a chance, Roy," Sari said suddenly. "Let him ..."

"What do the police know?" Anders asked. His face was flushed and I could sense the anger in him. "What do they know? What have you said to them?"

"Let me tell you," I said, my voice shrill with desperation. I knew that I'd have to talk fast. "Let me explain. They think I've had something to do with it. They think that it's some sort of inside job and that someone gave information."

"Maybe someone did. Maybe someone gave the police information."

He slapped me then, with the back of his hand, and it was like being hit with a mallet. The tears sprang to my eyes and I felt the side of my face going numb. But I kept on talking. I had to talk.

"Please let me explain," I said. "You see, they know that someone took the bullets from McKenny's gun."

He suddenly pushed me back so that I fell into the chair again. He looked at me, surprise on his broad pug-nosed face.

"The bullets from McKenny's gun?" he said. "What about the bullets?"

I saw then that he had not known McKenny's gun was empty and at the same time I realized that I could tell him about removing those shells and that it would be a point in my favor. It would convince him that I was on his side.

"Yes," I said quickly. "The bullets. You see, after I overheard you talking about the robbery and I knew when it was going to take place, I took the bullets from the gun."

The three of them were staring at me, amazement in their eyes. Sari looked at me as though I must have taken leave of my senses. Katz showed open skepticism, but Roy Anders himself had an odd expression and he watched me almost as though I weren't quite human.

"*You* emptied McKenny's gun?" he asked. "Good God, why?"

"Well, you see, I knew that the robbery was going to take place. I thought that it would help."

"Help?"

"Yes. Help. I wanted you to get the money."

"You mean," Anders said, and now his voice was barely above a whisper, "you mean you deliberately emptied your boss's gun so that he couldn't defend himself?"

I could see he was beginning to believe me and I felt that now I could convince him that I was on his side.

"Yes, yes," I said, speaking hurriedly. "That's it. I wanted you to get the money. I wanted McKenny to be shot!"

For a moment he just stared at me and I was beginning to feel a renewed sense of security. I was getting the situation in hand and I sensed a new feeling of confidence.

"Yes," I said, "I've helped you from the very beginning. I wanted you to get away with the robbery. I wanted McKenny helpless. Even afterward, when the police questioned me, I told them nothing. That was all a lie, that story the newspapers ran. About having told the police I saw any of you and would recognize you. I've protected you all the way through."

I could see they were beginning to believe me. It would be a good time to mention the money.

"And when you got the money and sent me the five thousand dollars, I knew you must understand. The only thing is, I am the one in the middle. I'm the one who must go on talking to the police and protecting you. Five thousand, out of a hundred and twenty thousand, hardly seems quite fair, don't you think?"

At that moment, just as I began to relax, his arm shot out again and his huge hand opened and then closed on my throat.

"Why you nasty little bastard," he said and before I knew what he was about to do, his other hand moved and he started slapping me. He didn't close his fist but he hit me first on one side of the face and then the other, swiftly and violently, until I thought my very head would fly off.

I didn't lose consciousness.

It wasn't the physical pain. Not, understand me, that I have an instinct for masochism. No, it wasn't that. But after the first couple of blows, I actually felt nothing. It would have been better if he had knocked me out.

What brought the tears to my eyes, the agony, was the humiliation. The utter and complete ignominy of being manhandled in front of this girl, Sari.

This man Anders was a sadistic beast and I would have attempted to defend myself, but I knew that to do so would only drive him into renewed frenzies of activity. I knew that I would be no match for his brute strength. And so I just stood there as he battered my face. It was Sari who finally put a stop to it.

"Roy," she said, "Roy, stop it. Stop it right now." For a moment he held back and turned to stare at her, still holding me with one hand at anus length.

"This sonofabitch," he said, "I should ..."

"Leave him alone, Roy," she said. "What's to be gained ..."

He dropped me and I fell back into the chair and buried my face in my arms.

"Listen," he said, swinging to the girl, "Listen. Why don't you keep out of this. Get up off your fanny and get out of here. I want to talk to this louse. If you can't stand to see him hurt, go and take a walk."

"There's no reason to beat him up," Sari said. "Not unless you're going to go all of the way. And you'd be a fool to do that."

"Look Sari," Katz said, "let Roy handle this."

She stood up.

"Well, for one, I don't want any part of it. I will go out. But Roy, just use your head. Don't go off half cocked. Use your head."

She didn't look at me as she passed my chair. A moment later and the door slammed behind her and she was gone.

Anders was back then and he pulled me from the chair again. He put one thick finger under my chin so that I was forced to look at him.

"We gave you five grand," he said, speaking between hard, thin lips, "to keep you quiet. We didn't have to—we could have shut you up another way. Remember that. I'm sorry now that we didn't get you at the same time we got McKenny."

He shoved me and I fell against the table.

"All right. In a minute I'm opening that door and you're leaving. I never want to see you, again. Don't come back here, don't ever try to find us. Stay away. Talk to the police and you'll find that you're as deep in this thing as we are. Remember that. You are just as much responsible for McKenny's murder as though you pulled the trigger yourself. So keep your mouth shut. And stay out of my sight. I don't like you and if I ever see you again, I'll take you apart for good."

He picked up my hat from where it had fallen on the floor and threw it at me.

"And one more thing. Stay away from Sari. Stop trying to see her. She wouldn't be interested. She's too used to having a man."

Katz had opened the door and Anders lifted me by one arm and pushed me toward it so that I almost fell. A moment later it shut behind me.

Blood mingled with the tears as I half fell down the hallway and found the button which brought up the elevator.

I staggered from the building and out into the street and two middle-aged women, standing at the curb talking, looked at me curiously. My handkerchief was in my hand and I wiped my face. I was half blinded as I started to walk up the street. I had gone less than a block when the taxi pulled up alongside of me.

At first I didn't recognize her and she had to call my name twice. It was Sari.

I climbed in beside her and she said something to the driver. We drove on for several blocks and then the cab stopped.

She turned and looked at me but I avoided her eyes.

"God only knows why I care," she said, "but I just hate to see anyone hurt. Anyway, you've been very foolish. Do what Roy says to do. Keep your mouth shut and stay away from him. He's more dangerous than you realize."

I muttered something, I'm not sure just what. I was afraid to look at her.

"Yes, stay away from him. He'll kill you if you don't. And stay away from the police."

For a minute or two she just looked at me.

"I wish," she said at last, "that I could understand you. That I knew what made you tick."

I started to reach for her hand but she pulled it away.

"I'm going to get out here," she said. "Go home. Get yourself cleaned up."

"Sari," I said, "Sari, listen. I've got to see you. I've got to talk to you. I must ..."

She didn't let me finish.

"No, no, I can't see you again." She moved to the door.

"Once more," I said. "Just once ..."

She hesitated a moment. Then she spoke quickly as she opened the door of the cab.

"Call the Middleton—tonight, late," she said.

A moment later and she was gone.

I watched her walk up the street and then I tapped on the window separating me from the driver. He slid the glass back and looked at me.

"Uptown," I said.

IV

The cab driver was a yellow-skinned Negro and he looked at my battered face with cold disinterested eyes. I didn't think he was going to take me at first, but apparently he was indifferent to anything but the possibility of a fare. He didn't ask where I wanted to go, but put the car into gear at once. It took me several minutes to gather myself, to collect my wits. And then I leaned forward and told him to take me to a bar.

He looked at me over his shoulder.

"What bar?" he asked.

"Any bar," I said. "Any bar, but not around here. Get away from here."

He drove on for a distance of several stoplights. Then, once more he turned and looked at me over his shoulder.

"Midtown bar or uptown bar?"

"Uptown," I told him.

That's how I happened to end up in Harlem. Apparently he was known in the place in front of which he stopped, because he left me in the cab while he went inside and then after a couple of minutes he was back.

"Friend of mine owns this place," he said, looking at me. "You'll be all right here. He'll help you."

I must have looked like I needed help. It suddenly occurred to me that there was blood over the front of my shirt and jacket. The wound in my head had been reopened, but the blood was mostly from my nose and my cut lips.

The cab driver helped me inside. It was a long, dark, narrow room and there were two young colored girls sitting at one end of the bar. The colored man in a white coat who tended bar walked around and met us, and without a word he too helped me and they took me into a back room.

I was in a half daze, only vaguely aware of what was happening.

I remember that someone put a drink in my hand. In my bruised mouth it burned and felt like acid going down my throat. They dampened a rag and wiped off my face, opening my collar and the first two buttons of my shirt after taking off my coat.

I seemed helpless, unable to move and not at all clear in my mind as they worked over me. But from their conversation, I got the impression they thought I had been mugged. There was a second drink and it was about this time that I got the strange, ringing sensation in the front part of my head just above my eyes, which never was to leave me. Perhaps it was from the blows I had taken, perhaps from something else.

Later I was stretched out on a couch. I must have fallen asleep because the next thing I remember was the Negro with the white coat leaning over me. I opened my eyes and saw that his lips were moving. He was shaking me gently.

I saw that he was holding my wallet in his hand.

"Gave Billy ten dollah," he said. "Rest of it's all here."

He put the wallet into my inside coat pocket.

"Billy?"

"Billy brought you here," he said. "How you feelin'?"

I sat up on the couch and he handed me a large ceramic mug. I must have been very weak because it felt almost too heavy to support.

"Coffee," he said. "Shot a whiskey in it. Bring you to."

The single window in the room was shaded and I noticed that there was a light on.

"What time is it?" I asked.

"You been here most all day," he said. "It's after eight. Thursday night—after eight."

He waited while I drank the coffee with the whiskey in it. He asked if I wanted something to eat, but I told him I didn't. A few minutes later and I was on my feet and putting on my tie. He told me that he'd call me a cab. He didn't ask any questions.

I handed him a twenty-dollar bill when I left.

For a moment I started to give the cab driver the address of the Middleton House. I changed my mind however, with my mouth half opened. I didn't know where to tell him to take me. I didn't want to go home. And then, as he sat half turned waiting for me to speak, I gave him the address of the office.

The night watchman let me in. He looked at me curiously, but he said nothing.

I didn't take the elevator, but walked upstairs. I was still half dazed. I moved like a sleepwalker. It wasn't until I was almost at the door of my private office that I noticed the lights were on. Some instinct made me stop with my hand on the knob.

And then, through the mist of my mind, came the realization that behind that door two persons were talking in low tones. One of them was Sam Fleckner; the other was my wife. It was Marian's voice I heard speaking when at last I began to understand the words.

"I can't believe it," she said.

"You shouldn't worry too much," Fleckner said. "He must be ill; something must have happened to him."

They were standing just the other side of the closed door with the light behind them and I could distinguish the silhouettes of their two figures, which seemed to blend together. I could feel the blood leave my face as anger overcame me. Again my hand went for the doorknob, but Marian's next words stopped it in mid-air.

"Oh, Sam," she said, and I shuddered at the way she used his given name. Wondering how long she had been calling him Sam almost made me miss the rest of it. But not quite.

"Oh Sam, you must be wrong. He couldn't have had anything to do with it. I don't care what that detective says. Harold just couldn't."

"I felt the same way," Fleckner said. "At first. But now, well, frankly, I just don't know what to think. We know definitely that he had been handling Tom's gun, that the chances are he took the bullets from it. We know that some woman saw him while he was in the hospital and probably left that candy box, although we don't think it contained candy. We know he has been hanging around a Third Avenue bar which is a notorious hangout for criminals. I don't know what to think."

For long moments then there was silence.

"But where is he now?" Marian asked at last. "Where is he and where has he been? I'm sure that something has happened to him. Oh, God, if I only knew what ..."

"You must do as I say," Fleckner said. "Return home and if he comes in, call me at once. Make some excuse and go out and call me."

"And if he doesn't return home?"

"In that case meet me here early tomorrow morning. Around nine o'clock. I would pick you up but I'm sure the house is being watched and we don't want O'Malley in on it."

"No, we don't want O'Malley."

"So meet me here. We'll find him. Somehow or other we'll find him and once we do, we'll take him to the rest home. For it's either one of two things. He was involved or else all that he has been through has temporarily deranged his mind and he needs treatment. I have private detectives checking hotels and rooming houses and he's bound to turn up. Once he's been located, we'll take the big car and pick him up. You will be able to sign the commitment papers."

Again there was silence and I could hear half-muffled sobs. The two figures fused together and I experienced a wild moment of murderous hatred.

"I'll call a cab," Fleckner said. "We shouldn't be seen together."

With extreme caution, I turned and tiptoed down the hallway as I heard Fleckner lift the receiver from the phone. A moment later and I had concealed myself in the men's room at the end of the hallway.

It was while I was sitting there, waiting to hear the sounds of their departure, that I decided that I would murder them. My mind was very clear at last. I knew exactly how I would do it.

I knew how I would do it and, at the same time, I knew what else I would do. I would solve the bank robbery for Detective Lieutenant O'Malley. And I would see that I had my revenge on a man named Katz and a man named Anders.

It was only just and fair that both Marian and Sam Fleckner should die. Just and fair and terribly essential for my own protection. Only by sacrificing their lives could I protect myself and deliver a solution to the robbery which would satisfy O'Malley. Only through their deaths could I have my revenge on Anders and Katz. Only through their deaths would I be able to have Sari.

They deserved to die!

What they may have been to each other up to this time I didn't know. But one thing I learned while listening to their voices through that partition, one thing of which I was as sure as I was sure that I was standing there living and breathing. If they were not already lovers, they soon would be. It was but a matter of time. Their very conversation, their plans to have me committed, were sufficient proof of that. Yes, have me committed and get me out of the way.

One can always tell. There was that certain timbre to their voices as they whispered together, a certain connotation in Marian's tone as she had said "Oh, Sam."

I knew. I knew only too well. Somewhere, deep down inside of me, I even understood in a way that those two, Fleckner and my own wife, were really made for each other. They had the same sort of animal vitality, the same ...

But I didn't want to think of that. I didn't want to set up excuses for them. I wanted to get on with what I had to do.

Fleckner might steal the profits of my years of labor with his firm, but he was through enjoying them. And Marian would never share them with him.

It was all going to be beautifully simple.

V

At nine-thirty, Sam Fleckner and Marian left the office. At nine forty-five I was again talking with the night watchman. He was very easy to handle. What I had to do would take an hour and I needed complete privacy for it.

He thought it odd that I should want the early morning editions of the newspaper badly enough to send him down to Times Square to buy them when they came out at eleven o'clock but he didn't question the order. I told him to take a cab and I gave him the money for it. I told him that I would accept responsibility for his being absent.

In order to insure myself plenty of time, I also asked him to stop and get coffee and sandwiches on his way back.

Five minutes after he had left, I was in the basement.

Thank God, Sam Fleckner had taken the Allard instead of his big car. It didn't take as long as I had thought it might. I had a little trouble attaching the four dynamite sticks under the dashboard, but making the wire connection to the starter was really very simple. I was, at last, finding a practical use for some of the odd fragments of information I had absorbed in college.

Later, when I was sure that things were as I wanted them, when I was sure that a foot pressed to the starter pedal would do the job, I went back upstairs. But I didn't go to my own office. I went to Sam Fleckner's office. I used his secretary's typewriter and I wrote the letter on one of the company's letterheads.

It was a very simple letter. It merely gave Roy Anders' name and address and the name Katz. It said that the writer had learned that Anders and Katz were implicated in the robbery and that he was writing this letter in case anything should happen to him before he was able to obtain conclusive evidence. The letter was insurance in case they suspected he knew about them, and were able to silence him.

I signed the letter with the typewritten initials "SF."

I was careful to wipe my fingerprints from the keyboard when I finished. My dealings with the police had not been without some benefit.

I folded the single sheet of paper and put it in the top drawer of Sam Fleckner's desk, carefully hiding it under a number of pieces of correspondence. I didn't want Fleckner himself to find it accidentally. I didn't want anyone to find it until the police themselves carefully made a search of his desk. A search which would without doubt be made sometime before noon the next day.

I was waiting downstairs when the night watchman returned.

We had coffee and sandwiches together and although I had forgotten his name, he seemed a quite intelligent man. But I was in a hurry to leave as soon as I could without arousing his suspicions. I wanted to leave and hurry to the Middleton House.

Because Sari was there, waiting for me.

I had called when I had finished the letter in Sam's office. Called and asked if there had been any messages for 1002.

There was a single message and the night clerk read it to me over the telephone.

The message was very brief and it had not been signed. It merely said, "See you at twelve." Only one person in the world knew that I was checked into Room 1002.

Chapter 8

I stopped at a Sixth Avenue barber shop and had a face massage and a shave. Later, the valet in the men's room of a Forty-second Street hotel cleaned up my clothes and somehow managed to find me a fresh shirt.

Still and all, when I entered the lobby of the Middleton House the desk clerk looked at me very strangely as I asked for my key. Looked at me strangely, but gave me the key nevertheless. I wanted to see if she was in the checkroom, but I decided not to risk it. Anders, or possibly Katz, could have been around watching. So I went upstairs at once and let myself into Room 1002. It was ten minutes to midnight.

I was pouring my second drink when she arrived.

For a moment, after I had opened the door and let her in, she just stood there, looking at me and saying nothing.

I closed the door and locked it.

She went to the couch and sat down and I noticed that she was wearing a different dress and that her hair was different and that she had on a very light wrap which only came to her waist and that she wore a long scarlet scarf across her bare shoulders. She placed her pocketbook on the small table next to the couch. I noticed the butt of the gun. I had never mentioned it to Sari because I assumed that she carried it to give her a sense of security. She encountered all sorts of dangerous people.

"I'm crazy to come here," she said, looking up at me.

"Thank God you did come."

"Crazy. Roy would kill me. He'd probably kill you too."

"Why did you come?" I asked.

For a second or so she just looked at me, as though she wasn't really seeing me at all. And then she shrugged.

"I don't really know," she said. "It's just—well, it's just that somehow I feel a little responsible for what happened to you today. For Roy's hitting you."

I felt my face redden. I was torn between humiliation for the scene which she had witnessed and hatred for that brutal man who had beaten me in front of her.

My emotions were too close to the surface and once again I felt the tears well up in the corner of my eyes.

She knew.

A moment later and she was up and had crossed over and her arms were holding me.

"I'm sorry—sorry," she said.

It was then that I broke down completely. I told her everything and probably I was a little mad. I told her I loved her and that I wanted her and that I had to have her.

She tried to stop me, she tried to keep me from talking. She said that

I was sick and hurt and didn't know what I was saying. Later, when I had kissed her and held her, she forced my arms from around her slender body and told me I would have to listen to her. I sat back on the couch and she stood in front of me and talked, but she didn't look at me as she spoke the words.

"I like you and I guess I feel sorry for you," she said. "But there are things you have to understand. What I feel isn't love. It is something different. Something ... oh, I don't know how to explain ..."

But once more I was on my feet. Once more my arms were around her and once more I closed her half-opened mouth with my bruised lips.

One of my feet tripped on the light cord and it jerked the plug from the socket and the room was in darkness then. We fell together back on the couch and suddenly, instead of fighting against me, I felt her own arms go around me.

Her jacket came off and my hands were clumsy and inexpert as they moved down her naked shoulders to the back of her dress. She didn't protest.

Once, in my frenzy, I heard the rip of cloth, but I was gentle with her and careful not to hurt her. Suddenly she lay still and I heard her breathing deeply, each breath ending in a sort of half-muffled sob.

The ringing was louder and louder and the blood churned tortuously through my veins. The blackness was coming and my body was trembling and quivering.

She was half crying now, pleading and crying and it sounded as though she were saying please, please, please, over and over again.

And then, at that very moment when I thought I couldn't bear it for another second, it happened.

It happened like it had always happened before. With Marian and even with the two prostitutes I had gone with years ago.

This wasn't Sari whose body was welded to mine. This wasn't a woman that I loved and who was young and beautiful and crying out in passion. No—no—it had all changed and I was back again in my childhood. Back lying in the arms of my mother, lying against her breasts and with my head buried in the soft hollow of her neck. Yes—*mother—mother*.

At one moment there was that complete, unquenchable ecstasy and then as the very gates of Heaven and Hell seemed to open for me, there was that old horrible sickening sense of paralysis and the quivering stopped and the blood ceased its mad surging and the limpness and decay came over me and I just lay there exhausted like a dead man.

I didn't love her. I hated her. I hated her for having wanted the one thing I didn't have to give her. The thing I had never had to give any woman.

She was like all of them, all of the rest of all women.

It was Sari who got up and found the plug and put it back into the socket and brought light again to the room.

I sat on the edge of the bed, white and sick with hatred and humiliation and fury as she went into the bathroom and straightened out her clothes. I found myself staring at the butt of the gun in her pocketbook on the table.

I was holding the whiskey bottle in my two hands, half caressing it when she returned and stood in the doorway and stared at me.

"I understand, now," she said, "about you and your wife."

I stood up then, placed the bottle on the table next to her bag, and I turned.

There was nothing but loathing in her face.

She didn't draw away as I went up to her. She just looked at me, the way she would look at something unwholesome. I guess she thought I was going to put my arms around her again and she didn't even bother to step back. Just stood there and stared at me.

It wasn't until I had swiftly snatched the gun from her pocketbook and, grabbing it by the barrel, raised it high in the air, that she realized.

And then it was too late.

II

I am back in Sam Fleckner's office. It is after four o'clock in the morning. It took me a long time to return here as I walked all of the way. I had to think and I have always been better at thinking while walking.

For the first time in as long as I can remember my mind is absolutely crystal clear. I have gone back to the very beginning and thought about everything which has ever happened to me in my life. I have thought about my mother and about my marriage and about my work. I have even remembered the little dirty barefooted boy who ran into me a few days ago with an ice cream cone in his hand.

It seems that it happened ages ago.

Yes, I have thought about everything. And for the first time in my entire thirty-six years, my mind is at last at peace.

I know what I have to do.

I am finishing this letter now and I have already torn up that other letter which I wrote earlier in the evening and left in Sam Fleckner's drawer and signed with Sam Fleckner's initials.

Yes, I am finishing this long and often tedious account. I'll be through in another two or three minutes.

And then I am going downstairs and I am going to open the door of Fleckner's big Chrysler limousine and I am going to get behind the steering wheel and I'm going to press my foot on the starter.

In a sense it is ironic that now when at last I have found the key to the tragedy and futility of my life—now that I have finally discovered the thing which has always been wrong with me—it is too late to do anything about it. Too late to do anything but destroy the fragile vessel which contains my body. I pray that my soul will find some peace and security in some other world after I have paid for the sins which I have committed in this world.

But one thing I have finally understood. It wouldn't really have mattered at all which turn I took. Right, left, or straight ahead, my own destiny has always been here waiting for me.

THE END

From the master of the big caper....

Lionel White

978-1-933586-87-7 **Marilyn K. / The House Next Door** $19.95
A lone driver picks up a beautiful woman and gets more than he bargained
for, and the perfect heist is made complicated when a drunken neighbor
climbs in the wrong window. "Pure noir."—James Reasoner, *Rough Edges.*

978-1-944520-19-9 **The Snatchers / Clean Break** $19.95
Two classic heist novels, the first one a kidnapping gone wrong, the second a
perfectly orchestrated race track robbery, filmed in 1956 by Stanley Kubrick
as *The Killing.*

978-1-94452037-3 **Hostage for a Hood / The Merriweather File** $19.95
A failed caper involving a bankroll heist and a missing wife; and a clever
mystery in which many secrets are revealed when a body is discovered in the
trunk of a husband's car. "Insidiously potent."—*Kirkus Review*

978-1-944520-83-0 **Coffin for a Hood / Operation—Murder** $19.95
"These two caper novels are gripping and tense, reading them is like
watching a lit slow burn fuse, you can hear it sizzle, see it spark and you
know where it's headed – an explosion, or in this case a blood letting...
noir to their core."—Paul Burke, *NB.*

978-1-951473-31-0 **Steal Big/The Big Caper** $19.95
"White's writing is brilliant throughout and just pure noir, stripped to the
basics and filled with tight detail."—Brian Greene, *Criminal Element.*

"I just can't say enough good things about this author and his stellar body of
work. What a remarkable legacy to leave behind for generations of readers to
enjoy and celebrate. When compared to Lionel White's contemporaries, this
author remains in the very top echelon of mid-20th Century crime-noir
creators."—*Paperback Warrior*

Stark House Press, 1315 H Street, Eureka, CA 95501
griffinskye3@sbcglobal.net / www.StarkHousePress.com
Available from your local bookstore, or order direct or via our website.

CPSIA information can be obtained
at www.ICGtesting.com
Printed in the USA
FSHW012252080222
88188FS

9 781951 473587